ellen mcCarthy

Guarding Maggie

POOLBEG

Crimson

This novel is entirely a work of fiction. The names, characters and incidents portrayed in it are the work of the author's imagination. Any resemblance to actual persons, living or dead, events or localities is entirely coincidental.

Published 2008
by Poolbeg Press Ltd
123 Grange Hill, Baldoyle
Dublin 13, Ireland
E-mail: poolbeg@poolbeg.com
www.poolbeg.com

1 3 5 7 9 10 8 6 4 2

A catalogue record for this book is available from the British Library.

ISBN 978-1-84223-322-1

Typeset by Patricia Hope in Sabon 10.5/14

Printed by
Litographia Rosés, Spain

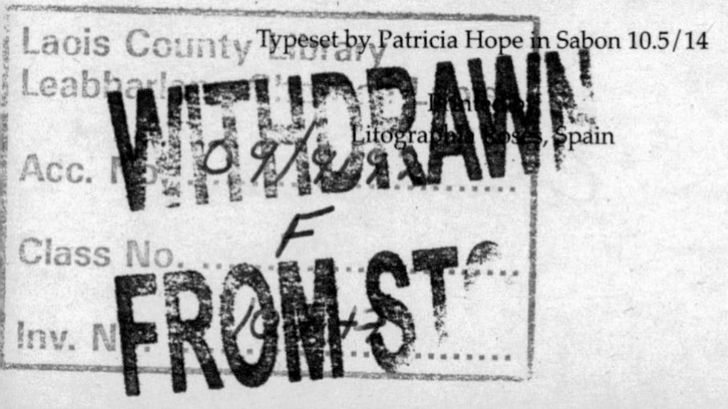

Note on the author

Ellen McCarthy grew up in West Waterford near the Comeragh Mountains. She has a degree in Literature and Sociology from DCU and was the winner of RTÉ's *Seoige and O'Shea/Poolbeg Press* "Do The 'Write' Thing" Short Story Competition 2007. *Guarding Maggie* is her first novel.

Acknowledgements

I would like to thank Paula Campbell of Poolbeg Press and *Seoige and O'Shea* for picking me as winner of their Short Story Competition.

Thanks to Gaye Shortland, my editor, for helping me breathe life into Maggie.

Thanks to my agent Ger Nichol for helping me take care of business.

And thanks to my family and friends for their faith in me.

To Denis
Thanks for everything

Reality surrounds us like a smoke screen.
Sometimes, when the wind blows, you can see
right through it.

Prologue

He closed his eyes and blew out his breath loudly. He'd always been cool and never lost his temper. But even in the darkness inside his head he could see the old man's retreating back. All he wanted was to talk to him. He needed to explain how he felt. Surely after all these years Pascal owed him that.

Tears threatened him. He couldn't reduce himself to a snivelling wreck in front of him. The wisest thing would be to go home but the pain was too much. He'd never felt such despair as he felt now. All his life it had been locked up inside, poisoning him. It had tainted everything. He needed to let it go.

God, he hated them so much! He realised he'd been moving after the old man despite his indifference. His stiff old back disappeared into the house and the door shut but then through the wood he could hear him shouting. He listened to the drama from where he stood and wished he could see what was happening.

Pascal must be taking his anger out on her. Finally the shouting stopped and the night dragged on.

He didn't know why he did it but at last he turned the handle of the door and pushed it open, then stood silently in the porch. They seemed to have gone to bed now. He opened the inside door quietly and stood looking into the kitchen which was void of life and stood in silence watching him back. He moved into the room, the inky blackness dissolving into a murky grey.

Then he heard something like a kick against wood to his left. The utility room. The door shook. Someone was locked in there. He heard her shout the old man's name. He must have locked her in. That was strange.

He knew where Pascal's room was. He moved forward.

He had no idea what he was doing now. He just wanted to talk it out with him.

As he approached the door he heard what sounded like drawers being dragged out and their contents dumped on the floor. Silently he entered the room.

At first he couldn't see him but he could hear his laboured breath. The room was in disarray. He certainly wasn't expecting that; Pascal was such a fastidious old goat. Then he saw him lying on the ground, still fully dressed. He hurried across the room and looked down at him.

Pascal was lying on the linoleum, gasping for air. Already his lips were turning blue and the panic in his eyes made them stand out, glassy and alive in his dead face. He was dragging his hand across the floor, his bony knuckles scratching on the floor's surface. The hand was gripped tightly around an inhaler.

Suddenly he felt cold determination. The old man made a more concentrated effort with the inhaler and without hesitation the man standing over him laid his foot on the back of the claw-like hand. He could feel it squirm slowly under his boot. It was like stepping on a mouse. The labouring breath was turning to choking rasps now and the eyes were slowing, letting go of life and moving on. He stared as hard as he could, trying to see the moment life abandoned him and left the shell lying there alone. He was disappointed. You couldn't see the exact time. One moment life struggled and some place along the way it gave up.

He sat back on the bed and looked at him. Gently the night faded and a brand-new day would soon be dawning outside. Pascal was gone. Gone from his life forever. Then he remembered her.

Part One

Chapter 1

Maggie sat with life pressing heavily on her shoulders. There was no point in lighting the fire. She would be going to bed soon. A roaring fire was a waste at this hour. She gave a jump, splashing tea over her wrist as a sound broke the stillness. Betty the tabby, attracted by the movement, jumped onto her knee.

The sudden disturbance in the dead of the night frightened Maggie. Her brain had slipped into a trance. The sound she'd just heard must have been the wind – it had whipped up to make quite a noise in the last few hours. Up here by the mountains its howling could be akin to shrieking voices as it beat against the eaves and echoed down the chimney pipe.

Pascal hadn't come in yet.

For a moment a silent tear slid down her face but she brushed it off. She had to be strong now. She couldn't lose control.

Maggie pushed the chair back from the table,

clasping Betty to her heart. The cat stretched out, her soft feet briefly exposing her tiny claws to grasp the wool of Maggie's jumper in a loving grip. She started to purr and tenderly rubbed her cheek against Maggie's face. The loving gesture again brought a wave of emotion to the surface. For a moment the woman and the tabby cat held each other in an intimate gaze; two old friends sharing the night, their hearts filled with love.

Maggie held the cat close and rose painfully. Her bruised hip ached and she knew if there was ever a time to act it was now. Life could be different if she could spend it with Tommy. She eased her body into the rocking chair by the fire. Gently she guided the chair into a rolling motion and watched the slanted eyes of the cat get smaller and smaller until the purring turned to gentle snores and the gripping claws withdrew. She mustered all her courage. Invisible bands were constricting and gripping her, stopping her from lifting the phone. Pascal was due back soon. Would she have the strength to tell her news before then?

She glanced back at the clock. A quarter of an hour had passed since she'd spoken to Reeney and soon she would have to do it. She hoped she had the nerve. The rocking of the chair was getting more agitated as she wrestled with her courage. America was five hours behind so it was the perfect time. The rest of the family were together having dinner in New York and she was going to tell them about Tommy, tell them right now if she could get her fear under control. Some of them would understand, some would disapprove but, once they all knew, Pascal would no longer have a hold over her. She would be free to go and spend time with Tommy if he still wanted her.

Again a thump rocked her heart. It had been doing that a lot tonight. These palpitations were just a reminder to her that she was still alive. She needed those from time to time. She gently lifted the sleeping cat and placed her on the warm cushion of the chair.

Maggie moved her stiff bones towards her bag and pulled a little wallet out of the middle zipped pocket. Inside was a small book where she kept her phone numbers and her reading glasses. She held them in her slender fingers as she took them back to the chair. Betty saw her coming and bounced off. She knew from experience that Maggie was gentle getting out of the chair but had a habit of sitting on her when she came back, so she decided it wasn't worth the risk. She sat on the hearth with her slanted eyes looking through the stove door at the dying embers.

Maggie put on her glasses and opened the book. Flicking the pages she turned to Brian's number. Her own brother and she couldn't remember the last time she'd spoken to him. Pascal would call him from time to time but Maggie only ever answered the phone the odd time he called here. But tonight she had to make the move herself, for Tommy, her little Tommy. The best day of her life had been that first day when he stepped out of the car in the yard and introduced himself to her.

She'd been baking in the kitchen all morning when she heard the car pull up outside. She already had a tray of scones cooling and was about to take out the brown loaf, which was just nicely crisped on the outside. She had two rhubarb tarts to go in after the bread came out. Maggie always overdid the baking, giving some to her neighbours as gifts. She came from a large family and she'd never adjusted properly to it being just herself and Pascal. All that week her neighbour Dolores Blaney, who lived in the next farm over from theirs across the mountain, had men in helping out with some land reclamation. Five extra men, on top of the three she already had in the house, ate a lot of food so Maggie was glad to help out.

Sheila barked. That was nothing unusual. Sheila did a lot of that but this time she continued on unabated. Maggie marched to the door to order the old dog to the barn but stopped in her tracks. Sheila was walking circles around a strange man. He'd driven up in a big car – people-carriers she believed they were called. The back was full of cases. He was leaning against the opposite side of the car, gazing around him at the yard.

Maggie watched him for a few moments without speaking, thinking there was something familiar about him but she couldn't quite put her finger on it. He didn't look particularly aggressive. He looked a bit overwhelmed. Then he turned and looked into her eyes. Again she got a strong sense of the familiar as she looked back into his face.

He was very handsome. His skin was tanned and his eyes from where she stood looked like brown orbs. He smiled at her. It was a shy smile that lit up his face.

He had an intense gaze and Maggie found herself blushing. Being sixty years old, this wasn't something that she experienced often.

"Are you Maggie?"

She nodded.

"My name is Michael."

He walked towards her and extended his right hand. Maggie wiped her buttery hands in embarrassment on the front of her apron. Then she took his hand in her own trembling one. She had to pull her hand away as he held on, looking into her eyes. Now that she was close she could see that they weren't brown – they were hazel like her own and swimming in tears. She wanted to ask him why he was upset but she didn't know how to broach the subject without embarrassing them both. She felt no threat, even though she'd never laid eyes on him before – Pascal was around somewhere and there was always a neighbour passing by. Contrary to what the townspeople thought, there could be a lot of foot traffic in the country. Without hesitation she invited him in and offered him some tea. Like a little boy collecting for the local GAA draw he followed her meekly into the house.

"Sit down there." She gestured towards the two-seater couch by the fire.

She wet the tea and got a tray ready with a plate of scones, butter and jam and a piece of the tart she'd made yesterday. While she worked at the kitchen table she had her back turned to him but she could still feel his eyes on the back of her neck. As she turned around she was amused to see Eddie Molloy, her neighbour from down the road, taking sideways glances at the strange car as he crossed her yard to the upper gate. Eddie had land taken up there where he kept some cattle so he was a regular passer-by. He walked up every day to a hide he had there for hay. He fed them the hay and when the hide was empty he drove up on the tractor to replenish his supplies.

He had a smallholding that was doing okay but he didn't have enough grazing close by for his cattle. He needed that, especially in the winter, to feed them.

Maggie crossed the room and placed the tray on the low table by Michael's side. He drank some tea, then munched on his scone, never taking his eyes off her face. He seemed to be having a struggle with words. He appeared on the verge of speech more than once and then he went back to chewing and watching Maggie with the same unwavering gaze. Maggie used that opportunity to go back and put the finishing touches to her tart and place it in the oven. When that was done and the bread was on the wire tray she went and sat in the chair opposite him.

"It's about time you told me more than your Christian name, isn't it?"

He nodded. "My name is Michael Reynolds. I've come from Boston to see you."

"You have?" By now her curiosity was at boiling point but she didn't want to rush him. "How do you know me? Are you a relative?"

Like most Irish families the Breslins had a smattering

of American relatives and they often came knocking on the door looking for their roots. The old stone walls in Ireland were like a call from the mother ship for them. A pilgrimage they all had to make at least once.

As she sat now in the dead of the night, thinking back, the impact of his next words still hit her like a clenched fist.

"Maggie! I'm your son. I've wanted to meet you for such a long time."

Maggie was glad she was sitting. If not her legs would surely have given away. For a moment she looked around her, confused, trying to formulate her thoughts.

"Are you sure?" was all she could come up with.

"I wasn't! Not until I met you. But I am now. Instantly I felt like I recognised you. Didn't you feel it too?"

Maggie had. She knew now that was what she'd felt. He had her eyes and he had a look of Pascal when he was his age, the shape of the brow and the earnest expression. But the boyish smile and the easy charm, those belonged to someone else. Someone she wouldn't be able to give him much information about.

"Tommy!" she said almost to herself. "My little Tommy!"

"Tommy!" he repeated, looking puzzled.

With a break in her voice Maggie explained that Tommy was the name she'd chosen to call him the day he was born but she'd never been given the opportunity.

Like a stab wound, the pain of separation still burned in her. She'd felt stretched all these years as if the child she'd had to let go still had a grip of her and was tugging at her from a great distance. She hadn't realised that distance crossed the Atlantic.

The brown-haired man sitting in her kitchen suddenly stood up and reached out his arms awkwardly. She stood and stepped towards him. Shyly she returned his embrace and felt his hot tears wet on her cheek.

A sharp voice broke the moment. "What is this?"

Pascal her brother stood in the doorway, his dark shape blocking the light. His face was hardened into a frown and his eyes were like granite in his wrinkled face.

Pascal was the eldest son. He had inherited the farm when their father died. He'd been twenty years old at the time. Maggie was just a baby then and he'd been the only father figure she'd ever known. He was father, brother and provider all in one and he was the tie that bound her to pain all these years. His presence was like a band of iron constricting the house, even now at eighty years old.

Pascal had been the head of the household since the death of their father and neither Maggie nor her mother before her death had ever disputed this. Sometimes Maggie questioned it in her own mind but life hadn't produced many alternatives. A suitable husband hadn't come along since her return to Donegal and she hadn't wanted to settle for less; she'd known passion, brief as it was, and somehow she could never see that in the men around her.

Life just settled in, enclosing her. Gradually she succumbed to the weight left behind by the residue of her dreams and hopes. By the time the sixties came around for Maggie, her mother was in ill health and it was her place to take care of her. Pascal had the farm and the stock to look after. Áine Breslin's life ebbed and with it went Maggie's youth. For the last ten years it had just been her and Pascal.

She knew him and his ways. She knew how to get around him when he suffered the dark moods that sometimes rendered him almost motionless for days, days when the farthest he'd venture was the opposite side of the yard where he'd lean on the edge of the open gate and look down the lane ruminating on the past. Maggie knew him and never questioned their roles. It had always been so. Even in her own mind she didn't have a satisfactory answer as to why she put up with it. He was her brother, her family, beyond that she didn't explore it in any more depth. She learned to live within a confined space and the outside world fascinated but terrified her. Up until now there had been nothing abroad to tempt her out.

Michael was oblivious to the politics of the house but natural wariness made him leave the explanations to Maggie.

"It's Tommy, Pascal, he found me." She smiled hopefully at him. Hoping for some reprieve from her lot of the last forty-five years, hoping for some pity at this stage of her life. But none was forthcoming.

Pascal stood back stiffly and gestured to the open door. "Leave, please."

"Mr Breslin!" Michael pleaded.

But it was obvious pleadings would fall on deaf ears. Michael, being a diplomat, thought best to leave it for now. He thanked Maggie for the tea and walked slowly to the door. He turned back in the doorway, his hazel eyes fixed on her as if afraid he would never see her again.

Maggie wailed.

The sound surprised both of the men and they stood looking at her.

"Pascal, please!" she begged.

Pascal walked to the table and sat down. "Say your goodbyes. He's not welcome in this house."

Maggie clutched at the small concession her proud brother had granted her and ushered her son out the door.

They stood in the yard facing each other but Maggie couldn't look above his knees. The buildings and walls felt like they were gathering around, squeezing her in and keeping him out.

Michael's voice broke into her thoughts. "I'm going to write to you. He can't stop you reading a letter. I'll be in the town for another week. Meet me in Letterkenny. We can have dinner and I'll tell you about your grandchildren."

"My grandchildren!" Maggie's eyes finally rose to his and opened wide in her lined face.

"Yes, dear. You have two grandchildren: a boy Darren and my baby Trudy. Darren is twenty – he's in college and will be going to medical school soon – and

Trudy is seventeen – she wants to study law. I knew you were my mother when I saw you, you know. Trudy is very like you." He leant down and kissed her cheek. "I'm staying at the Beachwood Hotel. Call me when you're in town."

He climbed into his car and drove out of the yard. As he passed her she noticed again the luggage in the back. He must have come here to Cooleen to find her before he even went to the hotel to unpack. Her heart leapt. That made her feel very special. Slowly she turned back to the house, her movements robotic with her thoughts speeding down the road in a rented car.

She'd expected an argument when she went back inside but Pascal presumed the subject was closed.

"Is there any tea in the pot? I'm starving."

She bustled around cutting bread and getting his tea. Life was too short for complacency but Maggie's life got shorter every day. Inside, she knew silence was the reason she lost Michael. Silence allowed him to be taken from her, kept her locked up here all her life and took her life away from her. Pascal had to preserve the silence; inside silence you could hide so much. When everyone knew, Pascal couldn't keep them apart. She knew she had to act now and take back the years he'd stolen. Her first step would be to break the silence.

Chapter 2

Maggie's plan to tell everyone about her son seemed simple in the light of the bigger world but Maggie was shut off from the bigger world. Its rules and opportunities didn't hold much sway here. Behind her door the world shrank from view and her options shrivelled with it. She watched Pascal as he ate. His old neck was stiff like the back end of a brush with a loose pliable covering of flesh encased in folds of skin. He sat proudly and turned towards the fire, effectively cutting her out of the picture. He'd taken his cap off and the white hair on his head stood stiff like cotton wool away from his skull. The pink skin shone through. Long single hairs protruded from his nose and ears and moved as he chewed. She could see the passage of food from the plate into his mouth and onwards. His bodily functions consisted of growing hair in all the wrong places and consuming food cooked for him with her hands. Her body had produced that beautiful human being that had just graced her table and he in turn had brought two children of his own into the world. The practical purpose of Pascal's life had long since been eradicated and he now held his position more from tradition than from necessity. Maggie, who never held any position of authority in her life, was being sought as a mother and grandmother.

One thing Maggie had learned over the years of dealing with her brother was to let him think he'd won. It gave her time to consider her options without the stress of conflict. So she cut him a slice of the warm tart and smiled sweetly in appreciation of the compliments he extended by way of an olive branch and quietly bode her time.

When he finished his tea he continued the daily drama. He scraped his chair back from the table and grabbed his cap.

"Um!" He nodded, smacking his gums. "That did it. I think I'll rest my eyes for a few minutes before I head over to the cards later on." He made no reference to Michael and left the room.

Maggie went about the rest of her evening, clearing the dishes and cleaning the kitchen. For more years than she wanted to remember that had been her daily life. Neither Pascal nor herself had ever married. There never seemed to be an opportunity to bring any new blood into the family.

Pascal left it too late. It had always been expected that he would marry somebody local and they would produce an heir. An heir to all this, she thought, looking around with a wry smile. But Pascal was never big on socialising. He was shy when it came to women and he thought he had all the time in the world. The sand left the glass before Pascal had a chance to reassess his chances. One day he looked in the mirror and saw time marching for the first time. Unfortunately, by then the lines were deep, his hairline had receded and a small farm didn't hold the same collateral it had twenty years before. He was competing with the smart young fellows working in the bank and the civil service who had regular hours and spent their days in a suit enveloped in aftershave with no whiff of what hung around Pascal's head for most of his life.

He developed a new batch of lines as the frown extended to become a permanent mask. He took to sighing at regular intervals, more to the ghosts in his head than because of any visible ailment. Resignation sat on his shoulders until finally he had to battle it in order to get out of his chair. Pascal's life was spent and he knew it.

Maggie had always been a very pretty girl. She was the baby of the family and grew up her mother's darling. She got to stay at school longer than the others. They were all away working then and sending something home so the pressure was off her to move out. But being smart had its price as Pascal told her afterwards. Maggie wanted to live. She bounced with an inner energy none of the other Breslins ever possessed. She was an insatiable reader and always the first thing out of her mouth was a question.

When Maggie was sixteen she asked if she could go

and live with Maureen in Glasgow. All the older girls had gone away to work. Grace and Olivia both went to New York, with the two younger boys following them. Later Olivia married in Canada. But Maureen was settled in Glasgow and she'd always been the closest to Maggie. It seemed like a good idea at the time. Maureen would look out for her bright young sister and maybe get her into an office.

She wrote to Maggie. The family she went to when she first went over would be delighted to introduce Maggie to their cousin who was looking for a nanny. Maggie was over the moon. She bought her ticket and all the others clubbed together to get her a decent wardrobe before she left.

The night before she left Cooleen, her mother gave her a lecture about the problems a young girl alone in a new city would face but she forgot the one problem a young girl anywhere had. Maggie didn't hear a word. She was so excited it went in one ear and just as quickly out the other. Pascal didn't say much to her. He just held out his hand and shook hers as though he were closing a deal with a buyer and pushed a roll of notes into her hand. Maggie understood. He wasn't big on sharing his thoughts.

She took the bus to the boat that night and met her sister on the other side. She was going to spend the first few days with her and start work on Monday.

Now, looking back, it seemed like pages from the book of someone else's life. She was going to be living with the family. They'd written to her and described her living quarters which were small, just a converted corner of the attic. She had a small staircase, with a door at the bottom, up to her living room. A tiny bedroom extended off it towards the back of the house. Her window was a little dormer overlooking an overgrown corner of the garden. It was the least formal side of the lawn and no one ever sat there so it felt like it was her private domain. The father was a QC so the house had an extensive library. Maggie had free rein to read any of the books she wished.

Her working day consisted of getting the children ready for school, cleaning their rooms and doing their laundry. Basically all the work they accumulated was passed to Maggie. She didn't mind. They were both school age so she had the afternoons to herself and at weekends they all went on day trips, with Maggie always included. They would visit the children's grandmother or friends of their mother's while Maggie sat in the garden and supervised. She usually kept herself occupied with a book. She was supposed to be more actively involved but the children didn't want her to be so no one really pushed the issue; as long as she kept an eye on them she could do as she pleased.

Everything would have continued in this ideal fashion but the children's uncle came to stay. He was their mother's younger brother and a bit overindulged. That summer he was twenty, tall, athletically built and endowed with a handsome impish expression. His smile was the first and only to cause a blush to colour her cheeks until she saw it return on the face of his son.

They were on a collision course from the moment they met. Maggie was for once away from her book and running with the children. He stood waiting to catch their attention from the patio. When they saw him they shrieked "Uncle Charlie!" and ran to his side. Maggie turned to look in his direction and he held her gaze and took her breath away. The knowledge in his eyes awakened the knowledge in her body. He set off a chemical reaction in her that was to alter her forever more. She'd never heard what happened to him afterwards but that feeling was still there when she thought about him.

Everything happened so quickly. He pursued her every waking moment. He was by her side talking to her or helping her with her chores. When she sat in the garden he sat with her. When she had time off he showed her Glasgow from an angle Maureen had never seen and could never show her. They ate in expensive restaurants and walked through galleries and public gardens. He talked to her about the places he'd travelled and the people he had met. Maggie absorbed it all like a bewitched sponge. The time frames had all blended together now in her head and it was difficult for her to tell how long it was before their runaway train finally hit a wall. She would never forget that night: their last night. She left the kitchen at her usual time and climbed the stairs, living in her head and oblivious to the shadows past the family landing.

As she placed her hand on her china doorknob she heard his voice behind her back. She turned and as she moved, he moved. Their bodies met and blended in the middle. His lips closed on hers and his hips ground hers against the door. At first she was terrified but the pleasure transferred from skin to skin undermined any second thoughts she had. He turned the doorknob and opened the door. Then they meandered like a drunk in the park up the stairs but they didn't get as far as the bedroom door before their bodies collapsed on the floor of her sitting room. As she closed her eyes she remembered seeing for the first time the cornices on her ceiling were in the shape of dripping fruit trees. Her body was soaked in the sweetest feeling she'd ever experienced.

The next day she remembered an atmosphere at breakfast but she thought she might be mistaken. The mother seemed to have taken on a frosty smile that teased the corners of her mouth but never spread any farther into her face. Her orders seemed less like suggestions and seemed to carry more weight.

Charlie never seemed to spend any time alone with her over the next few days and she interrupted more than one whispered conversation between him and his sister. She remembered the day it finally came to a head, because the little girl had home economics. Wednesday! She was crying, complaining that nothing was going right. She didn't have all her ingredients and now Uncle Charlie wouldn't be there for her birthday!

Maggie's head turned sharply though common sense should have told her any acknowledgement of what she'd just heard was a mistake. The mother cruelly held her gaze and that illusive smile finally found a bit more ground.

"Yes, darling, he's been seeing a girl in London. I think our Charlie may be smitten."

"What's smitten, Mummy?" the little girl innocently asked.

"Maggie will tell you, darling. I have to run."

She kissed the top of the little girl's head and left the room, popping her head around the door a few minutes later.

"Maggie! I've prepared your wages. They're in your room. I'd like you to be packed and out of here by this evening. Is that all right?"

She didn't wait for a reply. By the time Maggie nodded, the door had closed behind her.

Maggie arrived back to Maureen's house two months after her arrival in Scotland. Maggie didn't want to explain but her elder sister was wiser to the ways of the world than she'd been. She patiently listened to her little sister's version of the affair and then she bluntly told her the real version.

"Have you had your monthly yet?"

Maggie, unprepared for this level of intrusion into her bodily functions, stared blankly at her.

"Have you?" Maureen asked a bit more sharply.

Maggie shook her head.

Maureen started to cry and left the room.

The following months were painful for Maggie. She'd finally come to terms with her own stupidity.

She was working clearing tables in a teashop and reading wasn't top of her priorities any more. Finally, with a pain in her heart, she came to Maureen and told her what they both knew already. She was pregnant. She'd gone to the doctor and found out that day. Maureen shouted at her. Then she hugged her. Then they both cried.

"We'll think about it during the night," said Maureen. "We'll come to a decision in the morning." She kissed her sister's forehead and went to bed. Maggie sat a while longer gazing into the fireplace.

The next day they decided to tell Pascal and see if she could go home. It wouldn't be ideal but it certainly wasn't unknown for a girl to come home a young widow and bring up her child alone. Maggie waited for Pascal's letter but the day it arrived it didn't hold the answers she was expecting.

Pascal had gone to a lot of trouble. He'd contacted a convent where a cousin of their mother was a Reverend Mother. She'd offered to take Maggie in for the duration of her pregnancy and said if he wanted they could keep Maggie.

"It might be for the best," she'd gently pushed.

"We'll see," Pascal had replied. "We'll see how she gets on."

Maggie read the letter over and over until the lines ran into blue rivulets of tears and ink down the page. She knew she had no choice. She was starting to show and she couldn't expect Maureen to take care of her indefinitely. She had two small children of her own and another one on the way. So Maggie packed her belongings and caught the boat back to Dublin.

The convent was located near the city centre and was an enclosed order. When Maggie entered the grounds she knew her shoes wouldn't touch the street again until after the birth of her baby.

Some months after she arrived she experienced a sharp pain as she was working in the kitchen. The twinge nearly caused her to pass out. Jean, who slept in the bed beside hers in the dormitory, had to hold her or she would have scalded herself with a huge saucepan of boiling water – they were on dinner duty that week. Maggie wasn't sure if it was the shock of the baby moving or the smell of salt bacon that caused the pain. Perhaps the baby was hungry – he certainly wasn't happy. She remembered the shock and pain of thinking her baby was coming early but Jean had a lot of experience of births and knew the difference. "It's just practice, Maggie pet. A dry run!"

Maggie knew this precious time was all she would ever have with her baby so she talked to him as she lay in bed at night. She knew it was a boy. Nobody believed her but she didn't need anyone else to know. He was her little boy. She wanted to tell him all her hopes and dreams, thinking maybe one day he'd remember. She wanted to tell him all she wished for him. Give him all the good advice she must have been given but never listened to. Give him the wisdom of her sixteen years.

It was then she named him Tommy. She knew it

was an old man's name but when she tried to picture his little face she saw a little scrunched-up face like a little old man. Tommy just seemed right.

The night he arrived she tried to hold him inside her as long as possible. She didn't want to let him go but he couldn't be delayed for long. All the other girls had told her in detail about the baby being ripped from her still covered in blood. She felt every moment of the pain. It was the most real experience she'd ever had. But finally she felt him tear away from her body and heard his first cry as they wrapped him in a blanket. She pulled herself up and reached for him but they turned him away from her. She saw a tiny greasy arm and the top of his head. She knew he was dark and he had a strong healthy set of lungs. That was all she ever saw of him. She wanted to fight it but she didn't have the strength.

Eventually she went home to Cooleen after Pascal came all the way to Dublin to bring her back. She cried when she saw him and begged him to help her get her baby. Now that she could talk to Pascal face to face, she thought he would understand her need for her child. She told him again her plan to pretend she'd been widowed. That way no one would know and she wouldn't bring shame on the family.

But he refused to talk about it.

"You have no son, Maggie. That child will go to a family who can give him respectability. He'll never know of the shame his mother brought on him and her family. You should be glad we're taking you back. We could leave you here with Mother Imelda. Have some gratitude."

Any further tears would have fallen on deaf ears and a stony heart. Maggie came home and tried to put Tommy out of her mind. But every Christmas and birthday she did something special, hoping in some way it would reach her son and bind him to her. She bought him gifts and gave them to local children. She wrote him letters and burnt them at night. Gradually the pain eased, but now the memories were back clear as day and once again she had the opportunity to change her life.

Chapter 3

After Michael's visit Maggie had to work hard to keep the sparkle in her eyes from giving away her secrets. She didn't want Pascal to suspect anything. Moping wasn't her thing but she thought a certain amount of moping was necessary now. She kept all the housework in order but she didn't read and the television sat dead in the corner until Pascal himself decided to switch it on. The next day and the next she let slip by without being tempted to go to town. She knew Friday wouldn't arouse any suspicion. She always went into the town on the morning bus to do her shopping and Pascal would meet her off the bus on her way back, to carry the shopping up the hill.

A world of thoughts and feelings crowded her mind during those two long days. There were times when she thought she would explode. Throughout the years she had never forgotten Tommy but she had managed to subdue the feelings to maintain her sanity.

But now the longing was threatening to choke her at times. She had to swallow numerous times in quick succession to try and control her rapid breathing. Tears coursed down her cheeks, collecting in the hollow of her neck, when she allowed herself to think about the wasted years but then she would look around her at the farm and think what life would have been like here for him.

The house was old and hadn't changed in over forty years. Every year, as Pascal's years advanced, a few more weeds found purchase between the stones in the yard and the garden at the end of the house got a bit more overgrown. The trees were no longer trimmed and their branches could be heard scratching the roof when the wind blew off the mountain. David Blaney, Dolores' husband, offered to concrete the yard for Pascal but he wouldn't allow it. It had always been paved with stones and Pascal resisted change in all its forms even now when he was finding it more difficult to restrain the ever-growing weeds.

Maggie's own imagination stagnated over the years and she feared that soon she too would succumb to the rot that inevitably set in when you shut out the new and the unexpected. She no longer had the ability to converse at will with everyone; shyness controlled her now. She was aware of the separation between her and the people she met, the years of experience she'd missed out on here, keeping house for her brother and taking care of her mother. In both cases it had been a thankless experience. Her little boy wouldn't have benefited either from this harsh environment.

Her mother never lost her faculties. Her body gave up a little more of its abilities year after year but her mind was razor sharp and her tongue could and did cut to the bone. Maggie knew when to pull back from confrontation. The old lady's eyes would take on a cold look and her lips would purse. She would refuse to look you in the eye unless it was to follow up with a spiteful retort. Maggie would never let her see her bend. If necessary she would leave the room and cry, then come back to finish whatever job she was engaged in. Somewhere in the decay of life her mother's ability to feel pleasure and empathy withered. Perhaps the hard cold centre was the only part that survived the ravages of time. The indignity of having to depend, as Áine Breslin had to learn to do, on someone inferior was something almost too difficult to endure. She knew Maggie's secret and she never forgave her for it. From the day of Maggie's return she seemed to want to punish her. Maggie had been everything to her before that. She was the most talented, the most beautiful and the liveliest of her children. On her she had pinned all her dreams and Maggie had let her down.

Maggie promised herself that the day her mother passed on she would go and seek a life of her own. She thought, despite what her mother and Pascal said, no one else need know about her past and judge her subsequently. But though her mother was ailing for many years and was bedridden, she lingered on.

Maggie remembered the morning of her funeral clearly. She cried for the woman who gave birth to her and did her best for her growing up but she mourned more for her own lost opportunities than for her mother's passing. Maggie dressed in her best black coat and hat and a new pair of shoes. She stood in her room looking in the glass and tried to arrange her hair and clothes to a pleasing effect. Funerals and weddings were the only chance she got to dress up and she would spend the duration of the event sitting at a table, mortification at her lack of finesse gluing her to the seat.

Mother chose to go on Maggie's fiftieth birthday. She was ninety-one years old. Maggie inventoried her countenance in the mirror, making mental notes. The snow-white hair pulled back in an old-fashioned bun, the sagging neckline and drooping lines of her body couldn't be hidden by her good coat and hat. She'd heard recently that fifty was the new forty and the age at which the modern woman reached her prime. Perhaps this applied to a woman who had spent the first fifty years taking care of herself instead of a selfish brother and a spiteful mother. She tried to picture herself standing with Joan Collins at the church. It was beyond her comprehension. They were two different species and Maggie was the younger of the two.

The Thursday evening before her rendezvous with Michael dragged on and on and she was almost sick with longing to feast her eyes again on her son. She had to keep repeating "My son" over and over, trying to let the enormousness of it sink in slowly. It was difficult to do. Pascal was at Gallagher's again that night so she could indulge herself. She sat by the fire, in turn crying and smiling into the embers, stoking the feelings burning inside her. She crossed the room three times to pick up the phone and ring the hotel but she knew her courage would fail her and the words wouldn't come. If he'd gone, she thought she would die. Her heart couldn't take losing him again.

She wished he'd come back to find a different woman his mother. She felt so small. She watched the television for an hour and closely examined the faces and fortunes on the screen. Her grandchildren were going to go to medical school and law school. She had a sudden feeling of pride. How could her genes have produced such wonders? She supposed Charlie's had something to do with it too. Genes that would get a girl in trouble and abandon her. Anger swept over her then but she'd never indulged in that. It didn't help before, but that night somehow it did. Mentally she stripped Charlie down to his bones, letting her anger wash over them.

She looked at the clock. She'd sat up longer than she meant to. She heard the small gate below the house bang and Sheila gave an excited bark. Pascal was back. He'd obviously come up from the village cross-country and tackled the old style at the base of their land. It wasn't a long journey from the village as the crow flew but Pascal wasn't a crow and Eddie was convinced that one day it would be up to him to pull the old boy, pickled in porter, out of a ditch. Eddie ran young weanling cattle on the lower fields and walked the land early in the morning.

She flicked off the television and retired to her room. She didn't want to talk to Pascal. The only time he ever felt the need to exercise his lungs was after he wet them first with a few bottles of porter. She had enough going on in her own mind. She clicked shut her bedroom door just as the key turned in the kitchen door. In a few moments, she was tucked up in her bed. She thought she'd never sleep but it slipped over her like a blanket and she slept soundly for eight hours.

The next morning she woke at her usual time. Seven o'clock on the button. She was always the first up; her pottering about would wake Pascal and he would follow down a few minutes later, when she had the kettle on.

They'd always had very strict battle lines drawn regarding the workload. Pascal took care of the sheep and cows when they'd had them. He'd sold them five years ago when things got too much for him. Shortly afterwards he'd rented out the land. He still kept an eye on the garden, watching the weeds slowly take over the flowers, and he would spend a bit of time helping the young farmer, David Blaney, next door. This was more a matter of their neighbour keeping an old friend occupied than of any great practical input on Pascal's part. Though David often said how lucky he was to have a fountain of farming knowledge living next door. Perhaps it wasn't all for pity. David had always been close to the Breslins, having grown up close by. Now he, his wife Dolores and their two sons Jason and Dan would regularly come over to check on Pascal and Maggie. David had always been a quiet lad and had grown into a man of even fewer words, if that were possible, but despite this you couldn't fault him as a neighbour.

Everything else was left to Maggie. She took care of the dog, cat and hens. She took care of the house. She shopped for the food and cooked it and she took care of paying the utility bills. Pascal gave her the money on Friday. It had always been so since she came back and she couldn't see it changing any time soon. She hadn't received a wage since her youth and she was a few years short of pension age. Everything she had was courtesy of her brother. When her mother died she'd asked Pascal to take care of Maggie and keep a roof over her head for life and take care of her financially from the farm. One thing Pascal had was a sense of duty.

Maggie was floating inside with excitement about her trip to town but she couldn't let anything slip. It was killing her. She slowly went about her morning chores, almost going overboard with the bent head and the lifeless dragging of her feet.

Finally Pascal turned to her.

"You'd better get your bag or you'll miss the bus. It's nine o'clock."

"So it is." Maggie looked out of the corner of her eye at the clock.

She put on her coat and grabbed her bag.

"I'll see you later!" She called back to him as she left the house.

"I'll meet you off the bus . . ." his voice trailed away behind her.

In case he was still watching she crossed the yard slowly with her head down until she'd gone out the gate and turned down the lane. The moment she was away from the house Maggie's heart sang and a skip replaced her usual walk. A wave of tears choked her. The excitement was overwhelming. She was still a bit early for the bus so at the head of the lane she stood and nervously swayed from side to side. She turned her head to the right and watched the fuel lorry pull out of Eddie's yard and drive down the road, making a mental note for herself to order some coal.

She was just checking her watch again for the tenth time when she heard the bus coming. The bus was locally owned and picked up a bunch of people like herself dotted around the parish who had no other way of getting into town. The same bus picked them up in the evening and brought them back. It carried the same crowd on Sunday for Mass and on Friday night for Bingo in Letterkenny.

The bus rattled over the potholes, negotiating the bends on both sides of the narrow roads, the windows shook and a film of grime covered the outside of them – but it made the journey. The assembled crowd were all in or around fifty except for the teenagers who weren't old enough or rich enough to drive yet. They sat at the front in tight jeans and short tops talking to the bus driver, with the smog of cheap perfume mixed with cigarette smoke surrounding them. Their smart mouths and girlish giggles carried back to Maggie. She smiled to herself. The exterior wasn't fooling anybody and they couldn't hide the anxious shadow that crossed their faces when the teasing of the driver touched a raw nerve.

Maggie sat in her usual spot, centre of the bus by the aisle, feet closely held together, back primly straight, eyes fixed ahead. She stole another glance at Eddie's yard as they drove past. He'd painted the front door a nice glossy green; it lifted the little house out of the winter gloom.

She nodded and smiled at everyone on the bus and wished them good day but she could never be drawn into conversation. Her input would betray her lack of life outside the television and she really didn't have anyone to gossip about except Pascal. She didn't think it was worth anyone's time to listen to that. Behind her back they thought her spoiled and above herself because she'd worked for a wealthy family in Scotland years ago. Today they were probably correct: Maggie could only think of her son and her clever grandchildren.

When the bus stopped at the bus station she got off with everyone else. Every third week Eddie's wife Kate would drive her in for the company; lucky for Maggie they'd had their day out last week. Usually the bus group would all troop up through the town together for a look around before they headed back to Tesco and did their shopping. The supermarket was beside the station so it was handy for the bus, but today Maggie wanted them all to go on without her so she could go the other direction and meet Michael at the Beachwood Hotel.

Dora Scanlon, a nice wee girl, offered to stay with her but Maggie was adamant.

"No, pet. You go. I'll catch up. I have to make a quick phone call."

Dora needed no more encouragement – she was only being polite anyway. She ran to catch up with her friends. Maggie waited until they'd all gone, then walked out the door and turned the corner. She had a ten-minute walk and then she'd be there.

Letterkenny was a different town now than it was when she returned from Scotland. Back then few had cars and there were few big shopping centres. Now there was Dunnes, Tesco, Aldi, and Lidl – the list just kept growing but Maggie still preferred the small shops. She liked to go into a shop that was a piece of the town tapestry woven by generations of families and long years of commerce.

She couldn't help smiling as she walked along. She knew what people saw: a petite older woman in conservative clothing on an errand. But once upon a time she was a young girl with a bright smile and a sway in her walk. Pascal thought she was a fast woman that got caught. But the years had altered that perception. The appraising looks as she walked by were replaced by compassionate ones as youths held doors for her and offered to help her on the bus with her shopping.

Inside she still felt as though she were the same person but outside nature had wrapped her in a cocoon of lines and grey that concealed the energy and enthusiasm that still longed to make a mark. Only she knew what a mark she had left. From her body Michael was given life and generations would follow.

She could see the hotel up ahead. She stopped for a moment and just looked at it. Terror brought back the rapid gulping as she fought for control. She stood on the footpath looking up at the hotel, her feet rooted to the spot. She wanted so badly to go up to the lobby and breeze through the door and stride with confident steps up to the desk and ask to speak to her son, Mr Michael Reynolds. She could see her reflection in the darkened window of a car beside her. She looked diminutive and unimportant standing there in her good coat with her bag held protectively against her tummy.

Once again her mind brought her back though the years. She was standing on the footpath in Dublin looking at the convent door with her hands protecting her unborn child. She knew she was guardian of a very precious thing. Trees topped the walls in front of her and crows cawed from the branches. They were like heralds, black agents of doom lifting off the branches and flying back towards the building behind. There is no going back now, she thought. They know I'm here. She placed her trembling hand on the doorknob. She saw her white fingers, void of circulation, the knuckles yellow with fear, turn the knob. It was locked so she raised her hand to the knocker. As she did the door opened.

A nun stood there, pale and impassive, black eyes glinting through a pair of wire-rimmed glasses.

"Yes!" Her voice was cold. Her lips were surprisingly full, a bunch of lush cherries slashing an alabaster mask. Her eyes sank to take in Maggie's swollen stomach. A look of disdain finally altered the mask. Not for the better.

"You must be Margaret Breslin. You're late. We were led to believe you would be here an hour ago." Her face had changed from disdain to disapproval inside of a moment.

Maggie waited patiently for a welcoming smile. Perhaps that was the cause of the hesitation on the doorstep – perhaps she was struggling valiantly with herself to extend a welcome. Maybe even raise a glimmer of a smile.

Instead she stepped aside and obediently Maggie entered. The door was at least three inches thick and slammed shut behind her, echoing down the empty corridor, which was really a covered walkway stretching from the garden gate to the main convent building. The heels of her shoes tapped on the black and white floor, breaking an eerie silence. The walls stretched ahead like white ribbons. Recessed into the walls were statues of saints, whose eyes watched her progress down the corridor; the disdain of the nun seemed to have infected them too. Maggie's heart sank with each step she took and the baby responded to this disturbance by giving her a sharp kick.

A voice called out: "Maggie!"

For a moment the older Maggie stood confused, taking in the hotel and realising where she stood. The sounds of the convent slipped into the background and there in front of her stood Michael, a gentle expression on his face, his hand extended. Quietly Maggie walked into the hotel lobby holding tightly to her son's hand.

Chapter 4

Maggie had been in this hotel a few times in the past for family gatherings. She knew the layout. She walked with her head held high towards the dining room. Michael suggested that they have lunch so she wanted to look as though she were taking all of this in her stride. She hoped her trembling legs wouldn't let her down. Her sister Olivia was a big fan of the hotel dinner when she was home.

Michael helped her off with her coat and held her chair for her as she sat down. He pushed the chair in and her feet glued themselves together, firmly pressed against the floor with her hands nervously clasped in her lap. Michael sat opposite her. As they looked at the menu he couldn't keep his eyes from wandering off the menu to look at her face. He was memorizing every line, every gesture and every flicker of expression.

Maggie wanted to do the same and gaze into Michael's face but her eyes just weren't up to the task.

They hadn't the strength to face the intense scrutiny of his. Finally the waiter came and stood at their side.

"Sir, Madam, are you ready to order?"

Michael looked at Maggie. "Maggie?"

"A pot of tea, please, and some salad sandwiches: And a glass of water. Do you have ice?"

The waiter smiled and nodded.

Maggie's face relaxed. "Thank you."

She handed him the menu and he turned his attention to Michael. He ordered quickly and the waiter moved on. A long silence descended on the table.

Michael broke the silence. "Can I call you 'Mom'?" A big cheeky grin split his face.

"Oh, I don't know," Maggie answered, furrows of worry crossing her brow.

"I'm only kidding," he said hastily. "I'm so happy to be here with you. I won't do or say anything inappropriate to jeopardise that." He paused for a moment, retracing the lines on her face with his eyes. "I talked to my children."

"Did you?"

"They were very excited that I'd met you. One day we have to arrange a meeting."

"I don't know how we can manage that. Pascal wouldn't understand."

"We'll think about that later. Right now, Maggie, I want to hear all about you. Please tell me everything. I have so many questions I've wanted to ask you."

The pleading light in his eyes affected her deeply. She didn't want to let him down by telling him there really was nothing to tell – nothing worth hearing anyway.

To buy time she asked him a question. "How did you find me?"

"I knew your name was Maggie. Do you remember the blanket you made for me? The nuns asked my mother," he looked a bit embarrassed, "if she wanted to hold onto it. I found it in the attic after she died."

Maggie noted the blush when he said "mother". "I spent so much time working on that blanket. It was crocheted squares. You found the words?"

"I did."

"I thought my mother made it for me. I spread it out on the floor and ran my hands over it, tracing the stitching, and I saw it: *I love you ~ Maggie*. Then I read my mother's diary. She wrote in it every day of her life since she was a child. My daughter wants to edit it some day and try and get it published. That's when I got the full story. At first I felt deep anger at being deceived all these years. It was stupid, I know, but I felt abandoned."

"Or maybe you thought there was something wrong with your mother and they took you away." Despite her efforts, a hint of bitterness crept into her tone.

He blushed again. "There was an element of that."

The silence descended again on the table.

"Tell me about your mother." She was burning to know more about his life.

Michael cleared his throat. "My mother was born in Dublin. She was thirty-nine when she met my father. He was American – second generation Irish – and worked for an American corporation that was contracted to do some building work in Dublin. His contract lasted six months. During that time they fell in love and married. They always wanted children but they met too late in life. They tried for a number of years but they weren't successful. One day my mother's aunt, who was a nun in the convent where I was born, told her about a baby there. Maybe it was divine intervention but they thought I was perfect for her. We were very close. She did an excellent job as a mother."

Maggie could see that but she longed to have been that woman.

"Sister Rita said that an adoption could be arranged if Mom wanted. My parents hopped on the next Aer Lingus flight to Dublin and fell in love with me instantly and took me home." He reached across the table and held Maggie's trembling hands. "I had wonderful parents, you know. They gave me all that I could ever need. After my mother died I was left with a hole in my life that nothing could fill and I knew I had to find you and see who I really was."

Maggie couldn't answer him. She smiled through her tears and squeezed his hand. Then the waiter, arriving with the bread basket and a jug of water, interrupted them. They waited until he poured the water and left, then they resumed their conversation. During the lull, Maggie became uncomfortably aware of how possible it was that someone could see her here and wonder what she was doing, but Michael started talking again and suddenly she didn't care.

"I didn't contact you sooner because the time just never seemed right. First I was in college, then when I graduated I met my wife Lauren. We got married straight away and the kids came along a few years later so again the timing was wrong. Procrastination, I suppose. But early last year a work colleague put me in touch with an online agency that reunites family members. It worked for her so I thought I'd give it a go. It took them a bit longer than I thought it would. I mean I knew where I was born, I knew the exact date and I had your first name but it still took longer than expected to break through the red tape. My aunt was dead but the convent still held the records of my birth and eventually someone co-operated." He went silent again and went back to staring into Maggie's face. "Then I guess I just chickened out. I had your address but I didn't want to cause you any trouble so I held off as long as I could. But I was so scared something would happen to you and I would never forgive myself for not acting sooner. Finally my daughter Trudy threatened to do it herself if I didn't. She's very headstrong, your granddaughter."

Maggie's heart swelled with pride: her headstrong granddaughter. "I had no idea," she said. "No idea I had grandchildren and that they are now almost grown up too. I've always thought of you. You were my little boy but as the years went by I forgot you'd grown up. I recorded in my memory what I thought you'd be like until you were about ten but then the milestones got harder for me to bear. I preferred to hold you in my heart as my little Tommy. One day I sat down and cried like my heart would break because a neighbour's child who was born the week before you made her First Communion. I wanted to see you in your suit. I wanted to brush your hair for you before you went out the door. Put a clean hankie in your pocket for the church, but I couldn't. Somebody else cared for you when you had the measles, made your lunch for school and met you off the bus. You held someone else's hand and called her mammy. I had to stop picturing you growing or I couldn't have carried on. I placed you in a time capsule: like in *Star Trek*."

Michael laughed. "Are you a trekkie?"

"I love science fiction."

He exploded with laughter at her earnest response. "Now I know where Darren got it! Would you like to see pictures of the children?"

"Oh yes! Please!" Maggie's eager face shone. She held out her hands before the photos were even out of his wallet.

The first was of Darren. He was like his father, tanned and dark-haired.

"He has our hazel eyes too," said Michael. "But, despite her colouring, Trudy is like you, isn't she, Maggie?"

Maggie turned her attention to Trudy. She was round-cheeked and smiling with blonde hair and bright blue eyes. Yes, there was a resemblance though Maggie had been dark-haired.

Then Michael showed her his wife. She was a beautiful woman with blonde hair framing almond blue eyes and a lovely face with prominent cheekbones. Maggie asked why she hadn't come to Ireland with him.

"She passed away when they were little."

"Oh, Michael! I'm very sorry. What happened?"

"Cancer. She developed breast cancer in her early thirties. I guess we weren't looking for the symptoms because of her age. By the time we realised, it was too advanced for treatment. We spent an amazing summer together, the four of us, in Cape Cod for her last few months. That was her wish. She died peacefully with us."

Maggie was stunned by the maturity and acceptance of this man. His parents did a great job bringing him up.

"What about your father? You said your mother died. Is he still living?"

"No. He died when I was fifteen. He was ten years older than my mother. He was fifty-four when they got me. He lived to be sixty-nine. How old is Pascal? He must be a great age."

"Eighty. He's twenty years older than I am. I was the baby. I'm sixty now. I'll be sixty-one soon."

Michael's eyes misted. "I'm leaving Wednesday. Is it before then?"

Maggie again felt tears prick the back of her eyelids. "No, pet. It's not for a few weeks yet. We can write though, can't we?"

"You can count on that, Maggie."

Maggie's nervousness was starting to wear off now. She was having such a nice afternoon she forgot all about the shopping but the colour drained from her face when she remembered.

"Oh no!"

"What is it?" Michael looked concerned.

"The shopping, I forgot all about it. I have to catch the bus back and I need to do the shopping and pay the bills. I'll never get it done."

"I'll help you. Come on. There's no need to panic."

"You don't know Pascal. I can't face him tonight when I've had such a lovely day." Maggie knew how quickly the sharp words and the harsh expression could deepen into something more when he was crossed.

"Come on, Maggie, it will be all right." Michael called for the check and helped Maggie with her coat. "Where do you usually do your shopping?"

"Tesco. It's by the bus stop for handiness. Oh, I'll miss the bus! I've got to go."

Michael gently placed his arm around her shoulder. "I'll sort it out. Please don't get upset."

The tender tone in his voice was only accelerating Maggie's rising emotions. She followed him obediently out the door with the sinking heart of someone who knows they've made a fatal mistake and will have to pay for it.

Maggie stood by the side of the footpath as Michael got the car. How could she be so stupid? She knew Michael didn't understand. He would have no comprehension of the control Pascal had over her. Years of undermining her and subtly pinning her to the house had worked very well. She felt like a young animal that has been caged all its life. She was standing at the shed door sniffing the fresh spring air with two feet still inside. She knew there was a price to be paid for freedom. But Michael was a prize too precious to risk losing.

He drove up beside her and jumped out. He ran around to her side and opened the door. Everything he did was a mystery to her. She had never met anyone like him. He was gentle, sweet and intelligent; through life's tragedies he'd maintained a sense of faith and wonder.

Maggie gave him directions to the supermarket and together they went inside. They got halfway around the shop before Maggie saw some people from the parish. She saw the curious stares from twenty yards. There was no way around them, so she walked along, her head held high, pretending to be oblivious to the veiled question marks.

"Maggie!" Moira Bonner called out.

Maggie slowed, but kept moving. "Moira! I'm way behind. I have to rush."

"Will you be on the bus?"

Michael turned before Maggie could answer.

"I'm giving her a ride. You guys go on without her."

Moira was single and in her late twenties. Her eyes

bulged like a child's following Michael's stride down the store.

Suddenly, Maggie found she was delighted at the spectacle she was causing. She turned and followed Michael. She would place her hand on his arm when she required him to stop and get something off a high shelf for her. She knew the eyes of the store were watching their every move.

They paid for the shopping and Maggie waved to the gaping crowd of women as she followed her son out of the store. She giggled like a girl.

"I enjoyed that."

"I know you did! I think you have an evil streak, Maggie Breslin!" He hugged her and kissed her cheek.

His spontaneous shows of affection were frightening to Maggie and she didn't know how to respond. Each time he touched her, her heart gave a lurch, thumping into her chest wall.

They paid the bills.

"Where to next, Maggie?"

"I must pick something up for Pascal."

Together they walked to the chemist for Pascal's Ventolin inhaler. As the trip home loomed, Maggie's high spirits sank. She became very quiet.

"Are you okay, Maggie?"

"You won't get much of a welcome, Michael, at the house. As you've seen, Pascal can be very cold."

"I know but I'm still coming back tomorrow to bring you out for a drive."

"I don't know . . ."

"We have to, Maggie."

He held her small cold hand as the car ate up the last of the miles. Vast stretches of purple heather permeated by granite soaked into the distant darkness on either side. The loneliness of the landscape matched the pain in Maggie's heart. Too soon the lane appeared ahead.

They pulled into the yard and the first thing Maggie noticed was the closed door. The porch door was always open when they were at home. Pascal must be out still. She looked at the clock on the dashboard. She suddenly realised the car had been much faster than the bus. She wasn't due back for another half an hour at least. Pascal was nearly always late so usually she waited for him at the turn of the lane.

She turned to Michael. "I'd love to meet you tomorrow, so let's play it safe today. Pascal isn't back yet so could you help me in with the bags and then you go on." She stepped from the car before he could argue.

He followed with the bags. "Will you be all right?"

"Yes, I'll be fine."

"Okay, then, I'll see you tomorrow."

She waved Michael off at the door, then ran around the house putting everything away before Pascal came back so that he wouldn't know how much shopping she'd done. She was going to tell him she had bought only a few small things today so she walked up by herself.

A deep depression had settled on her as soon as Michael's car backed out of the yard. A part of her that lay dormant for many years had awakened when he was near, and there was a deep feeling of emptiness when he wasn't there. Trying to keep busy she went about her jobs, putting the shopping away and getting the tea on the table. Pascal would be more amiable if he was well fed. She'd just set the tart in the oven to heat when she heard Pascal at the door. She turned quickly but immediately lowered her eyes.

He stood there with a look of livid rage on his face.

"Are you trying to make a fool of all of us?" he shouted.

Maggie felt her bowels constrict with fear. She had seldom seen him so angry. Fear and the colour of his face rendered her dumb.

Chapter 5

"Pascal. I got back early, I have your tea ready." Her face pleaded with him to ease off his temper and give her a chance to explain. "Pascal, won't you sit down?" She pulled the chair out, ran to the range and grabbed the teapot. "I'll pour out your tea."

His face remained frozen. "I know what you were doing. Moira told me you were shopping with a Yank and he gave you a lift home. Now, I wonder who that could be?" He sneered the words into her face. "I'm left waiting for you like an idiot at the bottom of the lane after your fancy bastard drove you home. I told you he wasn't welcome in this house!"

"Pascal! I had lunch with him in Letterkenny. He didn't come into the house. I had to talk to him before he goes home."

"He's not your son, Margaret Breslin. You gave birth to him after a roll with your employer's brother. He's a symbol of your shame, your sin, in the eyes of your family and in the eyes of the church. The best thing you could have done for him was to let him be reared by decent people – what chance could he have, with the stuff he inherited from a tramp like his father and a slut like you!"

At first Maggie's fear and shame at being caught in a lie had stopped her in her tracks, but now anger grew inside her to match Pascal's. Anger was something she never felt. She'd been timid her whole life. But Maggie had never come as close to happiness as she had today. Pascal had no right to speak like that.

"Pascal!" she shouted. "You know nothing about the things that happened to us! You have no right to judge me. Michael is your nephew. He's an engineer and he's got two children in college. My sin produced more than your sanctimony ever did!"

She was breathless from her outburst. She rarely shouted and never with such intensity.

Pascal took two steps towards her. Before she could react he lashed out with his long bony hand and slapped her soundly across the face. Maggie, caught off guard, fell against the range. She placed her hand to steady herself on the hot plate and yelped with pain.

Her cry brought them both back to the moment. She swayed with the shock. Pascal immediately realised the folly of his actions and reached out to help her. Maggie was too upset to push him away. She allowed herself be led to the sink where he turned on the cold tap and ran it over the burn. The burning skin went numb under the cold water. He looked in the freezer and found a bag of frozen vegetables and, bringing a chair for her to sit on, he gently guided her to it and placed her hand on the cold bag. Tears started to course down her cheeks. She was too worn out after the excitement of the day to move.

"I'll see to the tea," Pascal offered.

Never in over forty years had he done that before. It was as shocking to her as everything else that went before it, but she didn't want to break the spell by passing comments. He brought her tea to her and fussed around her as she ate, buttering her bread and filling her cup.

Maggie knew there was going to be no happy ending to this story. Pascal was right. She allowed a man to use her and that moment brought a child into the world. A child that was better off without her. If he were better off then, why would he benefit from knowing her now? Maggie felt like a rotten piece of fruit with the bad centre hidden from view. She couldn't allow anyone to get close or they would see her for what she really was. She rose on unsteady feet from her chair.

"I'm off to bed now, Pascal. I'll see you in the morning."

"Goodnight."

He looked sadly after her. Why was that girl ever born? She'd been nothing but trouble. He sighed and turned to the dishes, but changed his mind. She could see to it in the morning when she'd had some sleep. He wasn't going to clean up any more of her mess. He switched off the light and closed the grate, then went to his own bed.

Maggie lay awake for hours staring at the ceiling. The pain in her hand matched the pain in her heart. She alternated between anger and tears. Pascal always spent Saturday at a neighbour's out in the hills. He never explained what they did but she knew they made and consumed poitín. Then he would come back drunk early Sunday morning. She knew he wouldn't miss that and the way things were between them tonight he'd probably leave right after breakfast. As dawn erupted in pale golds across the sky she drifted into a fitful sleep.

The next day Maggie awoke to a bright morning and the sound of dishes clattering in the kitchen. She looked at the clock. Nine o'clock. Maggie never slept past eight, even on a Saturday. She turned in the bed and a wave of nausea took her breath for a moment. Her hand was blistered and red. She hoisted herself up on the other arm and tried to gather enough strength to stand. After much self-berating, she finally took the plunge and swung her legs onto the floor. Wrapping an old dressing gown around her, she went up to the kitchen.

Pascal turned when she entered the room.

"You know how to create a drama, don't you?"

Maggie ignored him and walked to the teapot.

"Well, the mess will wait for you. I have to go. I have a bit of business to take care of."

He walked to the door but hesitated in the porch. He turned to her, as close to concerned as he could get.

"Are you all right? How's your hand?"

Maggie hadn't the strength to argue this morning.

"I'm fine. You go on. I'll get myself together and clean up. Go on. I'll see you later."

Grateful for the reprieve, Pascal went as quickly as he could. He really didn't think any of it was his fault anyway; Maggie had always been highly strung. She was difficult to cope with sometimes. A day in the hills and a drop with the men would cheer him up. He was smiling as he left the yard.

Maggie took stock when silence descended again on the room. She was bewildered from the stress of the past week. Her life's routine was shattered. She knew bitter decisions and recriminations would be her life for the foreseeable future. Pascal was a brick wall and she could see no way around this. She would have to blast through and that was one thing Maggie was ill-equipped to do.

She sat at the table and had her breakfast. There was enough time until Michael arrived. Nothing could come between her and her child again. She ran her mind over the situation from every angle, trying to find a solution. Her mother lived to be ninety-one; Pascal was eighty and in the peak of health, except for his asthma. She'd never change his mind and had no idea what to do. A longing like none she'd ever encountered before gripped her. In fifteen years her grandchildren would be in their thirties, Michael would be close to sixty. She would probably have great-grandchildren. She had been robbed of enough and couldn't bear any more loss.

Doubt grabbed her. Maybe she was a novelty and Michael just wanted a holiday. Perhaps he wasn't looking for a permanent addition to his family. She'd love if she could open her home to them and have holidays together and family meals.

The heart of the girl who stumbled across the room and into the arms of her lover was still beating in her chest. Maggie never thought about the good old days and often wondered what was good about them. She saw the changes in the world as positive. She envied the choices and freedom of young girls today. She didn't begrudge them anything. She was happy for them that they wouldn't have the life she had. She bought the papers and a couple of magazines every week and wasn't shocked at the land's shattered morality. Maggie's eyes and mind were open, despite the sparseness of her own life experience. She couldn't rot alone here with a condescending brother; the remainder of her life was too short. Maggie had to act.

But first of all she had to get ready. She cleaned the table and gingerly washed the dishes. When the kitchen was presentable again and she was ready to face the wider world, she relaxed. A glance at the clock reassured her that Michael should be along soon. Betty tiptoed her way across the flagged floor and jumped onto Maggie's knees, her green eyes blinking into Maggie's. The moment was broken by the sound of a car entering the yard. Betty was unceremoniously dumped onto the ground and almost stepped on in Maggie's hurry to get out of the house. Before Michael had a chance to come and get her, she'd grabbed her bag and coat and ran out. As she was locking the door she saw Eddie crossing the yard carrying a wire strainer and an old potato sack. He was always fixing something. He nodded at Michael and Maggie and went on his way, leaving Maggie wondering what he was thinking.

Maggie was losing the temerity of their first two encounters. This time she jumped into the car, greeting him with a wide smile and gleaming eyes.

"Hello, Michael. You're right on time."

He sat sideways, examining her face thoughtfully. He seemed to be speculating in his mind. He gathered his thoughts and smiled. "Hey, Maggie, where are we going today?"

"I don't know. Maybe we could go to Bundoran. It's nice down there. There's a nice beach. We could have lunch or we could take a look around Donegal town. We could drive back by the coast, drive through Carrick and Killeybegs. It's a lovely day. We'll have a great time."

Suddenly realising she was chattering like a monkey, she stopped.

"I know we will," he said, smiling. Then his expression changed. "Maggie! What happened to your hand?"

She was holding it upright in her lap to stop it from touching off anything. The large blisters were visible. "Oh, don't worry, love, about that. I spilled the kettle on it last night. I got an awful fright but it was fine. It will heal in a few days."

Michael still looked concerned. "Should you go to a hospital?"

"No, pet. It only needs a bit of rest and it will be fine. Pascal finished the tea for me last night and got his own breakfast this morning. I'm in good hands."

"If you're sure!" Michael started the engine and they pulled out of the yard.

For a while they drove in silence. Under normal circumstances Maggie had an inbuilt need to fill gaps in conversation and would talk constantly. To her, silence signified the gulf she felt in company. Maggie always put the empty space down to herself. But today she comfortably sat and watched the mountains roll by until they came into Glenfin.

"Michael, this is where your grandmother was born."

"Really!" Michael seemed genuinely intrigued.

"Yes. She married and moved to the Letterkenny area when she was a girl. She was married at eighteen. She had Pascal a year later." Maggie looked out at the swaying bushes. "A respectable nine months later!" She flashed a mischievous smile.

Michael roared laughing. It was a big belly-laugh. He threw his head back and Maggie's heart burst with pride. It felt so nice to make a joke about morality without the disapproving frown of Pascal.

Maggie guided him up narrow winding roads overgrown with high hedges infringing on the roadside. She warned him to be careful because some of the roads had channels for run-off water at the side. He wouldn't want to get his wheels stuck or he'd have to call out the garage. Finally the car pulled up outside the gateway of an old ruin. The house was a pile of rubble with a mountain ash growing from the corner of the toppling chimney. It was encircled by a ruby ring of fuchsia crying their petals into the grass.

It was a sad little hovel now. Maggie remembered that kitchen full of noise and laughter as her grandmother baked bread and fed the young mouths open like chicks' around her table. They would help her with the farm work and when times were tough at home a few of them would stay over with her to give their mother a rest. Whenever a new baby arrived they all stayed at Granny's to be out of the way.

The day Maggie gave birth to Michael was the loneliest memory of all. There were no children nearby to welcome the new baby. No family to help with the birth. No women to pass on the family skills to the new mother. Her baby was ripped from her and she had to recover in silence, the scars of the birth hidden rather than healed. The scar to her soul took precedence. As the stitches from the birth dug into her flesh and the milk meant for her baby dried in her breast she recited the rosary and said her penance and her little boy lay alone in a nursery, waiting for the Reynolds to come and claim him. But God had a purpose after all.

She didn't have the resources but Michael went to wonderful people who did, and now they were together again. Mother Imelda told her one day that God always had a plan. The nun thought the plan was to benefit the Reynolds in their quest for a baby but Maggie would love to be able to tell her now how right she actually was. God's plan had brought her baby back to her with a much better life than she could have given him.

Michael's eyes glowed. He jumped out of the car and climbed the fence. He ran around the tiny property, looking through fragmented window panes, raising briars out of his way.

"This must be the kitchen!" His voice was full of excitement. "Look, it's got the remains of a stove in there and a corner cupboard with pink stripy mugs."

Maggie laughed out loud. "Michael, it's a pile of rubble!"

"No, Maggie, it's my history, my past. It all feels strangely familiar. It feels like coming home."

Maggie was mesmerised. He turned and manoeuvred himself around a fat gorse bush to get into the cowshed.

"The home of the Breslin family cows!" his disembodied voice called out of the darkened entrance.

"McGlynchy family cows! Your great granny was a McGlynchy."

Maggie tried to open the gate and follow him but it was beyond opening. The only hope was to climb it and that was beyond her physical capabilities now.

But she didn't need to. She was one up on Michael; it was like having x-ray vision. She could see the path down to the door when it was scrubbed and trimmed with pansies. She could see that old shed minus the gorse bush when it was whitewashed bright enough to reflect the sun. She could hear her grandparents discussing the news in the kitchen on a Sunday over a pot of tea. Her mother would be at home, lying down having a rest, and her father would be out in the mountains having a drink of poitín with his buddies. Pascal kept a lot of his traditions going.

Maggie's father was a stern man with no spare emotions left to extend to his family. They were reserved for closing a deal at the fair and making sure someone didn't pull a fast one on him when they were settling up later. Reserved also for the inevitable argument that he always started in the pub on the way home. Nothing got his emotions going quicker than an imagined slight from a fellow drinker. He was a good man to make money and he intended his family to be well provided for, but he was just as good at spending it in the pub. Gallagher's public house extended their business on the money that should have fed the Breslin children.

Maggie didn't see the worst of it, being the youngest. Her father died young. He was out of the picture before she was old enough to understand. Her siblings paid for her clothes and food and sent her to school. Perhaps Pascal was right. Maybe she did get everything too soft. She loved all her nieces and nephews but, looking with pride at her son now, she thought even when it came to children she'd produced the best one. She wanted to throw a party and celebrate his arrival. The moment would come at last. Maggie couldn't feel shame for Michael and she couldn't believe that anyone else would. She knew they would be surprised, but they would get over that. She had to handle Pascal first.

Chapter 6

Michael popped out of the bushes on the other side of the house. He looked like a big kid.

"This is great, Maggie!"

She smiled at him.

"Awesome!" he said, half to himself. He came towards her. "Tell me about the layout. What was it like? How many rooms did the house have? How many people lived there?"

Maggie tried to order the questions in her head as she prepared to answer. "Well! Let me see . . . The yard was a similar shape to ours. On the left side of the yard as you came in the gate was the vegetable garden and on the other side was a row of outhouses. Between the sheds and the dwelling house there was another gate, as in our yard, leading out to the orchard and further out into the fields behind the house. Everything was arranged as closely as possible around a central yard for shelter in bad weather. If the farmer was called out late at night for a sick cow he never had to walk much more than thirty yards to the shed."

She pointed out the rooms as she described them so Michael could get a better view. She talked about the layout of the garden and the sheds. She talked about the animals she played with when she was a child.

"Oh, my!" She started to laugh. "I forgot Edward G!"

He laughed at the name. "Who was Edward G?"

Maggie had tears of memory and mirth in her eyes. "He was my grandmother's gander. He was a vicious creature. All us little ones were terrified of him. He used to live in the small garden behind that shed you were just in. It was the fruit garden. I think Granny kept him to keep the wee ones from stealing too much of the fruit. He would run at us and flap his great wings and make the loudest noise. We were terrified of him. My father came back here one night after the fair in Brocagh by mistake, thinking he was at home – he was steamed –"

"Steamed?" Michael interrupted and raised his eyebrows like two question marks.

"Drunk," she laughed back.

"Oh."

"Anyway, he went around the back to let himself in and he couldn't find the door. There was no back door in this house. He was just on his way around the front again when he saw the little hovel in the garden. My grandfather used the hovel for farm tools. Edward G used it as a bedroom at night. Daddy walked right into him in the dark. Edward G cut Daddy's face with his wings and gave him a terrible black eye. Daddy tried to pretend it was a fight and he'd won, but my grandfather had heard Edward G's raucous screams and, with my father on the path and blood all over his face, he got the picture!"

"How did he get his name?"

"Edward G Robinson. My grandfather liked gangster movies and that gander was a bit of a rebel."

"Did many people have television back then?" Michael had always been led to believe that Ireland in the forties and fifties was so backward there was no television.

"No – nobody I knew had a television set but there was a travelling film show that came around once a week. They set up a film projector in the parish hall and showed movies. The parish priest would sit in the front row and keep an eye on what they saw. Occasionally he would denounce one but usually I think he just enjoyed the film. People would go see the films when they were young but they wouldn't have much of a chance when they got older and were tied down with families."

"Did you go sit in the hall and watch those movies, Maggie?"

"Not often. I was only sixteen when I went to work in Glasgow. So I was too young to be out gallivanting on my own. Being the youngest I was a bit sheltered by everyone."

"Was it in Scotland you got me?"

Maggie blushed at the directness of the question

but she nodded. "Yes. I went to work for a rich family. But I only lasted a few months before it happened. Then of course I had to leave." Somehow she couldn't get herself to mention his father. "I went to live with my sister Maureen – she still lives in Glasgow. She's married and has six children and ten grandchildren scattered all over. I was living with her for a few months when I found out you were on the way. She was expecting as well and she couldn't look after me when I stopped working so I asked Pascal could I come home. But of course he would only allow me under certain circumstances."

"The bastard!" Michael spat out the words. The boy-like face hardened and for that moment he looked every inch the man he was.

Perhaps Maggie was trying to fill her soul with as much as she could of the boy she'd missed.

"I'm sorry, Maggie, for shouting. I know the memories must be hard but you wouldn't have given me up, would you, if you didn't have to?"

Maggie reached out and slipped her small hand into his. "No, my love. You were the most precious thing God ever gave me." With bitter bile choking her, Maggie realised all her pain was in the Name of God. They took her child in His Name and Pascal condemned her in His Name but Maggie often wondered what God Himself would have had to say about it all.

"Was there no other way?"

"I asked Pascal to tell everyone that I got married young in Glasgow and that my husband was killed. I thought a young widow sounded respectable. But Pascal went to confession and told the priest about his dilemma and that was that. Father Dee was his name. He wasn't from Donegal. He was from down the country somewhere. He told Pascal that a great evil had befallen my family. I had performed the evil act and was trying to take my sin and shame into the community and now I was asking my brother to lie for me. He told Pascal to look beyond his sister and her child and see the situation for what it really was. He said it was a community seeking to protect itself from outsiders' influence. It was a great time for spirited rhetoric from the pulpit with a good dose of fire and brimstone. On Sundays that priest would stand on the pulpit and pound it with his clenched fist, punctuating his words. A cousin of my mother ran the convent I went to in Dublin. She took me in and put me to work and when you were born they took you away. They knew I would be difficult so they took you immediately. They didn't give me any chance to bond but they forgot the nine months I carried you, and the long nights in the convent when I lay awake talking to you. I explained everything to you as best I could, hoping you wouldn't hate me later."

He flicked his gaze around the little yard. "I know you hurt a lot over the years. You missed out on so much but I did have a wonderful life. My parents were the best. I was an only child but the house was always filled with friends and life. They gave me the best education they could. I have the most amazing children. As soon as we can arrange it, you must meet them. They're dying to meet you. We've a lot to be grateful for." He paused. "Maggie – I'd like to ask you something."

Maggie's stomach churned. "What?"

"Do you think I'll ever get to meet my father?"

Maggie's shame burned in her heart. His inner thoughts were written all over his face. She knew he was finding it difficult to formulate the question because he worried his conception might be a delicate subject. He might even be wondering if she knew who his father was.

Her face burned red and she looked at the ground. "I can give you information on how to contact him if that's what you want." She couldn't raise her eyes to meet his.

"It's all right, Maggie. We'll discuss it some other time." His voice was gentle and Maggie loved him for his empathy. "Now, come on, Maggie Breslin. We have a lot of travelling to do today. I have to get to know my home county."

They got back into the car and drove on.

Before they got to Ballybofey Michael started laughing. "Do you know, I've waved to nine people, in an area where I know nobody? What's that all about? Do you know them?"

"No! Everybody waves up here, especially at strangers because they're wondering who you are. It's a gesture of welcome."

"It's great." He laughed again as a man in another

vehicle, a blue Hiace van, waved at him. He waved back and flashed his headlamps. The man in the van did likewise and winked as the two cars passed each other.

"That one's a distant cousin of ours. He's a nice fellow."

Michael's face glowed. "This is great."

Maggie agreed.

"So this is Ballybofey?" He looked around. "Is it always this busy?"

They were driving slowly though Glenfin Street.

"It is. It serves a large area."

"I looked up as much about these towns as I could on the Internet before I came over. I met a man in a pub one night in Boston. The Kinvara, it's an Irish pub. He was from Balleybofey."

"Oh. What was his name?"

"I have no idea. It was a work night out and we were all a bit drunk. I probably got a bit poetic because at that point I was so longing to find you, but I didn't have your full name yet. I did know you were from the northwest."

"Good thing you didn't have my name or you might have told him and he would have been on the phone that weekend to his Aunt Bridie or Mary who would have spread it around and it would probably have been back to me inside a fortnight. It was a nicer surprise to find you at my door."

"You're probably right. The demon drink – he gets blamed for a lot, doesn't he?"

"He does," Maggie agreed, "but he has plenty of co-conspirators."

Michael stopped at an intersection. The sign said right for Donegal town. "What's left, Maggie? Is there anything else worth seeing here in Balleybofey?"

"Would you like some tea? There's a nice hotel in Stranorlar."

"Where's that? Is that another town? Is it far away?"

"Take a left and I'll show you."

They drove on through the town. As they were crossing the bridge Maggie pointed out Finn Harps' ground.

"Have you heard of them?"

"Yes, I have. The brother of my friend from The Kinvara played with them and I looked up their results every week in the *Irish Times*. I have an online subscription. It's kind of small, isn't it? It's not Fenway."

"What's Fenway?"

"It's where the Boston Red Sox play. I'll take you to a baseball game some day. My son and myself try to get to as many games as possible during the season. But there are so many it doesn't always suit our schedules. He grew up so fast. A lot of the good times slipped away before I had a chance to appreciate them."

Maggie again got that twinge of pain. How she longed to get some time before hers slipped away too. She pointed out the hotel. "There it is, Michael, on your right there. Turn up that laneway and you'll find some parking. I'd say the street is full."

Michael indicated and sat in the traffic waiting for a clear run. Finally he got the opportunity and turned when a lady in a Volvo waved him across. He smiled broadly and waved back. Maggie was watching his face.

"You'd know you had Donegal blood in you."

"Why is that?"

"You're very easy with people. You'd fit right in here."

Michael parked the car and they went inside.

"We'll go into the bar." Maggie led the way. Her small frame strode purposefully ahead into the interior of the hotel with Michael bringing up the rear.

In such a small amount of time she was finding her feet and starting to take a little taste of her rights as his mother. She pointed to a seat in the corner. She didn't come in here very often, but she'd been here often enough to at least pretend to be au fait with the lie of the land.

"You sit there and I'll order a pot of tea. Would you like sandwiches or scones?"

"Scones would be lovely." He sat and looked around the bar. Two young girls were working behind the bar dressed in tight black skirts and white blouses. They both seemed to know Maggie well and smiled at her and launched into a conversation.

Michael noticed for the first time how obvious Americans were in Ireland. He spotted a couple just inside the door having an early lunch. He was trying to isolate what exactly set them apart when Maggie came back. It's not their shape, he thought. He'd always thought the Irish were very thin compared to Americans but not so much now. He'd seen plenty of people of varying ages and stages of obesity. One thing different was the expression on their faces, but he still couldn't put his finger on what that was. Their walk was a bit different too. But again he couldn't quite grasp what it was. Each Irish person that walked through the door strolled in casually and happy, smiling and chatting. Each American he'd seen walked in as though they'd taken a class in walking. It was as though each step had to have a purpose.

"What did you say, Michael?" Maggie was pouring the tea.

"American facial expressions. Do you think they're different?"

"Definitely."

Now he felt conspicuous. "In what way?"

She started to laugh. "I don't know. They look like they're on holiday. Like they're being the best tourist they can possibly be."

"Um!" Michael looked even more bewildered.

"We probably look different abroad too, pet. I wouldn't worry about it."

"I suppose you're right. Those two just bothered me. I want to fit in but straight off I knew they were from the US and I thought 'I don't fit in'. I stand out as being a middle-aged American doing the holiday thing."

Maggie started laughing. "They don't look relaxed. Maybe you should relax."

"Well, thanks, Mom, that's nailed it, no more confusion."

Maggie threw back her head and laughed loudly. The sound and the novelty took her totally by surprise.

"Hey, you could let yourself go once in a while too," said Michael. "You're a very wound-up little woman."

Maggie's face just erupted again into a huge smile. "You make me very happy."

"Ditto. Mom." He whispered it this time.

Maggie laid her burnt hand beside his and he held it gently, avoiding the blisters while she drank her tea with the other.

The hotel guests gradually found their way into the bar in dribs and drabs and peppered themselves around the room. Maggie and Michael ate their scones and amused themselves trying to figure where people came from and what their stories might have been. Maggie was exhilarated. Few people she knew ever took the time to people-watch as they were doing now. Gossip and interfere, yes, but actually watch, no. Maggie felt younger and more alive than she had in many years.

Finally Michael drained his cup and gathered himself to go. "Come on, my dear. We've been gone for hours and we've only travelled thirty miles. I'll never get to see my county."

They walked out together and Maggie realised she was greeting people with a smile and hardly a trace of the nervousness she had on their first day out and that was just yesterday.

Once more they buckled up and pulled out into the road. They turned left again through the town and headed south towards Bundoran.

"The mountains are gone. These are just green fields, not so pretty."

Maggie grinned. "Wait a minute."

Around the next corner the land started to get rough again and then they were in Bearnas Mór Gap.

"Wow!" Michel looked around him. "They're back! This is like a moonscape. It's great."

"You're never too far away from mountains in Donegal, Michael. They're like our backbone."

The car seemed small and insignificant as they wound their way along. The faces of the mountains rose high on either side. At that moment there wasn't another car in the gap. Sweeping arms of heather-covered mountains embraced them and they felt alone as though it was just the two of them after all those years.

Chapter 7

Michael manoeuvred through the traffic jams of Donegal town and entered the 'Diamond'. Each side of the town centre was a choked artery of traffic. They had travelled the last few miles in a companionable silence, which Maggie broke now, to inform him how to get around the back of the shops to find parking. There, they got out and checked the meter to see how long they could have. They paid for an hour and walked through, back out onto the street.

"It's so quaint." Michael looked around. The town square was diamond-shaped. The sides were lined with shops and hotels and then in front you could see the old structure of the castle. Michael spotted McGee's clothes shop and asked would it be okay if he went in and had a look around. He wanted to buy some gifts for his children. The knitwear caught his attention straight away. He held up an Aran jumper, asking Maggie if it suited him.

She smiled at him. "It does, pet. One of those and a tweed cap and you'll really look like a tourist."

"Then it's not for me." He smiled at her. But he still held it up. "I think I might get one and wear it at home: a nice grey one. I could face a Massachusetts winter in that with my Gore-tex jacket and a pair of cords."

"Is it very cold?"

He nodded. "We spend a lot of time shovelling snow. It's good exercise. We do it every morning to get to work."

"We haven't seen a good fall of snow in Donegal in a long time. I'd like to be in Massachusetts for the winter. I'd like to be indoors by the fire while a blizzard raged outside."

For the first time talk seriously turned towards a visit. Michael too had been thinking about all the lost time. He knew Maggie was still young enough to enjoy time with him and her grandchildren, but if she didn't stand up to her brother time would slowly slip away. Gently and as unobtrusively as he could he started to plant the thought in her head. At first she resisted, seeing only the obstacles in their way, but over the rest of the day the ideas were taking firm root.

Michael had more than enough money to help her out but Maggie's pride wouldn't hear of it.

"I have a bit saved for my funeral."

His heart gave an involuntary lurch when she said that.

They paid for the purchases in McGee's. A jumper

each for his children, a tweed cap and a jumper for him, and a few knick-knacks for friends. Maggie's eyes bulged at the final tally for the shopping spree. It was more than herself and Pascal would or could spend in a year on clothes.

They had always led a very frugal life. For many years Maggie had cleaned the church; it gave her a little pocket money. She always siphoned off a little from the shopping money and stored that away. But pooling all sources of income together wouldn't loosen enough money to do what she saw her son do this morning. What a different world! He probably lived like those people on the television programmes she loved, with their Cape Cod cottages and their swinging seats on their porches. Her grandchildren were probably like extras for *Dawson's Creek*. She bet he had lines of chrysanthemums on his porch and large trees dotted around his property, which opened directly onto the street with no garden wall to cut it off from his neighbours. Maggie had always soaked up American culture from every possible source – magazines, books, and television, anywhere – because it was so different from her own. For her it was the ultimate escape. She immersed herself in the daily lives of lawyers, doctors, tycoons and writers. She lived their colourful lives right along side them. Her son was a Bostonian engineer and her two grandchildren would one day be high-powered lawyers and doctors. If Maggie could get to be with them she would be living in the midst of all that excitement. Like *Dallas*; she would live like

Miss Ellie. She would be the matriarch of her own family. Her flesh and blood. The longing took her breath away. She could feel her breath quickening again.

She stood for a moment on the edge of the street and looked around her. She tried to open her eyes and see everything. She separated the indigenous Donegal or Irish from the tourists. What do we look like to the eyes of the rest of the world? Was Michael impressed with her the same way? Or was everything quaint like his description of the Diamond? To her the Diamond had always been the central hub of one of Donegal's busiest and wealthiest towns. She had never seen it as quaint before. Her parish was quaint. These were townsfolk. She'd been living so long out in the sticks she was in awe of everything and everyone. Even in her own parish she wasn't the smartest. She'd never married and carried a secret scar deep in her heart that sealed her inferiority in her own eyes and she knew in the eyes of anyone else that should happen on her secret. But in her heart, in the deepest recesses of her soul Maggie lived a thousand dreams. If she gave her mouth a chance to do its job and share those wonderful parts of her she could stand up and be counted amongst kings and queens. Maggie was that rare mixture of pride and inferiority rolled into one ambiguous package. Nobody knew quite what to make of her and it was very difficult to become her friend. But there was a floodgate waiting to open. Her son and grandchildren were her conduit to the world she'd always wanted.

"Let's walk." Michael held out his arm and without a trace of her old self-consciousness Maggie accepted it and happily walked along beside him, smiling with confidence at the people she met around the square. They walked around the castle. Michael wanted to go inside but it was closed up. He examined the walls and stood there, battles of centuries taking place inside his head.

Then they took a walk down to the pier. The tide was in. It gently lapped against the wall of the pier. Michael sat down and let his legs dangle. The toes of his shoes were inches from the white tips of the waves. A spray of moisture caught his face full on each time a wave broke.

"Keep sitting there," Maggie informed him, "and you're going to get wet!"

He smiled at her and put his hand up and held hers. "What was it like?"

She knew at once what he meant. She felt the familiar pain as she tried to resist the memory.

He saw the expression on her face and knew what she was doing. "Please. Let me share some of the experience."

She pulled her hand away and gently stroked the top of his head, looking out over the water.

"Maggie!" he prompted her, but only the wind answered. "Mom!"

That got her attention. "I'll never get used to being your mom, you know."

"Yeah, you will. It's happening already."

"I suppose it is, just a tad." She smiled down at the little centrepiece on the top of his head where all sides of his hair met. Then she began. "I just don't know how to talk about it. I've locked the feelings away for so long to protect myself and nobody ever wanted me to open them up. It was the most painful time of my life. I thought it would kill me. Unfortunately allowing myself to die would only compound my sin. I couldn't win. It was hard. I worked long hours in the convent and had no time to prepare myself to be a mother. Then to top it all I had to try to come to terms with the fact that I mightn't have you for very long. None of it was as difficult as the day they took you away. My labour seemed to last forever. Nobody spoke to me apart from push and stop when they deemed necessary. One nurse had kind eyes and she tried to smile with them without letting the matron see it on her mouth. I remember holding onto that look when the pain got so bad. When I thought I hadn't the strength to go on I held onto the thought of seeing your little face for the first time. But the powers that be had other ideas. They knew I was going to be trouble after the birth. They knew I wouldn't want to give you up, so as soon as you took your first gulp of air, they took you away. I heard you scream and saw your little hand reach up into the air looking for me. Then you were gone. I knew you were scared, such a tiny little thing alone in the big cold world without me to comfort you. From the moment I heard you cry my heart ached to love you. I saw the tiny little fingers on your hand and I could imagine those gripping mine as your little blue eyes looked up at me. All babies have blue eyes, you know. I cried and your wails got fainter as they carried you away. I never saw you again until you were standing in my yard a couple of days ago. But I never forgot you. I carried you inside for nine months and a little piece of you stayed there and it will be there forever, even if God takes one of us."

Michael stood up and held her head against his shoulder. The closeness confused her but she allowed herself to feel it, to let it sink in, that he was her son. At long last she was holding her son.

They walked back along the pier and across the street to go back to the car with both of them lost in their own thoughts. Maggie felt strangely lifted as she walked. For the first time in over forty years she had been able to talk freely and openly about that day and explain her actions to her son. She'd always feared that if she ever got the opportunity he wouldn't understand, but the look she saw on his face told a different story. She knew, not only did he understand, but also today they'd forged an alliance, a bond that would prevail forever more.

They pulled out of Donegal and drove on out of the town. A few miles out Maggie showed Michael the entrance for Rossnowlagh beach. He drove down, expecting a little cove like others he'd seen around the Donegal coast since his arrival. Instead he found himself driving onto a beach that stretched way into the distance.

"You can drive along the beach for miles," said Maggie. "I'd like to walk along if you wouldn't mind. I don't get to come down here very often."

Michael didn't say a word as he stopped the car on the sand. For a while he didn't move a muscle. He just sat there gazing out the window on his side of the car. Maggie was starting to feel nervous. Perhaps she was wrong about him understanding; maybe he did resent her. Her hands started to tremble.

Michael noticed the movement. For a moment he just turned his head and with his steady eyes he watched her bird-like fingers gripping and releasing in her lap. Then his eyes lifted and he scrutinised her face, watching all the confidence of the morning evaporating into the air. Maggie's face was crumbling before his eyes. Her face hung and her shoulders sagged and she closed her eyes to hide the shadows that she knew had covered them. She willed as hard as she could to keep the tears from sliding out but despite all her best efforts one did and slid silently down her cheek. Michael watched it. He watched it make its way down the thin covering of her cheek and hang on the sagging jaw-line of his mother.

Her eyes were pressed tightly closed and her lips were pursed together to stop them trembling; it caused the hollows in her cheeks to deepen and the wrinkles around her eyes to become more pronounced. He could see the wave of pain the memories caused, choking her, and at that moment all he could do was watch. He wanted to understand. He wanted to see what it was like for a woman to carry a child for nine months and have it wrenched away from her. He wanted to see when the mask of time slid off, the raw emotion underneath. He knew it was unforgivable. He knew he should reach out and comfort her; just a touch of his hand would make it all go away but he couldn't. He wanted to see first-hand that it did hurt her. She didn't just abandon him because it was difficult, he wanted to satisfy himself that she suffered, that her heart bled like his did the day he found out that Marianne Reynolds, the woman he adored above all others, had lied to him and betrayed him. He wasn't bitter but he wanted to know that there were real feelings, that it wasn't all a game.

The day Michael opened Marianne's diary and saw the entries regarding his birth inside, he felt the world momentarily stop its orbital path and stand still. He inhaled a breath and only the ensuing dizziness reminded him to let it out. Even later with children of his own he couldn't let it go, in fact his children made it worse because he found it even more difficult to understand how someone gave him up. Was he that unlovable? He knew rationally he should take it in his stride and thank God that wonderful people had found him and made him theirs, but he couldn't. He felt abandoned. Just like any little immature kid felt alone in the park, he suddenly felt alone in the world.

He'd kept the secret from all around him and tried to carry on as normal but time only deepened his sense of abandonment. His children knew something was seriously wrong. They'd always been the sort of family that if there was something, they shared it, and if someone didn't have the strength to share someone else would ask straight out "What the hell's the matter with you?" It was his daughter who finally had the delicacy to demand an answer and he loved her for it. He sat them down and explained what he'd read in the diary. His kids were hard-nosed and immediately set about helping him find their grandmother and now here he was watching her suffer to prove to himself that his pain wasn't alone. He'd had a wonderful upbringing, fathered two exceptional children and he was tearing apart this little woman who'd carefully hidden her past to protect herself. He felt more ashamed than he'd ever done in his life. He leaned over and held her in his arms and the pain of a lifetime flowed between them.

They walked the beach and talked and finally now that he had his real mother, there was no going back. He couldn't understand how he hadn't figured out he was adopted sooner, because he never felt this intensity towards his adopted parents. Maggie felt the same and her eyes followed his every move, terrified to miss any little detail.

Chapter 8

They sat in the car and watched the sun drop low over the horizon.

"Michael, do you still want to go to Bundoran? It's very late now."

"No, it's not." He looked at his watch. "It's only five after five. You're a grown woman. You can stay out as long as you like. Can't you?"

"I suppose." She was suddenly aware of the pain throbbing in her burnt hand. "I was just wondering if you wanted to head back to the hotel. You must be tired after all this driving."

He smiled at her innocence. "This isn't a lot of driving. If we go out into the country at home, it takes twice as long to get around. Donegal isn't that big, you know."

"It is to me. My horizon doesn't stretch too far." For a moment she weighed up her options. "Okay, pet, let's go have our tea in Bundoran then, if you don't mind the drive there and back."

"Not at all."

Michael drove the car up off the beach and once again they took a southerly direction.

It was dark when they got to Bundoran and Maggie had no idea what restaurants were there for evening dining. She knew there was a little coffee shop on the main street but it was closed as they drove past. After some searching they found a restaurant just out of the town. It looked like someone had converted a portion of their house. They drove into the yard, the car tires crunching in gravel inches deep, and got out.

Maggie had that worried look on her face again.

"What?" He looked at her with a gentle smile.

"It looks very fancy."

She'd been looking at the cars in the yard and there were BMWs, Mercedes and an auspicious-looking Jag. He saw her looking at the cars.

"Margaret Breslin, look at the car you got out of."

She turned and looked and for the first time realised she'd been driving around all day in a Mercedes. How had that slipped by her? She'd realised it was big but the colour was dark and she knew it was a rental – she never thought somebody would rent a luxury car.

"Oh my!"

Michael laughed and put a supportive arm around her shoulder. "Come on, Mom. Let's eat."

The inside made her feel worse. A woman in a cream twin set and a pair of camel-coloured leather trousers came and offered to take their coats. Maggie had her walking shoes on and a warm tweed skirt and felt very dowdy and out of place. Casually Michael handed the woman his coat and waited while Maggie slowly relinquished hers. The cream beauty wandered off in a cloud of Elizabeth Arden. A young girl in black trousers and a white shirt quickly took her place. She led them to the bar until a table was vacated and handed them the drinks menu. She smiled at Maggie.

"I'll be back in a moment."

Michael seemed oblivious to his surrounding as he perused the menu. "I'm driving." He spoke half to himself. "I think I'll have a mineral water now and a glass of red with my dinner." He turned to Maggie.

"What will you have?"

"Eh! A sweet sherry would be lovely."

"Excellent choice, Mother – too bad I'm driving."

The waitress returned and led them to a table. She took their drinks order and left them alone.

Maggie sat and stared around her. This was worse than lunch in the Beachwood. At least there her casual dress wasn't so bad considering the time of day but here she felt very drab. The lighting in the restaurant was muted. That was a blessing. Every table housed a couple. Nobody ate alone and everyone looked under thirty. Michael Reynolds seemed to be the only one who'd brought his mother. His mother! She repeated it ten times as she looked around the room. She wondered if everyone realised. She seriously wanted to stand up and tell them just in case they didn't.

The restaurant was surprisingly quiet. The murmur

of voices could be heard but no distinct words stood out. Maggie usually had excellent hearing – this must be what it felt like to be partially deaf. Half the diners were like her and Michael, looking around in silence. Perhaps genteel society didn't speak in public.

"Did you have a good day?" Michael's voice interrupted her thoughts.

"I did. It was a strange day for me though. I can't believe this is all happening. I can't believe you're here with me now. How long more do you have to stay?"

"I leave day after tomorrow. I have to get back to work."

"Oh!" Maggie's face said it all.

"I wish we had more time too. Have you given any more thought to what I said about coming to America to stay with us for a while? Pascal can't stop you from going."

"I know he can't. But he could make it so that I have no place to come back to."

"Would that be such a bad thing? You could stay with us full time. We have an apartment over the garage. It could be yours."

"Really! Who lives there now?"

"A college friend of my son's. He rents it for a nominal fee. His parents live out west now but they used to be my wife's best friends, so we have to look after Keith. He's a great kid. If you came to stay he could move into the house. There's always a way, Maggie."

She nodded her head but she was unable to put

into words the feeling of hopelessness she felt whenever she thought about standing up to Pascal. He'd been her big brother all her life. He'd made all her decisions for her. She wanted to be with Michael and his children but they were people she didn't know in a world she'd only observed on the television. Would a woman gone sixty from rural Donegal survive in the city, even if she did pluck up the courage to best her brother? The thought sent her heart into a downward spiral.

Michael held her hand. "It can't be that bad. We will find a way."

Before Maggie could collect her thoughts the wee girl arrived back with the bread basket and a jug of water. A young fellow followed behind with the tray of drinks.

"To us!" Michael raised his glass in a toast.

Maggie raised her glass and took a sip, then watched Michael as he resumed looking at the other diners. He was forty-three years old but he really didn't look it. He'd certainly looked after himself. He was healthy and fit. His hair was still thick and shone. His eyes sparkled in the dim light. He had turned out to be everything her wildest dreams had hoped for. She hadn't prayed for him in the conventional way over the years. The church had stolen him away from her so she couldn't invoke the Name of God on his behalf. But she had sent out love and all the best wishes her heart could muster and someone had obviously been listening. God or whoever was in charge got the message across.

Suddenly curious she raised her eyes and looked at Michael. "I know politics and religion are bad dinner conversation but I was wondering." She looked embarrassed and went quiet for a moment.

"Wondered what, Maggie?"

"What do you think of religion?"

Michael smiled. "Any particular one or religion in general?"

"Catholicism."

"I was raised by two very devout Catholics and went to Catholic school. My faith has taken a bit of a battering over the years so I guess now you would say I am a lapsed Catholic. I do go to Mass from time to time but it's usually when I want to feel close to my parents."

"Me too! Not lapsed in practices – Pascal makes sure I do my duty towards the church but he can't control what goes on in my head. The church has cold comfort for me."

The dinner menu had appeared like magic at her elbow. Maggie hadn't even noticed until she saw Michael pick his up.

Michael turned from her serious face and cast his eyes over the menu. "Right, Maggie. Let's eat."

Maggie'd eaten a lot today. She wasn't sure how much she could fit in. She thought she would start with a bowl of soup and then have a salad. She wasn't keen on pasta and there appeared to be a lot of that. Once again she glanced at the prices. If Pascal could see her now! Again the hand throbbed. Michael ordered a steak. For some reason Maggie had assumed

Americans didn't eat red meat any more. She thought he'd have salad or pasta.

"No, Mom, only Californians don't eat red meat," he said when she voiced this thought. "They exist on egg-white omelettes, mineral water and surgery."

She laughed.

"You think I'm kidding?" he said.

"I don't know." She stared at him and he stared back, then he laughed and turned away. He's a funny person, she thought, wonderful and funny. Minutes ticked by and then she said. "Why egg whites? What do they do with the yolks?"

Michael threw his head back and laughed again. Maggie wasn't sure what the joke was but she couldn't help laughing too. It distracted her and she never did find out what happened to the yolks.

The meal was delicious, so much so it was consumed in a happy silence.

Michael tapped his stomach. "That was a good steak. How was your salad?"

"It was lovely. It had a lot of strange additions to it. There were oranges and grapes."

She never got to finish her description as Michael was off laughing again. Anyone else would have Maggie in tears, laughing at her like that, but somehow it felt good, tender. It made her feel at ease.

They drank their coffee chatting about the meal and the restaurant and rating it against others they'd been to. Maggie rated it quite highly but her comparisons were sparse.

After the meal Michael helped her on with her coat and they left. Once again Michael had insisted on covering the meal. This time Maggie didn't argue. She was terrified to imagine how much it would come to. Michael just left down his credit card and signed a little slip of paper.

"How much do people tip here?"

"Oh! Whatever you think is appropriate." She tried to sound knowledgeable and say nothing quotable at the same time.

It was a lovely night, crisp and clear. A slight frost was setting on the car and the stars dotted the navy sky. The moon was a little slit weakly casting its glow onto the countryside. Suddenly and without warning Maggie felt the sharpest pang of sadness. What would she do tomorrow? How could her life go back to what it was before? Pascal would be waiting up for her when she got back and he would be in a foul mood. He wasn't someone who would come around and get used to things. He would simmer and brood and explode and eventually have his own way. It had always been so. Her tummy tied in knots as she sat into the car.

Michael chattered away. Maggie didn't say much but she said enough in the right places to feign participation. As they entered the Diamond again in Donegal, Michael noticed the buses and the queues outside the Castle Hotel.

"What's going on there?"

"Oh, some sort of a dance. The Castle is a very

popular place. I hear the wee girls on the bus talking about it."

"Let's go in. It could be fun."

"Are you mad? I'm sixty and you're forty-three."

"And your point is, Mom?"

"We're old is my point."

"Speak for yourself, Mother. Come on. Just for an hour. Have you ever been inside there?"

"No, I haven't! But that's because I have no business in there."

"Margaret Breslin, I thought you had a sense of adventure. You wait there then and I'll go in on my own."

"You will not!"

He turned his head like a cocker spaniel, his eyes wide and liquid in the glow of the street lamps, and looked at her. "Time is ticking, Maggie, and I want a broad view of Donegal. You don't want me to go home deprived."

"Go in there and you risk going home depraved!"

Michael went into peals of laughter and went back to looking at her, his head now resting on the back of the seat.

Finally she relented. "Oh, come on then! But when you're gone I'll be the laughing stock of the parish! Going to nightclubs with a handsome American. They talk a lot around here, you know."

"Mother, they talk a lot everywhere. Don't let them bother you."

Feeling like a cheeky schoolgirl Maggie followed

Michael across the street. There was a large queue at the door. Michael stood obediently in line with Maggie beside him. She couldn't stop herself from giggling. She wasn't sure if he was exaggerating obedience for effect, or if he was always that regimental about queues.

Next thing Maggie felt a strong arm around her shoulders. She jumped and turned. Joe, the young fellow who drove the bus to the town on a Friday, was standing there with a big cheeky grin on his face.

Maggie was mortified. "Joe!" She tried to keep her voice level. "How are you?"

"I'm fine, Maggie. You're the last person I expected to be queuing up for a late pint. And you brought a friend." He turned to Michael.

"Michael Reynolds!" Michael introduced himself with an outstretched hand.

"You're the American." Joe mixed statement and question.

"That's me."

Just then the crowd surged forward and before Maggie could change her mind she was pushed through the door. She'd just entered her first night club.

She turned her head. She was too far inside the door to turn and leave but she was still in a queue. Herself and Michael inched forward step by step towards the ticket window: a number of people needed to produce ID and seemed to be having problems digging the little cards out of pockets and bags. A row of bouncers in black suits and dicky bows stood giving directions and providing a silent warning against trying anything on the premises. It looked quite intimidating to Maggie, a far cry from the family nights in the parish hall. While she was looking anxiously at the wall of black, Michael paid them in. He handed her a ticket and walked a little ahead of her. She watched him hand his ticket to the ticket collector who was standing a little off on his own. He seemed a bit friendlier than the others. Maggie handed him hers as well. She was just walking off when he handed her back half the ticket. She looked at it.

"It's for supper later, Maggie."

"Oh, thank you." She smiled. "How do you know who I am?"

"I'm Connell McGlynn's son, Barry."

"Oh my! Little Barry. I haven't seen you for years."

A crowd was building up behind Maggie. Young girls with long legs and short skirts and a group of young fellows with gelled hair were getting impatient.

"Sorry. I'm in the way. Give my love to your family."

Michael was waiting for her. They walked together through the double doors at the back of the hotel lobby and Maggie felt like she was in another world. She turned to Michael.

"It's like *Buffy the Vampire Slayer*."

He gave another one of his loud guffaws.

The room was large and pulsating with life. Music pounded out of the speakers. Maggie had to push forward to make her way through the young crowd.

Beer bottles held in moving hands dug into her flesh. Body odours and perfume assaulted her nose. She thought she would hate it but she was exhilarated. The beat of the music was getting into her feet and she could feel her body moving in a new way. She felt younger and more alive than she had in a long time. She found it hard looking around her to see herself as anything other than one of the young people she saw making way for her to pass through, until she looked down and saw her hand reach out for the bottle of beer a drunken Joe held out for her. She saw the aged hand reach out and couldn't reconcile it with the life she felt surging through her veins. Maggie held her hand up and looked closely at the loose skin then looked around her. Where had it all gone? Why wasn't she born thirty years later?

Her son interrupted her thoughts.

"Maggie! Do you want to dance?"

"I'd love to."

Joe still hovered by her elbow. "Maggie, don't leave your drink unattended. I'll hold that for you."

"Can you trust him?" Michael whispered into her ear.

"He's a good lad," she whispered back.

She turned to Joe and handed him the bottle. "We need more like you around, Joe," she said, patting his cheek.

Joe's beer breath hit her full in the face. "I'd do anything for you, Maggie."

"Thanks, pet." She followed Michael to the dance floor.

Chapter 9

Maggie knew her legs were past dancing, but they didn't. They were a bit slow and stiff but they were catching on fast. They danced for two songs. Then Maggie's lungs were starting to scream. Before she got a chance to speak Michael beat her to it.

"Come on! Let's sit down for a while."

She nodded. There was barely enough space to park their feet, never mind sit. Joe was still holding her beer when she got back to the edge of the floor.

"I'll leave you two alone for a while. I have to see a couple of bucks over there before they get lost in the crowd."

Maggie watched him meander his way out of sight. "He's a nice young lad. His parents are lovely people too. It's no wonder he turned out well."

Michael looked after the youth that had turned out well. He was clutching his beer like it was the staff of life and, whoever the two bucks were that he was looking for, his beer-clouded vision was having trouble picking them out of the crowd. Maggie said he was a bus driver. He was young – maybe it was a part-time job or his dad owned the company. Michael thought of his own son and their shared dreams and vision. Life here moved at a different pace.

Maggie stood there swaying to the rhythm. Her smile was wistful. Since Michael had first seen her just days ago her features had softened and a sparkle had entered her eye. Every so often she waved at some people and a broad smile split her face. Michael realised how young she was when she had him, just seventeen. She was only sixty now and he was forty-three. The age gap was negligible.

"You know a lot of people."

"Donegal is that kind of place. People may move around and generations come and go but if you've known someone once or known one of their family, you'd always speak when you meet. Do you see that young girl over there?" She pointed about fifteen feet away to a girl with brown hair and sallow skin chatting loudly to a bunch of lads. "I went to school with her grandmother. I knew her parents when they were wee ones. I've never spoken to her before, she's one of the youngest, but you'd know her out of her mother."

As she spoke the girl looked in her direction and gave her a big smile and a wave and to prove a point she turned and marched over to Maggie.

"Maggie, how are you? Do you remember me? I'm Mary Boyle's granddaughter."

"I do, love. It's lovely to see you. How are you and all the family?"

"We're all the best. Róisín's pregnant again."

"My! She only had one yesterday."

"I know – not one – it was twins she had the last time. The doctor says it's not twins this time but you should see the size of her, she's as big as a house – and look at me!"

She held up her right hand where a tiny solitaire sparkled on her engagement finger. "Oh, that's lovely! Congratulations. Who are you taking down the aisle?"

"Stephen Breslin. I think he's a distant relation of yours."

"He is. I never heard that. It's funny Pascal didn't know. We don't get around much sometimes. You'd miss out on the gossip."

"You're getting around tonight." She looked at Michael.

Michael held out his hand. "I'm Michael – family from Boston."

"Kathleen! Pleased to meet you!"

They shook hands. She turned again to Maggie.

"We've built a house in Killybegs. Stephen is on the fishing these days. We're saving for the wedding. I'm working in the factory on the machines."

Donegal was a big textile producer. Many of the women found their way into the factories.

"There's some organising in a wedding, Maggie!" She waved at the group of lads who were moving off. "I've got to go. I'll tell Nan I spoke to you. She's very forgetful these days. She's in the Home now, you know."

Maggie's heart gave a little lurch. Poor Mary wasn't much older than her. She swallowed hard to quell the tears in her throat. Before she composed herself Kathleen had moved on.

Michael had noted the look. "Was she the same age as you?"

Maggie shook her head, her eyes blinded by tears. "No! She's a few years older than I am but sure that's nothing. The years will slip by in a blink." She spoke almost to herself. Her mind could slip away too like poor Mary's and she'd never get to spend time with her son and grandchildren. Maggie knew she couldn't let that happen.

"Do you want to leave?" Michael was getting concerned.

"We've been here an hour. Maybe Pascal'll be worried." Despite his faults, he did worry. They got the coats and waved to Joe as they left. He was still searching for those two bucks. Michael suspected he was chasing a moving target.

The road was really moving outside now. The line for entry had doubled in size and a few scuffles had broken out. But again Maggie felt alive and suffered no anxiety about being out so late. The only anxiety she felt was deep in her heart. A feeling of impending loss that like the tides was beyond her control. Her new-found flesh and blood was going to slip away, leaving her with some tantalising memories and expectations just beyond her grasp.

The moon was high in the sky as they travelled back through the Gap. It really looked like a moonscape in the dark. The faces of the cliffs loomed up dark and impenetrable towards the skyline. Trees and scrub dotted the ground like spirits of the night reaching out to entice them off the path into the darkness. The old people often talked of the creatures of the night roaming the heather-covered mountains looking for souls to steal away. Donegal was a haven for the mysterious, she always thought. The lines between this world and the next became thinner once you passed Bundoran and left the south behind. It was as if you'd entered another realm, especially at night.

There were many superstitions still alive out in the mountains. When you entered a house in parts of Donegal for the first time, you were offered a cup of tea. This was more than hospitality. It was an old superstition where it was believed that malicious visitors could turn the milk sour but if you accepted refreshment in the house then you wouldn't curse the cow. But if you refused, you'd given your intent away.

The Fear Gorta was another popular tale in the mountains. It was believed that a ferocious hunger consumed those walking alone on the mountainside. It seemed to occur most long ago when people had less to eat and worked long hard hours on the mountain.

Maggie had never felt it but Pascal did and always claimed it was from another world. Many believed it was felt on the spot where the famine coffins were laid down to rest on the way to burial.

Others talked of the Seachran that caused those alone on the mountain to lose their way even in an area well known to them. Many had walked miles, lost on their own mountain. Maggie had her own suspicions, knowing the secret contents of the holy water bottle often kept by the door. Poitín had a profound effect on her when she sampled a drop in the kitchen at home – she could imagine the impact on a dark lonely hillside with the waving branches of scrub trees and gorse bushes pointing you in alternate directions.

Ballybofey was a ghost town too as they slipped through. Tonight the young ones had taken the buses to Donegal and emptied the smaller towns for another night. That way the commerce was spread around and the young ones had a night of fun away. It would be Glenties another night or Ballybofey or Letterkenny.

Maggie was directing Michael on the main road. The traffic would be less now and they would make better time. She showed him where to make the turn off for her house. The light was on in the kitchen when they drove out of the darkened lane and into the bright yard.

"I'll walk you to the door." Michael was already halfway out of the car.

Maggie jumped and tried to tell him not to bother,

hiding the tremor in her voice, but he was already at her door. He helped her from the car and she tried to protest again but he ignored her and led her to the porch door but before they reached it, it opened.

Pascal stood there, his old face chiselled from bog oak. His dark eyes flashed with anger at his wayward sister. He tried to eliminate *The Yank* from his field of vision but, with Michael's arm protectively around his mother's shoulder, that was impossible to do.

Pascal stepped aside to let her enter, then stood squarely back in the doorway to keep Michael on the path.

"You'll be going now." The cold tone invited no argument.

"Mom, I'll see you tomorrow."

She turned to answer but the door slammed between them and the big old iron key turned in the lock.

Pascal walked into the kitchen and waited by the stove, his back turned to her. Maggie lifted the tail of the net curtain in the porch and looked out into the night. She waved at the silhouette by the car and watched a blob-like arm wave back. She stayed there until the tiny red tail-lights disappeared from her view, then slowly she walked into the kitchen after her brother.

A cold voice penetrated her thoughts.

"Where were you?"

"I don't need to tell you."

"Oh, don't you? Whose house is this?"

She answered in a tiny voice. "Yours."

Maggie had never questioned the validity of this statement. Pascal was the son and heir. Her existence had always been bound with his until the day she would marry. But fate had never deigned that to be an option.

"Pascal, I don't want to argue. I want to go to bed."

"Where were you?" he said quietly.

Pascal's voice was unlike that of the rest of mankind – in anger it went down an octave at every sentence until finally he was barely audible. That was the moment his rage was so white hot he couldn't get any more words out. Maggie had seen him get this angry only a few times. She still didn't answer.

"Only one more time, Maggie – where?"

Maggie stepped back in anticipation. His hand grabbed the rolling pin from the hook by his head and he lunged, grabbing her right arm. Even at his age he was an intimidating figure in his rage. He didn't speak, just looked into her twitching eyes and raised the pin. By now Maggie was too scared to speak so she just ducked her head. She was expecting the blow but it still took her breath away. It hit the soft part of her buttocks. That she knew was the last warning. The next time the rage would be beyond him and the pin would crunch bone.

"Bundoran and Donegal town!" She shrieked it at him. "We had dinner and looked into The Castle for a drink!"

"I can smell it off you. My sister in The Castle on

a Saturday night when the county will be laughing and pointing at her with her bastard son. Your shame is determined to show its ugly face and ruin the family name before I die. It was a fitting place for a slut and the spawn of her sin. Even your mother's prayer couldn't keep the evil streak in you from coming out. Maybe you might think of how this affects other people besides you."

Pascal stepped back and looked hard into her face, allowing the loudly ticking clock to hammer home the point.

"We'll say the Rosary and then we'll go to bed. It's been a long day and we have Mass in the morning. You need to be ready so we don't miss the bus."

Maggie knelt on the stone floor, a throbbing pain in her buttock. She dropped her head and listened to Pascal call out the mysteries. She watched her fingers tracing the prayers on the pearl beads her grandmother gave her going to Scotland and watched her tears form a little pool underneath. Each tear as it appeared momentarily suspended in the air seemed like a tiny pearl itself. She answered automatically when it was her turn, silently cursing each mention of God as her heart condemned him for all her suffering. Tonight Pascal outdid himself with the trimmings. He droned on and on until finally he kissed his beads and blessed himself. Without looking at Maggie he left the room and went to bed. He'd said all he needed to tonight.

Maggie couldn't move for a while. The pain was spreading up into her lower back. She took a few deep breaths and raised herself up slowly, wincing. She put the beads in her pocket and hung the rolling pin back up on the nail. Slowly she moved about the kitchen, piling Pascal's dishes in the sink and washing them. She filled the kettle for the morning and had a final look about. The fire was going out and the clock was wound. She lowered herself painfully onto the hard settle by the fire. If she sat on her soft chair she'd never be able to hoist herself out of it. The cat jumped onto her knee and gently butted her cheek with her little face, purring her delight at seeing her.

"Thank you, little pet," Maggie whispered to her holding the tiny animal close in her arms. "I'm glad to see you too."

The little warm body and the small gentle green eyes finally unleashed her pain and tears streamed down her lined cheeks. She had to do something.

Maggie eventually recovered enough to retire to bed and switched off the light. It was only when she was lying down that she realised she'd never filled her hot water bottle. The cold of the bed seeped into her bones but the pain in her hip was too much to face the rise off the old mattress. It was too soft to support her and the pain was too severe for her to turn around. Through the wall she could hear the contented snores of Pascal, oblivious to the pain he'd caused. She lay like that a long time listening to the sounds of the night. Eventually she too slept.

Chapter 10

A loud bang and a sharp pain woke Maggie the next morning. At first she lay there with her heart pounding, trying to determine what had happened. Another loud bang on her bedroom door finally drove away sleep for another day.

"Yes, Pascal. I'll be up in a minute."

"I'm away outside for a few minutes. If we don't get the breakfast over we'll miss the bus." His nailed boots tapped across the stone floor to the kitchen door, punctuating his words.

Maggie examined her bruised hip in the mirror. An angry purple stain spread across her buttock and over her hip. She winced when she touched it. She dressed with care, choosing loose clothes to avoid any pressure on the area. She unlatched the bedroom door and went about her Sunday morning ritual. Breakfast was just a fancy name to describe a cup of tea. They never had breakfast until they came back, to observe the fast. When the tea was poured the miracle of Sunday occurred with Pascal immediately appearing through the door. Sometimes she suspected he loitered outside, fearful in case he'd have to tackle the hot kettle by himself. Silently they sat opposite each other and drained their cups. Maggie finished first and got up to gather her things together, for the walk down to the road. They usually arrived a couple of minutes early, although on a Sunday young Joe wasn't his usual punctual self. Pascal always said one day they'll breathalyse that caddy and he'll be off the road.

As Pascal turned to lock the door a car pulled into the yard. Pascal watched Michael alight from the car and walk towards Maggie.

Michael saw straight away that the sparkle of last night had died in her eyes and been replaced by moving shadows which got darker when she turned towards her brother. Tension was suspended in the air like a veil. He placed a hand on her elbow.

"Maggie, I'd like to drive you to church."

"Not in this parish!" Pascal shouted.

"If that's how you feel. What do you say, Maggie? Mass in Letterkenny and lunch afterwards in the Beachwood Hotel?"

Maggie gave a sideways glance at Pascal and nodded. "That would be lovely, pet. Pascal –" she spoke with a lot more bravado then she felt, "you'll have to get your own lunch today. I'll be away for the whole day."

She walked slowly to the car, feeling his eyes burn into her back. As they drove away he was still standing on the path like a wooden carving, a formidable figure in his suit and hat.

All the way down the drive Maggie was willing a bright smile onto her face to divert Michael from any awkward questions. The strain on her face would have been obvious when Pascal was there, she knew that. She wanted her Sunday free of fear and reminders of her sins. She twisted her gloves in her hand. Michael stretched out his left hand and held her hand in his. The twitching in her hands stopped but resumed in her heart. Michael made no comment. Maybe he would leave well enough alone, for now anyway.

"What church would you like to go to, Maggie?"

"I'd like to go to the little church in St Patrick's, if you don't mind. I know a lot of people who've passed through that sad place and I like to say a prayer for them."

"What sad place?"

"It's the local psychiatric hospital."

"Oh!" Michael didn't seem to relish the idea of Mass in such a place.

Maggie sensed his apprehension and for the first time in their lives she took a firm hand with her son. "The least we can do, Michael, is share a prayer with them when we send them out of our society into such a place. Many of them were people like me who did something to disgrace the family and were hidden away."

"You're right. I'm very sorry, Maggie."

"That's okay, pet." She spoke vacantly. "We should

thank God. For the most part we were the lucky ones. Things could have been so much worse."

Michael's eyes glistened with tears.

She guided him up the Port Road and showed him the way to the hospital. A few cars were parked outside. Michael wanted to march ahead and pick a seat in the emptiest corner of the church but Maggie had other ideas. Despite the pain in her hip she took the lead and sat four rows from the top behind some people that looked like staff or perhaps fellow visitors. The row behind them was empty.

Maybe it wasn't going to be so bad, thought Michael. The Mass started and everything was fine. The congregation was quiet and the priest's lilting accent kept him amused for a while. But gradually the extreme cold of the church took hold. How on earth could a building used by the public be allowed to get so cold? The cold burrowed into the wool of his overcoat and sank its sharp fingers into his flesh and finally drilled through to his bones. He started to shiver. Any minute now his teeth were going to start chattering and embarrass him even more in front of his mother.

Just as he thought he had the cold under control, keening started at the back of the church, building into a crescendo as the service continued. Every so often the sound was punctuated by a monotonous thumping. His teeth forgot their wish to chatter and now decided to grind of their own free will and a pounding headache was starting in his temples. In misery he wrapped his coat as tightly as he could around his shivering ribs and tried to get some positivity from this experience. As he sat there he tried to avoid looking at a group of women about Maggie's age sitting to the left of him. They huddled rather than sat in a tight group with their eyes fixed on the priest while he spoke. Their expressions were void of any life or experience. They reminded him of young Sunday School children who heard God's word as a story but had never processed it in the context of real life. Though in varying stages of rapid physical aging they still had the demeanour of adolescents. At some stage in their early lives they'd experienced a state of arrested development and he wondered how they would fare in the world today if someone came to take them home.

Finally the service drew to a close and the last hymn was sung. Michael and Maggie stood up and edged their way out of the church. Michael tried his best to stop his mind from picturing Maggie shuffling along with these people if Pascal hadn't taken her home. Forty-three years would have been a long time for anyone to keep it together in an institution. Again tears were pricking the backs of his eyes and he acutely felt a stab of pain as his origins finally became clear to him. When he set out on this journey into the past to find the place of his birth he really hadn't stopped for long to think about what he would find.

Maggie stopped at the water font, dipping her finger in and blessing herself. She caught Michael looking at the gesture.

"Force of habit!" she ruefully commented. "Come

on now, Michael. I need to get some food – I haven't had any breakfast. I could eat a sheep off the mountain."

He kept his eyes slightly diverted from Maggie so she couldn't read his thoughts. "Gosh, Maggie, there's no need for that. Come on!" He forced a laugh and linked her arm as they walked towards the car.

In two minutes they were turning into the hotel car park. It was full today.

"Sunday lunch is very popular. People don't want to eat in their own homes any more. Maybe they're right." Maggie had seen the benefits of slaving for your family. "It must be a lot of hard work catering for a whole family. It must be a nice break for the women of the house." She chattered on as they walked into the hotel.

In the dining room Michael had to tap her elbow to get her to wait to be seated.

"I don't think that's necessary here, not at lunch anyway," she said. She stood looking around. "It's very full – we'll never get a table. Sure maybe we'll try someplace else."

Michael ignored her and waited for the manager to be free. A handsome woman in a black suit walked towards them.

"Mr Reynolds!" She indicated to the right. "This way, please. It's all ready for you."

"Thank you." Michael smiled at her and guided Maggie in the direction of the pointing hand.

The restaurant sounds were loud. Voices echoed around the room and children cried. Metal scraped on dishes and a loud pop caused Maggie to jump as somebody's birthday champagne went off.

"A bit fancy for lunch!" Maggie hissed into Michael's ear.

Finally the manager halted them at a large corner table by the window with a reserved sign on it. She stood with the menus while Michael pulled out Maggie's chair and waited for her to remove her coat and sit down. Six roses sat in a crystal vase on the table. Maggie noticed there wasn't anything like it on anyone else's table. The manager left the menus and said she would send over the waiter in a moment.

"What's going on?" Maggie was bewildered.

"I booked this morning before I went to pick you up. Now order some food. The sheep on the mountain are getting nervous."

Maggie knew what she wanted. Sunday lunch meant a nice roast and Maggie's favourite was lamb so one sheep had to die. She was never going to embrace vegetarianism. For a starter she ordered a hot bowl of vegetable soup.

"It will warm me up after the cold of that church."

Michael agreed and ordered the same followed by a large medium rare steak.

When the waiter took the order Michael started playing with his napkin. Maggie guessed the questions would come next.

Sometimes a day, a week or years at a time are spent auditioning or practising for the main show. Maggie's whole life was in preparation for the last few days. When the day arrived she knew her lines and played the part to perfection. Even though she had only met Michael on Tuesday, a little part of her soul hoped this would last forever.

Michael looked sad and uncomfortable on the other side of the table. His red paper napkin was ripped to shreds, the pieces like spots of blood in fresh snow. Maggie was afraid to ask why. She didn't want to hear the words. It wasn't going to be questions about Pascal or her bruise. He was leaving. A dark hole was opening up inside her. If they didn't speak and they held onto this meal maybe she wouldn't fall in.

The first course arrived and they ate that in silence. Maggie was finding it very difficult to swallow but if she drew attention to this she knew it would break the spell, give him the opening she knew he was desperately seeking. The waiter came back and cleared the table and they returned to examining the dining room and its occupants. Michael seemed on the cusp of speech when the main course arrived. The lamb was succulent, the vegetables crisp just like she loved them, but they tasted like chalk in her dry mouth.

When they finally foraged their way through the mountain of food on the plate, Maggie had to admit she couldn't stop time.

The waiter threw her one last lifeline in the form of the dessert menu.

"You have room for more?" Michael was incredulous, unable to see where she put it – she couldn't be much more than one hundred pounds!

"I love desserts!" She grabbed the menu. "Let's splash out."

Maggie was halfway through spooning the sickly sweet food into her mouth when she heard the words. She tried to feign deafness but Michael just repeated them a little louder.

"Maggie! I have to go to Dublin. Tonight."

"Why?" The single word was all she could get out before the tears started to choke her.

"I have to catch an early flight from Dublin tomorrow. I have to get back to a big city project I'm working on, plus my daughter has some important exams that I have to be there for. It's only for a while. I'll be back or you'll come over yourself."

"A while is a long time when you pass sixty," she whispered.

"Sixty is nothing, Mom. My Uncle Harry is ninety and healthy in mind and body. Please, Mom, don't cry or you'll start me off too. You could leave with me today if you wanted."

"No!" She shook her head. "I couldn't go without sorting things out. I can't run away. But I might follow you later?" She made the statement sound more like a question.

"You know you're always welcome."

"I know. You have no idea how bleak it will be here without you."

"I'll miss you too."

They finished the meal in silence.

Chapter 11

Michael pushed his chair back from the table.

"Maggie, I have to go upstairs for a minute and finish packing and check out. Then I'll spend the rest of the day with you. You can come up with me, if you want." Maggie nodded and followed him to the elevator. She'd never been in a hotel room in her life. Wasn't that funny, she thought, a woman of sixty years old in the twenty-first century in an economy booming with the success of the Celtic Tiger? The last few years had just slipped by. The last two decades for that matter. Maggie's routine was exactly the same this year as it had been in her forties or her thirties.

The elevator stopped on the second floor and they walked down the corridor to Michael's room.

"It's lovely." Maggie looked in every corner.

"Um, I suppose." Michael looked around as well, but didn't see much.

Secretly Maggie was a little disappointed. She'd

told the truth when she said it was lovely. But entering her first hotel room she hoped would be like walking into a five-star hotel in Monaco or Paris.

Michael picked up things from the bathroom and the floor while Maggie sat on the edge of an armchair watching him.

"How long will the flight take?"

"Six or seven hours."

"That's a long flight."

"It's not too bad. There's a movie and I have work to do anyway."

"You carry work with you on holiday?"

"Yes. I didn't know if I would even get to see you so I thought I might have a few days hanging around with nothing to do. I wouldn't really be into sightseeing by myself. I would have looked around the town, had a look at where you lived and spent a lot of time working in my room, abused the room service menu maybe."

Maggie perched on the edge of the bed. "I would have cleaned the house, cooked the meals, done my shopping on Friday and gone to Mass on the bus with Pascal on Sunday. All the hours in between would have slipped by happily enough. I'm never bored. I would have read, watched some television and dozed by the fire with the cat. I was happy enough doing that before, now it will feel like waiting to die." Her head sank wearily onto her chest. "I was never meant to have a life, Michael, only moments."

Michael sat on the bed opposite her and held his

head in his hands. Finally he looked up. "Why don't you leave? What's keeping you here? I don't understand."

"It's my home, pet. If I went to Boston, I'd be your guest. All my life I've been a guest. But here I know the place, I know the people, I know the way of life. An old tree is difficult to transplant without causing some damage. Pascal is eighty, he won't be around forever. He's twenty years older than I am and even though he hurts me and has hurt me, he's my brother and my mother asked us to look after each other. I'm not saying I'll never go to visit, but myself and Pascal both need time to readjust to the changes of the last few weeks. He's an old man despite his noise."

Michael moved to the floor by her side and put his head in her lap. For a moment Maggie wanted to push him away. She had never been physically close to anyone in her life except his father and that was what it was, one of her moments. This was life in one of its strongest forms. Maggie's body felt weak and her heart vulnerable. She tentatively reached out her hand and touched his hair. Her tummy muscles tightened and she felt like there was ice water in her belly. Her breast ached like the day they took him from her in the hospital. Suddenly her grip strengthened and she held his shoulder and tears streamed down her cheeks. How did she give birth to a baby and have to wait over forty years to hold him? Like The Pietá they sat there. Once again she was watching him leave her and for all she knew it could be another decade or maybe never before she saw him again. Maybe it would take another lifetime.

Michael raised his head and reached for her hand. "Maggie, don't cry! I give you my word we'll see each other soon. Either we'll come over or you'll come to us."

He rose and closed his bags. Then together they left the room and descended to the lobby.

The girl behind the desk dealt with the bill professionally without any sign of overt interest but some of the other staff that dotted the lobby cast glances at them.

They walked to the car.

"What do you want to do this afternoon? Would you like to visit your grandparents' grave?"

Michael's eyes lit up. "Yes, I would. That would be great."

"Okay. I'll show you the way."

They drove out of the town and headed back into the country to Maggie's parish, Cooleen.

"What if we bump into Pascal?"

"It will be all right."

It had to be. Pascal had stood in her way long enough. But when they got there the churchyard was deserted. She hadn't needed to worry. It was built on the edge of a hill with a terraced graveyard underneath and to the left. The terraces were almost like the rings on a tree trunk. You could tell the age by following the lines across the hill. The oldest part was at the bottom where the old church used to be in the eighteen-hundreds. A part of the old gable still stood with a small window visible. Someone had planted roses on a grave there many years ago and the roses had grown up and over the fragment of the church and spilled its petals on the ground underneath.

As the years went by the graveyard spread up the hill. When the old church finally succumbed to the ravages of time it was deconsecrated and the new one was built in its place on the hill above. The Breslin graves were in the section in the middle. The first people went into that plot in the eighteen-hundreds and more Breslins had been keeping them company ever since. It must be quite crowded but there was space for Pascal and Maggie. For the first time in her life Maggie doubted this. She looked at Michael. If she did get to go to Boston, perhaps her grave would be there, but then the whispered voices of Breslins past asked: "Is that what you want, Maggie, to desert your roots after all these years?" She looked at the stone and it seemed to say: "You belong to us, Maggie. This is your home."

Michael was worried when he saw her face. "Mom!"

She didn't seem to hear.

"Mom!" He touched her arm.

She turned slowly and looked at him.

"Sorry. I was miles away. Well, what do you think of the family plot? Many generations of your bloodline lie buried here. Breslins back to the eighteen-hundreds. It's a bit untidy looking now. Pascal and myself need to do a bit of work on it."

Michael thought it was charming. Being so old, it was built on uneven ground with stones from the old church buried in the undergrowth. Flowers had been planted in the hollows to give the stones a purpose rather than dig them out completely. Over the years, honeysuckle, roses and other climbers had become twisted around themselves and now the stones looked like green bodies sitting huddled around the grave. The headstone, topped by a Celtic cross, had succumbed to the pull of gravity and was leaning down the hill. Sprigs of roses grew through the arms of the cross. It did need a bit of trimming but he liked the wildness of it. He didn't like the manicured perfection of many of the graveyards back home. He imagined resting in those would be like dressing up for Sunday every day, always wearing a suit and tie. Here you could lie back for eternity in jeans and a checked shirt and happily watch the clouds roll by.

Michael pulled back the leaves and looked at the writing. He read aloud: "*The memories of life, the love of a wife, with hope for my family and sweet repose of death, here lies the body of . . .*" It was difficult to read but the first name on the list was Thomas. "*Thomas (Tommy) Breslin. Born April 17th 1775. Died June 2nd 1875.*" Michael looked at Maggie. "Wasn't that supposed to be my name?"

Maggie nodded. "Yes, and you were born April seventeenth too!"

"Wow! Did you remember this when you were going to name me?"

"No, I didn't. It's a funny coincidence, isn't it?"

Michael was spellbound. "Do you know anything about him besides him being a centenarian?"

"No. I don't even know if he was the first Breslin buried here or if he was the first person to have his name carved on the stone. This graveyard dates back to well before the famine so I'd say there's many forgotten souls buried in it. We could go ask the priest if you like and see what they have in the parish records."

"That would be great."

"What time is it?"

He checked his watch. "Quarter of three."

"What?"

"Oh, sorry." He laughed. "I mean two forty-five."

"Oh!" She smiled. "I never heard it said like that before. We say quarter to three."

"It's the same time either way!" Michael laughed and hugged her.

"The priest should be in now after his lunch," she said. "We'll go up and knock on the door and see what he says. He's only a few hundred yards up the road."

Together they walked up the road to the priest's door. He did have a lovely house, Michael thought. It wasn't exceptionally big but it was well proportioned and big enough to lose one priest in it. The site was elevated. There were steps up to the front door flanked by two sweeping banks of grass edged in flowerbeds and dwarf trees. The house was old. There was a date carved over the door: 1885. Michael guessed that when the first priest walked through the door of his new house, he would have passed cabins and hovels on the way with parishioners tipping their caps to him, honoured to have bumped into the priest that day, the day the parish priest walked into the mansion that they paid for.

When they got to the door he turned around. Parish priests for over a century could stand here and literarily keep an eye on the whole parish. It was like the original Big Brother. The eye of the priest watching down off the hill into their lives, the eye that followed Pascal Breslin and forced his little sister to give up her baby to strangers and even now was trying to keep him out of her life.

Father Landers opened his stained-glass hall door personally after the third knock. He gave a huge smile when he saw who it was. "Maggie! Come in! It's lovely to see you."

They walked in and stood in the hall as he closed the door.

"Walk into the parlour there." He indicated an open door to his left. "I'll go put the kettle on."

"No, Father," said Maggie. "Don't go to any trouble."

"It's no trouble, Maggie. It's a delight to see you."

They entered the parlour. It was a lovely room situated at the front of the house. The floor was covered in small black and white tiles and the walls were painted a pale cream. The shelves and floor were relieved by pots of greenery, ficus plants, ferns and numerous cacti. A bright fire burned in a black iron fireplace inlaid with patterned tiles. Bookcases lined one entire wall. It was filled to capacity with hard-backed books. In contrast one small shelf by the fireplace held paperbacks. Michael examined the hardbacks. They seemed mostly theology and history; some appeared to be very old, probably valuable judging by the condition they were in.

"They go with the house." Father Landers had come in behind him, carrying a laden tray, which he placed on a small table. "Those are my own." He indicated the less exalted paperback titles. "I'm a bit of a crime fan. I like a good detective story."

Maggie smiled indulgently at the attempt at normality from the priest. Though the clergy weren't her favourite people she liked this fellow. He wasn't all pomp and collar. You could see a human heart beating in his chest. He was quite young. When she saw him first she thought they must have got a new curate. She couldn't believe he was the parish priest.

Meanwhile Michael looked coldly at him and distastefully at his books. All his life he'd been thought to believe in the mercy of God and his unfailing goodwill to all men. Michael prayed daily when his wife was sick and waited for God to reach out and wipe her body clear of the cancer that was slowly eating her away, but he didn't. Michael spoke to religious men on both sides of the family and they all told him that the Lord worked in mysterious ways. Michael bought none of it but he did struggle daily trying to reconcile himself with the security of his childhood beliefs. Over the years he had formed an uneasy relationship with God but now the old pain came rushing back. This God they were all referring to seemed anything but merciful and now Michael was faced with his representative on earth. He couldn't take his anger out on God himself but he could certainly ask some hard questions of Father Landers.

By now Father Landers had become more interested in Michael's visit than Maggie's as he noted the strain on the American's face. He looked expectantly at Michael.

Michael looked at Maggie, for a moment cruelly waiting for her to explain who he was.

She sat wrestling with her courage. The silence ticked on, marked by an ornate clock on the mantelpiece. Father Landers realised the answer would have to come from her and he turned also and watched her face compose itself for speech.

"Father, this is Michael Reynolds."

The priest held out his hand, still looking at Maggie.

Michael refrained from shaking his hand. He couldn't do that. Not until he finally heard the words "my son". Before he left he wanted someone to hear him introduced in Maggie's voice as her son.

There it was.

In a barely audible voice Maggie said it: "Father, this is my son Michael."

Michael offered his hand now, looking straight into the priest's eyes, daring him to react in some way to the news.

Father Landers grasped his hand in a firm grip. "Michael! I'm delighted to meet you. Well! We all need a cup of tea. It's such a cold day. We need something to take the shivers out of the air. Who likes it strong?"

Maggie bubbled enthusiastically. "I'll have the weakest one, Father, and Michael likes his strong."

The priest placed her tea on a little table beside her, a few biscuits in the saucer. She lifted the china cup and held it tightly in her hand. She left the saucer on the table. She knew her hands would shake too much.

Michael took his and sat by her side on the couch.

The priest spoke first. "Maggie, I had no idea you had a child."

"Why should you, Father?" Michael spoke looking directly into the priest's eyes. "It was a secret."

Maggie held his hand protectively. "I was very young when I had him, Father, only seventeen. Michael found me this week. He lives in Boston. We've been spending the last few days getting to know each other. It's all very new. We have a lot to talk about."

"I'm sure you do." The priest looked again at Michael. "I sense some anxiety on your part, Michael. Is there something you would like to talk to me about?"

"Anxiety, Father?" Michael raised his eyebrows. "I think something stronger than anxiety would be a better word. I mean it's time we all started to be honest here, isn't it? Anger! There's a good word. I never met my mother before this week because she was forced to send me away. I was like a blight on this parish. Your predecessors would have seen me every day from that front stoop." He halted his flow for a moment to gaze out of the window down the hill into the valley of his ancestors. "I don't particularly want to talk to you but maybe some answers would be nice if you have the time?" Michael was dangerously close to tears even though he thought he'd dealt with this part of it years ago. But feelings long buried were being churned up inside, choking him. He knew he was behaving like a surly child but he just couldn't seem to stop himself.

"Michael, things were different back then. A lot of mistakes were made."

"What's your position today, Father, on unmarried mothers?"

For a moment the priest was quiet. "Are you asking me that as a minister of the church or as a person, Michael? The church's position is still clear – sex before marriage is not condoned and neither is contraception – but as a person I can see how everything isn't as black and white as we'd like it to be."

"You should go into politics, Father. That was very diplomatically put."

"I can't change canon law, Michael."

"I suppose not, Father." Once again Michael lapsed into silence.

Maggie spoke again. "Father, we didn't come here to try and change the past. We were down at the grave and we noticed reference to one of our ancestors, Thomas Breslin. We were wondering if you could look him up in the parish history and see if there is any mention of him."

Father Landers jumped at the opportunity to do something useful for his troublesome visitors. "Thomas Breslin, yes, indeed! Indeed there is!" A big smile on his face, he took down a large leather-bound book from the shelf and laid it on the table. "Let me see – what year would that be?"

"He was born in seventeen eighty-five and he died a hundred years later."

He rapidly thumbed through the book and remained deep in his reading for a few moments. "Yes, here he is. This is quite a coincidence, your coming here. I've actually been meaning to talk to Pascal about this. We're setting up a heritage centre here and we wanted to include some of Thomas Breslin's life in it." The priest turned to Michael. "Have you ever heard of the hedge schools in Ireland?"

Michael shook his head, wondering what that had to do with anything.

"Usually it was a school set up in a remote area on the sunny side of a bush or in an abandoned hovel. The children would bring a sod of turf to keep their small bodies off the cold ground and afterwards give them to the master as a payment for their education. The children would take it in turns to keep an eye out for the landlord's men or the police who would arrest the teacher and maybe even take the children in as conspirators against the British government of the day. Many people were transported to the colonies on a one-way ticket. Tommy Breslin taught in the hedge schools in this area. Even after primary schooling was available to everyone in the country many people preferred to send their children to one of their own, one who wasn't a countryman of the queen so to speak, so Tommy's school still flourished. He was compensated for his time by the people of the area. They fixed his house, helped on his farm, supplemented his crops. People had little money but they were happy to contribute in any other way they could. They learned Latin and this book says he spoke a little Greek."

Michael was astounded. "So the poor spoke Latin and Greek in those days!"

"Latin was the language of the church, Michael, until well into the twentieth century. I'm sure Maggie here knows her Latin too."

"I do, Father. I have three languages – Irish, English and a nice bit of Latin, though I've forgotten a lot of it."

"Wow! I didn't know. What happened to Tommy afterwards?"

"Well, by the early eighteen-hundreds Tommy was married and he had six children. Two died in childhood and the others lived to be adults. Two of them emigrated during the early famine years and two stayed at home. Of the two that stayed at home, a boy and a girl, only one survived the famine. You and Pascal are his direct descendants, Maggie."

"How do you know so much about them? Wouldn't records have been sketchy back then?"

"Usually they were, Michael, but your ancestor was a scholar and kept diaries and left a rare view of that time. He was a strong and exceptionally healthy man and survived the law, famine and outlived every one of his generation and generations that followed. Tommy Breslin died in Gweedore in the home of his friend Seán McGlynn at the age of one hundred in eighteen seventy-five."

Maggie looked stunned. "Father, I'd never heard of him."

"It was in this old parish history." He held up the book in his hand. "My predecessors hadn't much of a taste for history and the volumes weren't available to the public. Tommy's papers were left to the church by a relative after he died. We're in the process of setting up the local heritage centre, but it will take a while. We need a lot more funding than we have now. We've applied for lottery money and we're setting up a government employment scheme to cover the labour but there's still a long way to go. During my research I found all this information on the events of the eighteen-hundreds and your family's connection. I wanted to make it a major piece of the centre. I wanted to speak to you about it first, but your visit got ahead of me a bit. So, do you think it's a good idea?"

"I think it's a marvellous idea, Father. I'm sure Pascal will be delighted when we tell him."

Michael was only too aware that Maggie had given the priest a way out of their earlier conversation but he hadn't the mental energy to go back and rehash and perhaps Maggie was right to bring an end to it. It wasn't possible to rework the past.

He stood up and extended his hand stiffly. "Thank you for your time. I have to travel to Dublin tonight. I'm flying back to Boston tomorrow. I'll watch out for the centre."

"It was nice meeting you, Michael."

A sod of turf settled suddenly in the grate of the fireplace and sparks flew into the room onto the rug. The priest rushed to put the guard up.

"We'll be off, Father," said Maggie. "We've taken up enough of your time."

With sad eyes he watched them let themselves out into the blustery day and his heart was heavy with the burden of history. He had a lot to think about.

They made their way back to the car.

"So you hadn't heard any of that before?"

"No, Michael, I hadn't. Our family will be a central part of the exhibit. There was a lot buried in the past, wasn't there? I'm going to make things right, Michael. I'm going to let the whole family know about you – and the parish as well. It's only fair. You made this trip to Ireland to find me, I owe it to you."

"Maggie, I don't want you to have problems after I've gone back home."

"Michael, there won't be any problems. I wasn't the centre of society around here anyway and I'm sure we're not the only ones in this situation."

They were sitting in the car and Michael seemed in no hurry to start the engine. His mind was far away and in another time. Maggie watched his face concentrate on the trees blowing shadows across the road. Large pieces of hail were now hurtling themselves onto the ground and against the windscreen of the car. There was nothing more vicious against your skin than a Donegal hailstorm. Many times Maggie had to walk home in one. Each drop would sting your face as it struck and by the time you arrived home your flesh would be red and raw and your head would throb with the pressure. For a time the noise was deafening on the roof of the car so they sat silently and let the sound drum into their brains. Eventually it eased off and the sun broke through again, sparkling like crystals off the wet road.

"Maggie, tell me some more"

Her heart lurched. "What do you mean?"

"I mean the whole experience. There are so many questions I should have been asking you over the last week but there was never enough time and now there is no time. I have to go and I need to know more before I leave."

Tears stung the back of her eyes.

Michael's hand gently held hers. "Please, Maggie, I need to know everything."

She nodded but she felt she'd told him enough. What more could she tell him?

"My father Maggie, tell me about him."

"Your father . . . what can I say about him? This sounds bad but I can barely picture his face now. I was only sixteen when I met him. I was working in that house I told you about, his sister's house. He came to visit, we had a brief affair and she terminated my employment. It was after I left that I knew you were on the way. I told you I was living with my sister and she was expecting herself and they already had enough mouths to feed so we wrote to Pascal. You know he wasn't big on the idea of you and me coming back here. He thought the convent was the best option. I was four months gone when I arrived at the convent so I was showing. From the moment I walked in the door and everywhere I went the nuns and the priests looked at my belly before they looked at my face. The one memory I can't erase is the look of contempt for you before they would even deign to look at me. I was sent to work straight away in the laundry. I read a piece in a newspaper once where someone said bad girls do the best sheets and, do you know, we did. We washed and ironed and starched until they were immaculate, hoping the snow-white piles would redeem us and someone would cast us a pleasant smile or a word of gratitude but it rarely happened. After your birth I asked constantly where you were and if you were all right but no one would tell me. As soon as I was ready to leave the infirmary I was sent back to work. Not in the laundry – I did lighter work dusting and polishing for about six weeks to make a full recovery, then I went back to the sheets." Maggie's voice faltered and she started to shake.

"How did you get back to Donegal? I know in those days many women never came out of those places?"

"Oh Michael, I'm so ashamed! I tried to take my own life. I tried to hang myself with one of those goddamn sheets."

Michael wanted to laugh at her choice of blasphemy but it was a fleeting moment born of shock and he held it in.

"Somebody found me and I ended up back in the infirmary again. The Reverend Mother told Pascal. To give Pascal his due he couldn't have the death of his little sister on his conscience so he sent for me immediately to come home. The convent and the priest tried to talk him out of it but Pascal was the head of the household so he had his way. But there was no possibility of you coming back – you were gone for good. They wrote to my mother when you were adopted and that was the last I heard of you until the day you arrived on the doorstep. I never knew where they sent you. On returning here my options were limited. Girls didn't rent flats in the town or go back to college. I suppose I was suffering from depression too. I slowly sank into a deep rut."

Chapter 12

They sat in silence for a long time.

"There's an evening Mass on in a little while," said Maggie. "The car park will be full soon. We'd better move."

Michael still sat silently looking out the window on the other side. A mist had started to fall, turning the parish to grey. Everything was still and very quiet. He could hear his own breathing and when he looked down he could actually see the movement of his heart, as it hammered in his chest.

Looking back over the years he had such a wonderful life. When he found out about his adoption he thought he needed answers. He resented not being told before but he hadn't appreciated how perfect things were for him, growing up. His adoptive parents gave him the best education they could afford. They left him very well provided for when they died. Even the birth of his own children was a blessing he took for granted. He felt a tear trickle down his cheek as he remembered the first day Trudy stood up by herself. He looked over the top of his paper and saw two blue eyes looking at him over the edge of the table. She'd pulled herself up with all her strength and stood on tiptoes watching him. It was such a milestone in her life and he'd barely registered it.

He was worried now. He'd opened up the past for Maggie and now he was leaving her to deal with it. Michael wanted answers and he got those. He hoped he'd form a bond with his mother and he'd done that. Now he was going back to his children, his home and a job he loved. Maggie's world had been turned on its head. Was he so arrogant to think that the pleasure of his company for one week was worth all the problems he had unleashed for her? Maggie was going to tell her family and friends with no idea how they would react.

"Maggie, you don't have to tell anyone about me. I don't want to cause you any more trouble."

"It's too late to go back now, Michael. Even if I could I don't want to. You're the best thing I ever did and I'm very proud of you. I want to show you off. It's a different world now. Don't ever regret coming back to find me. I'm very glad you did." She gulped loudly. "I'm just sorry you have to leave." The first cars were arriving for Mass. "Anyway, I'll have to set the rumours straight now. God knows what they're saying about us. It's five to six – do you have to go soon?"

"Yes. I do. I'll drive you home first. Are you sure you'll be okay?"

"I told you I would. Come on! I don't want to hear any more sadness."

Maggie watched the car disappear down the lane in the dark. She ran into the yard and stood there in the frost, feeling like her soul was being wrenched from her body. She tried to be uplifted and positive but she was terrified.

She walked back inside and sat down. Pascal hadn't come back yet and she had no idea where he was. He usually went rambling around the neighbours on a Sunday evening and Maggie watched *The Practice*. Tonight she couldn't settle into anything. She tried reading but the words swam in front of her eyes like alphabet worms. She couldn't even muster enough energy to cross the room and press the button on the television. Finally she picked up the phone and dialled a number. There was one person she had to speak to.

Maureen answered on the third ring. "Maggie! I was thinking about you the last few days. I was going to call you."

"Were you?" Maggie was delighted. "Reeney, I met Tommy."

For a moment Reeney was quiet. "He found you?" She didn't even need to ask which Tommy she meant.

"Yes. He did."

Maggie told her all that had happened during the last week.

"Oh Maggie, I don't know what to say. Is it a good idea to open all this up again? Maybe you should let it rest."

"Reeney! I can't. I'm going to tell all the family about him. He's my son and I want to have a relationship with him."

There was quietness again. "What about us? What would mother say?"

"She's dead."

"Maggie! Pascal is still here."

"Only barely!" Maggie muttered the words into the receiver.

"Maggie, what's come over you?"

"Maureen, Pascal is eighty years old. How long has he left? How long have I left for that matter? I want to spend some time with my son. I lost enough time. Don't I deserve what's left?"

"I suppose you do. Did he ask about his father?"

"He did. I had to be honest and say I knew nothing, that it wasn't the great romance I thought it was at the time. I don't know anything about what he's doing now."

"He's married!"

"No. He's a widower." Maggie hadn't understood.

"Not Tommy. His father."

"What?" Maggie's heart began to pound.

"He got married and had four other children. He lives in Glasgow."

"Maureen, why didn't you tell me that before?"

"He got engaged while you were in the convent. He was married by the time you went back to Donegal. I thought you'd be better off not knowing."

"Maybe. Where is he now?"

"He became an investment banker, made pots of money and has lived in bliss for the last forty-odd years."

A pang of pain pierced Maggie.

"He retired last year," Maureen went on. "Himself and his wife moved to their country house full time. My friend still works for his sister. She's kept me up to date."

Maggie thought she was overloaded before the call. She was wrong. Outside, she thought she heard the little garden gate opening. Pascal must have come back cross country.

"Reeney, Pascal's back. I have to go talk to him. I'll call you soon."

"Okay, Maggie. Talk to you soon."

"Don't tell the others, Reeney. I want to do that myself."

"All right. They're all in Brian's tonight in New York."

"Thanks, Reen." Brian's birthday, she'd forgotten all about that. These family occasions weren't relevant to herself and Pascal.

She went back to the fire and sat down. She knew the time difference between Donegal and New York. Had she the courage to tell them tonight? Maybe she'd wait a while. The party would surely go on for some time. Everyone apart from herself, Reeney and Pascal would be there tonight for Brian's birthday. It had gone clean out of her head in all the excitement.

Now was as good a time as any. But circumstances dictated otherwise.

Time ticked by with no sign of Pascal coming in. She must have been mistaken about the sound of the gate. It was probably the wind anyway, it had whipped up outside since she was out last and she could hear it moaning around the eaves. She held the cat close for warmth and looked at the photographs of Michael and his family that he'd left with her. She plugged in the two-bar electric fire. They'd been out all day so the grate sat cold and empty. Just as she was about to make her call Pascal walked in the door his cheeks reddened from the cold air and alcohol. You could tell by his face when he'd had a few. The frown lines deepened and he was always ready for an argument.

"So he's gone then, is he?"

Maggie nodded. "He left this evening back to Dublin. He's flying out in the morning."

"And what have you decided to do? I hope you've decided to forget all about this."

"I don't want to talk about it, Pascal. Michael is my business."

"What are you going to do?"

"Nothing now, Pascal. It's late."

"Don't be smart, Maggie. I'm talking about from now on."

"Please, Pascal, go to bed."

Pascal grabbed her wrist. "Who did you ring there?"

She'd left the phone off the base. He was sharp tonight despite the poitín.

"Maureen," she whispered.

Pascal's hand moved before she could react and slapped her sharply on her cheek.

"You told her about the Yank, didn't you?"

"Why not? She knows the whole story already. You know that."

"Well, you didn't have to remind her, did you? You won't tell anyone else."

"Yes! I will. I'm going to ring Brian's and tell them all tonight."

"You won't." Pascal's even tone was more chilling than a scream.

Maggie backed away from him. "Pascal, maybe I won't tonight. We can talk about it in the morning, figure something out."

"I want to talk about it now, Maggie. I promised our mother I'd take care of you and the family."

"Pascal! I'm a grown woman. I have a grown son. All the family have left home and moved on. Mother is dead. There's no one to protect any more."

His eyes were haunted. He looked around the room with Maggie following his gaze. The chairs stood silently in place around the sides of the table. They no longer scraped on the flagged floor as the members of a large family sat down to a meal, arguing and discussing their day while plates of food were placed in front of them. The stove was silent too. Maggie had been gone for the whole day so there was no cooking done and for once it stood silently observing the Sabbath. Usually a pot with food simmering and bubbling up under its lid wafted delicious smells around the room. The kettle would sing along beside it with a promise of comfort and sustenance in the air. A debate on the radio and the dinner on the range and Pascal could almost hear mother's voice in the background. Imagine that any moment now his father would come back from the fields and Maureen would hand him a heaped plate of food. Now his life held lots of space. It seemed to grow around him with the ticking clock getting louder and louder. They'd all gone and he was left here surrounded by emptiness and memories.

Today Pascal looked around this room and saw only loneliness. He'd made tough decisions for the family and, like the mountain could grow over a tumbled house, the hands of time stole back his efforts. He never thought about how determined a mother and son would be. But in Pascal's heart it would never be right. She had sinned. The priest told him that. It couldn't be condoned. He could never understand the new liberalism that was diluting his church. Since Vatican II so many of his beliefs were being undermined. But he didn't believe in all this change. He worried in case the church was just trying to be popular, now that the numbers were down, to appeal to the masses again. What if the new rules were wrong? What if God still followed the old ones and expected him to do likewise? He only had a short time left on this earth.

He didn't have time for redemption, if he got it wrong now. His church had backtracked but he wouldn't.

"Maggie, I can't let you humiliate the family and me. I won't."

"You can't stop me, Pascal. People have seen us together already. I'm sure they're talking."

Pascal grabbed her arm. "We'll see." He dragged her by the arm to the utility room and shoved her into the darkness. The light switch was on the outside of the door. She hit the washing machine hard and it knocked the wind out of her momentarily. Before she got to the door she heard the key turning and then being pulled from the lock and slammed onto the small table in his rage. Normally it was hung on a nail high on the wall for security.

"Pascal!" She screamed his name, pounding her fists on the door. "Let me out!"

The crack of light under the door disappeared and she heard the catch close on Pascal's door. Everything went quiet in the house. She screamed and pounded on the wood but the silence reverberating back to her finally slowed her hand. Then she heard Pascal slamming things around in his room. This was so unlike him – that room was a shrine to order.

In her mind she could see the layout of the room as if the light were on. She tried the back door that led out into the orchard, on the off-chance someone had forgotten to lock it, but she should have known better, it was locked tightly and the key safely on its nail. She was meticulous in her cleaning and nothing was ever moved in here except by her. Pascal had never used the washing machine in his life or taken a piece of meat out of the freezer. She knew the washing basket was in the corner. She was due to wash the bedding tomorrow so the bedclothes were in that. One by one she dragged them out and wrapped herself into them in the corner until gradually the shivering subsided. She listened. Was that a door she heard opening? She shouted again and threw a mop-head at the door. Then she listened. Nothing now. Pascal's room had gone quiet. She must have imagined it.

She tried to make the night go quietly by slipping into slumber but it wouldn't happen. She never expected Pascal to be this bad. She thought he would calm down and they could talk.

Then she found her mind drifting in odd directions. She thought how other worlds can exist inside such familiar space. She entered this room about twenty times a day to open the freezer or get some detergent from the shelf. There was always some washing to do, but she never saw it in the dead of night from behind a shut door before. The smell of detergents clogged her nose and the hum of the freezer was growing by a decibel a second. Large bulking shapes surrounded her in the gloom. If she narrowed her eyes a certain way they seemed to move towards her and when she concentrated really hard she could hear the silence or was it a buzzing inside her head? Shadows played across the glass in the outside door as the trees swayed in the wind outside. The odd time a light swept across the ceiling as a car passed on the road below.

Periodically Maggie turned in her makeshift bed to restart the blood supply in her hip and ease the pressure on her bruise. She heard the clock in the kitchen strike three o'clock. There was a bunch of Pascal's socks in the bottom of the basket. She put all of them on to keep her feet warm. Her mind was just succumbing when she heard the garden gate bang. She wondered if it was the wind. For a moment silence resumed, she even managed to filter out the sound of the freezer as she concentrated on the sounds outside trying to break them down into their individual parts, but then the silence shattered with the sound of footsteps coming down the garden path.

Maggie's heart was pounding and she considered calling Pascal but she knew that would be no use. He slept like the dead. She was starting to wonder which world these footsteps came from. She snuggled deeper into her blankets as the footsteps came closer to the back door. Her prison was small and she was only three feet from the door.

The footsteps stopped right beside the outside door and she could hear a hand trying the handle. When the door refused to open the owner of the hand started to laugh. Maggie's shivering resumed. The laugh was that of a male and either he was very small or had crouched down by the handle.

"Maggie," the voice whispered. "Yes, Maggie."

Maggie remained silent and listened.

The whispering started again. "Maggie, Maggie, Maggie!" He chanted the name in a whisper and then started to laugh again. "Locked in and nowhere to go, eh, Maggie? Well, I'll see you, Maggie. I'm on my way home. Sleep tight, Miss Breslin."

The voice disappeared into the night and Maggie was once again alone.

"Damn Pascal!"

Maggie wasn't a superstitious woman. She knew Pascal was out drinking tonight. There were a few houses that Pascal and his buddies gathered in. Pascal always loosened up when drink was taken – he had probably discussed his predicament with someone. Now she knew why Pascal went so far. Someone had been winding him up. Maggie was more scared of small minds than anything else and some of the smallest in the world drank with Pascal. They could have been in the *Guinness Book of Records*. Whoever it was could walk home off the mountain though their yard. That narrowed it down to half the parish and the bottom half where most of the population lived.

The rest of the night slipped slowly by, as she dozed on and off through exhaustion. She started awake as the clock struck seven. Pascal was late getting up so she waited and waited. The clock struck every hour until eleven. Maggie resumed her knocking on the door, shouting in panic. Nobody came. There was no sound from Pascal's room. Could he have gone out after all?

Midday came and went. The postman hadn't arrived yet. What a day to have no post! Nobody else was due until he arrived tomorrow. Eddie never went up to the cattle on a Monday. He went to the mart instead and wouldn't be up again until tomorrow morning.

The afternoon wore on with no sign of Pascal.

Maggie looked around the room again. The window was small and double-glazed. Even if she opened that she wouldn't be able to get through. The back door was old and the lock was heavy. She shook the door. It was solid and so was the lock.

She turned back to the kitchen door. That was a modern door. They put it in a couple of years ago as a temporary measure but they never got around to changing it. It wasn't solid – it was one of those filled with cardboard. She looked around. There was nothing heavy enough to break it.

Then she had a brain wave. She opened the freezer. There was a nice leg of lamb in it that might come in handy. She picked it up and wielded it like a hammer. It was heavy enough if it didn't disintegrate on contact. After about ten bangs Maggie broke through the surface on her side; that seemed to be as far as she could go. She looked around again. The fire shovel was poking out from under the washing basket. She picked that up and put the edge of it though the slit in the door and used the lamb as a mallet. Her arms were aching and sweat trickled down her shoulders. She rested briefly and started again. Finally as the sun was sinking in the sky she broke through. Then it got easier. With a couple of socks on her hands she ripped bits of wood off the door, praying as she did so that her arms could reach the small table. She stretched out her arm as far as she could, with the needle-like points of the wood scratching her arms through the opening in the door. Her fingers just reached it and she edged the keyring back slowly towards her. If she knocked it on the floor she'd have to wait another hour until she widened the hole in the door.

At half five she finally turned the key in the lock and stepped into the cold silent kitchen.

For a moment she stood looking at Pascal's door, too scared to open it. She hoped he'd just crept out early and would arrive back in a couple of hours upset about the state of the door. But she knew that wasn't the case. The heaviness of the silence alone told her there was no point calling out to him. When she raised the catch the click made her jump. She put her hand in first and turned on the light, then slowly pushed open the door and stepped into the room.

Part Two

Chapter 13

Every door in the house creaked loudly but Pascal's creaked louder than any of them. Over the years it had sunk and now it scraped on the linoleum. The bed was right in front of the door, untouched. There was no sign of Pascal but his room was in disarray. The wardrobe door and the bureau drawers were both open with their contents strewn onto the floor. She pushed the door back further until it stuck on the uneven floor but still she could see no sign of Pascal. She walked into the room and looked behind the door, her heart hammering. Nothing.

She went to the locker, shutting the door before she turned her attention to the bureau. She was relieved. Pascal must have just ransacked his room in a temper getting up or going to bed, then he must have gone out early. Maybe he made his bed before he left. She was pushing in the first drawer on the bureau when her gaze was drawn to her right. Pascal was lying on the floor partly concealed by the dust ruffle. For a moment she was rooted to the floor, too scared to move. Was there a burglary? Was that why the drawers were all pulled out? Had poor Pascal been assaulted? Was that what her midnight visitor was doing? Did he hurt Pascal? Questions were running around in her head.

She bent down and pushed back the frills of the dust ruffle to examine him. She had to turn his body over. He was a lot bigger and heavier than she was. Pascal was a tall man. His arm was bent and so was his knee, his back arched as though he had succumbed to a spasm. His body lay awkwardly with the sharp bones of his joints pointing accusingly at her from his Sunday suit. The side of his cheek that had lain against the lino was a dark colour. The skin on his face was cold and rigid with a marked blue tinge. Then she knew what had happened. Pascal had asthma. He must have been searching for his inhaler. That was why everything was pulled out. "Oh, poor Pascal!" she crooned, stroking the white hair back off his forehead. He always kept his inhaler by the bed. She went over again and looked in the locker. There was the inhaler. She tried it and found it was empty. She went back again to Pascal. Then she saw there was another one in his hand. She tried to remove it but his fingers were too tight. She couldn't see if that was full or not. It must be. She bought him a new one in town with Michael.

He was always so meticulous about filling his prescriptions; he'd never let two of them run out. Maybe the stress of the last few days had taken its toll and he was too far gone by the time he found the second one. She started to cry. Poor Pascal got no pleasure in cruelty. He must have been so upset last night over what happened between them he had an attack. While she was in the dark fighting for her freedom Pascal was in here fighting for breath. Slowly she walked to the phone to call the doctor. With mechanical movements she dialled the number and spoke to him. She couldn't remember afterwards a single word she'd said.

In the kitchen she put the kettle on the gas stove and sat back at the table, thinking about which neighbour she should call to help. Her visitor in the night had made her wary of her neighbours. She decided Eddie's wife Kate was her best option. She was a nurse in the local geriatric hospital. She'd know how to arrange the body. She was just dialling the number when she heard a car stop in the yard outside. Over an hour had gone by. She reached across the table and pulled back the hem of the curtain and saw Doctor Barton walk towards the door. She rushed down and turned the key and at the same time he tried the knob. The door didn't open. She'd been so sure Pascal would have locked the door last night – she certainly hadn't unlocked it so it must have been open all night. She turned the key back, opening the door and directed the doctor into the bedroom.

The doctor bent down to check Pascal over. Maggie couldn't stay and watch. She needed something to do.

"Would you like a cup of tea, doctor?"

"Sure, Maggie! I would."

Maggie left him to it and went into the kitchen. She poured a cup for herself and sat at the table and waited for him to finish. She looked up when she heard him enter the room.

"Doctor, sit down. I'll pour your tea."

He sat and as Maggie poured he observed. His dark eyes looked around the room and paused momentarily when he saw the broken utility-room door.

"Have you got someone to come over to keep you company, Maggie?"

"I was just about to call Kate Molloy."

"Good idea." He spoke almost to himself.

"Doctor, are you all right? You look tired."

"I'm fine, Maggie. I'm just worried about you."

"I'm tough, doctor."

"Maggie!" His voice was strangely gentle as though he were talking to a child. "Before anyone else gets here, tell me what happened."

His eyes were staring at her feet. She realised she still had four pairs of wool socks on. Self-consciously she wiggled them under the table and made sure her sleeves were covering the now angry-looking scratches on her arms, where she'd broken through the wood. The doctor still had his overcoat on. The cold was sharp.

"Doctor, I told you already. I went into the room found poor Pascal there and called you straight away."

"But, Maggie, he's been dead for almost a day, I

would say. That door over there is broken through and Pascal's room is a mess. Why didn't you notice this morning that he was dead?"

Maggie hung her head. "I didn't know he was there."

"But, why, Maggie? You were in the house. Did you not go and look for him? And what happened to that door?

Maggie stood up, ignoring the questions. "I'll go and call Kate. I'll need help with the body."

"Maggie, I'm going to have to call the guards."

Maggie gazed into space for a few moments. "We'll have a lot to do, doctor, over the next few days." She stood up and dialled Kate's number.

Doctor Barton went outside and used his mobile to call the police. When he came back inside Maggie was clearing the table. He sat down and watched her silently setting the kitchen to rights before everyone arrived. After about twenty minutes Kate opened the door. Nobody followed the ceremony of knocking around here. She walked over and put her arms around Maggie.

"Poor pet! Show me where he is and we'll sort everything out in no time. But didn't you light the fire, Maggie? It's freezing in here."

Again Maggie ignored the question.

"Kate, can I talk to you for a moment please, outside?" the doctor asked.

Maggie's eyes opened in fright. "Doctor, there's no need for whispering behind my back."

"Maggie, the police will be here soon and they told me to make sure nothing was moved. Kate will have to wait here with you until they've finished."

"But, Doctor, there's no need for the guards."

"It's standard procedure, Maggie."

Maggie sat down again and stared in mute silence at her hands.

"Do you want me to ring the others, Maggie?" Kate asked. "They need to be told."

Kate was a neighbour for many years so she knew them all. Maggie thought about her options. Last night she was going to talk to them and tell them about Michael. Now she didn't want to. She knew they'd be the same as the doctor, asking questions, judging her. But she couldn't avoid it.

She nodded. "Thanks, Kate. The book is by the phone. All the numbers are in it. But you'll probably find most of them at Brian's."

Kate was delighted with the opportunity to break the silence and do something useful. This was going to be a long evening.

When Kate was halfway through her list the police and the ambulance arrived. The police went in and examined the room. The next hour passed in a blur for Maggie. She watched them move and heard them talk but none of it sank in. Finally, they loaded Pascal onto a stretcher and covered the body. This roused her.

"Where are you taking him? This is his home."

"Maggie, we have to do an autopsy."

"Doctor, he has asthma! You know that. His inhaler

was empty. I checked the one in the locker when I found him. Poor Pascal had an attack."

"There was a second one in his hand, Maggie, that wasn't empty. He should have been able to use it. We just need to explore some details."

A female guard walked over to Maggie. "Margaret, we need to ask you some questions."

"Okay."

The guards sensed the unease in the air. Maggie personified the essence of innocence but she was very nervous. Something felt wrong here. Maggie was definitely more scared than grieving and this felt odd to everyone in the room. Nobody knew quite where to start with the questions.

"Margaret, would you like some more tea or coffee?"

"Tea, please!" Maggie smiled but her heart fluttered inside.

The smile further undermined their efforts at a stern front. Despite themselves they found themselves smiling back.

"I'll get the tea." Kate went back to the cooker.

Maggie sat and wriggled her toes inside their layers of wool. She had seen so much crime television that she wondered if they were doing this to intimidate her. Were they expecting her to crumble under the pressure of tea and sympathy? Would they expect her to quietly confide in them about how she knocked off her brother in the dead of night, then sat in her room in the freezing cold till the next day when she decided to confess? She guessed they were confused over who'd be bad cop – none of them looked tough enough to be stern with a sixty-year-old woman. Well, they were underestimating her. She had done nothing wrong but if she told them of her problems with Pascal that would give them her motive for killing him. She needed time to decide what to do.

There were two detectives, one male and one female. They introduced themselves as Detectives Grant and Ryan.

"Margaret, we're going to ask you a few questions," said the woman, Detective Ryan. "Is that okay?" Her voice was peculiarly flat.

Maggie nodded.

"Can you just start by telling us what happened?"

Maggie described how she went to bed before Pascal and fell asleep.

"I was very tired last night, so tired I slept a bit late this morning. There was no sign of Pascal when I got up so I assumed he was gone out. Today is Monday. I thought he might have gone to the mart."

"When the doctor arrived, Margaret, he said the door was locked as though you hadn't opened it yet," said Detective Grant.

"He's mistaken, Detective. I thought I'd locked it earlier so I turned the key but doing that I accidentally locked it. I was flustered. My brother is dead."

"The doctor also noticed that the utility room door was broken right through. How did that happen?"

"I don't know about that. When I came home

yesterday it was broken. I'm assuming Pascal did it but sometimes he can be a bit stubborn – he wouldn't tell me what had happened. I think he lost his temper and broke it."

Maggie mentally patted herself on the back for remembering to put the leg of lamb back in the freezer. That would be harder to explain.

"Did he have a temper, Margaret?" asked Detective Ryan.

"Oh, he did, Detective. He knew that so he always took a deep breath and smashed something: a door or a cup."

"Why didn't you hear him last night, Margaret?"

"I don't know, Detective. I can only suppose that it happened quickly and I was so tired I slept through it. Do you think I hurt my brother? Am I under arrest?"

"No, Margaret! You're not under arrest but we may need to speak to you again."

"Good. The animals need looking after – I need to be here. What about Pascal?"

"The state pathologist needs to have a look at him. We'll let you know when you can make arrangements. It shouldn't be too long. One more question, Margaret . . ."

"Yes?"

"Why were you sitting in the cold? Why didn't you start a fire?"

"I don't know, Detective. The odd day it just doesn't seem worth the effort." For the first time she saw a spark of sympathy in the detective's eyes.

She smiled. "Good night, Margaret. We'll talk to you soon."

Maggie walked outside with Kate. The night was dark. There wasn't a star in the sky. It was almost midnight.

"I'll stay with you and Eddie tonight, Kate, if that's okay?"

"Of course. Let's get your things."

Kate, Eddie and their young son Seán were her closest neighbours. Their daughter Rita was in England so there was a spare room. Maggie was despondent; from now on she was responsible for herself only. The whole picture of her life had changed in twenty-four hours. Pascal had always done everything for her and she now felt the oppressive emptiness around her as she stood in front of the house and felt real and rigid fear. Maggie didn't know how to start to lead her own life.

Kate helped her shut up the house and together they walked down the lane.

Later that night Maggie lay on the bed in Kate's unfamiliar room. It was fitting that the night after Pascal died she slept in another house. Her sentence was finally over. She was free. Her feet were on a new path now but there were no signposts to tell her which direction to turn. She analysed the night over and over in her head.

The chips of wood scattered around the floor by the utility room door must have looked very suspicious. They would be even more suspicious if she'd told them about Michael and Pascal. Maggie needed sleep. For the next few days she would be inundated with phone calls, well-wishers and crowds. Before they arrived she wanted to think. She was glad of the peace and quietness of Kate's.

She knew her siblings. She knew the image of her Pascal and her mother had cultivated amongst the family over the years. Poor little Maggie, she needed to be watched. The first thing they would do was take over and interfere. She'd never thought about the long-term future before. She wondered now what was going to happen to the farm and how much money she would have. Michael would probably help but she didn't want it to come to that. Any relationship she built with her son should be built on love and not on financial dependency or obligation.

Maggie wondered if God would come out of the woodwork now and look after her or if he would stand back as he'd always done in the past.

Chapter 14

The next few weeks dragged on for Maggie. The expected family and well-wishers came and hung around for what seemed like an eternity. Her life became full of questions and rhetoric. The only blessing in all of it was that her siblings had other commitments far away. She couldn't keep them away from them indefinitely. There was an end in sight.

The media was the biggest shock for Maggie. The news broadcast "*the mysterious death of a pensioner in Donegal*". One said someone was helping them with their enquiries. The papers went into more detail though it was all speculation. Someone who knew her well had obviously spent some time talking to them.

The most popular belief locally was that Maggie attacked Pascal and he suffered an asthmatic attack as a result. The police spoke to her on a few occasions but the coroner's report and the forensic result showed nothing unusual as Pascal did indeed die of an asthma attack.

She came back to the house after a few days. It wasn't the same though. All the family were there by then and the house was full of people for days. Pascal's body was released and once again she stood by the family plot as they lowered him into the ground. She cried. Even though they had a turbulent relationship they'd lived together for a long time and shared their lives. She cried mostly because nothing was ever going to be the same again and she had no idea what the future held for her.

Through all this Maggie spoke to Michael every night on the phone. It was a shining light during those dark days. He introduced her to her grandchildren and she learned a little more about them every day. She used the phone in her room so the others wouldn't hear. They barely noticed her anyway. It was nice for them to be at home and all together for the first time since their mother died ten years before. Brian and Niall stayed in Pascal's room as it used to be their room and neither of them were particularly squeamish, but the girls couldn't even bring themselves to enter the room while they were there. Olivia and Grace stayed with Kate and Eddie and Reeney stayed with Maggie in her room. Each morning they came together in their old home for breakfast and hung out together during the day.

Maggie knew that soon she would have to tell them about Michael. Now that she was face to face with them her courage was failing her.

The farm was home but in a way she wished it would be sold. She could live on the money. She had no income, as she wasn't yet at pensionable age. The one thing in life she was too young for. Her savings weren't going to last for much longer.

The will was to be read a month after Pascal's death. They all stayed until then. Every day as though she weren't there they discussed the outcome of the will. The very existence of a will had been a surprise at first. Unlike many people, the Breslins were fastidious about keeping their paperwork in order. Pascal's father left the farm and stock to Pascal when he died. Many times they'd referred to the will, hoping he'd discuss it with someone but Pascal played his cards close to his chest. They assumed the farm would be left to them all when Pascal passed on. It would have to be sold and Maggie would get her share. They had even taken it upon themselves to ask an estate agent how much it would make on the open market.

As agricultural land, they found the farm was valued at a quarter of a million euro. But it was becoming a popular area for town people to move out to. Many people around were selling sites for houses. Olivia even suggested they could sell a few sites to start with. As it was, divided between the six remaining brothers and sisters they would each get over forty thousand. Maggie felt sick inside. The prospect of so much money took her breath away. The night they discussed it with her she was elated. She knew then she could have a life with Michael. She wouldn't be a dependant. She would have wealth in her own right. She was so excited she decided there and then to tell everyone about Michael.

That evening in the midst of their euphoria about the money she dropped the bombshell. Maureen looked at the floor. Her name came up in the telling so they knew she'd known all along and never told them.

Olivia stood up. "Maureen, Pascal, Mother and you kept this secret all these years?"

"I never wanted to do that. All I wanted was my baby."

Grace looked sadly at Maggie. "I wish I'd known. When do we meet him?"

"Soon, I hope."

Brian was the youngest boy. He'd lived in New York for the last forty years. None of them really knew much about him. Grace lived there too but even she didn't see much of him. He sat quietly in the background tonight listening to Maggie's tale. She turned to him when he didn't interject and saw his eyes filled with tears. She held out her hand and he gripped it tightly.

Olivia spoke again. "I can't believe you jumped into bed with somebody your first two months away from home. Didn't you even stop to think of the consequences?"

Olivia was the eldest girl. She'd married in Canada and had only been home once in ten years. Her children were grown up and she had six grandchildren. Olivia was the female equivalent to Pascal. She was a devout Catholic who spread her conservative beliefs to her children and beyond. Her eldest daughter was a nun and her middle son became a priest. She believed beyond all doubt that God laid down his law and we had to follow it to the letter or we would suffer consequences in this world and the next.

"Pascal was right. You were a disgrace. The suffering Mother must have gone through because of you and she bore it in silence!"

Maggie turned, her voice shaking. "When Michael was out of the picture Pascal never threw anything back at me. Don't you start now."

"Well, he should have stayed out of the picture. How can you think about telling people? People haven't changed that much, you know – they'll still be laughing behind your back – even more so now at your age!"

"Shut up, Olivia!" Brian said.

"Who asked you?" Olivia's temper exploded. "I'm only thinking of her. You'll be heading back to God knows what in New York. She'll have to stay here and face the music."

Brian sat beside Maggie and held her hand. "I'm gay."

Olivia started laughing. "Brian, you don't have to divert me with shock tactics. It won't work."

"I knew it!" Grace said. "It's Greg, isn't it?"

He nodded.

"Who is Greg?" Niall asked.

"Greg owns the condo next to mine in Queens.

Grace met him. We've been together for twenty years. We're still part of the old school. We have our own friends who know us as a couple and then we have family, neighbours and work colleagues who know us as neighbours and friends. Even in New York it's hard to leave behind the chains of your youth, Maggie. When we sort all the finances out, I'd love if you and Michael could come and visit."

"I'd love to."

Grace turned to her sister who was gathering her coat without a word. "Olivia. Your brother and sister have just showed you their souls. Can't you support them? What will you do if one of your grandchildren is gay or in any way *less than perfect*?"

"I'm going to Mass – is anyone else coming?"

Nobody answered so Olivia left alone. They heard her car speeding out of the yard.

Niall started to laugh. "Well! Sis, you're full of surprises. You too, Brian!"

"I know," Grace said. "We should be ashamed our sister is an unmarried mother and our brother is gay and this has been the case for decades and none of us knew. We're in our sixties and seventies, not children. When were we going to face the world?" Maggie laughed gently. "You can't know when nobody tells you."

"That makes it worse, Maggie. All these years you felt you had no one to turn to. That's shame on us."

"Well, you know now, Grace."

The next morning they all had breakfast together. The

revelations of the evening before seemed to have changed the group. Barriers had dropped and carefully applied faces crumbled in front of their eyes. Everyone but Olivia seemed happy with this. By eleven o'clock the kitchen was cleaned and everyone was dressed to go visit the solicitors. They were going to make a day of it. They'd booked a table in Alberto's in Letterkenny for afterwards.

They brought three cars. Parking was hard to find on the Port Road where the solicitor was so they parked in the Tesco car park and walked up the hill. They were a bit early and someone was still inside so they all waited, talking and internally speculating on the will. The appointment time came and went and Olivia was getting agitated. She was about to complain when the inner office door opened and a middle-aged couple appeared. She was crying and he held her gently against his shoulder. The solicitor left them at the receptionist's desk and led the Breslins into his office.

He shook hands all around and guided each of them to a seat. Shortly afterwards a tray of coffee and biscuits was passed around. When the formalities were taken care of, the will was taken from the safe.

"Now, as you know, we needed two executors of the will. I was one and Danny Boyle, Pascal's best friend, was the other. Unfortunately, Danny died a couple of months ago and Pascal never got around to nominating a second. Pascal left aside some money to cover his funeral and all the legal expenses, and the rest" – you could hear the sharp intake of breath around the room, as they waited for their inheritance – "the rest he left to his sister Margaret Breslin."

A cold silence followed his words.

"What did you say?" Olivia was the only one strong enough to speak.

"Everything goes to Margaret, with one condition."

"One condition," Olivia repeated.

"Yes. It all goes to her now. It's a life interest but she can't sell it and on her death it goes to the immediate family here present. He specified it's not to go to anyone outside of this room whilst any one of you is living."

"When did he write this?" Olivia was still the only other voice in the room.

"Three years ago."

He didn't even know if Michael would ever show up and yet he had to provide for that situation just in case. All the pain of the last few weeks exploded inside Maggie. For the first time in her life she felt hatred. Her brother was a spiteful vindictive old fool who died alone and bitter. He was tying her to the farm for life. He was so sure Michael would only surface for her inheritance after one of them died. Even from the grave he couldn't give her peace.

"Is that it?" Niall asked.

"Yes, after the expenses were taken care of, there was nothing else left."

They thanked the solicitor and left the office, maintaining as much dignity as they could. But when they stepped onto the street they erupted.

"We all have family and commitments abroad," Niall said. "We can't help you run it."

"Maggie, do you have any savings?" Grace asked.

Maggie shook her head. She felt like she had been run over by a train.

"Well, I don't feel like dinner," Olivia said. "I'm going to pack."

"I'll go with you," Niall said. "I have to get home to Sharon." He pecked Maggie on the cheek. "It's not your fault, sis. We'll fight it."

"You're right," Olivia said. "He was seventy-seven when he wrote it. He could have been suffering from dementia."

The two of them strode with purpose down the street to retrieve their car. The others continued on to the restaurant.

The restaurant was just off Main Street in the square. It was designed in the Mediterranean style with bright tablecloths, candles and bottles in baskets. A large table was prepared for them in the front corner looking out onto the street. Grace informed Alberto as he bustled over that there were two less in the group. They sat at the table and perused the menu. Maggie chose pizza, everyone else opted for pasta.

Maggie first ate pizza about fifteen years before. It was in this same restaurant – she was in town one day and decided to treat herself to something nice. It had just opened so she thought she'd take a look. She was hooked on pizza from day one. After that she used it to celebrate or commiserate depending on the occasion. Her favourite was a margherita with a side order of garlic bread. The garlic bread was flat bread soaked in oil, garlic and rosemary. She always finished up with a mocha. Maggie had discovered that a few years later. It was her little piece of decadence. When the food was ordered and on its way there was silence.

"I'm sorry. I know you all wanted your money."

"It's not your fault, Maggie."

"It is, Brian. Pascal got it into his head that he had to look out for me. Save me from my impulses – that's what he's doing now."

"I know," Grace answered. "We all have our own homes. We're established. He wanted to make sure you were taken care of."

"But, Grace, I made a mistake when I was sixteen. He's dead. He's still making my decisions for me. I'd be an independent woman for the first time in my life if we could sell the farm."

"Olivia is going to fight this. You can be sure of that."

"I know, Grace. For a moment there I thought about getting my money and going to spend time with Michael. Now it all feels like a dream just out of my reach."

"Maggie, you do need to be careful," Brian said. "Forty thousand isn't a fortune, if you don't have a house as well. We'd all have forty thousand as well as our homes." Maggie's face froze for a second and all the previous decades slipped away. She wasn't sure of anything any more. He was right, of course. Maybe

Pascal did know what was best. She felt scared and powerless.

Maggie's distress was obvious to everyone so they spent the rest of the meal trying to cheer her up. By the time her mocha came around she was smiling again. Unconsciously they were all taking on Pascal's mantle of being Maggie's guardian.

Chapter 15

When the others returned to their homes Maggie felt the oppressive emptiness of the house. She'd never lived alone before. It was the first day in March and a slight thaw appeared in the air. The previous week was bitter and cold, but this morning could fool you into thinking spring was coming. The intermittent drip of melting ice could be heard from the eaves as she stood in the kitchen.

Getting out of bed was the hardest part of her day. There wasn't anything really to get up for. If it wasn't for the animals she didn't think she'd bother. The cat slept with her and the dog slept on Pascal's bed. Poor old thing! Every evening she checked his room to see if he was back yet and when she saw he wasn't she would lie on his bed and wait. Each morning when Maggie opened her eyes they were sitting side by side on the mat by the bed, watching her face until she got up and fed them. When her eyes opened the dog's tail would wag and she'd chase it for a moment before following the cat out of the room. It was like having children.

Michael couldn't come back to visit until the summer. He wanted to bring his children and the only time they were all off together was in June. Maggie assured him she would be all right until then. She hadn't said much to him about the questions she'd had to answer about Pascal's death. Nobody except her mysterious night visitor knew Pascal locked her in the utility room the night he died.

As time moved on she was realising that little things made a huge difference in your daily life. When she returned from town on Fridays there was nobody waiting at the head of the road to carry her bags and no one to talk to in the evenings when the sun dropped and she turned the key in the front door. But the local people were very helpful. She mentioned some of her worries to Kate and she insisted Seán her youngest be there to help her in the evenings. Maggie made him his tea afterwards and he would sit and talk to her for an hour before he went home. He would tell her about school and any local gossip he'd heard. He was thirteen and becoming one of Maggie's closest friends.

Kate called in most days on her way home from work. She brought her milk, the papers and the odd treat – a cake or a bottle of wine. She'd always tell her a few anecdotes from work. In an old people's home there was always something going on. Maggie was toying with the idea of doing a voluntary afternoon in the day care centre later on when things settled down.

The postman always stopped in the morning. Any gossip that evaded her other sources didn't get past him and he had a way of turning a tale so she wasn't sure whether or not he was winding her up. He always swore it was gospel but she was never quite sure. One morning in the middle of a story she realised she was laughing more now than she'd ever done in her life.

The clock behind her struck eight. She'd got into the habit of drinking her tea standing daydreaming at the window. The dog sat at one side, the cat sat on the sill, watching her through slanted eyes. When the clock struck she sat down to her porridge and opened yesterday's paper. She didn't get up again until she'd read it cover to cover. The news was always one day behind but she didn't care. By the time she'd cleaned up and finished her chores the postman arrived and they had another cuppa together. Mid-afternoon she watched a movie or went for a walk. In this vein Maggie's life took on the semblance of happiness but another storm was brewing.

It was a couple of weeks since the others had left. The thaw didn't last and the bitter weather returned. The road was a skating rink of ice and warnings were sent out to people to stay off them if possible. Young Seán came up to make sure she had fuel and a fire lit for the night. His mother sent her some soup she'd made earlier. He left about seven-thirty, shortly before the snow started.

The kettle was singing on the hob and she was watching a new drama on the television. Every so often the dog would appear at her side and nudge her arm, then after a pat on the head she'd trot back to her room. By ten o'clock Maggie's eyes were closing. She got up and filled her hot water bottle. She thought she might as well go to bed and relax there. She did her usual locking up and switched off the lights.

Her bed was so old it sank almost to the floor in the centre. She cuddled into this and opened her book. She always read a few pages before going to sleep. At ten-thirty she switched off the light and must have slept immediately. She had no memory after that.

She didn't know what woke her. At first she just looked at her clock and saw it was two-thirty, then she lay down again in the warm spot, glad of another five hours' sleep. But two seconds later she shot up again with her heart pounding, sure now of a sound out of the ordinary. Her room faced the back of the house, Pascal's the front. She listened again. There was a path past her window which went into the fruit garden. She heard it again, a footstep on the path. Slowly she eased out of bed, trying to minimise the creaking of the springs. She couldn't remember if she'd closed her window or not. She pulled back the curtain corner and looked at it. She relaxed slightly; at least that was closed.

Everything was quiet for a few minutes and she was just considering maybe she'd imagined it when the dog started barking. Maggie crept from the room and met the excited dog in the kitchen. She didn't have to be careful now, as Sheila's hysteria would cover any sound she made. As they stood in the dark listening, a wailing started outside and something began beating the water barrel by the barn. The noise was loud and Maggie and the animals were terrified. Maggie grabbed the phone and rang her neighbour Dolores Blaney. There were three grown men in that house. When she answered Maggie explained what was happening and held the phone close to the window.

"Stay inside, Maggie. I'm sending the boys over now."

It was only a ten-minute walk to Maggie's across the fields. She stayed inside the door listening and waiting. The minutes ticked by and silence returned to the darkness. She was a bit worried about the boys – Dan was only in his late teens and Jason in his early twenties – but they were fit and together could probably frighten away a single prowler.

A knock on the door by Maggie's ear started Sheila barking again.

"Maggie, it's Dan and Jason."

She opened the door and they walked in.

"Are you all right, Maggie?" said Dan.

"I'm fine. Is there anyone out there?"

"No – we had a good look around," said Jason. "The ground is a bit messed up around the water tank. You can see a lot of footsteps. I don't know if it was him or Eddie earlier on. There are some around the back of the house too."

"It wasn't Eddie. He has no business dancing around the water tank and what would he be doing around the back of the house?"

"He might have been washing his Wellingtons at

the tank," said Dan, "and maybe he went around the back of the house to the cattle."

"Maybe." But secretly Maggie refused to believe it was Eddie. "Tell me, did you hear anything as you came along?"

"No," Dan replied. "We carried a torch because we came across the hill. Maybe they saw us."

The boys sat with Maggie for a while but normality seemed to have returned to the yard.

Dan turned to Jason. "Give Maggie your mobile number, Jay, I've lost mine."

"Good idea," Jason said. "I'll have it on every night in case you need us. Next time, Maggie, we'll come in the dark. There'll be no light to warn them off."

"Do you want us to stay the night, Maggie?" asked Dan.

"No, don't be silly! You have work in the morning. He's gone now."

"Do you think it was a '*he*', Maggie, not 'them'?"

"I don't know. Figure of speech, I suppose."

She thanked the two boys and they went back home.

That was the first night Sheila forgot her vigil for Pascal and decided to sleep with Maggie. Maggie wasn't sure who was the most scared but from then on Sheila was at the end of her bed.

Next morning Maggie woke at the usual time and hurried into her clothes to go out and check the yard.

But first she got the fire going and put the kettle on to boil. By that time the sun was completely awake and warming the front step. When she opened the door the snow was melting rapidly off the eaves onto the ground and the yard was covered in a quickly disappearing slush. With Sheila at her side she went to the barrel and looked at the cover. It was battered in. The yard brush was beside it. That must be what made the noise. The ground was churned up around it but with the thaw there were no discernable footsteps.

Sheila was nosing around and looking up at Maggie.

"Will we go around the back, girl, and see what went on there?"

Sheila did her little dance and together they started out the back gate and around the back of the house. Here the thaw hadn't started. The sun hadn't even touched it yet and a soft blanket of crunchy snow had blown off the mountain and bubbled against the back of the house, dotted here and there by protuberances of heather and rushes. A mountain spring ran off the mountain and down behind the fruit garden; it could be heard louder than usual, swelled by the thaw.

Footprints were clearly visible at the back of the house but there must have been another fall of snow since they were left as the thread marks on the soles of the shoes could no longer be seen. Instead they looked like large oval depressions with no distinct patterning at all. Like a Yeti or something sinister had sloped by. But they were large. Size twelve or more. She followed them down the path and through the little garden gate into the front yard where they disappeared into the puddles. Well. She was none the wiser. One of her taller neighbours was having a laugh at her expense. At least she knew she wasn't going mad. Someone had been there. Ever since the evening she'd found Pascal she had worried if her prowler had hurt him. She knew it was an asthmatic attack that killed him but what brought it on? Was it just the stress of fighting with her or was it the prowler?

She went back inside and made her porridge and sat down. One of the first things she was going to do was take a look at her security. There had been some break-ins in this part of Donegal over the last year and now that she was living alone security should be more of an issue. With the sun up and so bright, without a cloud in the sky, she found her spirits rising and she couldn't keep her thoughts focused on threats and fear.

It was Friday. She was going to town today. She might as well take a look at the lock shop while she was there and get some advice on security. She got to the road just as the bus was rounding the corner. She greeted Joe the driver with a big smile and sat in her seat. It suddenly dawned on her that her newfound happiness and confidence must be confusing to the parish. She'd never discussed Michael with anyone local, especially as they already thought she might have a hand in Pascal's death. Sad as it was, being without Pascal had opened up her world and life was flowing in and nothing would be able to stop that. She couldn't feel guilty about it.

The lock shop was an eye opener. Window locks, Chubb door locks, security chains, sensor lights – the list was endless. For now she got locks for all her windows and a security chain. She'd seen a show on TV once where someone cut a hole in a window and reached in and opened the catch. Well, that was one trick her prowler wasn't going to use. When she had enough money or reason she would think about the sensor lights.

When she'd finished the rest of her shopping she went to Alberto's for pizza and her weekly mocha.

The Bellini family had come to Ireland and settled in Letterkenny in the eighties. Alberto's wife worked in the kitchen and ran it like a military zone. Two of their children, boys in their early twenties, worked as waiters and Alberto worked the tables, chatting to the regulars and encouraging them to come back.

Today he came and sat by Maggie. "Hello, madam." He spoke in very precise English.

"Alberto! How are you?"

"I'm fine, very busy, but that is no reason to complain, now is it, my dear?"

"No, Alberto, it's certainly not. I'm glad things are going well. I don't know what I'd do without my weekly visit to your restaurant."

"What a lovely thing to say, Margaret! May I call you Margaret?"

Maggie smiled. "Of course!" With his accent it sounded exotic.

"I read the story in the papers."

Maggie's heart sank.

"My dear lady, don't look so sad. I wanted to tell you. You've been coming in here a long time and you brought your family here and we're sorry for your loss."

Maggie reached out and held his hand. "Thank you. Since Pascal's death people have been reaching out to me from all sides and I make new friends every day. Thanks for your kind words."

"No, thank you, Margaret. Now, no arguments, this meal is on us and we hope to see you again."

Maggie's eyes filled with tears. All she could manage to say was, "Thank you." Alberto squeezed her hand and went on to the next table.

All the way home on the bus Maggie fought back tears. She had never been so touched in her life. She'd forgotten about young Seán. There he was, standing on a rock doing a balancing act, waiting for her to get off the bus. Dan was with him.

"Maggie! Give us those bags." The three of them walked along the lane, quietly at first, then Dan brought up the events of the night before.

"Did your prowler come back?"

"No, pet. No sign of him, you and Jason were bricks last night."

"Any time, Maggie. And we mean it about the mobile. Ring that the next time and we'll be over in a shot and no lights this time. We'll risk falling in the bog to catch the bastard."

Maggie laughed at his earnest face, and his language.

They entered the yard and Maggie invited Dan in for his tea.

"No, Maggie, I have to go. My mother has my tea on. I'll ask Jason to come around tomorrow to fit those locks for you – I'm working away in Killybegs so I can't do it. It's just a matter of taking off the old latches and putting on the new lockable ones. Jason will get it done in no time. Good night, Maggie." He waved to them and went out the mountain gate.

Maggie made a mixed grill for herself and Seán and they ate it side by side watching *Buffy the Vampire Slayer.*

As soon as he left she locked the door and checked all the windows. With the house tightly shut and the curtains closed, she relaxed by the fire until bedtime.

Chapter 16

Pascal's room hadn't been touched. During his lifetime he kept his space off limits to everyone in the household and for some reason Maggie honoured that even two months after his death. This morning she stood in the doorway, looking around her as she sipped her tea. There was a church sale in the Church of Ireland hall in the parish and Rachel Fairchild had asked her for a contribution. Maggie told her she didn't have a lot to give. She hadn't thought about Pascal's stuff at the time. It almost felt sacrilegious just opening a drawer in there.

After breakfast she went back in with a collection of bin bags. She was going to get started before she changed her mind. Originally there were three bedrooms in the house: the two used by Maggie and Pascal and a third smaller one that was made into a bathroom when the other children left home. At one time eight people lived in this house. There was a bed beside the fireplace, which was traditional in the old days. It was enclosed by curtains to give privacy to the sleepers; Maggie's parents slept there when they produced too many children for the other rooms. The small bedroom was Olivia's, being the eldest girl; and the youngsters were piled into the other two. This was a big house by the standards of the day. Other families only had the kitchen and one room.

Maggie remembered as a small child sleeping in a double bed in the midst of her sisters. It was warm and you were never alone. They would talk and laugh into the night with their parents shouting at them at intervals to keep quiet. Maggie's mother baked her own bread, churned her own butter and made her own clothes. They all helped, even little Maggie; it was like a mini co-op. In their spare time in the evenings the girls knitted socks for McGee's and their mother knitted Aran jumpers.

There was a waiting list for that small room; a room so small that a single bed and a locker were all you could fit into it. Olivia left first for America so the room went to Maureen, then she left for Scotland and it went to Grace and Maggie and the two big rooms were divided amongst the boys. Pascal always kept the same room. He'd slept in it for most of eighty years. A long time, so many dreams and memories encased in a single room. When Maggie moved to Scotland, she was never expected to come back, at least not so soon. Her mother was in the bigger room which was now Maggie's, the small room became a bathroom and the bed by the fire was to go but with Maggie's return they kept it for her. Finally, when her mother died she got her own room. Somebody slept in the kitchen of this house until the eighties.

At least they stopped using the bucket in the barn as a privy when the bathroom came along. All the girls hated that. Pascal made a bench out of plywood with a hole in the centre where the bucket was suspended. He made a kind of cubicle with a curtain at the front. The toilet roll hung on some twine just inside. It was shocking to think what people considered poverty now and what they had considered normal then. There was young Jason giving her his mobile number last night, bless him – until the seventies in this parish the nearest phone was a mile away in the post office. There was a phone box which you entered, with a small window if you needed change from the post-mistress. Though it had a door that closed, there was always someone leaning against it and privacy was out of the question. None of the kids today would know how to operate that phone; she smiled in memory. You had to wind it with a lever on the side and the call went through a central exchange where the telephonist would connect the call. If there happened to be nobody leaning on the door you could never guarantee there wasn't a lady with her feet up eating a custard cream and having her afternoon tea listening to your call at the exchange. The local post office was closed now and they had taken away the phone booth. Too many people had house phones or mobiles and the box was broken into twice.

At times like this, nostalgia was akin to pain. She ached for the sounds of her family and the knowledge that someone bigger and wiser was right there to answer her questions and assuage her fears. Her family in a lot of ways had nurtured and fed her mind. They told stories, laughed and loved each other. Her problems when she got pregnant were beyond their control. You can question anything you like and feed your imagination with books but in those days and in this parish the church was untouchable. You tipped your hat to the priest and you took out the best you had when he came to visit. To fly in the face of religious protocol was to risk open scorn from the rest of the parish. She could have lived with that but not her mother. The church was her mother's primary shield in this world and the vehicle that would transport her to the next; it was Pascal's place to honour his mother. Unconsciously Maggie blessed herself. It was beyond her comprehension where they were now. She'd been trained to believe in heaven and in her heart she still held a thread of hope but the solid belief of her parents and Pascal eluded her.

There was no one here now. The people of her memories and dreams lived in another world, she was the only one here and like them she deserved the opportunity to move on. She felt guilty about entering Pascal's space but it was time to bury her guilt forever.

Systematically she removed his clothes from the cabinets and wardrobe. She checked the pockets and arranged them in neat piles on the bed. When all the piles were neatly in bin bags and labelled she turned to the papers and knick-knacks her brother had accumulated over the years. Now she was delving into his soul. For that she needed another cup of tea. She moved the bags to the kitchen and brought her mug back to the room.

In the top of his wardrobe he had a collection of shoeboxes. In amazement Maggie looked at the clear labelling on each box. Her brother was more meticulous than she was. No wonder Tommy Breslin's words survived into this century. His diaries were like Pascal's boxes. Was there a pathological need in her family to live beyond their time?

The first box held deeds and bills, the second instruction manuals all the way back to their first vacuum cleaner. The last one held letters. She started at the beginning. Most of the bills were old and unnecessary. She screwed them up in a ball. They'd do to start the fire. Anything of value she put to one side. The same was done with the instruction manuals. Only three of them matched anything in the house. She sat back on the bed and looked at the letters. Should she open the box or just burn it intact and let the past stay in the past? Her grandfather always said there was nothing more inquisitive than a woman or a hen. With shaking hands she took the lid off; today wasn't the day she was going to prove him wrong.

Like everything else Pascal did there was a scheme involved. Little bundles of envelopes held by rubber bands nestled innocently inside. He obviously knew the writing so he didn't bother labelling the bundles, they were never meant for the eyes of anyone else. Maggie took them all out and lined them up on the counterpane. There were about fifty in all.

The first bundle was yellowed and brittle. She was about to open that when she recognised Maureen's writing on the first envelope of the second one. Pascal had kept every letter Maureen had ever sent him.

A thought came to her. She flicked through the letters looking for a particular date. There it was, the letter Maureen sent when Maggie was pregnant.

Inside the envelope the letter consisted of a single sheet. It was brief and to the point.

'Maggie is expecting, Pascal. I myself am due in three months and can't look after her. She would like to go home. Write to me and tell me how you feel about that. Something needs to be sorted out soon before she starts to show. If she can't go home we need to arrange something else. How is Mother? Maureen.'

Maggie sat back, shocked at its abrupt tone. She'd assumed Maureen went out of her way to coax Pascal into taking her home. The next letter was the answer to Pascal's. It was as short as the last one.

'Okay, Pascal, you know best. She's not showing much yet so it would be best to get her into the convent as quickly as possible. I'll get her ready and send her to the boat. Mother Imelda will look after her in Dublin.'

Maggie thought she was going to be sick. The betrayal from her only ally hurt deeply. During all these years Maggie never questioned Maureen's support; it seemed as unwavering as night and day in its dependability.

The next letter was after Michael's birth.

'Pascal, I've spoken to Mother Imelda and she agrees with us that no useful purpose would be served by letting Maggie have time with the child. It would only prolong the agony so they took him from her immediately. He's to go to a good family in Boston. She'd only bond if we let them be together, things would be hard for everyone. The child will have some future where he's going'.

In white-faced shock Maggie read the next letter.

'Mother Imelda was delighted with the contribution to the convent fund. Maggie's suicide attempt will remain a secret. Though you know our views on Maggie going home, Mother Imelda has agreed to send her back to Donegal. You're out all day and Mother isn't well – who'll provide the firm hand needed to keep Maggie in line? She's a wayward girl. Good luck, Maureen.'

Maggie's tears flowed down her cheeks and the shaky foundation on which she'd maintained her strength collapsed. How could Maureen betray her and condemn her like that? If it weren't for Pascal she would have been like the others and rotted in an unmarked grave for she would have eventually died. She couldn't have survived that place. Being a suicide, they certainly wouldn't have commemorated her passing.

She lay on the bed amongst the letters and let the pain wash over her like a cloak. She immersed herself in it and let the coldness of it sharpen her anger. Anger at the church was an old wound but she'd never felt anything like the sharpness of what she felt towards her sister. Maggie had never even questioned her on what she'd said, so convinced was she that Maureen pulled out all the stops to do what was best for her little sister. The fact that she was in direct contact with the convent and wanted to leave her there was like a kick in the gut. She even knew her little Tommy went to Boston. Now the significance of her knowing what happened to Michael's father sank in. Maureen was a person she'd never really known.

At last she pulled herself together and gathered the letters into the band and placed them back in the box. She would read them all later.

Now the devil in her wanted to know the rest. She picked up the next bundle, a smaller one and opened that. She read the name. *Breda*. Who was *Breda*? She lay back again on the bed and tried to remember. Was the name familiar? Most of the letter was just local gossip from when Maggie was a little girl. She laughed through her tears at some of the references. Breda was talking about people Maggie knew as middle-aged to old-aged. Gráinne the old post-mistress was referred to as '*the post office rip*'. '*If she goes near Kathleen's man again there will be a war.*' Gráinne would have been about twenty-five years older than Maggie. Nothing in here, she thought, putting the letter back on the pile. She opened the next one.

This letter was getting more personal. It was obvious an intimacy had formed between Breda and Pascal.

They'd held hands, danced and enjoyed a lot of eye contact across a crowded hall over a bottle of orange. Maggie smiled at the idea of her brother as the romantic hero.

Letter after letter went on in the same vein. Finally only a few letters remained. Maggie was bored by the simple love of her brother and his sweetheart. But she knew something must have broken them up and that was the only reason she continued to read. In the third last letter the beginnings of the reason became apparent.

'Packie, what happened last night was beautiful. I was touched by your tenderness and can't wait to see you again. You're in my heart and my soul. Breda.'

Maggie read the line again. Did that mean sex? It made sense reading between the lines of the other letters. They were getting closer and more intimate and Breda was gaining confidence.

She jumped to the next letter. It was written two months after the last one. From the beginning Breda was upset.

'Pascal, I've been to Duffy's every week since our night and you haven't been there. Why are you ignoring me? Didn't it mean something to you too? Why am I alone now when I need you the most? You know what I mean. I'm two months late. It's you and it's only been you.' Breda ended on a plea for him to contact her.

The last letter was dated a month later.

'Your words stung and I'll never forget the hurt. I married Peter this morning. My baby will have a good

home. Peter will be a good provider; I couldn't wait any longer. I'd be married to Peter now anyway if you hadn't swept me off my feet. I know I can rely on you to never breathe a word of this to anyone. The secret is ours. Breda.'

Oh Pascal! You abandoned your own child! She wished she could see the replies and speak to Pascal. Breda and Peter, she kept repeating the names. Whoever Breda was she didn't know how to write a letter. She didn't have her name and address on the top. There was no way for Maggie to know who she was. She read the letters again from the beginning, carefully this time, and there wasn't a hint as to who Breda might be. Maggie had a secret niece or a nephew somewhere, unless something happened with the pregnancy.

All the other letters were just general correspondence between family and friends. She scanned them all but none of them held a hint of Breda or her baby; Pascal must have completely blocked it from his mind and never confided in anyone. Was that why he never married? Was he consumed by guilt over his great romance or was there something deeper inside only Pascal had known? Breda said he was tender, so why did he abandon her?

The light was gone from the room and the dog was tugging her sleeve for her food so Maggie put everything back in the shoebox and with a sort of reverence placed it back inside its dust square in the back of the wardrobe before leaving the room. How many more secrets could there be in one family?

Chapter 17

Pascal let another man bring up his child when he should have done that himself. Then he forced Maggie to give up her child when she wanted nothing more than to bring him up at home. Was it just a matter of propriety? If she'd come back as a young widow with a baby the rumour of illegitimacy would always hang over Tommy. If Pascal and Breda had got married the term 'shotgun' would be added to the wedding banns. In those days those would have been serious issues. His baby would have been the first; he would have been the one to bring the family name into disrepute. Maggie herself was only a child then. Perhaps he couldn't let Maggie have her baby when he couldn't have his. Was that why he brought her home? His guilt was too much for him. A chain of events had been set in motion by his actions and that chain would have ended in her death inside a convent laundry if he hadn't at last made a mature decision and stood apart from propriety. For that she loved him. He was barely thirty when another man walked his girlfriend and child down the aisle. He was thirty-six when he sent his nephew to Boston to strangers and when he was eighty years old he died alone and scared in his bedroom while his sister slept in a prison of his making at the back of the house. Pascal's life was built on the shifting sands of fear, guilt and bitterness. For that she loved him too; he was as lost as she was. People had suffered because of him but Pascal was no less in pain.

Rachel had taken the bags of clothes for the sale. Maggie dumped the bedclothes, floor covering and bed from the room. She couldn't bear to look at them after the night she found Pascal. The floor was uneven so Jason and his dad spent four weekends taking up the floor and putting down a new one. David was a tall strong man. Jason was small but wiry. Between them they ploughed through the work. She bought a new piece of lino and a new bed, which she covered in a white bedspread dotted with embroidered roses. The furniture was good and she couldn't afford to change that but with the right accessories she had a lovely guest room.

The addition of a guest room to her home lifted her momentarily out of the blues. She held the best of her brother along with the worst in her head. She didn't need to surround herself with him in her home too.

Every trip to town she swapped a piece of the past for something nice from the present. She took some things into the second-hand shop on the Port Road and bought something new in return. Lamps and pottery dotted her shelves and she'd introduced some greenery to give life to her room. She never spent much and tried to offset her cost by selling something she didn't want any more. She found that Pascal's tools were worth quite a lot. She wasn't sure if it was legal to sell these things but she decided not to ask.

Over the following months she tiled the kitchen with linoleum tiles as she couldn't afford ceramic but they altered the whole room. She painted the walls a pale yellow and replaced the curtains her mother made twenty years before with a pair of new ones in autumn colours. She trawled the second-hand shops, thrift shops and pound shops in search of cheap and cheerful. Maggie hated tacky but if you searched hard enough you could find quality at discount.

Her own appearance was changing too. Just recently she'd had her hair cut into a neat bob that swished around her face as she walked. She'd considered colouring it but somehow it suited her as it was. She felt light now that she was free of the long hair she painstakingly scooped up every morning of her life into a bun. Her clothes were finding their way slowly into jumble sales and she was becoming a regular at Dunnes Stores. She was wearing trousers for the first time in her life and teaming them with soft colourful jumpers. Light anoraks and blazers replaced her cardigans. A wine-coloured ankle-length coat that she found in a local jumble sale replaced her belted brown one. It was hanging at the front of the rack. Maggie had seen one exactly like it in McElheny's in Ballybofey. She looked at the label. It was the same one. How could someone give away a brand new coat? The price was slightly more than she had intended to pay but she couldn't resist. One good buy was better than a dozen little things she probably didn't need. A nice pair of boots for the winter weather and she felt like a million euro.

Her biggest loss was Maureen. Maggie hadn't contacted her since the finding of the letters. She'd had to get an answering machine after Pascal's death to screen out pest calls and she'd added Maureen's calls to that list. The please-pick-up messages had finally stopped. Every day she wanted to talk to her, tell her what she'd discovered, maybe get her sister back but the words of the letter kept coming back to her.

One morning Maggie looked around her home with pride. It was warm and comfortable and she was very happy. In two months Michael and his children were coming to visit. The anticipation was growing with each day. A sound in the yard caused her to turn from her thoughts. The postman was there. It wasn't Terence, her usual one. It was his locum Alan. She didn't know much about him. He was a nice enough fellow, but a bit quiet. Maggie went to the door.

"Good morning, Alan."

"Miss Breslin." He handed her the letters.

"Lovely day, isn't it?"

"It is. Alan, would you like some tea?"

"Yes, I'd like that." Maggie was kind of hoping he wouldn't – he never had a lot to say in total contrast to the engaging Terence.

When Maggie was getting the tea ready she remembered something else she didn't like about him. He looked at everything.

"This place has changed a lot since the last time I saw it."

"Has it?"

Maggie blushed despite herself. She knew what he was thinking, what everyone was thinking, that Maggie got rid of Pascal and redecorated. The cup of tea seemed never-ending. She regretted taking out the Jaffa Cakes. He seemed to savour and linger over each one. He spoke sporadically and took in every detail of her kitchen before he finally left. Maggie was delighted to see the back of him. He'd dampened her whole day.

That night the trouble started again. Maggie had been asleep for a while when she heard the footsteps outside her window. There was no snow this time to insulate the sound. The steps were clear. Sheila lifted her head, quietly at first, and they both listened as one. Then the sound of a hand checking the window could be heard. Maggie thanked God she'd got the window locks. She'd checked each one before going to bed and removed all the keys, they were in a bowl on the sideboard in the kitchen. She crept out of bed with the dog following at her heels and went to the phone. Quietly she called Jason's mobile.

She crouched in the kitchen and whispered, "Hello, Jason. There's someone outside the house. Can you come over?"

"Maggie, I'm in the village – just leaving Duffy's. It'll take about ten minutes to get up there – stay inside until I'm at the door."

She could tell by his breathing he was walking and talking.

She hung up the phone again. Sheila was growling deep in her throat. Whatever the dog could hear Maggie couldn't hear anything now. Suddenly the night was split by the same wails and banging as the last time. Surely the neighbours must hear, she thought.

After a while there was silence again. She was standing at the window. The curtains were closed and she was gathering her courage to peer out. Without warning a rock flew through the window, slowed thankfully by the thick material of the curtain. By now Sheila was going crazy, her own fear coupled with Maggie's escalated her growls into a volley of vicious barks.

Maggie jumped back from the window and sat in the corner away from the glass. Sheila backed into her arms, still growling and barking at intervals. Then she too grew quiet, listening. For a short while there was total silence.

Then the voice from the night of Pascal's death could be heard in the yard. "Maggie! Hey, Maggie! Did I scare you? You killed Pascal, didn't you, Maggie? You're wearing your fancy clothes now and throwing bits of him out every day. I saw his clothes in a jumble sale. I saw you sell his things in the town. Did you kill him, Maggie? Now look at you spending his life. I'm sure the miserable old bastard didn't have much but you're stealing what he had."

She could not recognise the voice – it sounded thick and muffled.

Then there was silence again. Minutes ticked by, finally broken by the approach of footsteps and a knock at the door.

"Maggie!" Jason's voice was like a beacon in the night.

Sobbing, Maggie ran to the door, falling over the dog. She opened it and dragged Jason inside.

"Look!" She showed him the glass. "I was standing right at the window when the rock came through. Did you see anything, Jason?"

"No, I didn't. I think I might have heard him though going down through the bottom of your garden as I came up through the fields."

"Why didn't you see him then? Where did he go?"

"He must have gone out your little garden gate and taken that path down to Eddie's sheep pens. When I got to your garden gate there was no sound and he certainly didn't pass me. I'll ask Eddie tomorrow if he saw anyone down around their land. In any case, he's gone now. But I'm staying here and I don't want any arguments."

"I was hoping you'd say that. I'll make up the spare room. Will you have a cup of tea? I'd love one myself."

"You do the room, Maggie. I'll make the tea."

By the time she had the room sorted and a hot water bottle in the bed Jason had fitted a piece of cardboard to the broken window to keep the frost out. He was just sweeping up the glass when she entered the room.

"I'll help with that," she said.

"No, you won't, sit down and drink your tea. I put a nip of whiskey in it."

"You're the best – did anyone ever tell you that?"

"Every night, Maggie. I had to tell them I was busy tonight."

"You're bold!"

He laughed. "It's nice to see the smile back on your face."

They sat at the table and drank their tea, munching on the last of the Jaffa Cakes. After a while Jason turned to her.

"Did you kill him?"

Maggie's first reaction was anger and it flickered briefly on her face.

"I'm sorry, Maggie." Jason leaned across the table and held her hand. "I never thought it was cold-blooded murder but I did think that something didn't add up, you know. That you didn't tell them everything.

Was it an accident? I'm babbling, it's embarrassment, I feel bad for saying anything."

"It's okay. I know it's what everyone is thinking. At least you didn't throw a rock through my window and you're right, I didn't tell everything about that night."

The fear, whiskey and the presence of a friend loosened Maggie's tongue for the first time since it happened.

"Instead of exonerating me it would only have made me look guilty if I'd told the truth."

"Why?"

"Jason! How old are you?"

"Twenty-two."

She smiled. "I don't want Dolores telling me off for talking inappropriately to her son."

"There's not much, Maggie, I haven't heard."

"Well . . . I have a son."

" What?" Jason's coffee sprayed over her shoulder. His dark eyes locked into hers.

"I'm sorry, that was rude, why wouldn't you have a son?"

Maggie smiled. "I had him when I was seventeen and he was adopted."

"Wow! But what does that have to do with Pascal dying?"

"He was the reason I had to have my son adopted. Recently Michael found me. He was the American relative that was visiting. Pascal blew his top and told me not to see him. But I saw him anyway. The night

Michael went back to Boston, Pascal heaved a sigh of relief and then forbade me from telling anyone he existed. I said no. I'd already told my sister Michael had found me and I was going to call the rest of the family and tell them. Pascal lost his temper and locked me in the utility room. He had his attack while I was locked in."

"So that's why the door was broken! You didn't break out until evening – no wonder you didn't know he was lying in there all day. My God!"

"I know. If I told all that to the guards they would have locked me up."

"Why?"

"It would look like a motive to get rid of him, wouldn't it?"

"Perhaps."

"That was the night the prowler first arrived. He was talking through the door to me when I was locked in."

"How did he know you were there?"

"I thought about that. The only thing I could think of was that wherever Pascal was that evening he must have walked back with someone. Maybe he heard our fight and knew Pascal locked me in – or heard me shouting." Maggie got really quiet and a worried frown split her brow.

"What's wrong, Maggie?"

"I think my prowler killed Pascal or at least may have frightened him into an attack. He was there at the house – Pascal died – he jeered through the door at me. None of it makes sense of course but I know somehow he did it and now he's tormenting me more and more. And I'm wondering am I next."

"Don't you think that's a leap, Maggie?"

"Why?"

"That was a Sunday night, wasn't it?"

"Yes. Why?"

"Pascal used to drink in a house out on the mountains on a Sunday night. I don't know if he ever talked about it to you but that place has a terrible reputation."

"What do you mean?"

"Well, I know it by reputation but my mother would skin me if she caught me up there. Everyone knows who drinks there. One of them was Pascal."

Maggie felt ill. "Why is it such a terrible place?"

"They drink a lot of poitín."

"Well, that's hardly unusual – a few places around do that."

Jason lowered his head. "Now my mother will kill me for telling tales out of school to you. Another generation frequented that place. Let's say before boy bands and gay bars, being gay wasn't the open thing it is today."

"Jason! What! Are you sure or is this a rural myth?"

"No, Maggie, it's no myth. It's not like a massage parlour or anything like that – it's a sad place where sad old men congregate. I think they need the poitín to get them in the mood. Anyway, what I think, Maggie, is this: any man up there socialising must be a confused puppy. And if he met up with Pascal there I'd be careful. Let things lie. Those men don't want people knowing their secrets."

Maggie's stomach was churning. Pascal must be turning summersaults in his grave at all she'd discovered of his private life.

"Maggie, if you want my advice, tell everyone about Michael. Secrets rot your soul. Those guys up there are living proof of that. A bunch of old men with bonds as strong as family needing a pint of poitín to get laid. Sorry – I'm saying too much."

"I watched *Queer as Folk*." Maggie spoke earnestly.

Jason laughed himself breathless. "I can't picture you watching that, Maggie."

"It was a good show. I was a bit shocked but I couldn't look away. I remember Pascal got very upset and went out."

"Now you know why."

"Poor Pascal, I find out something new about him every day."

"Maggie, don't look like that – don't think too badly of him – those guys are lonely sad old men afraid to come out of the shadows."

"I know, Jason. No, I was just wondering who that guy in my yard is. Jason, should you ring your mother?"

"No. I'd only wake her up and worry her. I'll tell her in the morning what happened. We'll sleep on it."

As Maggie was succumbing to sleep that night it

finally clicked into place in her brain. Pascal should have been able to use his inhaler. Her intruder killed Pascal. Somehow he prevented him from using his inhaler. It had to have been personal because he didn't steal anything. Maybe Jason was right, maybe he fell out with a friend. But what did it have to do with her?

Chapter 18

Maggie got up early and wouldn't let Jason go without cooking him breakfast. "Maggie, you need your rest after last night!"

But she wouldn't hear of it and while he was arguing she had porridge, toast and coffee ready. He knew she just needed some company after the night, so he let her carry on. He'd be a few minutes late by the time he went home and picked up the car but he'd lay a few extra blocks during his lunchtime. He wasn't usually that conscientious but he needed the money and being paid by the block was a good incentive.

When they'd finished breakfast Maggie walked him out the door. The morning was dry but the ground sparkled with the remains of a frost.

"I'll be back tonight to fit that window for you, Maggie. It will be cold today. You'd better put a few extra sods of peat in the stove. If you don't mind I'll come and stay again tonight and make sure that prick doesn't come back."

"I don't mind, Jay. I'd be delighted. Wee Seán down the road comes up for his tea a few evenings. He'll be here today. It'll be like a dinner party."

Jason stepped out of the doorframe and looked back at Maggie. Then his focus shifted and his face froze.

"What's the matter?" She walked out after him and looked back.

"*MAGGIE IS A HORE.*"

The words were written in black paint on the wall of the house.

"The bastard came back," said Jason. "I should have sat up and watched."

Maggie was stunned and very frightened.

Jason tried to make light of it. "Well, now we can narrow him down a bit farther."

"Can we?"

"Yep! He can't spell 'whore'!"

His humour was lost on Maggie; her heart was heavy with fear. She'd just painted the front of the house a few weeks previously and there was loads of paint left over. She was going to have to redo it right now.

"You go on, love," she said. "I'll paint over that later."

The frown lines in Jason's forehead deepened considerably. "Maggie, I'd rather young Seán or the postman didn't see that. I'll stay and paint it and go in late."

"No, you go on!"

"Don't be silly. Get me the paint. It's a bit high up for you. It won't take me long."

The painting was just finished and the wall was pristine again when the postman arrived. Alan again. Maggie was going to wash the brushes but she handed them to Jason, then tipped him on the elbow and he went into the house to wash them. Alan handed over the letters. Maggie said hi and for once declined to extend any hospitality. She hoped he'd think herself and Jason were too busy with the painting.

Alan drove out of the yard and down the lane.

"Is Terence on holiday, Maggie?"

"I think so."

"What have you got against Alan?"

"How do you know I don't like him?"

"Well! Your facial expressions are a bit transparent and you didn't want to be alone with him."

"He gives me the willies."

Jason laughed. "He's quiet."

"No! He's watchful."

"Quiet people often appear that way."

"I suppose you're right. I can't wait until Terence comes back – he always makes me laugh."

"Now, *he* gets on my nerves," Jason said.

"Why?"

"What's he got to be happy about all the time? He's an awful gossip too."

"Aw, I know he is but he does a social service keeping old folks like me happy."

"Well, Miss Breslin, this time I have to go or I'll be working full time for you as I'll have no job to go to!"

"Oh, I'm sorry!"

"No worries, Maggie. I'll be back this evening."

Much of Maggie's bravado disappeared after he left. She had another cup of tea. She sat with it facing the broken window: So much information and in such a short space of time. So that was Pascal's secret. But why didn't he jump at the chance of a marriage of convenience? He could still have had his nights drinking in the mountains. Pascal's code of honour, she supposed. His child was brought up by its mother, without the influence of a man living a daily lie. Maybe one secret in the beginning was better than a secret that had to be lived every day. Was that the same with her baby? He'd been tucked away in a good family where he didn't have to face his dubious origins every day. For all Pascal's adherence to rules he was just like everyone else: he made them up as he went along.

He obviously wasn't alone. Other men in this parish were leading double lives as well, if what Jason said were true. Were they married, single and what age were they? Jason had said they were old. It was very sad and she thought they deserved to be left in peace but one of them was harassing her and probably killed her brother.

After lunch she thought she'd like some fresh air. She pulled her bike out of the shed and cycled down to the graveyard to visit Pascal's grave. Maybe he might be able to give her a little clarity. She had a bunch of snowdrops in her basket for the grave. Spring had come to the churchyard. Soft mint green was spreading like a thin layer of gauze over the trees. Flowers were dotting through the grass. Daffodils, crocuses and snowdrops appeared like confetti in the greenery. The only sound in the yard was the swishing of the wind in the trees and the cawing of crows from the roof.

She laid the flowers and sat on one of the tumbled stones by Pascal's grave. The ground was settled now and Pascal was blending nicely into his surroundings. She hoped he'd finally found some peace. It was funny how peaceful a graveyard can be. She leaned back a little against the ivy-covered wall and looked back up the path. She was sitting directly in the sun. Sheltered from the wind, the spot was warm. After the night before and all the excitement she was very tired and dozed off. It seemed like just a few moments until she opened her eyes. It would be more comfortable to go home and sleep in her bed, she thought, getting up stiffly and reaching for her bike. The sunbeam she'd been sitting in had moved around the dial and she supposed it was the cold that woke her up.

When she focused on her bike she saw there was a post-it between her handlebars. '*Nice paint job*'. She looked around; there was no one in sight. She was so scared she could barely grip the handlebars of the bike. She pushed it up the hill and cycled as fast as she could down the other side to come to a crashing halt against the wall of the bridge. The front of her bike was twisted but miraculously she was unscathed. A car beeped behind her and went quickly on down the hill. Her heart hammered. She couldn't tell the make or model of the car or read the number plate because she was so frightened. All she knew for certain was that it was a small dark hatchback. Anyone she knew would have stopped to help her – except whoever put the note on her handlebars. Slowly she pushed the hobbled bike back onto the road.

Father Landers was just driving by as she started to push the bike home. He slowed down.

"Maggie! Are you all right?"

"I am, Father, but my bike's in tatters."

"What happened?"

"I was going too fast and I took a spill. Thought I was Michael Schumacher. Could have been worse, I suppose. I'll have a few bruises in the morning"

He stepped out of the car and opened the boot. "I have some cord in here. We can tie the bike on and I'll drive you home."

"Father, you're a lifesaver. Thanks a million."

They pulled up outside the door just as Jason stepped into the yard off the mountain. "Maggie! What happened?"

"Oh, I came off my bike."

Jason's eyes locked onto hers. He knew there was something else to the story but in the presence of Father Landers he couldn't ask.

"Father, come in for a cuppa," said Maggie.

"No, I was on my way to a funeral. I'll come in some day next week and see how you're getting on."

The moment he stepped into the car and the door shut, Jason turned to Maggie.

"Okay! What really happened?"

She told him the story briefly.

"I can't believe I fell asleep in a graveyard."

"Is that what you can't believe? Someone was watching you while you slept, someone put a note on your handlebar, someone who's prowling your property at night! Maybe you should speak to the guards."

"Jason, they'll have to know more about Pascal and the night he died. It's too late now to tell them about that. I'd look guilty of something after all this time. It will probably stop anyway, Jason."

"Why do you think that?"

"Oh, you know what it's like around here – something is a big deal for a while and then everyone forgets about it. I'm sure if he wanted me dead, I'd be dead by now." It sounded funnier in her head before she said it.

"Maggie, I know all the messers in this parish and, if this was just a prank, they'd be laughing about it in Duffy's. Whoever is doing this isn't talking to anyone."

Just then they heard Seán dropping his bike on the path.

"Don't say anything to Seán," she said hastily. "I don't want to upset his mother. Seán's a bit young and he wouldn't be able to keep a secret."

"Okay, Maggie."

Seán breezed in the door. "Jason! You're here as well?"

"I just came over to check on Maggie."

"You're both staying for tea," said Maggie. "I need the company."

Seán pulled his hand out from behind his back. "I brought a video over." He started his infectious giggle and looked at Jason. "Maggie doesn't have a DVD player. I have to make videos for her"

"Yes pet! We know – Maggie is old. Right, we can watch it after tea." Maggie feigned exasperation with a big smile on her face.

Jason started laughing. "What are you entertaining Maggie with?"

"*The X Files*."

"Oh great, I'll really enjoy that!" She looked genuinely delighted.

Jason raised his eyebrows.

Maggie put her arm around Seán's shoulder. "Seán is a fellow science fiction fan."

Jason nodded at her and smirked.

As if she could read his mind, Maggie patted his arm. "Don't worry, I'm not doing a Fox Mulder on it."

He roared laughing and Seán looked a bit dazed. His usual state, Jason thought. Well, well – he had a date tonight and instead he was spending the evening with an old lady and a sci-fi freak.

It turned out to be a really good evening. Seán told them about school and had them in stitches. The poor kid wasn't even trying to be funny. They nearly cracked up when he told them he had to break a date with Annie because she drank too much.

"Alcohol?" Maggie asked, tears in her eyes from laughing.

"No! Orange! It's as expensive these days to drink minerals as alcohol, and I haven't got a job. Would you want to spend your pocket money on Football Specials when you'd rather be at home watching football on television for free?" The Football Special was a soft drink probably not widely drunk outside Donegal. Sometimes the local kids drank doubles in bars to look cool. If you poured two into a pint glass it had the deep colour of a pint of Smithwicks. It was pure sugar but that didn't matter; it saved many a post-pubescent male's face when confronted by a slightly older or at least more mature female. It was tragic, though, if she'd developed a taste for a guy with a genuine pint in his hand. Seán was too young to value the woman who tasted sugar and liked it. Those who preferred the hard man would one day chew up and spit out a gentle creature like Seán.

Jason stoked the fire and looked around the room. He'd been in here before Pascal's death and the contrast was stark. The house was cold then despite the stove and Maggie's warm personality. It hadn't changed for over twenty years. It was stuck inside the mindset of Pascal Breslin. All over this parish houses reflected the decay of their inmates. Dulled peeling paint, once bright but every year degenerating to a dirty wash of grey-covered damp walls. Curtains once hung with some semblance of care were dotted with rips and smears of food. They hung down like the sagging lines of a careworn body. The windows were like glazed eyes, looking out and seeing nothing. When you walked through the front door piles of junk mail stood inside the hall like pillars supporting the portico of cobwebs suspended over the doorway. The façade was a reflection of the interior and the interior was ultimately altered by the reaction to the façade. It was a self-sustaining system almost beyond the perception of the inmates. Maggie had been a dormant entity lying within, waiting for the moment when the conditions were right for regeneration. People like Maggie could be slowed and go into a state of inertia but they could never be stopped. Jason fully believed that opportunity would eventually present itself for everyone, that's what kept him going. His life too was waiting to be discovered.

Maggie's hooded brown eyes turned to him and softened. "What has you so deep in thought?"

"Just thinking about life, Maggie."

"I know. I do it myself. It takes me by surprise all the time."

"You two are a bit much for me tonight." Seán got up and walked towards the door. "I'll tell my mother you'll be in tomorrow if that's all right. She wants to come up for a chat."

"That would be great, Seán. I'd love to see her."

Seán waved and left.

"He's lovely, isn't he?" said Maggie.

Jason laughed. "He's a pain in the arse but he means well. There's no harm in him. You've had a tough day, Maggie. Are you tired?"

"I'm a bit wound up. Falling asleep in the graveyard with someone putting notes on my bike and watching me didn't help. Do you think he's been around at other times in the daytime?"

Jason sat back in thought. "Maggie, you do realise that he is someone who knows you and your habits so it could be anyone that comes up to your door."

"Like the postman." Maggie's voice lowered to a whisper.

"Alan!"

"I told you I didn't like him."

"Not liking him doesn't make him a prowler."

"He was around here today and yesterday!"

"He's the postman, Maggie."

"Yes, but . . ." Maggie trailed off, knowing she had no real case. "Do you know much about him, Jason?"

"He's not very old. He looks older than he is."

"What age would you say he is?"

"Twenty-five, I'd say."

"Um!" Maggie went silent again.

"Um what?"

"Nothing." Maggie had a little niggling thought in the back of her brain.

Could all this have something to do with Pascal's child? No one else around here had any reason to torment her. If Michael found her and he lived in Boston, surely a child left locally could do the same? But Alan was too young if he were only twenty-five. The hammer fell on her enthusiasm. It could have been a daughter anyway.

Chapter 19

Maggie's tea went cold again. She took a sip and the cold insipid liquid made her gag. She went to the teapot but that had gone off as well. It was unusual for Maggie to let a whole pot of tea go cold. She shifted the kettle into the centre of the hot plate and emptied the teapot. All her actions today were mechanical. It seemed like seconds she'd been looking at the lid of the bin when she heard the kettle boiling over. Today wasn't going to be a very productive day. She made more tea, poured out another mug and sat down again, gazing out the window. A crow was sitting on the windowsill cawing intermittingly at his reflection. His feathers reflected blue-black as the sun shone on them. He was like a little serious black gentleman in shirttails with his hands behind his back, thoughtfully looking around. Jason told her last night that Alan wasn't originally from the parish but from Kilcar. Kilcar was a village with roughly three hundred residents, east of Killybegs on the coast. It was a beautiful barren place, difficult to make a living from if you were a farmer. He'd moved here for a job in Duffy's when he was about sixteen. He was related to the family. He'd been here ever since. He still did weekends in the pub and he lived in a small bed-sit in the back of the property. He worked in a number of positions. He did relief in the pub and relief for the post office either in the back office or in the van. He was always available for farmers or small businesses whenever they needed him.

Jason speculated on where he kept his money. He didn't drink. The only time he spent in the pub was when he was behind the bar. His bed-sit was part of his remuneration. Nobody socialised with him. He was a regular loner.

If she weren't so scared of him she would pity him. She knew better than anyone what it was like to be alone. He certainly couldn't be Pascal's son. Pascal's child would now be approaching fifty at least.

Just then she heard the reason for her disquiet approaching. The post van stopped outside the door. Maggie had the door firmly locked and she knew the house looked deserted. She stood to the side of the window, looking out through the net curtains.

Alan was leafing through a bundle of envelopes. When he found hers he sat looking around the yard. After a few moments he got out and walked towards the door. He reached out and tried the handle. The door didn't yield to his touch. He pushed the envelopes through the letterbox and turned once again, looking around the yard. Maggie was too scared to breathe. She watched transfixed as he turned straight towards her. Shielding his eyes from the sun he tried to peer through the glass. Thank God for net curtains – he probably couldn't see much inside. Once again he walked out into the centre of the yard and stood by the van, looking back at the house. Pascal's son or not he was certainly behaving suspiciously. Either he was a disassociated weirdo or he was her prowler. Whether or not, she knew she didn't like him and now she had proof enough that he was a weird one. He didn't stop long; in a couple of minutes he sat back into the van and sped out of the yard.

With a long sigh of relief she watched him go. She was sick of the silence of the kitchen. The one item from the past that she couldn't remove from the room was the old radio. Crossing the room she turned the dial and tuned into Highland Radio. She couldn't go through a day without a dose of Daniel O'Donnell. He was singing 'The Tennessee Waltz'. Maggie loved him. Jason said he appealed to the granny brigade and Seán said nothing, just went into peals of laughter when he saw her tape collection by the video. She didn't care. She was a card-carrying member of the Daniel Club. He was always a comfort and brought a smile to her face. Seán would have agreed with the last part because he certainly made him laugh.

Now that the post had come and she knew she wouldn't have to face Alan she could go about her day. She opened the door and walked outside. The sun always shone straight into the yard in the morning so even in winter it was warm. Sheila was glad to be out and about. Herself and the cat raced each other into the yard. The dog in her excitement nipped the cat on the shoulder and the cat having none of it whipped her across the nose with her outstretched claws and left a dot of blood on her muzzle. Sheila yelped and sat for Maggie to kiss it better while the cat haughtily picked her way across the path. The dog left her old head against Maggie's side and lifted her paw, waving it in the air as if to re-emphasise her pain. "Humbug," Maggie whispered in her ear and kissed her furry cheek again. She turned the key in the lock and, with the dog trotting beside her, walked up the mountain path. A few months previously and she would have left the door open without a thought. In a strange sort of way she liked turning the key in the lock. It set boundaries between her and the rest of the world. In the past she'd always shared so much of her space with other people, the most she'd ever gained for herself was her own room when she was fifty. Now she had a whole house with a front door she could turn the key in and lock the world out. She liked the little click the lock made when it engaged. It was her click, the sound of her jurisdiction.

A morning on the mountain was a pleasure. It was cold but the air was fresh and clear. The mountain lark could be heard singing in the rushes to the east of her. The stream tinkled along, smaller now, without a recent fall of snow or rain to swell it. The path wound up the hill for about a mile and then disappeared into the bog. It was built for tractors going to the bog to haul turf. Only people like Maggie with no purpose in life wandered up there to take the mountain air. There were about twenty cattle on the land at the moment belonging to Eddie.

On the way back down she caught a glimpse of a shape in the yard rounding the corner of the house towards the orchard. *Oh God! He's back!* She crept down, holding onto the dog's collar to keep her from bounding ahead. Taking deep breaths she walked around the back of the house and prepared to peer around the corner and see who it was. At the same time a head appeared on front of her. Maggie shrieked and jumped backwards. Sheila started barking.

Kate Molloy jumped back as well. She wasn't so lucky at keeping her purchase on the ground – she slipped and landed on her buttocks on the path.

"Kate!" Maggie rushed to her friend's aid.

"You gave me such a fright! Maggie Breslin, you've aged me ten years. What are you doing creeping around?"

"It's my yard," Maggie bristled. "You were creeping yourself."

Kate laughed. "You're right! I was just checking up on you. Alan said he was here this morning. There was smoke out but no sign of you anywhere. He was afraid you might have fallen or something. He didn't want to break in and look like an idiot so he told me to come up and take a look."

Maggie thought for a moment. Could that be true? No! He just wanted Kate to find out if she were hiding on him. Make it look like neighbourly concern. "I was up the hill for a walk. With the dog."

"I told him he was being silly. But he thought you visited the grave yesterday and you go to town on Friday so he couldn't think where else you would be on a weekday."

Maggie tried not to register her shock when she mentioned the grave. "How did he know I was at the grave?"

"He said he passed you on the road. You were pushing the bike but he couldn't give you a lift because the van has no insurance for passengers."

Maggie couldn't remember seeing the post van. That explained the beep when she crashed. A concerned citizen would have stopped to speak to her, even if he couldn't give her a lift home, not beep at her. What about the little dark car? Were there two cars? Did he pass when she was on the ground after falling off the bike? She really didn't know.

"Are you all right?" Kate was watching the flickering emotions on her face and was starting to get worried.

"I'm fine. Come on in and I'll make you some tea." Maggie unlocked the door. "When did you start locking your door when you're around the place?" asked Kate.

"I was a way for an hour or so. I thought it was a bit long to be leaving the door open."

"I'm at the bottom of the lane. I look out for you.

We've never had any problems around here with break-ins." She hesitated a moment. "Did your prowler come back?"

"How did you know about the prowler?"

"Dolores told me."

Maggie couldn't explain why but she didn't want to confide in Kate. "No, but you can't be too careful when you live on your own."

"Has something else happened to scare you?"

"No! Perhaps I'm watching too much of the news and making myself nervous! All they ever give is the bad news. Now please come in and have some tea. I made a tart."

Kate stepped inside, saying, "Well, if that's all it is . . ."

"It is, love. Don't worry about me."

"I could ask Seán to come up more often."

"Don't be silly. He does more than his share as it is. I have young Jason looking in on me as well. I'm more than looked after."

Maggie was quiet as she made the tea. With the circumstances of Pascal's death and what happened this morning there was a growing possibility that people would think her insane. The last thing she wanted when she was alone for the first time was for someone to take that away from her. Ever since her youth she'd lived in mortal fear of being sent away again. If it ever happened she would die, she knew that. She loved life and her freedom too much. Maggie wasn't stupid. She was the only thing between her siblings and the proceeds of the farm. She wondered what would happen if she left for whatever reason. Could they sell? Or, more correctly, under what circumstances could they sell? Olivia she didn't trust at all. How many of her fears were genuine and how many were paranoia she didn't know. She just knew she'd been locked up before and she believed that under certain circumstances it could happen again. It nearly did after Pascal's death.

Kate only stayed a little while. She was on a split shift and she had to get back to work. Maggie thanked her for coming up and tried to put sufficient enthusiasm in her voice to dispel Kate's fears. But when the door closed all her resolve gave away. She felt like she were teetering on the brink. Many of her fears seemed so plausible to her but she knew if she could hear them with another's ears they would sound very different. Her postman prowling her property at night, her sister maybe waiting for an opportunity to lock her up, her neighbour's concerns giving Olivia the very opportunity she would need. It all sounded like madness.

Pascal's secrets! Did they have anything to do with all this? She couldn't help believing a gnawing feeling in her gut that it was all connected to his child. That connection in itself was insane. There was no proof or even reason for suspecting that this child had any idea of the identity of his or her real father. But someone had a grudge against her and Pascal and she couldn't for the life of her even think of any reason that anyone would hate them this much. She was positive it was personal towards Pascal. The abandonment of his child was the only thing she'd ever heard out of the ordinary about him . . . apart from Jason's story. But on the surface he was the straightest, most God-fearing man in the parish. Secrets and more secrets, her family was built on a foundation of secrets. Were they unusual or were there other families like them? If Jason were to be believed about the house in the mountains, then there were others like Pascal and there were certainly others like her. She'd lived amongst them in the convent for twelve long months. She knew they were hidden. She'd never gone back to look them up. She was afraid they'd realise their mistake and keep her there. Maybe some of the others were still there now.

She ran a list of names and faces through her memory. How would they have managed to survive? Gertrude was like her. She was sensitive and delicate and she had told Maggie if one died the other would too. Maggie never looked back when she went out the door. It was like a symbolic death. It was the same as the real thing for Gertrude. Her friend was gone and she'd never seen her again. Did Gertrude survive? Maybe it was a trip she needed to make – go back and face her past. Put it to rest once and for all. The nuns would be old now; many would have died. The institutions were crumbling and she was glad. She knew what they'd been built on. She knew what it took from people to support it. Draining the life-blood from families and communities to maintain a front for the world to see: a web of abuse and exploitation maintained by co-operation between Church and state.

She remembered after Vatican II thinking about it all. The rules that the Church told her were enshrined in God's own words were now changed at the whim of that same Church. If they could be changed to suit the Church why could they not be flexible for the people on which that Church was built?

Michael's father didn't go through the indignities she had, yet he and his had prospered and his actions and their consequences went unknown. Would they too come back to haunt him someday as the hidden deeds of Pascal Breslin were now seeping out of the grave? Maggie hadn't lost her faith. She still believed there was a higher order that oversaw everything and it had its own way of doling out justice. It was the institution she had lost faith in and she rejoiced in its collapse.

Chapter 20

By that evening Maggie was calming down a bit and feeling silly. Perhaps Alan was just looking out for a neighbour but, each time she said that, an inner voice said no, open your eyes, Maggie, who else could it be? Who indeed?

About five o'clock she went out into the yard to make sure the barn was padlocked. There was a shiny silver lock on there now. It was brand new, only bought last Friday. She was tightening her security every week. Last week it was the lock and the security chain for the door. The paint her graffiti artist used on the wall came from the barn. If he's going to do that again he can bring his own, she thought. She'd checked the barn afterwards but the tin was gone. It had definitely been there earlier because she'd seen it on the shelf shortly beforehand. If she couldn't stop him messing her about, she'd make it difficult for him in future.

As she closed the lock and pocketed the key she

heard Sheila woof down in her throat. A cold sweat broke out on Maggie's back. Slowly she turned around and looked about the yard. There was no one there but Sheila was getting more agitated. The evening shadows were leaving pools of darkness around the buildings. The front yard became dark early. Sheila sat back on her butt and turned her nose up in the air and split the evening with a howl. Maggie felt tears welling in her eyes. She held Sheila's collar and tried to steady herself. The kitchen door was about thirty yards away. Behind the porch the trees and shrubs spilled off the fence into the overgrowth that used to be their garden. That area was now a dark expanse of shadows moving slowly as the breeze danced through the trees.

Maggie swallowed and took a couple of faltering steps across the yard. She quickened her pace as she got closer to the door. In relief she grabbed for the handle. At the same time a laugh came out of the shadows.

"Good night, Maggie!"

Sheila tried to pull away from her and run to the voice but Maggie had a firm grip and pushed the agitated dog through the door. She locked the door behind her and stood in the shadows. She placed her eye against the crack of the curtain and peered out into the evening. She could see nothing and everywhere was silent now.

All the windows were locked and she had the chain on the door. Jason or Seán weren't due in tonight. Jason was going out and Seán was going swimming with his school. Talking to herself, Maggie did an inventory of what needed to be done in the house, anything to keep her mind calm and work off her nervous energy. She finished her washing up and put everything away. After the floor was washed and the laundry seen to she ran out of chores. She wanted to talk to someone but she had to remind herself of the danger of being seen as mad. She had to keep herself and the house looking well. That was the first step and the second was to be very careful – *about what,* she asked herself again and again.

When she finally sat down and switched on the television she thought about the voice. Was it familiar? It always sounded funny. A bit muffled like he was talking through his jumper. Her heart hammered again. Only someone she knew would bother to disguise his voice. That brought her mind around to Alan again. Nobody knew anything about him. He was a cold fish and you couldn't warm to him. There was always a distance about him. When he spoke directly to you it never felt like a conversation. Maggie would have considered herself a friendly person but her response to Alan was 'keep your distance and mind your own business'.

I wonder why he's never called me on the phone, she wondered. Almost as she thought this, the phone rang. She looked at the number. Michael! She almost wept with relief. She picked up the phone.

"Michael!"

"No, Gran, it's Trudy."

There was a silence on both sides.

"You don't mind me calling you Gran and calling out of the blue, do you?"

Maggie couldn't speak for a moment.

"Maggie!"

"Trudy, my love, I'm delighted to hear you call me Gran. It just took my breath away for a moment. How are you keeping?"

"I'm great. I have exams now and I'm going to pull an all-nighter for Psychology. I thought I'd speak to you first. My Irish gran might bring me good luck. I'm in Harvard but Dad wouldn't let me stay in student accommodation so I converted the attic. Darren has his own study. Typical boys – they get everything first. What were you doing today, Gran?"

Maggie savoured the word 'Gran' for a moment. "Well, I don't need a study. I took a walk on the mountain and spent time with my dog. I don't do very exciting things."

"Hanging out with a dog sounds cool to me. We're really looking forward to coming to see you. Dad's told us so much about you. I've marked a calendar on the wall by my bed. I'm colouring in a square for every day that's passed. There are fifty-five days left."

"That's a lovely idea. I'll do that too."

"Oh, that's wonderful – we could synchronise times when we colour them in. What time do you go to bed?"

"Eleven o'clock."

"That's six o'clock here. I'm home by then so you

colour yours at eleven and I'll do mine at six. I think about you all the time, Gran. I can't wait to meet you."

"Me too, Trudy – your dad is the best thing that ever happened to me and now I have you and your brother. You're a gift from God."

"I love you, Gran, stay well. I got to go."

"You too, pet. Don't study too hard."

Trudy hung up with a tinkling laugh.

Suddenly Maggie felt rich beyond her wildest dreams. Where did it all come from? Life was a tapestry. The dark hues and bright colours all blended together in almost blinding brilliance. Even a prowler was an exotic if unwelcome twist. Whatever she died of, it wouldn't be boredom. That thought sobered her up. The clock struck eleven. She walked to the dresser and picked up a sheet of blank paper. She dug out a red marker and an old wooden ruler and drew lines of little squares on the sheet. Now she too would have a calendar. Another day dissolved into sleep and sweet dreams replaced the darker ones of the previous nights.

The next morning Maggie woke in the dark and felt a wet tongue licking her face. "Sheila! Go away. It's still night!" She shut her eyes again but a great paw landed flatly on her nose. "Ow! What's up with you?"

Sheila yelped.

Maggie picked up the clock and looked at the face of it. Nine o'clock. It's stopped, was her first thought. But no, it was fine when she went to bed at eleven and once the fog of sleep faded she could hear its rhythmic ticking. She opened the curtain and looked out. The glass was pitch dark. This must be the twilight zone. She grabbed her dressing-gown and went into the kitchen. Opening the curtain there the same sight greeted her eyes.

"This is crazy!" she snapped at the equally perplexed dog.

She opened the inside door which was solid wood and went into the porch. She looked out that window and bright sunshine bathed the yard.

"What is going on?" she shouted out.

She opened the front door and went out into the yard. She stood looking back at her kitchen window. It was like soot. Someone had painted the panes a uniform black.

"That's a strange idea, Maggie."

Maggie jumped and turned.

Eddie stood about twenty feet behind her.

"Eddie! Someone's having a laugh."

Eddie wore his usual uniform of dung-stained cords, torn jumper and an old anorak with the hood over his head and his two arms outside. He never used the arms of the jacket – he said they were too short. For a small man he had remarkably big feet or at least he wore big Wellingtons. His eyes twinkled as he looked from her to the window.

"There's some cruel bucks around all right, Maggie. Is it dry yet?"

She put her finger against it. "It is, Eddie. What am I going to do?"

"I'll sort that when I come back from the hill. Do you have any paint stripper in the shed?"

"I don't think so but you can have a look."

"I will on my way back down. If I can't find any I have loads at home. I'll get it from there. I'll be back in about half an hour."

He walked off, laughing to himself. Sheila enjoyed the walk so she trotted along behind him. Maggie was glad he thought it so funny, but she was a bit put out at Sheila's turncoat attitude this morning.

Maggie cooked her porridge by electric light. It didn't feel right. Whoever did it knew the layout of the house and her habits. The only windows painted were the bedroom and the kitchen window. He must have known that the porch door was closed so that one didn't need to be done. She was getting heartily sick of this. She couldn't be getting up every morning to see what was in store for her. A knock sounded at the door.

"Maggie!"

"Eddie. Did you find paint stripper?"

"You have a padlock on the shed, Maggie. I couldn't get in."

"Oh, I'm sorry! Give me a minute and I'll get the key."

Like his wife the day before, Eddie was amazed at the new lock.

"When did we take to locking things up around here? Are you still scared about that prowler there a few weeks back? Has he been back? "

"No, he hasn't." She snapped the words at him. "I just want to be prepared."

Eddie thought for a moment. "Do you think it was him that blackened your windows?"

"I don't know." Maggie desperately wanted him to stop asking questions.

"Are you sure you should stay here alone? It's probably just high jinks but I can see why you'd be upset."

"Eddie! I'm fine."

"Right then, Mags. Give me the key and I'll get to work."

Eddie ambled off across the yard and returned a couple of minutes later with the stripper and a ton of questions.

Eddie had been at school with Maggie. Kate was his second wife and was quite a bit younger than he was. His first wife died in childbirth. For years they all thought he'd never get married again but one day he met Kate Kennedy, a nurse who'd moved to Donegal to work. She was from Monaghan originally. They married and had two children, Seán the youngest and an elder girl who went to England last year to be a nurse like her mother. Rita was a nice wee girl and Maggie was very fond of her. She missed her around the place. Eddie and Kate were lucky people. Eddie hadn't called her Mags in a long time. When they were kids he used to call her that. She was his first crush in school. She was a few years older than he was. He lost his infatuation when she went to Scotland.

"I suppose, Mags, you're not used to being alone. Maybe it's just the strangeness of it all and an incident like that night would give you a fright. But you know yourself there are funny people about so maybe you're right to lock up a bit more."

"Please, Eddie – I like my own company. I'm fine. There's nothing the matter with me that a little peace and quiet won't cure."

For a moment the expression froze on his face, to be replaced by anger.

"Eddie, I don't mean you! But I don't want pity. I'm well able to take care of myself."

"Well, I've finished the front window for you – maybe since you're so capable you can finish the back yourself!"

"Eddie! I'm sorry."

Wordlessly he handed her the stripper and walked out of the yard.

"Eddie!" she called after him but he continued on his way like a little goblin in a cloak and a pair of large Wellingtons. Some things never change. They'd been fighting all their lives. If it was anyone else she'd had words with she'd be upset but she knew Eddie would come round.

Eddie was practically reared in their house. He was an orphan and spent equal time between the Breslins and his grandfather. His grandfather lived in the old house next door to the one himself and Kate lived in now. The ruins still stood on the edge of the garden. Whenever his granddad had a few too many, Eddie'd come up and tell Maggie's mother and that night he'd sleep in with the boys in their room and she'd make him breakfast in the morning. Now he'd have been taken away from the old man but in those days people ignored the problem and there was always a well-meaning neighbour such as Áine Breslin to pick up the slack.

He married very young and with his first wife Abigail he built a small house, when the old house was condemned. The old man had neglected to maintain it and one day the kitchen ceiling caved in, thatch and all. The old man ended his days in the same hospital Kate worked in now, though he died a few years before she arrived. He was the smallest man Maggie had ever seen. He was like a little skeleton with a thin yellow muslin cloth stretched loosely over it. Eddie and herself used to think he was born like that; he never changed as long as they knew him except perhaps to shrink a little more over the years. Eddie and Maggie had a long history.

She was so absorbed in her memories and her paint-stripping out the back, she forgot about the postman. She was strolling casually back around the corner when she saw the van pull quickly into the yard. At that speed it could only be Alan. Terence had more respect for farm animals. There was nowhere to hide so she boldly walked up to the car.

"You look well today, Maggie."

Even though it was worded considerately, as usual his concern grated.

"I'm fine."

"Where were you yesterday?"

'Mind your own business' was on the tip of her tongue but the old adage 'keep your friends close and your enemies closer' sprang to mind.

"I was out on a walk. Kate told me you were worried. There's no need. I was fine."

An attempt to smile teased his mouth. "We have to look out for our neighbours, Maggie."

She tried to hide a shiver but she failed.

"You'd better go inside out of the cold. You have no jacket on you. You'll catch your death. Here's your letters. I hope they're worth getting. There are a few brown windows there. That's never a good sign."

And with that flow of speech and attempt at hilarity he departed the yard at an even greater pace than he'd entered. Maggie shivered again. That young fellow just gave her the willies.

Chapter 21

Maggie tried to run through in her head everyone she knew in the parish but she couldn't think of any couple named Breda and Peter. Breda was an unusual name around here. Usually they would be called Bríd. Names evolved over the years. She took out a sheet of paper and wrote down all the combinations of each she could think of: Bríd, Biddy, Breda, Bee, Bridey. Then at the bottom she made a list of every woman she knew with some combination of those but not one of them was married to a Peter or any variation of the same. It was a futile effort anyway. What would she do? Go up and say "Excuse me, was your child fathered by Pascal Breslin?" But it would be nice just to have an inkling, at least. Maybe Breda (whoever she was) deserved privacy for herself and her child. There really wasn't any reason to believe that it had anything to do with her prowler. It was just her overactive imagination.

A car entering the yard broke into her reverie. She

looked with her accustomed caution out the window. It was the priest.

"Hello, Father!" she greeted him brightly at the door.

"Maggie! I said I'd call and see how you were after your spill."

"Oh, I'm fine, Father. Not even a scratch. I have to get the front wheel of the bike fixed but at least that took the worst of the fall. Sit down. The kettle is just on."

"Thanks very much. It's a cold day, isn't it?"

"It is but I never really mind the cold myself. Warm blood."

"We have a bit more news on the heritage centre we're setting up."

"I'd forgotten all about that, Father. Tommy Breslin is still in the place of honour, is he?"

"He is. He's not alone any more though. There are a few other notables buried in the graveyard. We have the building sorted now for the centre. We have the old school and we made a deal with Hughey Slevin. He's given us the acre of land around the schoolhouse for a model farm."

"A model farm? What do you mean?"

"We're going to set up a small farm with a thatched cottage and everything as though it was in the eighteenth century. We thought in the summer we could have volunteers or maybe a Back to Work scheme set up as storytellers. They could dress them up in costumes from the time. Maybe set up a hedge school with Tommy Breslin in the master's role. It's all still in its infancy but we're getting very excited about it."

"Did you want to talk to me about it?"

"Well, we're looking for some volunteers and I was wondering if you'd have a few hours a week."

"That would be great. What role did you have in mind for me? Baking bread over a turf fire to feed the family, I suppose."

He laughed. "Eventually, yes, but at the moment I need someone to read through the parish histories with me and make a list of the best examples to exhibit."

"Father, I'm no historian."

"We're not looking for a historian. We just want someone to flush out the interesting pieces. I brought a few books with me today – if you have time over the next few weeks?"

"I'd love to, Father."

"Great! I'll go get them from the car."

By the time he returned she had decided to ask him.

"Father, have you met any couple in the parish since you arrived named Breda and Peter?"

The priest gave it a moment's thought. "No, I haven't. Why?"

"Michael met a woman in Boston who says she had relatives in this area by those names," Maggie lied. "No surname – just two first names."

He looked sceptical.

"That's all I was given," she said truthfully.

"Maggie, if they are like Michael and yourself maybe you shouldn't meddle. They mightn't thank you."

"I think it's a blessing I found Michael."

"I know you do, Maggie, and don't get me wrong. I'm happy for you both but not everybody would be ready for such a revelation. These things sort themselves out eventually."

Maggie was quiet for a while, digesting this.

"How are you and Michael now?" he asked.

"We're the best. I have two grandchildren as well. They're all coming to visit in a couple of months."

"Did it cause you any family problems?"

"Well, only three of us and our mother knew, so the others weren't happy at being kept in the dark."

"I'm sure."

"They're just going to have to get used to it, Father."

"Yes. But, Maggie, we have to consider everyone in these situations."

"I did, Father, that's why I lost my son."

Noting the stone in her tone he tactfully changed the subject. "Do you get lonely up here, Maggie? It's quite remote, isn't it?"

"I suppose." Unsure why, Maggie's inner voice warned her again. "I have good neighbours."

"They're a good bunch around here all right but you know yourself there's always a bad apple."

Now she was sure he was fishing. "Has something bad happened in the area?" she asked innocently.

"Have you heard anything yourself?" he countered.

"Nothing, Father. Not a thing."

Just then Jason walked in.

"Maggie! Father!" He nodded to both of them.

"Jason, there's a fresh pot made."

"Thanks. I'll just wash my hands."

"I'll be away." The priest stood up. "If you need a chat any time, Maggie, you know where I am."

Mystified, Maggie watched him leave.

"Chat about what?" Came Jason's voice.

"I have no idea, Jason. He was fishing for information there, about strange goings on. Someone has been talking to him."

"You know yourself, Maggie. Gossip is the favourite pastime around here."

"Have you said anything?"

"You know better than that, Maggie." He looked hurt.

"I know, love. Somebody has, though."

"Maybe someone went to the priest as a concerned citizen."

"Maybe."

She'd just come to the same conclusion herself. They were all watching her now. The neighbours, the postman and the priest and yet she had someone painting her windows and laughing in the bushes and nobody could find a trace of him.

Though she couldn't imagine why, she knew there was someone or some people out to drive her insane. She knew she wasn't crazy. Instinct told her people were watching her and she knew it wasn't all in the interest of her well-being. Well-meaning or not, people could put her away under the guise of safety or concern. Rather than a long-term commitment to look out for her, many would just find a reason to pass the buck to a hospital and then sit back vindicated. Yet this place was no more remote for her than it had been for an eighty-year-old man who walked the mountain alone at night half-steamed and yet nobody wanted to put Pascal away or look out for him.

"Hey!" Jason broke into her thoughts. "Nobody will harm you while I'm looking after you."

She placed the palm of her hand against his cheek and smiled. "I'll get your tea ready."

"You don't have to cook for me all the time."

"Don't be silly. You've been working all day. You need your nourishment."

She needed to look after someone. Taking care of Jason was like getting a real chance to be a mother.

"That little twit isn't coming up tonight, is he?"

"Don't be so mean. He's just young."

"He does my head in, Maggie. I don't know how you put up with him."

"Give him a few years."

"Even for thirteen, Maggie, he's very immature. Rita was never like that. She's not yet eighteen and she's away in London nursing."

"Well, she's the opposite. She was always grown up."

"I suppose she was." He laughed.

Rita was his best friend at school and he knew

exactly what Maggie meant. She had a squat figure about five foot two and was built like a little shot-putt thrower. Her whole family was small in height but she was the only one that was compensating with width. She started wearing her hair in a tight bun in her early teens and with her naturally ruddy complexion he could see her as matron by the time she reached thirty.

"Can you imagine her bedside manner?"

"You're very cruel tonight. She's just capable."

"That's one way of describing her. Don't get me wrong – I love the girl – she's one of my best friends but can you imagine her coming at you with a hypodermic?"

In Maggie's current frame of mind the image was both comical and sobering.

In the days that followed Maggie felt eyes following her every step. She watched over her shoulder every time she set foot in the yard. She created a ritual for herself every night of checking the house for intruders. Before the weekend was over she'd locked the attic door with a padlock and she did it by herself. She thought her staunch supporter Jason might even balk at the level of security she wanted in her house. The one thing she kept to herself was the gun. She knew it wasn't licensed: Pascal had never bothered. It came from a time when regulations weren't as stringent as they are today. When she held it for the first time she couldn't imagine ever shooting someone with it but now she thought if he entered her home she really didn't know. Would she have the nerve to pull the trigger? She'd watched Pascal and her father clean it and take care of it when she was a child and now with the same meticulous care she did likewise. This could one day save her life. When she finished preparing it for use she wondered if it would still work. She'd been a good shot in her childhood. Wouldn't people be shocked today if they saw a man taking his nine-year-old daughter out on the mountain to practise firing a rifle? But her father thought there was no harm in her knowing. Himself and Pascal mightn't always be around. She decided that the next day at first light she would go up the mountain and test it. She prayed it wouldn't backfire on her. The last thing she wanted to be remembered for was going insane on the mountainside with a gun.

Sheila didn't like being left in the house but Maggie was afraid that she would get in her way and accidentally get shot. She carried her raincoat over her arm to camouflage the gun. She left her yard through the mountain gate and passed the orchard behind the house on the path which wound its way up the mountain to the bog. Great gaping scars gashed the surface of the bog where years of turf-cutting had taken place. She walked to the end of the path. She lined two tin cans up on the rock her father used to use and stood back until she guessed she must be about fifty yards from the target. She aimed her gun and fired. Perfect shot each time. The cans went skimming across the heather into the stream.

Advancing age certainly wasn't affecting her eyes, she thought with pride. For once she almost hoped he was watching her. If he was he might think twice before messing with her again. But this was not for idle threats, she knew that. The gun was only to be used as a last resort – if she felt her life was in serious danger.

As quickly as she could she made her way back down the mountain, being careful to keep an eye out for her neighbours. Eddie wasn't due up yet but someone could come to investigate the shots. Wrapping the gun neatly in an old dress, she laid it on the bottom of her wardrobe, concealed by an innocent-looking line of shoes. The ammunition she placed in the pocket of her mother's old coat that still hung in the wardrobe. Satisfied that she wasn't completely helpless, she made her breakfast. She'd finished putting it out when Eddie knocked on the door. He stuck a disembodied head around the corner.

"Did you hear shots?" No 'good morning' from him today.

"No." She gave an equally curt reply.

"Somebody was up on your mountain early on firing shots. It sounded like a rifle."

"Really."

"Maggie, don't be so stubborn. There could be dangerous folk around."

"Oh, I'm sure there are but I haven't seen any today."

The head disappeared with Sheila following at his heels.

"Turncoat dog!" Maggie hissed. If Pascal wasn't

dead, that dog would ignore her completely. She was a real man's dog. Women came second best.

In a temper she shoved her dishes into the sink and turned on the tap. Splashing water around she viciously washed the plates and slammed them onto the worktop. The last dish balanced precariously on the top and slipped off, bouncing off her hand and smashing on the floor. Her lip quivered and tears slid down her nose. In the depths of self-pity she allowed the tears to flow, standing with her hands immersed up to her elbows in hot suds. The heat moved by conduction up her arms and gradually calmed her down as it spread across her shoulders into her chest. First she sniffed and then she hiccupped. I think I'll go lie down for a while, she thought. A nap will do me good after my early morning on the hill.

She locked the door and shuffled back to bed, the heaviness of her thoughts weighing her down. This was a luxury she couldn't repeat too often. If she started sleeping away the day they'd be sending up a doctor. Despite the stress of the morning she fell into a sound sleep punctuated by dark dreams.

They were appearing now in her mind as crowds of eyes peering from the shadows and watching her every movement. All her neurosis were taking a physical form and laughing a hideous laugh. After what seemed like two minutes she woke up with a pounding in her head. I am going mad, she whimpered to herself. Now I'm hearing banging.

I *am* hearing banging, she thought as the fog

cleared and the reality of her surroundings sank in. Focusing her eyes again, she realised it was dark. Did he paint my windows again, she thought confused. Her curtain was open.

She walked into the kitchen but caution told her to leave the light off. The kitchen curtains were open as well. Maybe Eddie had brought Sheila back. But Eddie wouldn't normally knock and not this loudly. Usually he just left Sheila at the door and went on.

Maggie crept along by the wall and looked out the window into the yard. It was dark. She couldn't see the time but the moon was up and it was late. The pounding continued. Someone was banging on the door. Whoever was there wasn't really visible from where she was standing. She could see a hulking dark shape but it was standing too close to the dwelling wall for her to make out who it was. She went into the porch and stood behind the door. Whoever was there halted the banging and the night listened.

There was total silence now. Finally a cold and lonely Sheila left out one of her dramatic howls outside.

"Who's there?" Maggie called. It couldn't be Eddie – the shadow was too big.

No sound, just another howl from Sheila. The minutes ticked by and Maggie listened but there wasn't a sound in the quiet yard. She peered out the porch window but there was nothing out of the ordinary in the yard. Maggie fixed the chain, turned the key and opened the door a crack. Sheila's cold snout pushed into the opening and snuffled. Again Maggie listened and waited. Sheila whined. Quickly Maggie opened the door wide enough for the dog to come in and slammed it shut behind her, turning the key again. The noise caused the dog to jump and dart forward, casting a terrified look at her owner.

"Sorry, pet," Maggie whispered to her.

Maggie was about to walk from the door when the laughing started. It was right outside the door and close to the level of her head. The banging resumed and stopped again as abruptly as it started. Maggie ran back to the kitchen window and peered out at the front door. There was nobody there now. He was gone again, back into the shadows he came from.

This time Maggie wasn't giving in. She decided not to call Jason. If anything happened she knew now she'd have no hesitation in using her gun. She took the rifle and sat in the rocker by the fireside.

Chapter 22

Her eyes were threatening to close despite all her best efforts and she was afraid she'd drop the gun on the floor in the night and maybe shoot the dog or the cat. She had better go to bed. Maggie laid the gun on the table and quietly slipped into the utility room and poured some food into Sheila's dish – the poor dog had been outside most of the night. She should have been starving but she sniffed at it, nibbled a few pieces and waddled away.

"Well miss, wherever you've been you've been fed. Trust you."

Maggie was afraid the dog could knock over the rifle in the night if she left it by the bed so she took the bullets out and left it on the floor under the bed so she'd find it if she needed it. If Pascal could see her now, she thought. The locks were rotting off the door for most of his days. Now there were new locks, chains and deadbolts all over the place. Whoever was tormenting her was just doing it to mess with her head anyway, she thought. They're just trying to make me look crazy.

What were his plans for her? What would it look like if the two of them died so close together? Was whoever it was playing with her, until they could engineer an accident? The cat snuggled in behind her legs and she heard Sheila groaning in pleasure on her blanket. But the spectre of a dark shape inches from her hands as she opened the door wouldn't let her sleep. If she'd just looked around the corner she would have been looking into his eyes.

Sheila isn't scared of him.

Her eyes shot open in the dark.

She was just cold. That's why she was fussing to get in. Sheila knows him well. It was amazing how clarity could be achieved minutes before succumbing to sleep and suddenly sleep was the farthest thing from your mind. Who could he be? How many people was Sheila especially friendly to? But reason returned. She'd been Pascal's dog and went everywhere with him so obviously she knew whoever he knew. The possible pool from which the prowler could have crawled got bigger and in turn smaller only to get bigger again. If only she could talk to Sheila and get her to give up her buddy. But the prowler's accomplice was gently snoring on the floor. After much twisting and turning and despite sleeping all day Maggie finally returned to sleep and slept until the sun came up.

With another pounding head she crawled out of

bed. Everything was as it should be and there was no sign inside or out of her prowler. She finished her breakfast and got dressed for town. It took her longer than usual. She gathered the contents of her bag together but it took longer now to check her security. Why am I bothering, she thought. Nobody's going to open any of the locks. I have the keys. I only use the front door. That's all I need to check.

"And you, madam," she looked at the dog, "since you keep such bad company you can't have your own key."

Eddie's droll voice came from behind her. "It's that cat leading her astray."

"You're in a better mood today." Maggie glanced at him sharply.

"Ah, you know yourself."

She raised her chin and looked down her nose at him. He must have had a good night's sleep, she thought.

"You're off to town," he said.

"I am."

"Leave the pup with me. I feel sorry for her locked in on her own."

Maggie suddenly had a thought. "How long did she stay with you yesterday?"

"You mean before she went off to meet her bad friends?"

"Funny, Eddie!"

"I had her for a couple of hours."

"Did she go back down to you afterwards?"

"No. She didn't. Why are you interrogating the dog?"

"When I let her in last night I thought someone had fed her, that's all, and I don't like her getting food from strangers."

"I didn't give her anything. Maybe she went over to Dolores?"

"Maybe. But that's a quarter of a mile away. She never strays."

"*Puppers* can look after herself – she's a cute one."

Maggie looked at the cute one as she gazed in adoration up into Eddie's face. She turned and locked the door. "You're welcome to her. Keep her out of mischief and I'll be back for her this evening."

"When Seán meets you off the bus, he'll have her with him."

"Right!" She watched the two walking up the mountain and glanced at her watch. "Oh lord, I'm late!"

She tried her best to run. The bus was waiting patiently for her at the bottom of the lane. Maggie could hardly catch her breath as she handed Joe the money.

"Slow down, Maggie. You know I'd never go without you."

"What if I was sick and wasn't going?"

"The ladies could wait two minutes while I go up and check on you."

"You wouldn't do that."

"Well, I'd get Eddie to go up and look in on you."

"You're the best, Joe!"

He winked at her and put the bus into gear.

All the way into town in her mind's eye Maggie was going over the layout of her house. She had locks on the windows, double locks and chains on the two doors, a padlock on the attic and a padlock on the sheds. Also she had the rifle. What else could she use? Sensor lights for the front door. If she'd thought of that before he wouldn't have got so close to her last night. She smirked to herself. He was in for a shock the next time he entered her yard.

She made her purchases and went for her pizza. As usual she savoured it like nectar from the gods.

But when she went to pay for it she saw a paintbrush in the bottom of her basket. It was a small brush caked in thick dried black paint. She held it up and could feel her face going pale. Customers watched in curiosity as she held the brush.

"Are you okay," the cashier asked.

"Yes! Oh! Sorry, how much did you say?" She paid.

"Were you painting?"

"No," she replied. A quick lie tripped off her tongue. "Not for months. I haven't carried this basket for a while. I'm annoyed at myself for not washing it. The brush is ruined."

"Oh, a little turpentine on that now and it will be fine."

"Thanks."

Maggie moved quickly out of the shop. She wanted as little to do with this brush as she could. If she were on speaking terms with the guards she might have thought of fingerprints but they'd done enough business already at her house. There was a cell with her name on it either in Mountjoy or the central hospital for the criminally insane.

Her mind raced as she sat on the bus on the return journey. This basket left her hands last Friday when she emptied it and she didn't use it again until today. Was this the brush that painted the message on her wall or put the paint on her windows, she wondered? She kept the basket in the porch, ready to grab on the way out. Anyone coming to her door could have dropped the brush in. Whoever it was knew her very well, of that she had no doubt. She wanted to believe it was Alan because she didn't trust him and didn't like him but other people had access to her property as well.

But they were her friends. Seán, Jason, David, Dolores and Dan Blaney, Eddie and Kate Molloy and Father Landers. Could one of those be her prowler? No! There was no way. It had to be Alan. The others were her friends. She wouldn't believe it. Her hands were starting to shake and she was fighting back waves of emotion. She wasn't a good judge of people. She'd always been told she was naïve, but those people, in her view, were the salt of the earth. She pulled at her fingers to hear her knuckles crack.

"Maggie! Are you coming home with me?"

At the sound of her name Maggie jumped.

"Joe, sorry, I was miles away." She stood up and walked to the door of the bus. "I'll see you next Friday."

"I'll still be available." He winked at her and laughed.

She nodded back vaguely but gave no response. His worried eyes watched her step off the bus and walk towards Seán Molloy.

"Well, pet, how are you?"

"Are you talking to me, or the dog?" He had his usual cheeky smile.

"My two pets!" She put her arm around his skinny shoulders and nudged the dog with her knee.

"I got you a great video tonight, Maggie, as long as that smart arse won't be there."

"Don't you like Jason?"

"Ah, he's too full of himself, that fellow. All polish."

"I don't think so."

"He looks down his nose at all us fellows around at home. All he cares about are the town lads. He goes to Dublin a lot too at weekends. He's a dark one. You wouldn't know what he's up to."

"What's the video?" She pushed Sheila's nose out of the basket. "Mind the bread, Seán, or Sheila will have it."

He gave the dog a push. "I got *Scream*, the first one."

"What's that about?"

"Ah, Maggie, you'll have to see! If I tell you anything it will destroy the suspense."

Great, Maggie thought. More suspense. "Where do you get these? You don't rent them all, do you?"

"No! It would cost me a fortune. My friend has satellite and he tapes them off the movie channel for me. I have a shelf of them at home. You haven't seen the half of them. Some of them are a bit violent."

"Does your mother mind you watching them?"

"I'm fourteen."

"I suppose you are. Fourteen is different now than when I was fourteen."

"That's what my father says."

"Your father was always old."

"He says you never left the cradle."

Maggie started laughing. "We've known each other a long time, Eddie and myself."

"Did you know his other wife?"

Maggie was a bit taken aback. "Yes, I did."

"What was she like?"

"She was a good friend of my sister Grace. She was a very nice girl. Good fun."

"Was she beautiful?"

Maggie wasn't sure she should be answering any of these questions. "She was the best-looking girl around here. They were very young when they got married. I was away at the time. They were only together a year when she died. Then he met your mother and they had you and your sister and now he's a happy man."

"But he wasn't happy for a long time before that, was he?"

"Why are you asking me all these questions?"

"One night I came in and Mammy was still at work."

It was very endearing to hear a lad Seán's age still call his mother "mammy".

"He had an old box of photos out and one of them was his wedding photo, his first wedding. I think he was crying. He was a bit steamed and he got very angry with me when he caught me looking. He never shouted at me before."

Maggie felt very intrusive having this conversation but she couldn't stop the child from talking or he'd think she didn't care. Eddie would be mortified. "He was just thinking about the past. We all do that from time to time – it doesn't mean we don't appreciate the present."

Seán's earnest face turned to her. "You don't think he's sorry he lost his first family and ended up with us?"

"God, no! Seán Molloy, don't you ever even think that! You said yourself he was a bit steamed. It was probably just the drink making him a bit sad."

"I'll stick to the Football Specials if that's what drink does to a man."

"I'm sure you will," Maggie laughed.

"Just you wait, Maggie."

Something about his face made her think he probably would. He was a strange young fellow. He thought deeply about everything and worried beyond his years and yet he was as naïve as a small child in other ways. She really enjoyed his company. But her words of comfort didn't seem to reassure him much. He was subdued and seemed to have a lot on his mind.

When they'd finished their tea and the kitchen was cleaned up Seán took out the film and a bag of peanut

M&M's. They were Maggie's favourites. They closed the curtains, turned on the low light and sat back to watch. Seán was laughing almost from the start, turning to her to see the appreciation on her face. Maggie's reaction was different. "Drew Barrymore is a pretty girl, isn't she?"

"Not for long." Seán laughed out loud.

"Do you want to die?"

The words echoed out of the television and Maggie jumped like she'd been shot. She grabbed a pillow off the other chair and held it to her chest. The two hours or so of the movie flew by. Terrified yet too intrigued to turn it off she sat with her head in her cushion for half the show. The film ended at half past ten.

Seán's bright eyes were watching her face to see her reaction to the movie.

"Seán, how can you watch those films? I won't be able to sleep."

"Ah, you will, Maggie! It's only make believe."

"Are you all right going home on your own? Wouldn't the dark bother you after watching that?"

"Of course I'm all right. I only live at the bottom of the lane and if you walked me down my mother would only go and make me walk you back up again."

That was certainly true. "Okay. But be careful."

"What is there to be careful about? Maggie, you're watching too much television."

"All right, go home. But don't dawdle."

He gave her a hug and walked out. He really is a pet, she thought. If Jason or his father were around there was no way he'd hug her but he was still a little lad when he was by himself.

She straightened up around the house and sat for a while by the dying fire. Sheila was lying across her feet and they were so toasty warm she didn't want to move. At eleven fifteen the phone rang. It was Kate.

"Maggie, have you seen Seán?"

"I sent him home at half ten. It was getting too late for him."

"Well, there's no sign of him. Did he say he was going anywhere else?"

"No!" A feeling of dread crept over Maggie. Her prowler. Would he harm a fourteen-year-old boy?

Kate was obviously trying to remain calm. "I'm sure he called in on someone and forgot to let us know. Don't you worry, Maggie. He'll be all right."

"I can take Sheila and go out and walk the lane with a flash lamp."

"Don't be silly. Eddie is due back any minute now. I'll get him to have a look."

Maggie's terror was growing by the second. "Let me know when he gets back or I'll worry all night."

"I will." The line went dead in her hand.

Chapter 23

The next morning still brought no sign of Seán. Kate was frantic with worry and sat by the phone all day, waiting for him to call. Eddie was out searching with the neighbours and the police.

Maggie got up early. It was impossible to sleep. She spent the morning baking bread and cakes. She brought them down to Kate's so the searchers and well-wishers could have a cup of tea when they called in. Dolores and a few of the other women in the area helped her. By lunch-time the search appeared futile. There wasn't a sign of him anywhere. He'd vanished without trace. Everyone knew Seán and knew there was no way he'd be out this long without letting his mother know. He was considerate beyond what was expected.

At one o'clock the guards asked Maggie could she come up to her house with them, as they wanted a word with her.

Fearfully she got in the garda car and they drove the short distance.

Detectives Grant and Ryan who dealt with Pascal's death were waiting at the house.

"Hello, Margaret."

The hairs on the back of her neck stood on end.

"Hello." Fear was evident in her voice.

The other gardaí were told to wait outside and Maggie led the detectives into the house.

"Would you like some tea?"

They looked at each other briefly.

"Yes," said Detective Ryan. Her serious eyes never leaving Maggie for a second. "Thanks."

When they each had a cup and the three of them were sitting at the table they asked her to repeat the events of the night before. She did, as concisely as she could.

"*Scream!* Are you in the habit of watching violent movies with a fourteen-year-old?"

"It was one of his films. He brought it up to me."

"Really?" The single word rang in the air.

Maggie could feel palpitations starting. Poor little Seán was missing and until now she'd just been worried for his safety but suddenly she realised they might suspect her. Two tragedies inside her space and not one of them of her making – what was happening?

Seán's loss was breaking her heart. A lovely boy, earnest and sweet, she ached with a greater intensity than she'd felt for Pascal. She loved Seán as though he were a child of her own. A sob broke free before she could control it.

"What's the matter, Margaret?"

"I'm sorry, I just can't believe this is happening. Seán was like my own family. His mother is my friend. I grew up with his father – he's like the extra brother. How could anyone think I would hurt his child?"

"Did we say you'd hurt him?"

"No. But I know you think it." Maggie got up, walked to the dresser and took down a bunch of keys. "These are the keys for every lock in this house. Take them and search everything. Do what you want. You don't need search warrants. You can go anywhere on the land. I want to know what happened to poor little Seán as much as anyone. I don't have a car. My bike is parked in the shed." Tears slid down her nose. Her pain was evident but too many questions circulated around Maggie Breslin.

"All right, Margaret, we'll take you up on that offer." The male detective reached for the keys.

They called in the other two gardaí and while Maggie sat at the table they began to go through her home carefully.

"What's up there?" Detective Ryan's sharp eyes had spotted her attic.

"Nothing. Yellow key-ring marked 'attic'."

"Thanks," her flat voice responded. "Do you have a ladder?"

"In the shed, blue key-ring marked 'shed'."

Nobody answered and she remained sitting, looking at the stove. All she could think about was how could this be happening again.

Detective Grant walked out of her room and placed the gun on the table in front of her. "What's this, Maggie?"

"It's Pascal's rifle."

"Did he have it registered?"

"I don't know."

"Why is it in your room under your bed with ammunition in the locker?"

Bells were ringing in Maggie's ears. Guilty, Your Honour! She could hear the gavel strike the bench and the murmur as the press left the court. Speculation would abound that she killed her elderly brother as well as murdered a young boy. The gates of an institution would bang behind her.

"I live alone. My brother is gone so I got some extra locks and resurrected the gun. I meant to check if the licence had expired. I didn't get around to it."

"We'll need to take it in for examination."

"The last time it was fired was about two weeks ago. I tested it on a couple of cans up the mountain. I don't have the cans but I'm sure you can tell by the gun. Examine it as much as you need."

"Do you fear being alone, Maggie?"

"What sixty-year-old woman doesn't?"

"You could always sell and move away."

"I can't. Pascal left me the house for a life interest. I can't sell it. If I die it goes to my siblings."

"Is that so? Did you know all that before he died?"

Maggie went back to mute silence, gazing at the embers.

She couldn't bear to see the look on their faces. They were smug. Confident now that they knew why she killed Pascal at last. It would be only a short time before they discovered the existence of Michael and then it would all fit into place. She killed Pascal so she could inherit her share of the farm and use her money to get away and spend time with her son only to find out with the reading of the will that she couldn't sell. Perhaps they would think Seán stumbled on her secret or perhaps after killing Pascal she had a thirst for blood so she watched bloodbaths on video with Seán and then couldn't contain herself any longer, snapping and finally killing him. Well! They could have as much access to her property as necessary. It would prove she didn't kill Seán. If, God forbid, the lad was dead whoever did it couldn't hide from forensics. They would have made sure to dispose of the body as far away as possible to protect themselves. That would absolve her too because she didn't have a car. Unless the gardaí thought she had an accomplice.

When they had finished searching the house and returned their attention to the lane between her house and the Molloys', she sat alone at the table. She was too ashamed now to speak to the family. Soon it would spread that the old maid of Cooleen had struck again. This time the victim was a fourteen-year-old boy. She took her phone off the hook and looked around trying to find something to do. Seán was only missing; he could be alive and well and off on the bus to Dublin with some young girl. Or he could be hurt somewhere in a hospital or something. Maybe he just wanted to be alone. She knew he'd recently had a row with his dad. Maybe she should have told them that but then would she be shifting suspicion onto Eddie? No, she was better off saying nothing.

There wasn't a crime so far. They had nothing only suspicions. They would be searching twice as hard now. They didn't like Maggie. She suspected if they could pin something on her they would. Murders didn't occur very often in Donegal. If they smell two and both times they can't find the perpetrator, that certainly wouldn't look good.

Maggie didn't feel well. It was five o'clock and there was barely any daylight left. Jason hadn't come up to her today. Maybe he thought she did it too. She reached for the phone and rang his mobile. He answered straight away.

"Hello, Maggie. Are you all right?"

"Not really. Have you heard about poor little Seán?"

"I have. I was out searching all day with the police. There's no sign of him. I was going to go over to you but I could see the police at your house. What was that all about?"

"He was leaving here. They're just afraid I might know something that might help. It's only natural for them to be suspicious of the last person to see him."

"I suppose. It's just unfortunate that the thing with Pascal happened."

"What thing with Pascal? What do you mean?"

"Well, they suspected you of his murder as well, didn't they?"

"I don't know. But they know I couldn't harm a little boy."

"How would they know that, Maggie?"

"You think I could have done it, don't you, Jason?"

"No, Maggie, I don't. I'm just saying what other people might think. Don't be so defensive with your friends."

"Are you still my friend?"

"Of course I am. Don't worry. I'll look out for you and if things start going bump in the night again make sure you still call me."

"I will. Thanks, Jason."

"You're welcome, Maggie."

For an hour she sat and watched the blank television screen. The disappearance was bound to be covered; she was too scared to see if she was mentioned again. Sheila and the cat were with her but nobody else had come near her all evening. She wondered what was going on down the road but now she couldn't face them. The phone rang. She'd forgotten to take it off the hook again.

She looked at the number. It was a private number. She hesitated for a moment and then decided to answer – maybe Seán would ring her if he were too scared to call home.

"Hello?" There was silence at the other end. "Hello!" she called again. The line went dead. Must be something wrong with the connection, she thought, pushing the other possibility out of her mind. It rang again. Once again she picked it up. "Hello?" Silence. "Who is this?"

A muffled voice answered, as she was about to hang up. "They say once you've killed once you'll do it again. Do you agree with that?"

Maggie hung up as if she'd been stung. It rang again instantly. It was another private number. She picked it up and this time she said nothing, just stood there as silently as the listener on the other end.

"What's it like, Maggie? Where is he? Did you bury him on the mountain? They will find him, you know!" He started to laugh and the familiar laugh filled the room.

"You know I didn't do it!" she said. "You've been watching me long enough. You probably did it, you cowardly bastard!"

An angry tone entered his voice. "I'm not a coward, Maggie, just remember that. I'm capable of anything. I'm going to tell the guards about you. They'll be getting out the straitjacket, Maggie, you know that? I'm ringing from an untraceable mobile. And believe me, my voice is disguised. I'm not stupid. There is nothing linking me to your property."

"Yes, there is." She was suddenly very calm.

"What do you mean?"

"You're somebody who regularly comes to my farm. There're not many people in that group."

"Good night, Maggie." The line went dead.

She knew he wouldn't be calling back tonight.

Now she was certain. Somebody she knew very

well was her prowler. And now she was afraid his tormenting of her had escalated to the murder of a little boy. Could that be possible? Of course it was possible. Eddie, Jason, Dolores, Kate, Alan, Terence, Father Landers and the odd person helping out Eddie. Those were her regulars. Maybe it wasn't a regular but someone who could easily explain their presence there. Sheila knew him very well. She barked like crazy at strangers. This was no stranger. Maggie was surrounded by enemies.

The night loomed long and lonely. Freedom had been a beacon to her for such a long time and now she had it. She turned the lock on her front door and took the phone off the hook and sat alone in an empty room. That was her freedom. She might as well have stayed with the nuns.

At ten thirty a sharp knock sounded on her door. Quietly she walked to the door and stood listening.

"Maggie, I know you're in there." It was Kate.

Quickly Maggie opened the door. "Kate! Come in."

Kate walked into the room.

"Sit down." Maggie indicated a chair by the fire.

Kate sat down and seemed to be trying to speak. "Seán was besotted with you." Maggie was too overcome to answer her.

"I can't believe my son would get it so wrong."

A long dead silence followed each of her sentences because Maggie couldn't speak.

"I won't believe that a friend could steal my son

from me. But somebody did. He's gone. My baby would never leave me worried like this of his own free will."

"No, he wouldn't."

"Thank you, Maggie."

"Thanks for what?"

"Thanks for your honesty. Everyone else says 'Kate, you know what young fellows are like'. But Seán wasn't like most young fellows. They didn't know my Seán. We know he's gone. Don't we, Maggie?"

"He could be in hospital – maybe he got hurt."

"We've searched the hospitals, Maggie. He's gone."

Maggie started to cry again. "I don't know what to think, Kate. I'm praying harder than I've ever prayed in my life but I don't have any faith in my prayers. It doesn't look good."

Kate got up with the haunted look of someone who's seen the heart of pain. "Keep praying. If the worst comes to pass we'll need them even more. Good night."

Kate opened the door and disappeared into the night.

Chapter 24

Maggie was left with an empty feeling she hadn't felt since Michael was taken from her. Her breath was coming in pants. She grabbed a pillow and held it to her breast, burying her face in its soft ruffles. The span of a life was so short. Hers was entering its final phase and she could see no end to pain. Rocking backwards and forwards she tried to get a grip before she went to bed. The house was too quiet but it didn't seem right to switch on the television. She wished she had someone to share her feelings with. She'd effectively cut herself off from everyone and everything.

Finally when the dizziness subsided and her breathing normalised, she took herself off to bed. It was hours before she slept but not long after loud banging shattered her dreams and as the clouds of sleep parted she heard the bang of the door and instantly knew it was her front door. She was totally aware and knew she was wide awake. The banging door wasn't in a dream. She got out of bed and reached for the metal pipe she'd brought to bed with her. It wasn't there. The pillow she'd been holding in the kitchen was there instead. What was happening? She scrabbled around, not wanting to switch on the light, but there was no sign of the pipe. Was she so crazy that she picked up a pillow and thought she had a pipe? No, she wasn't, she thought emphatically. She walked slowly to the bedroom door and immediately felt the draught of the open front door. She edged her way out into the darkened kitchen. She stood quietly until her eyes adjusted to the darkness.

The feeling of being watched and close to humanity hit her as the shroud of darkness held her in its arms. Her eyes were drawn to the door. As she watched she saw him emerge into her vision. He was standing inside the door looking straight at her. She stood immobilised. He was totally encased in black. It could have been the shadow but she thought he had a balaclava or some type of hood over his head. She really thought she was going to die. Nobody entered your house at night and stood as he was standing in solid black looking at you if he didn't intend to kill you. For what seemed like an eternity Maggie stood gazing at the shadow and it stared right back.

It wasn't bravery that caused her to hold his gaze. Maggie was too scared to move. There was no hope that she could fight this person. She had no weapon and she was sure it was a man or a very strong woman. There was roughly fifteen feet separating them. Was this what it had all been leading up to? Was she going to have a heart attack here or suffer a sudden accident? She stood as a little girl would on her Communion Day with her hands behind her back, leaning against the stone for support. Her nightdress was long and her bare feet were rooted to the spot. From where he stood she could be a little girl. Often she'd wondered how she'd die but this had never entered her thoughts.

Gradually or so it seemed, he glided towards the open door and went outside, closing the door behind him. As soon as the door clicked shut her feet found motion and as quickly as she could she flew to the door and turned the key in the lock. The key was on the inside. How could he have opened the door? There were two locks: the old lock and a new Chubb one for safety. The spare set of keys. She ran to the dresser and looked in the old china teapot. They were there. She took them out to see if any were missing but they were all there. She ran back to the door again and put the chain on. Moving quickly she checked all the windows and the back door. Everything was shut tight. Did she forget to lock the door? She couldn't have. But she was very upset when Kate left, so perhaps she did.

Oh God, he just stood there looking at her!

Was that what Seán saw? Did he leave her house and spot him lurking outside and confront him? No wonder Jason didn't see him when he came to check all those times – he was probably standing back in the dark. She could only barely see him herself that night at the door and not at all the night he stood at the bottom of her garden. Seán carried conspiracy and alien theories around in his head. He was always on the lookout for the unusual. His quick eyes and active mind would have spotted him straight away. Oh, poor little Seán, what did he do with you?

Sheila! There was no sign of the dog. She did another search of the house calling her name. She wasn't there. Stupid dog. She probably heard a sound and went to investigate. Recognising the person she would have just invited him in. She was probably with him now. He wouldn't hurt Sheila, would he? If he hurt a child he would be capable of hurting a dog, but why didn't he hurt her tonight? In her heart she knew whoever it was, was too clever to club her in the night. What ever was meant to happen would be unexpected and look like natural causes? Maggie knew that Seán must have stumbled across something by accident and forced the prowler's hand.

By now Maggie had the light on. The pipe she'd brought to bed wasn't there. She looked at the pillow. That might have been in her hand when she came in. He must have stood by her bed and taken the pipe away. How would he have seen it? Now Maggie doubted her own sanity. She went back into the kitchen and there it was, sitting on the bench by the fire. Did she leave it there after all? Maybe she had left the door open. How could she be so stupid after all that happened to leave herself vulnerable like that? She looked at the phone. Should she call the police and explain all that had happened? No! They would never believe her.

On Friday she was going to get a deadbolt for the inside of her bedroom door and she wasn't going to tell anybody. She didn't believe in ghosts and the living could be outwitted. Well, she could start outwitting them by locking her door carefully. Poor Sheila would have to wait until morning – there was no way she was going out in the dark looking for her now.

With stiff cold legs Maggie returned to bed and mercifully she slept but when she did her dreams were peppered with images of Seán reaching out to her and screaming. As he called out to her, he was whisked backwards from her at great speed – ripped from her by a dark invisible force. She was trying to catch up, with her arms extended to grab him, but it was useless – he was just out of her grip all the time. Suddenly in front of her from behind him she could hear the laugh from the phone and behind her she could hear the eerie muffled voice shouting "Go on, move it! She'll get him!" She shouted "Who are you?" The answer came from a voice behind her: "Who do you think we are? Who, Maggie? Whoooo?" The voice trailed off like a collection of demonic owls into the night.

Maggie woke up, crying in a film of sweat. Her hands were gripped in fists holding the damp sheet to her breast.

The next morning she thought about the events of the night as soon as she opened her eyes. At first she remembered them by feeling rather than a memory of pictures. The sick taste of fear polluted her mouth and knotted her stomach but it took a moment to remember the events. She got out of bed and dressed quickly. The house was exactly as it was every morning, quiet and cold. She stood in disbelief in the same spot she'd stood in last night. Last night the room was like an alien landscape. The distances seemed longer and the corners deeper. She was standing only a few feet from a light switch. She knew that even if she'd thought of that last night she wouldn't have used it. At that point she was part of that alien darkness, the two of them together sharing the shadows. If light had flooded the room he would be a man and she a frail woman. She would probably know who he was and he would know that now he would have to act to make sure she could never tell anyone. The thickness of the darkness was her only protection.

She walked to the spot he stood on and looked at the floor as if some substance from him would be still there clinging to the linoleum tiles. But they sat silent and shiny, mocking her in their innocence. She stood and looked back where she had stood; so close. She sidled out the door as he had done except first she had to halt to open the locks and the chain. The morning was fresh and clear, the ground dry and hard. There was no sign of anyone having been in the yard. Poor Sheila. She wondered where she was. "Sheila!" she called loudly but there was no response from the dog. Surely he hadn't taken her dog? There was no one left if her animals were gone. They were the extent of her immediate family. Without them she really was alone.

"Sheila!" she called again and again but to no avail. The cat stood on her back legs and gently unsheathed her nails into Maggie's tights. Normally she'd be annoyed at the unnecessary expense of another pair of tights but today she was glad of the gesture of affection. She bent down and gently picked up the cat. "Good morning, little woman. Did you see anything last night?" The little slanted green eyes blinked into her face, the little hard nose butted her chin and the physical contact started a purr deep down in her body. She was vibrating like a little engine. Maggie held her against her heart and went back into the house, not wanting to be in the yard if searchers went up on the mountain.

That day and the next went by in a similar vein, and Sheila did not come back. Maggie hid from the world and mercifully for a while they forgot about her. The mountains were searched and the phones were manned but no sign was seen of Seán Molloy. Maggie walked out in the yard once to call to Eddie but he went on without stopping. He could have avoided the yard and walked around it but he chose the short cut so she hoped that meant he was softening and no longer believed that she could have hurt his only son. Kate never called after that first night. Maggie reminded her of the black hole that had swallowed her child.

Every night Maggie coloured in a square on her calendar and thought about her other family. She couldn't tell them what was happening now. Her heart lived with the hope that by the time the coloured squares covered the page everything would be as normal and she could introduce them with pride to her neighbours and the nightmare of the moment would be just a memory. For now she would have to live in solitude and wait out the storm.

Nearly a week after Seán's disappearance Maggie opened the door and Sheila's excited face met her in the doorway. She bounded about, jumping up on Maggie, and barking with her nose pointed at the sky.

"Where did you come from?" Maggie dropped to her knees, oblivious to the hard floor and hugged her wayward pet.

Sheila licked her face furiously and ran in excitement to steal the cat's food, getting a slap on the snout for her troubles. She saw Maggie smiling at her and she smiled back, full of good humour after her adventure.

"If only you could talk!"

"What would she say?" Jason's happy voice interrupted her.

"Hi! She's been missing for a couple of days now. I was very worried about her. How are you, Jason? Come in and have a cup of tea." Maggie was almost as excited at having a human visitor as she was at having her dog back.

"I'm okay. I met Sheila in the fields. I walked across the mountain. She was wandering around by herself."

"Was she? Why didn't she come home then?"

"She probably was on her way home."

"It took her long enough. She's been gone for days."

"Well, she looks in good condition wherever she

went, Maggie. Don't worry about her. She's a wise old girl."

Sheila looked up into his face as if she could read his thoughts and thumped her plumy tail on the ground.

"I don't know how wise she is."

Jason turned, recognising something uncertain in her tone of voice. "What's been going on? Has something happened?"

"No, nothing happened, nothing except Seán's disappearance. There's no news yet?"

"Not that I heard. We've searched high and low. It's a mystery."

"It's been nearly a week now. That probably means bad news, doesn't it?"

Maggie looked to Jason for some form of reassurance but none was forthcoming. What could he say? Bad news was inevitable and they all knew it.

They sat and had their tea in silence. Jason's usual chat was absent and he seemed lost in thought. Finally he excused himself and said he had to go. Maggie walked him to the door.

"Maggie, if anything happens, please call me. You know I'll come right over if there are any problems."

"I'll be fine." She was unsure why she wasn't telling him what happened the night Sheila went off. She wasn't sure of anything at the moment.

The guards still hadn't returned with Pascal's gun. She was afraid to ask them about it. They were leaving her alone at the moment and she thought any questions would only re-ignite their interest. Perhaps they were waiting until they found Seán and then they would come and arrest her for something. He couldn't be on the land or they would have found him by now so whoever took him transported him somewhere else. That should clear her because she didn't drive. That was cold comfort. She missed Seán so much. His happy face and strange theories had brightened her life.

She missed Jason too. A distance and watchfulness had developed between them. Maybe that was understandable. He'd obviously had a little doubt about Pascal's death or he wouldn't have asked her straight out if she had done it. When people keep dying or disappearing in your space you are going to attract speculation. There was nobody around the last few months more than Jason. If their suspicions about Maggie were justified then the odds were stacked against him too. Perhaps he was giving her the benefit of the doubt from a safe distance. It was understandable; things did look bad.

She had no doubt in the world now that her prowler and a brutal murderer were one and the same. She was watching the events from the bottom of a pit of her own digging. Jason knew of her prowler so perhaps they could go together to the police and tell them the whole story. No! Jason had a car. History was steeped in killing teams and she and Jason could be moulded into that cast as well as anyone. At times like this society cried out for justice. The public definition of justice was someone to point at: someone to take the fall. Maggie knew already that she couldn't subject Jason to that as well. Her heart cried but her eyes were dry. Maggie couldn't see the threads to pull to unravel her pain. Days would slide together to become a dull mass of empty time before clarity started to replace the blindfold she wore now.

Chapter 25

Maggie sipped her tea and wondered. Something was simmering just below the surface of her brain. She had no idea what stimulated it and what it was trying to tell her but she knew it was important. Something someone had said or something she'd seen was in the back of her mind. Maybe she forgot to do something. She ran over everything she could think of from the events of the last few days. Finally she dropped her head into her hands and closed her eyes. She tried forcing the memory but by now her mind was blank and there was no breaking down the barrier that had sprung up there. Squeezing her eyes shut and concentrating didn't help, it only made her head hurt.

Maggie had a stack of books she'd bought over the last few months in the second-hand bookshop in the town. She ran her hand down the line of titles. A Patricia Cornwell caught her eye. There was a lot of talk about her. She'd seen her once, interviewed on the

Late Late Show. The Body Farm, an ominous title considering everything, but she'd give it a shot. The story consumed her from the start. A woman against the world just like she felt right now. She sat back after an hour or so and closed her eyes and just let her mind wander and follow its own course. It thought about the plot of the book and connected with the growl in her stomach reminding her of hunger and then it connected with that nagging thought that had been trying to make itself heard all evening.

Then it stepped right into the spotlight. It took centre stage and then stepped back, taking a bow. Oh my God! Was it imagination or had her troubles multiplied?

It was her dream. The night he stood in her kitchen she had a dream. It was difficult to piece it all together now. Seán was dragged away from her by a hidden hand but the voice that spoke came from behind her. She knew it was only a dream but sometimes they existed to highlight something that you needed to analyse in the laboratory of your sleeping brain. There were two people present in the dream besides her and Seán, one dragging him away from her and the other talking to her from behind. Were there two people involved in this? Or was it a symptom of her fear that the police would think her and an accomplice had taken Seán? No, she felt that her subconscious thought there were two people involved. She didn't know anything but she did trust her instincts, though she didn't always have the courage to act on them. This was important, of that she was sure, some portion of her inner fibres had connected with a slip on the part of her tormentor but she couldn't process it yet. Time would help.

Her dinner that night consisted of a boiled egg, wholemeal toast and tea, followed by yoghurt. She went back to her book afterwards, for once ignoring the spectacle of the dishes. Tonight she wanted to treat herself and a good book, a full stomach and a warm fire were all she needed. Her animals lay on the rug at her feet. Still that nagging feeling of something pressing on her brain continued. A man or a strong woman, that's what she'd thought the night the dark shadow had stood in her kitchen. She'd thought he could be a small man or a woman. Then her brain twitched and she thought of the shadow that stood outside her door the other night as she looked through the curtain. There was no doubt in her mind that was a much bigger person. She hadn't seen anything beyond an outline but it was certainly a different shape, a bigger bulkier shape. And the footsteps she'd seen in the snow behind her house earlier in the spring – those were large with long steps between them. There were two people. There were. She knew that. In her heart she knew that for sure. Two people. Her breath was coming in labouring pants and her vision was blurring – this was no time to get a panic attack. She eased back in her chair and allowed her heart to quieten.

At ten-thirty the phone rang. The panting started again but she forced herself to the phone to answer it. For a moment there was silence except for the sound of traffic in the background.

"Hello!" Maggie said it a few times and then she hung up. The phone rang again and she answered it, her anger rising.

"Who are you? Stop tormenting me! Leave me in peace!"

She was about to hang up again when Kate spoke.

"Maggie! Don't hang up – it's me."

Maggie's hands were shaking. What must Kate think of the way she answered the phone? Her life, such as it was, was crumbling.

"Kate, pet, how are you?" She spoke in a soft voice void of life.

There was a pause again as Kate collected her thoughts.

"I had to call you. Let you know what happened."

"What happened?" Maggie parroted a response though she knew what the answer would be.

"I wanted to hear for myself your reaction when you heard."

"Heard what, Kate?"

"Don't act stupid on me now, Maggie."

"It's Seán, isn't it?"

"Yes. They found a body." Kate's voice sounded hollow.

Maggie let out a wail before she could stop herself. Afterwards there was a silence while she regained her composure.

"Where?"

"In the bogs in Glenveigh."

"Glenveigh! How did he get there?" The minute

the words were out of her mouth she heard how awful they sounded.

"I presume he was driven, Maggie. I mean fourteen-year-olds don't walk twenty-odd miles at ten-thirty in the night without their clothes."

"He was naked!"

"He was, Maggie. My baby was found in the bogs. Naked. A group of hill walkers found him." For a few moments there was silence as if Kate was too overcome to speak.

Maggie gently broke the silence. "Did you see him?"

Kate continued on as though she hadn't heard. "They saw him floating off the edge of a small bog lake near Sliabh Sneacht. It's been over a week – in the water. They had to identify him by his teeth." 'Teeth' came out like a squeak.

"It can't be."

"Maggie, I'm hardly making this up. I've just had the guards here."

"I'm so sorry."

"I'm sure you are. You have no one to carry your shopping now or sit with you at night and watch movies I forbade him to see."

"He told me you knew, Kate."

"Did he? He was fourteen, Maggie. He'd tell you anything. If you weren't such a sad damaged old woman you would have seen all of that. Acting like a young one hanging out with young boys – what kind of a sad bitch are you, Maggie?"

"Kate!"

"Oh, shut the fuck up, Maggie! I just wanted to hear your voice when I told you. They suspect you did it but I know you didn't. You needed him as much as I did. But he was mine. He was mine, and the little shit seemed to love you more. My baby is gone and you were the last person he spent time with besides the monster who took him."

"Kate, please –"

"We're both alone now, Maggie."

"You've got Eddie and Rita."

"Rita lives in London now – and Eddie? Eddie's yours too, Maggie, you and your family. We never speak. We just occupy the same space."

"You had two children together."

"He was just collecting his conjugal rights, Maggie. That was all."

"Oh, Kate, don't say that!"

"I told you to shut up. Shut up! You know nothing about me and mine. Nothing." Maggie was left with a dead phone line in her hand.

Maggie sat and rocked, tears slid silently down her cheeks as she thought about Seán. What a terrible thing to happen. It was understandable why Kate was so angry. She was right about how much Maggie was going to miss him and in a perverse kind of way it comforted Maggie to know that he had been fond of her too, even though she knew that already. Kate was only confirming what her heart already felt.

Sheila came and jumped onto her knee. Though she was a grown collie she forgot that when she thought you were very upset and reverted to being a puppy. Maggie's tears wet her coat as she held her tightly, the dog's head resting on her shoulder. The cat sat on the bench beside her, licking the dog's outstretched paw. They were so sweet sometimes. Often she walked into her room or Pascal's and the two of them would be lying cuddled up in the duvet sound asleep. They fought when one upset the other and showed love to the other when she was down. We could learn a lot from you if we bothered to, she thought, looking into their eyes. They looked back at her, wondering if they had made her cry. Whatever it was, they were reaping their reward now as she lavished attention and affection on them.

Less than an hour later the phone rang again. Maggie was almost in her bed at this time.

Cautiously she answered it. "Hello?" She never gave her name any more.

"Maggie."

"Jason. I'm not in the mood to talk at the moment."

"You heard."

"I did. Kate called me."

"She called my mother as well and Mum told me they're all in tears in my house."

"There were a few tears shed here tonight as well. I can't believe it."

"You spoke to Kate. How is she?"

"She's very angry."

"She would be. Do you want me to come over for a chat?"

"No, Jason. I'd prefer you didn't. I really need to go to my bed and sleep."

"Right then." He spoke abruptly and the line went dead.

Maggie stared at the phone. What's the matter with him? I suppose, she thought, he's feeling it too. It was a terrible shock for everyone.

That night Maggie slept a dreamless sleep of the dead.

It was just under four weeks until Michael and the children were arriving. They were going to be long weeks. There was no news yet of when Seán's funeral would take place. No one had come near her house all day and even the postman had nothing for her. When she stood in the quietness of the yard she could hear the cars stopping and starting at Kate's. They would have a full house. She really wanted to go and pay her respects to the family, especially to Eddie, but she knew the way the rumour mill worked around here. She could imagine the hush that would fall over the room when she walked in and the uncomfortable looks that would pass amongst the mourners. It was customary to stay a while and just be with the family but her presence would be no benefit to anyone.

Paralysed by fear and inadequacy, she just stood in her yard listening to the cars and the voices travelling on the wind from the yard. As the crow flew it was only two fields away. By the lane it took longer. The lane veered off a bit to the left, travelling past the ruin of an old house, then turned back to the right and straight down.

The ruined house was last lived in about forty years ago. A small lane known locally as Foy's Lane split off the main one and went uphill about one hundred yards. Maggie hadn't been up there in a long time. Mrs Foy lived up there when Maggie was a child. She was an old lady who lived alone. Her children emigrated to America and her husband died a young man. Maggie and her sisters loved her and used to spend a lot of time in her house. Maggie gulped. Maggie was the old lady up the lane now.

It was a pretty house surrounded by a ring of mountain ash trees interspersed with a couple of evergreens. The yard was surrounded on three sides by the dwelling house and two lines of outhouses. All the houses including the dwelling house were brightly whitewashed. The main house was covered in a thatched roof and the sheds were covered in red tin sheaths. In a mountain area like this it was impossible to stop the sheep from eating your flowerbeds so Mrs Foy hung flowerpots from wall brackets and planted hanging flowers in hollows at the top of the shed walls. Her house was like a Constable painting, a study in rural beauty. She churned her own salty butter, made her own baked goods, killed her own meat (by her own hand), had a flourishing vegetable garden and ran ducks and chickens in her yard. She was completely self-sufficient and operated a barter system with Maggie's mother. She supplied her with bread, milk and eggs supplemented by seasonal vegetables in return for the girls after school to help with the work. She died before Maggie went to Scotland and though she left her farm to her son he never lived there. The farm was sold to Dolores' husband and the plot the house was on was kept as a holiday home. Gradually over the years the son stopped coming to Ireland and now it was just left to rot. The thatch fell in many years ago and the garden was an overgrown wilderness. It was still the most beautiful property around here, facing into the sun for most of the day and up on a height so you had a great view of the valley.

Suddenly Maggie had an urge to go and see it. She needed to connect with something outside herself and her house. Maybe the happy memories she still had of that house would be therapeutic for her. She locked the door and with Sheila at her heels she walked down the lane. It was only a few minutes' walk to the bottom of Foy's Lane. Maggie stood there listening to the sounds coming up on the wind from Kate's. Cars stopping and starting and a mixture of voices carried on the evening air. Kate's was quite close now. It would have just taken another few minutes for Maggie to go there if she could pluck up the courage.

Sheila nosed around in the undergrowth and Maggie, wary now of every sound, kept her senses on high alert. Together they ascended the lane to the old Foy place.

The lane was overgrown now. Halfway up Sheila got a bit restless, snuffling around in the grass. Maggie turned her eyes on the grass to see what was bothering her. Car tracks were visible and a condom discarded in a bush was turned up by Sheila's probing snout.

"Don't be a silly mutt! You're not that much of a puritan, are you, getting out of joint about a courting couple?"

Sheila's eyes stared up at her and her head moved from side to side as though she were following every word she said.

"Come on, girl!" She nudged the dog on her way and in a moment the two of them were leaning on the old gate looking across the remains of the yard, Sheila barking her head off at some crows.

The place was more rundown every time she saw it. The whole thatch roof had fallen in now and the tin had blown off the sheds and was lying on the grass that had grown up amongst the stones. It was a very old property and the yard had been paved in stones rather than concrete, just like Maggie's. The trees and bushes had encroached on the yard until they practically covered it. Maggie pushed at the gate expecting it to be stiff but in amazement she noticed it had new hinges and a brand new latch. The grass behind the gate was flattened where the gate passed over it when it was opened. Um, she thought, someone is spending a lot of time coming up here.

"Maybe we should go back. It's creepier than I remembered it."

But Sheila had bounded ahead towards the sheds that bordered the opposite side of the yard. Maggie followed.

The shed the dog ran to was the only one with a full roof still covering it. Oblivious to Maggie's calls she ran into the darkened doorway. Maggie followed cautiously. It took a few minutes for her eyes to become adjusted to the shade. Sheila was at the back of the shed, nosing around in a dish.

"Sheila!" she shouted, terrified her dog was about to be poisoned.

Sheila looked up, shocked at the harsh call. She wagged her tail and looked again at the dish and back at Maggie. Maggie walked over. The dish was fairly clean and a new bed of hay lay beside it. The dog seemed very at home here.

Then she saw the collar and chain attached to the wall by the bed of hay. She picked it up and Sheila obediently sat down for her to put it on. Maggie's chest tightened and she suddenly saw as clear as day where Sheila disappeared to those days she was missing. She was tied up here with food and a comfortable bed. She looked at the collar and saw tufts of black hair stuck to the leather. She dropped the collar and chain and turned to go. Then a tin in the far corner of the shed high on the wall caught her eye. She grabbed Sheila's collar so she couldn't run off and paused to check out the tin. In her heart she knew before she looked at it what it was going to be. It was up on the top of the wall and was partly obscured by old twine and cobwebs. She pulled her jumper down over her hands and gently slid the tin along the wall behind the cobwebs and lifted it down, trying not to disturb anything. It was a tin of black paint. Though the twine was old and cobwebs hung down from the rafters in front of the box someone must have put it up the same way she just took it down. The tin was old but the paint drips down the side hadn't been there that long. There was no dust or dirt on it. Maggie had known even before she took it down that it was the tin from her barn. Pascal put a mark on everything. There on the side was his scrawled initials scratched into it.

With trembling hands Maggie carefully placed it back where she found it and hurried out of the shed, dragging the dog by the collar. Her fear was close to panic. They crossed the yard and went through the gate, closing it behind them. As they descended the path a sound could be heard over Maggie's footsteps. It was the sound of the gate banging. Knowing she'd closed it properly, Maggie ran now, bent over, dragging the grumbling dog along. Maggie didn't know if it was imagination or what but as they neared the end of the lane she thought she heard a second set of footsteps. Sheila was twisting in her hand and trying her best to go back to the sound behind them and it was slowing Maggie down considerably. Maggie thought he must be right behind her by then. She couldn't outrun him. But then the bottom of the lane appeared under their feet. Maggie turned towards her own house. As she did a car rounded the bend behind her and pulled up by her side.

Father Lander's twinkling eyes looked out at her.

"Do you want a lift home?"

"Yes, Father!" Maggie gasped. "Thanks!"

She scooped the collie up into her arms and looked back at the lane she'd just run down. The distance was short but it had felt like a marathon trek to her. The lane was quiet now. Once again she wondered if she'd been imagining things but instinct told her that no she hadn't. This evening something was definitely out there. She sat into the car and held the large dog on her knee.

"Isn't she able to walk?" The priest wasn't amused.

"She runs off sometimes, Father."

"Oh."

As the car went on up the lane Maggie sensed a pair of eyes watching them, but she didn't dare turn her head. Playtime was over.

Chapter 26

Maggie poured as much tea as she could into the priest and kept a steady flow of small talk going. But, with all her delaying tactics, she could only manage to keep him there for forty minutes. He'd been down to see Kate and he thought he'd pay a quick call on Maggie. He stayed as long as he could, obviously thinking that loneliness was getting to her. Maggie used the few minutes that it took for him to break away and get into his car as an opportunity to let Sheila go to the bathroom. That dog wasn't getting out of her sight for the rest of the night. As soon as the priest's tail-lights disappeared down the lane Maggie dragged the dog straight back inside and double-locked the door. Remembering the night before, she went back and put on the chain. She checked every window and door; they were all shut tight.

Like a prisoner on the mile she paced up and down the room trying to process the events of the evening.

Someone who knew Sheila and was kind to her took her away and tied her in an old abandoned house for three days. Someone, probably the same person, was right behind them as they left the farm. How did they know she was there? Sheila was barking at crows as they arrived. The prowler must have heard her. He must have been very close then to get there so quickly because they weren't at the house for more than a few minutes. Perhaps it was someone at Kate's. They could have heard Sheila from there.

Then she thought of the black paint. It must have been the paint used on her wall. Without knowing when the shift had taken place, she realised she couldn't talk to Jason about this. Some place along the way he had fallen into the camp of suspects; he was no longer an ally. Seán didn't like him – he told her that the night he died. What did he call him? A dark horse! That would explain how he never caught the prowler. If *he* were the prowler. But that didn't make sense. The night she rang Dolores when the prowler was first in her yard, Jason and Dan were at home and Dolores sent them across the hill. So it couldn't be him. But still, somehow she couldn't bring herself to confide in Jason any more. Besides, she still felt there had been two of them. Maybe he worked with someone. From now on she couldn't trust anyone.

The priest disturbed her as well. Too many times and in a number of ways he'd hinted that she wasn't coping well on her own. He even said people were worried about her. Was someone doing what Jason said and going to the priest as a concerned citizen to undermine her and get her put away? But why? Who would want to do that? Someone who wanted the house and land? Her family would inherit the land if she wasn't here and then they'd sell it. Who would they sell it to? There were two perfectly good reasons right there, why people might work together to get her out. A family member would make some money and a neighbour could grab a bargain . . . no . . . she couldn't believe it . . . not murder for profit . . . not her friends and family . . .

Her head was spinning and she could feel a noose closing in around her and cutting off her air supply. Her freedom was getting more claustrophobic every day. She had more freedom when Pascal was alive and she was getting pocket money and a food allowance. Her bright home was deepening in colour and taking on the shape of a prison. The air seemed stale because she never opened the windows. Even Sheila was imprisoned.

Numerous times that evening she went to the phone to ring someone but there really wasn't anyone she could talk to. The things she'd experienced over the last few months were so fantastical even she didn't believe them. Involved or not her family would certainly think she was suffering from dementia if she told them. They'd put her in a home and her neighbours would remember her as a maniac.

The next morning brought the police back to her door.

"Margaret, we need to talk to you." The female detective sweetly manoeuvred her way through the door as if she just wanted tea and a chat.

"Come right in?"

There was no need, beyond formality, to speak as they were already in and sitting down before Maggie was herself.

"Aren't there procedures the police need to follow when entering somebody's house?" she said boldly.

"Yes, there are, Margaret," said Detective Ryan. "We asked politely – unless you want us to get a warrant."

"I have nothing to hide. But maybe next time you could phone first. Would you like some tea?"

"We'd love some. Thank you."

Maggie got the tea ready, aware that their eyes were taking in every detail of her behaviour. She laid the tray on the table and left them to pour their own.

Detective Grant poured while his partner kept her sharp eyes locked on Maggie's. Maggie broke the silence. "You'll be very disappointed, having wasted all this time on me, when you find out that someone else killed Seán."

"This is just a process of elimination, Margaret." Detective Ryan was doing all the talking. "We're just here to clear up a few points."

"I'm listening."

"We've been informed that you have a son."

Maggie's face froze. She was trying to be cool and calm but the question caught her totally off guard.

"Is that true?" the detective continued.

"Yes." She gulped and nodded simultaneously.

"Why didn't you tell us that before?"

"It never came up."

They braced themselves at her evasion and exchanged a glance but obviously mutually decided to let it slip.

Finally Detective Grant opened his mouth. "Why didn't you tell us someone vandalised your house?"

"It didn't seem serious enough to call the police."

"Really? We're beginning to think you're not being very co-operative, Margaret. Tell us about the harassment"

"I wouldn't call it harassment."

"What would you call it?"

"Just high jinks. You get a lot of that in the country, young fellows coming home from the pub, that kind of thing."

"Well," said Detective Ryan, "like we said this is a process of elimination. Even if you had nothing to do with Seán Molloy's disappearance, don't forget one thing – he was leaving your house. For your own sake you should co-operate. We don't want to find your body sunk in a bog lake."

On that friendly note they put down their cups almost in unison and got up to leave.

"Just one question," Maggie said.

"Yes?" said Grant.

"Who told you about Michael and the vandalism of my house?"

"A concerned citizen, Margaret."

"Did you ever consider maybe that's the person you should be looking at next?" They paused for a moment as if weighing up what she'd just said. Then they both smiled at her, giving nothing away, and bade her goodbye.

Maybe she'd finally put them in the right direction, she thought, as they turned and left. She hoped so as she watched them leave the yard. Was this a new tactic, a few quick visits to catch her off guard? She wondered what the person feeding them information was hoping to accomplish.

They'd only just left when the postman arrived. Terence had been back for the last few days. Maggie was delighted to see the back of Alan.

"How are you, Terence?"

"I'm fine, Maggie. Was that the guards?"

"It was."

"I was thinking I recognised Miss Ryan. She was stationed here a few years ago. You mightn't remember."

"No," Maggie said, not wanting to talk about guards.

"How are you feeling after all the goings-on down the road?"

"I've been better, Terence."

"Poor Kate is in a terrible way."

"Is she?" Maggie remembered the hollow voice on the phone.

"Um, it will be a while yet before the body is

released to her. The poor little fellow was too badly decomposed for her to see him. It's just the way it's hanging over her, I think, at this stage."

"Do they have any idea what happened? The police only ask me questions, they never tell me anything."

"No." Terence's blue eyes looked into hers for a moment, then he went on talking. "Hikers found his body in one of the small bog lakes out on the mountain in Glenveigh. They're saying he was put there shortly after his disappearance but they don't know as yet what happened. They know he wasn't drowned in the lake."

"How."

"I suppose there wasn't any water in his little lungs."

"Do they have any idea why someone would leave him naked. Was he assaulted?"

"Maggie!" He seemed upset. "There's things you don't talk about."

Maggie blushed. She was finding it harder these days to speak without embarrassing herself.

"It's an awful thing. Maggie, they said he was floating there, snow white against the dark water. Maybe it was quicker to hide him that way than to dig a hole. Bodies don't float straight away I'm told."

Maggie's stomach churned when he said that. The thought of that little boy down in the dark water sickened her.

"Water is a good way of destroying DNA too." Terence's voice droned on in the background.

Maggie's fear was palpable now. Death was so close to her.

Terence looked at her anxiously. "Maggie! Are you okay?"

"I am. I just can't bear the image of the poor little thing like that. Who could do it to him?"

"I wish I knew. I haven't felt right since I heard. I'd better get on. I'll see you tomorrow, Maggie."

"Right, Terence. See you then."

Maggie paced the house. For close to an hour she walked the room full of nervous energy and too scared to go out. Should she talk to the police? Would they believe her or would she convince them she really was mad? What practical thing could she do on her own? Sleep on it that was all she could do.

The car came to her yard that night at eleven o'clock. Sheila lifted her head and gave a low woof as she heard the knock, her grey-flecked head cocked to the side and her ears standing straight up like a hyena's pointing towards the door. Maggie's own ears, though not as flexible, were just as fine-tuned. Cautiously she stood behind the door listening.

"*Maggie*!"

It was Alan.

She thought she'd seen the last of him when Terence came back.

"*Maggie*!"

He sounded like he was agitated, not his usual placid self. Maybe she'd been right about him.

The knock repeated, a little louder now. She ran back and grabbed the phone. Who could she trust? Should she call Jason? There was no one else who would come over at this short notice. She didn't know what to do. There was a speed dial on the phone and Jason's number was number two. She held the phone with her finger over the button. A crash sounded beside her as Alan kicked the door.

In fright her reflexes caused her to press the button.

"Maggie! Don't be so stupid! I need to talk to you."

"What is it?" She called out to Alan. "It's very late – I'm ready for bed."

"I need to talk to you, Maggie, please let me in."

"You can tell me in the morning."

"That could be too late and you won't talk to me tomorrow. You don't like me."

"Don't be silly."

"I'm not. It's very important."

"I don't open the door late at night."

"I'm not going to hurt you." His voice was softer now.

"All right, I'll open the door a crack and we can talk on the doorstep." She reached to put the chain on at the same time she opened the door.

He didn't give her a chance. He shoved and the chain whipped through her hands, opening the door. She screamed and Sheila went hysterical.

He pushed past her and stood in the porch. "Shut the door, Maggie, so we can talk."

The phone landed on the mat when the door opened and now it was pushed behind the open door. Maggie didn't know if Jason had answered or not.

"Maggie, I heard people talking tonight about you and I came to warn you."

"You're just trying another tactic to scare me."

"No, I'm not, Maggie. I promise you, you have enemies in this parish and you need to be very careful."

"What are you talking about?"

"I live over the pub and tonight I had the window open and I heard some people out the back talking about you. You've got to believe me you're in a lot of danger. Please, shut the door and come inside."

In what seemed like slow motion Alan turned and walked into the kitchen. Maggie stared after him. A shadow fell on the porch floor and the next thing Maggie knew Jason came bounding through the door straight at Alan with a shovel in his hands. Catching him off guard as he turned, he struck the back of his head with it and the larger man landed with a dull thud. A snapping Sheila attacked the prone body.

Jason turned to her. "That's enough, Sheila!"

She lowered her head and backed away.

Maggie watched the show of obedience and observed the black outfit worn by Jason and a slow realisation dawned.

Jason was staring at the man on the ground and Maggie was staring at him.

"What are you doing here?" she asked.

"You rang me."

"Oh, did the call go through?"

"It did. You're lucky I was just down the road and I heard everything. I ran as fast as I could up the hill."

He wasn't panting too much – he must have been very close.

Maggie smiled at him. "Thank God you're fit."

For a moment he seemed to be sizing up the situation, as if wondering was she being serious or having him on.

"What will we do with him now?" Maggie bent down and felt Alan's pulse. "I think he's still alive but he needs a hospital. He could have a concussion. You could have cracked his skull."

"Hold on a minute, Maggie. Slow down. Considering the happenings around here lately, if we call the hospital or the doctor they'll get the police and do you think they'll believe that you had nothing to do with this?"

Maggie's downcast face told him she thought he was right.

"Even if they believed I wielded the shovel they would be sure that you were involved. Getting a young impressionable neighbour to do your dirty work."

Maggie didn't know what to do. Was Jason being a friend or was he being smart to cover himself? He was right about the police.

"But we can't let him die!" she said.

"What do you want to do with him? Put him to bed?"

Now she knew he was mocking her.

"I'm not being smart, Maggie, but he's a big man – he'll be difficult to hide."

"Jason, we can't let him die."

Jason touched him with his shoe. "Maybe we won't be able to stop him. At least help me to tie him up and gag him, Maggie. You don't want him coming around and hurting you."

Maggie didn't know who was going to hurt her but somehow she found herself complying with his wishes. He was right. She'd never hurt a soul in her life and she was suspected of being involved in two murders. Now here she was with a man lying unconscious in her kitchen.

"We have to at least get him inside the utility room, Maggie, and close the door."

"What about his car?" Her eyes were open wide. "I heard him drive up."

"We'll sort that in a minute, come on." He was already reaching for Alan as he spoke.

Together they dragged him inside the small room. Maggie had a roll of nylon twine in the utility room. Jason measured and cut lengths. He tied Alan's hands together to the front of his body. Then he tied his feet. As he did this he pressed his two fingers against his neck and turned his gaze on Maggie.

"He's gone, Maggie."

"Gone?" Maggie asked in shock.

"Dead. Now, we have to take care of ourselves. You don't want to be locked away again, do you?"

Maggie could feel herself turning green. This was too much trouble for one lifetime.

Quietly she nodded her head, too scared to meet Jason's penetrating gaze. He was testing her out to see how she was going to react. Jason locked the door behind Alan and pocketed the key.

"Jason, why are you locking the door?"

"You don't need to be in there with him. Now, Maggie," his voice was soothing and gentle like he was talking to a small child, "I'll get rid of his car. You don't move. I'll be back in about half an hour."

"Okay." She sniffed. What was she into now? She needed time to think! If Alan was the murderer then maybe Jason had saved her life. If not . . . let him go off with the car.

He turned around as he got to the door.

"Don't call anyone, Maggie. They won't believe you." His voice softened again. "I'll take care of you – just wait for me."

She sat on the couch after he left and stared at the phone. Thoughts whirled around in her head but always came back to the same place. She couldn't phone anyone. Who could she turn to? The police would think she had been involved, her neighbours would think she was crazy and incapable of taking care of herself, and long before it ever got to that stage Jason would kill her. He said he'd be half an hour but he could be back much sooner and catch her on the phone. Maybe this was a test to see if she'd go along with him. If going along with him now was what was necessary, then so be it. If she turned against him, he'd kill her.

The clock ticked and the minutes slipped by until she was sure it must be at least half an hour since he left. She looked over at the clock. Twenty-five minutes.

Something was bothering her. Why had he locked the utility room door and taken the key? His answer didn't really make sense.

His hands. She watched his hands again in her head tying the knots. He was wearing gloves.

A bolt of pain caused her to gasp. He wasn't coming back. How could she be so stupid? He'd set her up to be found with Alan's body. She jumped up and ran to the outside door. Alan's car was still there. Had she heard Jason leaving in a car? She was so stressed she couldn't remember. She tried the door of the utility room. It was unlocked. He'd just taken the key to make her think he'd locked Alan in. She looked inside. She checked Alan's pulse herself to make sure he was in fact dead. He was. Jason had told the truth about that. She bent to untie him. Knowing now that he was probably innocent she wanted to give him back some dignity. In truth she didn't know what she was doing. Looking back later she remembered feeling numb. She knew people were on their way to get her. She'd been right all along – someone was trying to get her put away and it was the only person she'd really trusted.

It took her ages but finally the knots on his hands were coming loose. As she turned to work on his feet, thinking they might be easier, she heard cars and commotion in her yard. Fear immobilised her and she just sat there on the floor beside Alan.

People burst through the door and removed her. The two detectives stood looking at her.

Part Three

Chapter 27

Maggie refused to speak to anyone. She watched through blurred vision as Alan's body was taken, shrouded in white, out of her utility room. Voices surrounded her and questions were hurled in her direction but she found she couldn't speak even if she knew what to say. Her face felt like it was frozen into a mask. Finally they felt there was nothing more to do but take her to the police station and get the doctor on call there to advise them.

It had started to drizzle since she'd been outside last and she felt its gentle mist touch her cheeks as soon as she left her porch door. Its whispering touch on her earlobes finally tuned her in again to her surroundings. She felt as though it were all whooshing back at her from a long tunnel.

Hands directed her into the back of a waiting squad car but she wasn't really aware now of any individual, just a background hum.

She knew her life was over now. Sitting in the car waiting for the lead cars and the ambulance to move, she looked back at her brightly lit house. This could possibly be the last time she saw it. Jason had covered his tracks well. Her fingerprints were on the twine and she was with Alan when the police arrived. They weren't going to believe she was trying to untie him – it probably looked as though she were doing the opposite. There was no way she could talk herself out of another death. After years of watching television she felt like she'd been sucked into her own thriller. A panic attack was beginning and it was constricting her breathing like the metal bands on an old blacksmith's barrel. To his credit she could see the guard driving watching her in the mirror with concerned eyes.

The drive took her past Kate and Eddie's house. This was the first time she'd been down the road since they found young Seán. All the lights were on in the house and the yard and both sides of the road were lined with cars. A group had gathered in the street to watch Maggie's cavalcade go by. Kate was in the centre, flanked on both sides by her neighbours. Dolores held her on one side and Kathleen, Dolores' sister, stood on the other. They faded into the distance and the road turned pitch black with the high fences blocking out any moonlight.

The heater was up very high in the car and Maggie was finding it difficult to breathe. The scent from a cheap pine air-freshener added to the stuffiness. Nobody spoke. She supposed that since they obviously all thought her guilty, it must be disturbing to be riding in a car with a petite sixty-year-old woman who was capable of multiple murders. They all had mothers and grandmothers.

When they got to Letterkenny she was led through the halls of the station to a room with only a small window high up on the wall. The furniture was sparse with a small table and a few chairs. They directed Maggie to one.

The young guard they left with her had a gentle face, but he wouldn't meet her gaze. She couldn't take her eyes off him. For some reason, she wanted to tell him the whole story. He looked like he could listen. They couldn't lock her up. A sob was building up. She could feel it. How would she survive being in a small cell?

"Can I have a cup of tea?" Her voice was small and brittle.

"I don't know, Margaret. They'll be back in a moment to talk to you."

"How old are you?"

He looked straight at her for a moment and turned away again.

"You look very young. I can't believe you're a guard already."

He smiled at her and pointed to the pale blue badge on his arm. "I've still got my L-plates."

"You'll do very well." The earnest look on her face seemed to unsettle him.

"Relax, Margaret. They won't be long more."

She lifted her chin and clenched her hands tightly. The minutes ticked by.

The door opened abruptly and her two detectives entered, accompanied by a robust man in a grey suit. He doesn't have to wait for his tea, she thought. They sat down. Two of them sat opposite her and the grey man sat beside her.

Maggie turned to him.

"Are you my lawyer?"

"No, I'm not. I'm a doctor. Doctor Wilson."

"Well, isn't it customary to have a lawyer present in an interrogation room, not a doctor?"

"Do you think you'll need one, Margaret? A lawyer, I mean?" asked Detective Grant.

"I don't think I have enough experience to figure that out. My solicitor would be better placed to tell me."

"Give us his name and we'll call him." Detective Ryan's patience was wearing thin. This was going to delay everything and keep them here all night.

Maggie gave the name and her young guard disappeared.

"Okay, let's get started," said Detective Grant.

"Ahem!" Maggie cleared her throat. "I'd rather he was here when we talk."

"Of course, Margaret," said Detective Ryan with a sigh. "You sit here until he decides to come in. We'll be back later."

The detectives got to their feet and made for the door, leaving the doctor sitting beside Maggie.

"Can I have a cup of tea?"

Detective Grant turned sharply but thought better of what he was going to say.

"Would you like a sandwich?" His tongue dripped with sarcasm.

"Yes, please," Maggie, answered as sweetly as possible.

Detective Ryan laughed and guided her partner out the door.

"Communicative bunch," said Maggie to the back wall.

"That's their job." Her young guard had slipped in when her back was turned.

"Are there two-way mirrors in here?" she asked, taking a good look around.

"No. We're not allowed to violate the privacy of suspects."

"Really?" She sounded surprised.

He laughed at Maggie's innocent expression.

Doctor Wilson nodded to the guard who opened the door bringing in a female guard, before exiting again himself.

"Okay, Margaret," said the doctor, "let's have a look at you."

"I'm fine, doctor. I just had a shock."

"I can give you something for that."

Panic erupted in Maggie again and her eyes opened wide. "No, doctor. There is no way I am taking any medication and I won't go to hospital"

"Please, Margaret, just let me check you out first."

"Fine." She pouted as though she were a teenager and let the doctor continue with the examination.

The doctor checked her heart and lungs for signs of palpitations or irregular breathing – in case she collapsed under the pressure, she supposed.

"Well?" She raised her eyebrows to heaven and glared at the doctor as he put away his equipment and she fixed her clothes.

"You're fine. In fact you're healthy as a trout. There must be some fine air out in Cooleen."

Finally Maggie relaxed a little and even managed a smile. "Doctor, could you please be sure and make everyone aware that I am well?"

"I certainly will, Margaret. Don't worry. Relax and co-operate and you'll be fine."

The medical examination over, the female guard was replaced by the young guard and the doctor left.

The room lapsed again into silence, which was broken after about ten minutes when Detective Ryan arrived with her food. The tea was hot and weak as she liked it but the sandwich left a lot to be desired. The bread was pasty, the ham curling at the corner and the butter was as thick as the bread. She looked at it, raising her eyebrows and the pert tip of her nose unconsciously.

"The chef's night off?" she said.

Detective Ryan smiled. "Bon appetite, Miss Breslin!"

Maggie couldn't resist smiling and thanking her as she left the room in silence.

"Don't wind her up," the young guard said. "You'll need her on your side."

"I have no one on my side."

"Why do you say that?"

"It's true."

"What about your family?"

"I have a son. I suppose you know that."

He didn't answer immediately. "Margaret I need to caution you. You've asked for a lawyer so be careful what you say to me before he arrives."

"Its all right. We're just talking." For a moment Maggie paused and gathered her thoughts. "My son was adopted when he was a baby and he lives in Boston. He spent a week with me earlier in the year before my brother's death. He'll be back in a couple of weeks."

"Have you told him what's happening now?"

"No. He's under no obligation to look out for me. I don't want to become a burden just after he meets me."

"How did he find you?"

"He just turned up at our house. He found me through the Internet. Do you use the Internet?"

He laughed again. "I do, too much. My girlfriend is away at the moment and we spend all our time instant-messaging."

"Instant-messaging?" Maggie's natural curiosity kicked in.

"Yes. You know, I type to her and I can see my questions and her responses. It's like she's right there – but I miss her smile."

"Will she be away long?"

"Another week. Then I'm never letting her out of my sight again."

"Oh no. Don't say that."

"Why not?"

"A little break does people good. But you'll have a lot to talk to each other about when she gets back."

"You're a wise woman, Margaret Breslin."

"No, pet. If I were a wise woman I wouldn't be in here. I didn't kill anyone but I still landed myself in this situation."

"What happened tonight, Margaret?"

Maggie thought for a couple of moments and before she could change her mind she told him the whole story from start to finish. He listened to her without interrupting.

"Why didn't you tell anyone this before?"

"I thought after Pascal's death that they had their minds made up. I didn't want to be locked away."

"We don't lock people away, Margaret, without good reason."

"I've already been locked away without good reason – here I am now."

"I don't know what to say."

"You don't have to say anything. I wasn't brought in for a little chat, was I?"

"No. But you can help yourself by telling them exactly what you told me."

"Will that help?"

"It can't hurt."

"I wish I could believe that."

They lapsed back into silence.

Finally the door opened and Detective Grant came in alone. He spoke directly to Maggie.

"Margaret, it's too late to get anyone to speak with you tonight. You're going to have to stay here for a while. Come on, I'll get someone to show you where you're going to spend the night. Your solicitor will talk to you tomorrow."

Her chair was bolted to the floor. When she tried to push it back she banged her hipbone off the table. She felt tears pricking the backs of her eyes.

A female guard she hadn't seen before led her away and her young friend stayed behind.

Her heart was breaking into little pieces with each step. Her footfalls sounded hollow and empty and echoed back to her. She was led into a small room with a narrow bunk. The bunk was actually built into the floor and wall; it was like a concrete shelf. A toilet stood at the other end. She stepped in and turned to speak but the door had already closed behind her.

They'd searched her earlier and confiscated her bag and the contents of her pockets. She was wearing elasticised trousers – they'd even checked that, pulling out the band. She supposed it was in case she hung herself with her belt. They weren't as thorough as they thought, though. She was wearing nylon hold-ups under her pants with socks over those. It would be almost worth it to use those as a noose to spite them. Maggie knew from experience how effective those could be. They obviously didn't know her history from the laundry.

She thought she wouldn't sleep at all but she did and needed to be awakened next morning for breakfast. Her watch said eight o'clock. She couldn't believe it.

Insomnia certainly wasn't one of her failings – even this experience couldn't keep her awake. As she chewed on her toast she found her mind indulging in a fantasy of room service eaten amongst crisp cool white sheets in a hotel room. Some day soon she was going to do that, she promised herself, even if she had to sell her soul. A trip alone to a country house hotel would be a dream come true.

After breakfast she was left alone again with her thoughts. She asked when she could speak to someone but the officer on duty just smiled at her and closed the door. Finally, approaching lunchtime, the door was opened and she was led outside and back to the room she'd occupied yesterday. A man she'd never met before was waiting for her. He shook her hand.

"Margaret. I'm James Rowe, your solicitor."

"Mr Rowe, I've never heard of you. I think there's some mistake."

"Your son has retained me, to represent you."

"My son!" Maggie's heart sank. She'd so badly wanted to keep all this from Michael. "How did he know?"

"Your family solicitor contacted your brother Brian in New York but as neither of them are criminal lawyers they felt they couldn't do an adequate job for you. Brian contacted Mr Reynolds and they will be here later today. They're both flying in this afternoon."

Maggie couldn't speak. Finally she sat down and looked at her hands spread flat on the table. "How did he find Michael?"

"His engineering business is listed as Reynolds Engineering. Your brother wouldn't be much of a lawyer if he couldn't figure out that much."

"I don't want Michael to see me like this. I wanted to be out before he got back."

"Margaret! That's the attitude that got you in here."

She frowned. "What do you mean?"

"You kept a lot of secrets from everyone. I can help you if you talk to me."

"How?"

"I've talked to the police. After your conversation with Guard Leahy yesterday they decided to have a chat with Jason Blaney."

"What did he say?"

"He denied everything. Tell me again what happened, including the night of your brother's death."

That's what she did, in the most minute detail she could. He listened silently.

"Margaret, we have a lot of work to do but right now we need to get you out of here."

"Can I go home?"

"No, Margaret. At the moment it's a murder scene. We're also checking that old house you were referring to. We need to examine the paint tin and the shed you and the dog were in. Don't worry."

Maggie wasn't feeling very reassured.

By late afternoon Maggie was released. But they said they would certainly need to speak to her again.

Maggie left the police station in the company of

her brother. Michael wasn't going to be in Letterkenny for another couple of hours. Maggie would rather have multiple teeth extracted today than speak to him. She was burning up with shame. Brian tried to talk to her but she had retreated back inside herself again. It was five o'clock when they got everything sorted and they could both leave.

"Okay, Mag's! We need to get you to your hotel."

Her eyes frozen in pain, she looked at him. "Brian, I have no money. I don't know what to do."

"Darling, it's all right, we're taking care of everything, Michael and I."

Michael's name piqued her interest. "Have you met him?" An unexplained pang of jealousy pierced her.

"No. I just spoke to him on the phone. He seems like a good guy."

"He is. How am I ever going to pay him back?"

"Will you stop worrying about the wrong things, Margaret Breslin," he said in exasperation, "and worry about the important issues of life?"

"Like what?" Her brother's sharp tongue had surprised her.

"Food for a start! I've come all the way from New York and if someone doesn't feed me soon I'll pass out."

At last he raised a smile in Maggie.

"Come on then," she said. "Where will we go?"

"The hotel until we find something more permanent for you."

"But a hotel!"

"Maggie, you're turning into a parrot. Yes. A hotel. You're not sleeping on the street."

They covered the short distance to the Beachwood in a few moments. Brian had already checked them into two rooms so they just collected their keys and went straight up. They stopped at his room first and he nipped in and came out with a large paper Dunnes Stores bag.

At Maggie's door, she stopped, reached up and kissed him on the cheek. "Thanks."

"Go on, have a bath. I'll be back in fifteen minutes and we'll go get some food. Oh here!" He looked uncomfortable and handed her the bag. "I got a girl in Dunnes to put this together for you."

Maggie took the bag and went into the room.

What a day! This was the first time she'd ever stayed in a hotel and it came about by the death of someone who was probably an innocent trying to protect her. Why did she press that button on the phone? Then she remembered that technically she hadn't. It was an accident. Maggie wasn't religious but she couldn't help believing in a guiding hand. It didn't always make sense but one day when the master put the finishing touches to the canvas, then it would all become clear. She wondered if that was just the Irish way. Were we searching for meaning that made sense to us or was there really divine intervention? Perhaps Trudy would bear a son some day and he would produce the cure for cancer but why didn't all this happen without the misfortune of others? It was cold comfort for Alan if

Maggie's life brought about a medical miracle. Surely there was a more direct route that wasn't littered with the wrecks of others? Nothing made sense to Maggie tonight but her gut was growling for sustenance. Awareness could wait.

Chapter 28

Maggie looked in the mirror. She'd showered and changed into the clothes that Brian bought for her. She felt like a million euro despite the circumstances. He'd included toiletries and make-up; it was obvious he'd forgotten which sister he was buying for but she appreciated that more than anything. Olivia would have bought the basics, knowing that Maggie wouldn't be used to anything else. She showered in dewberry gel almost sweet enough to eat and plastered herself in a matching body lotion. Even the underwear fitted perfectly. They did say gay men had a good eye. That made her think of Pascal again – was he really gay or was that more of Jason's lies? At this stage she had no idea what to believe.

Brian had included a long blue dress, which was plain but nicely cut, and the blue brought out the colour of her eyes. She always knew there was a fey element to her family. It was as though a hint of her was right there with him when he was shopping. With her new hairstyle and clothes she felt elegant. The lady in the mirror smiled at her through a light touch of make-up. Michael wouldn't know her. Suddenly she smiled broadly at herself. For the first time she thought that he wouldn't be here if his mother wasn't an attractive woman. She pushed back the mantra she'd been taught over the years: that beauty was her downfall. Tonight she looked a lot younger than she'd done the day Michael left her; maybe she could become a woman he'd be proud to call his mother. Damn it, she thought, the tears were threatening again.

The evening was cold. She brought the cardigan she'd had on in the cell with her. She kept her own shoes as well; she wasn't ready yet for the delicate heels Brian had included. Her feet were moulded for flats, regardless of what the rest of her looked like. Maggie left the room and walked to the elevator. She smiled serenely at an American couple; they grinned back at her showing four rows of perfectly proportioned white teeth. I'm just out from questioning for double if not treble homicide, she thought. Suddenly she wanted to laugh out loud but managed to hold it in.

Maggie stood in the elevator, eyes glued to the crack in the centre of the door. In her imagination she could see the next day's headlines: *'Killer Living It Up In Luxury'*. What a mess! When she stepped out of the elevator, she turned towards the lobby. Brian was sitting there and she recognised the back of Michael's head. Suddenly all her strength disappeared. This time her beautiful son was coming to meet his mother out of prison. She was standing on the edge of the lobby, frozen in mortification, about to turn and go back upstairs when Brian saw her.

"Hey, sis!"

Michael turned to look at her.

For what seemed like an eternity Maggie and Michael were bonded in a gaze that shut out the rest of the room. His face was serious and intense and seemed to appraise every little detail of her. Maggie just stared. He looked even more wonderful than the last time. Brian discreetly stood back and let them get on with it. Finally Michael's smile came out like a break in a bank of grey clouds and lit up the room. He strode towards her. "Hey! You look wonderful! Despite everything!" He put his arms around her and held her.

"I'm so sorry!" Maggie was starting to weep.

"For what!"

"What must you think of me?"

"My God, you don't imagine I thought for a second that you did any of the things they said you did?"

"Why not?"

"You're not a killer, Maggie Breslin. Come on, don't be so silly! We'll have dinner and talk."

"Don't you think, Michael, it would be better if the three of us had room service sent up to my room?"

"No. We won't go out on the street but the dining room will be okay. Don't worry. We'll be with you."

Luck was with Maggie that night. The room was quiet and the only people there were hotel guests from out of town who didn't seem to know who she was. But all the staff were local and she knew that in less than an hour the whole town would know the killer was residing in the hotel. At first they avoided the subject most on their minds and talked about Brian and Michael's life in America. Maggie listened to her big brother talk openly for the first time.

"You're quite successful, aren't you?" she said wonderingly.

"I suppose I am. I'm no Fortune Five Hundred but my business is doing well. I have a nice apartment and a good lifestyle. Don't worry, sis, I can more than adequately look after you."

Maggie felt a stab of embarrassment that sent her rocketing back to the days of her drab brown coat and smock dresses. Her fine clothes and cosmetics seemed to melt and she saw Pascal and Olivia lurking behind the veneer of polish and sophistication surrounding her brother. Why did her family always reduce her down to this, a burden that it was their duty to carry?

Michael felt her embarrassment as acutely as if it happened to him and tears welled in his heart. Right then he knew his mother more intimately than anybody ever had before. In that moment of empathy he felt her pain and could see the years of hurt she'd endured. He vowed that he was going to find a way to repay her for his life and all she gave up because of him. Brian carried on smiling his way through his dessert, oblivious to his faux pas. Michael clasped Maggie's hand under the table and briefly held her eyes. That gesture gave her more pride than anything they'd experienced so far. With a son like this she was going to be all right.

When the waiter arrived with their coffee, Brian turned the conversation to the case.

"Maggie, Maggie!" He shook his head. "How did you get involved in all this?"

His talking down to her was really starting to grate but he was after going out of his way to help and she didn't want to embarrass him in front of Michael – at least he was trying. Nobody else had bothered to contact her.

But then in a moment she knew why: Brian had taken on the job. He was the representative for the family. Tonight he would go upstairs and report back to the others and let them know what was happening. He was the only one without family commitments, and he was a lawyer. She knew criminal law wasn't his thing, she thought it was contract law or something like that, but he would be able to understand more of the proceedings than anyone else. The others would be watching the outcome closely. If she were locked up they would probably start proceedings to sell the farm and split it, if they could.

How much should she tell Brian? She wasn't sure. She took a deep breath and told the whole story again from the moment Michael left the yard and Pascal locked her in until the moment she found herself in prison. They both listened intently.

"Maggie, it should have been obvious that he was manipulating you," said Brian. "You need looking after."

She opened her mouth to speak but Michael got there first.

"Why? Why should she have known? You just heard the same conversation I did and I certainly can't see how she would have known."

"Well, he was obviously unstable."

"Really! Was he indeed? What do you base that on?"

"Well, at the end, when he knocked out Alan."

"At the end!" Michael spat the words in sarcasm. "It's a bit late to try and alter a course of action at the end, don't you think? At that point I see a woman who took a calculated risk. If she knew he was capable of murder, then it seems obvious that he could kill her. She was buying time. Look at her! Do you think she could overpower a young man in his twenties who labours for a living?"

"That's my point! She's not capable of looking after herself."

Michael scoffed outright at that. "Brian! Alan was a grown man over six feet and well built. He was strong and aware that this person was dangerous. He didn't survive him. Jason is cunning. Maggie did the best she could – and survived."

"Look, I don't have to listen to this after coming all this way to help. I'm going upstairs. Goodnight, Maggie." He tossed his neatly coiffed hair, grabbed his jacket and left the room.

"Well, you blew his cover certainly," said Maggie.

"Sorry. Did I cause you more problems?"

"No, pet. It's fine. They're all in it together. Jason

was right about that. They would lock me away again in a heartbeat. They come from another generation. If I'm found innocent they will probably find a nice little retirement home somewhere paid out of my share of the farm and they can enjoy the rest of it. They don't think they're doing a bad thing. If I'm guilty . . ." She never finished the sentence – it just hung in the air.

"They have two of us to deal with now, Maggie. You're not a girl alone with a new baby. We're both adults."

Maggie picked up his hand and kissed the palm of it. "You're the best thing I ever did."

They sipped their coffee for a while in silence.

"What are we going to do about a place for me to stay? And then my court case?"

"Well, for a start I'm going to rent you a house tomorrow. Can you drive?"

"No."

"All right, it will have to be in Letterkenny. Is that okay with you? It will mean you won't be dependant on anyone. We won't use any money from your family so you won't be under any obligation."

"I don't know, Michael. I'm very embarrassed that you and your family are seeing me like this."

"Don't be daft. We're glad to do it. Come on, we'll go to bed now. Tomorrow we're going house hunting."

At first a house seemed like the best option but most of the houses were too big or in bad repair. They started to look at apartments next and finally they saw the perfect one. It was a two-bedroom and quite cosy. After they moved her clothes and some of her things to it, it looked like home. Secretly she was happy to be in town. Her neighbours had let her down. She knew it wasn't their fault, but she was still a little hurt. The only two she'd trusted were Seán and Jason: a boy who was murdered and the other who probably did it.

In town she was near the shops, the cinema and her coffee shop. She wondered if they would still welcome her after this fiasco but to her amazement Alberto sat Michael and her at the best table and ordered them a bottle of wine on the house.

"Either he really thinks I'm innocent or he's a ghoul."

Michael laughed. "Grab it with both hands – you need your friends."

"Friends like Jason Blaney?"

"Well, not him."

With her apartment sorted and lunch out of the way, next they had an appointment with her solicitor.

Maggie got up and excused herself. "I must brush my teeth."

Michael started laughing again. "Do you need to announce that?"

"I don't want the man to think I'm an alcoholic."

"As opposed to being a murderer?" Michael's eyes twinkled.

"Don't be smart." Maggie feigned annoyance but the shine in her eyes matched his. "Go on then, Mom. Hurry up."

Mom, she thought, walking away. I'm a mom. No matter how many times she said it she couldn't believe it.

Her solicitor had to drive up from Dublin to meet her.

"Couldn't we find anyone nearer to home?"

"He's the best."

"How do you know, living in Boston?"

"There's a lot of Irish in Boston and he was well recommended by many of them."

"But he does homicide. What sort of friends do you have in Boston?"

"You'd be surprised."

She was and it was genuine.

He laughed again at her face. "Come on." He grabbed her elbow. "He's expensive."

"How expensive?"

"He's too expensive to keep him waiting but don't worry about it."

"That's no answer."

"Will you come on?"

"All right, all right!"

They were still arguing when they entered the room.

Mr Rowe shook her hand. "It's nice to meet you again, Margaret."

"Mr Rowe."

"Call me James, Margaret, please?"

"James." She smiled.

He was doing a good job of breaking the ice. They sat down and he had a pot of tea and some chocolate biscuits brought in. When they each had a cup and Maggie had stopped shaking, they got down to business. The first thing she had to do was repeat her story again from the beginning. Every so often she had to stop and answer questions if things didn't make sense. By the time she got to the end he was deep in thought.

"Margaret. Go back to the night Pascal locked you in. Tell us again, in detail."

She repeated it again.

When she had finished James Rowe was silent for a while, lost in thought. They waited. At last he spoke.

"Margaret, your visitor at the door that night – you think he killed Pascal?"

"Yes."

"Okay. So let's say Jason was the intruder. He enters the house and hears you banging and shouting and trying to get out. Did you make much noise?"

"At first, yes."

"Your noise would have masked the noise of him entering. So he enters the house and you are in the room and Pascal is going to bed. In a high wind and over your own yelling you heard nothing."

"I suppose so."

"He enters Pascal's room. Pascal would have realised his first inhaler was out and gone looking for the second one. Supposing he has the inhaler in his hand and he has his back turned to the door. He's upset over his fight with you so he has an attack. Did he have them often?"

"Yes, at times."

"So he is using the inhaler or is about to and then he turns and Jason is in the doorway. There is a good possibility it would have worsened his attack and distracted him from the inhaler and possibly he collapsed. The police suspected it was possible that Pascal's death wasn't an accident. There was some trauma to the hand that Pascal held the inhaler in. It could mean that someone stood on his hand and stopped him from using it. That's what the police suspected but they couldn't prove it. The coroner said it could also be a spasm that caused him to clench tighter on the inhaler. His hand was bruised inside where the plastic pressed on his flesh but the back of his hand was only slightly marked. So after he gets rid of Pascal he goes out and torments you and has been brainwashing you ever since."

"But, why get rid of Pascal?"

"We don't know yet. He's manipulative and unstable and very clever. Tell me, did he prompt you in the conclusions you came to?"

"I can't remember. Maybe he did. He's the only person I spoke to and he did give me advice. I just don't remember if he led me." She gasped. "The hood!"

"What?"

"I told you I walked out and saw him in the kitchen with either a balaclava or some kind of hood over his head. If Pascal saw that in the night in the middle of an attack it would be enough to make him collapse. And that would explain why I didn't hear any raised voices from Pascal's room. Nobody spoke the night I saw him in the kitchen. I was too scared and he probably didn't want to be recognised."

"How come you didn't recognise his voice when he taunted you from outside the house or on the phone?" Michael asked.

"I always thought it sounded muffled. He was probably talking through something."

"Were you guys always close to him? How did he end up spending so much time with you?"

"We knew him and he was around from time to time. The first night the prowler was outside I got scared and called his mother."

"Why her?"

"There's three men in that house. Eddie down the road isn't very big and poor little Seán was only a lad."

"So that first night Jason and his brother came over," James kept probing.

"Yes. But the prowler was gone when they got here."

"What a surprise! Do you think the brother is involved too?"

"I don't know. I don't think so. I mean their mother sent them over when I called and the prowler was outside then so they couldn't be in two places at once. Unless Jason was already there and Dan was at home . . . at least one of them must have been at home or Dolores would have told me they were out." She paused. "You know, I dreamt one night after Seán disappeared that there were two people involved in taking him away. Then I realised that the person who stood in my kitchen was smaller than the one I saw by the door that night. Maybe I'm mistaken. I don't know."

"Possibly he was – or perhaps it's just intuition."

"Seán didn't like him. There was something on his mind the last night he was up with me. He said Jason was a dark one. That night Seán was worried about a fight he'd had with his dad. He'd seen him some time ago crying as he looked at old photos and he got annoyed when he realised Seán was watching him."

"Maybe just embarrassment," James said. "But why did Seán bring it up that night?"

"I don't know. I got the feeling Seán thought his dad was sorry his first wife didn't live. That Kate and her children were a consolation prize. Perhaps it was playing on his mind. I told him he was being silly." For a moment emotion choked Maggie. "You know, Jason didn't like him either. He said he was a little twit and immature. He asked me why I bothered letting him come up. He asked me did he annoy me. I said no. He was just young. I enjoyed his company."

Michael looked thoughtful. "Perhaps Seán guessed something. Perhaps that's why he killed him."

"Maybe." James chewed the butt of his pen.

"Poor Seán!" sighed Maggie. "And poor Alan! Alan really was coming to warn me that night and I called Jason! Brian was right. I was easily manipulated."

"Margaret, he was just very clever and very disturbed."

"How do we get him?"

"I don't know." Michael's face had a worried frown.

"I was wondering, Margaret," said James, "how safe you are now?"

Maggie was wondering that too.

Chapter 29

Maggie couldn't get thoughts of Jason out of her head. She was humiliated that she had been so easily manipulated. He'd led her by the nose since the night he'd come over to her house. His concern, his interest in her life was all phoney. She should have guessed. What did an older woman have to offer a young man like that in the way of friendship? But as the days slipped by and turned into weeks she found it harder to see herself as old. She had cable TV in her new flat. She could walk to the shops as often as she wanted without arranging a lift. Every morning she went to her coffee shop for a quick cappuccino. She got into the habit of starting her day with the paper and a gossip with Alfredo. The mantle of victim wore thinner every day until she had to concentrate to keep focused on her situation. She was having regular meetings either on the phone or in person with her solicitor and even they were turning into occasions. She found herself laughing out loud without thought. At first it was like a puppy's first bark – it took her by surprise popping out of her like that.

The thing that was hardest to deal with was losing Sheila. The poor old dog would be lost in Letterkenny. Maggie worried about her until Brian came back with the news that the night the police took her away, Sheila wandered down the road and moved into Eddie's barn. Despite her owner's possible misdeeds Eddie didn't hold the dog responsible and by all accounts she was very happy. In her heart Maggie knew Sheila was a man's dog and would be happier with Eddie. She put up with Maggie because Pascal was gone. Maggie had brought the cat with her – she couldn't bear to lose everything. They both had to get used to confined spaces and litter boxes.

Michael checked out of the hotel as soon as they found Maggie's apartment and he moved into her spare room. He took a pen and paper and made a list of everything she needed. He brought as much as he could from the house and bought the rest in the town. Maggie had more appliances in this little space than they ever had in the house. She had a new washing machine and tumble drier combined. There was a dishwasher, which to her was a total waste. After seeing the glow on Michael's face as he demonstrated it for her, all she could come up with was a feeble "I haven't got enough dishes".

"Oh, I forgot!" and he unveiled an ovenproof, dishwasher-safe forty-piece tea set. "I got tan to match the kitchen tiles."

Maggie took a quick glance at the tiles. He was

right – they did match. How did he remember that? Most men she knew, if you asked them to close their eyes in the kitchen they'd have forgotten what colour the tiles were.

"I'll have the microwave mounted on the wall by tomorrow – they're ordering in the brackets for me."

"I don't need a microwave."

"It's good for leftovers."

"I never have leftovers. That's why I brought my scales, for measuring."

"Oh, Mom, you worry too much. Let's go out for dinner."

"But, pet, you bought me all these cooking utensils and now we're going out to dinner?"

"You'll have plenty of time to cook."

"I'll get my coat then."

Michael flicked on the television as she got ready. Maggie felt like she was playing house. Her bedroom was cream and white. The units were built in and very plain, just as she liked them. There was so much space. She had bought a little bunch of fresh flowers for each of the rooms. Hers were daffodils and they sat on the edge of her dressing table. The moment something was moved out of place Maggie had to move it back. Everything was placed for maximum beauty and enjoyment. She kept sitting in different places and looking around at all the corners and nooks to make sure there were no ugly places or clumps of clutter. Maggie was never going to accumulate again. Life was better stripped down.

That night after a delicious dinner in yet another

restaurant she'd never been to before, they sat together and watched television. Maggie had a lump in her throat. She had to keep swallowing. This was the best time of her entire life. She didn't miss Pascal or her home. Everything was perfect now. She had her own home and her son. Michael had just been talking to Trudy on the phone. He was going to stay until his children came to visit. They'd all been due to visit in a few weeks anyway. They would be with her for two weeks and then they were all leaving again.

She was trying to forget that the apartment was only rented and her family lived elsewhere. She was going to really make the most of their time together and cherish the memories.

"Are you all right?" Michael looked at her serious face with concern.

"Just thinking."

"Don't do that." He misunderstood her. "There's nothing to be scared of. You have an unlisted number and we'll be with you for a few weeks. Something will turn up before then. If Blaney has murdered three people, he's bound to make mistakes."

"Do you think so? He's been one step ahead of me all along."

For a few minutes they were silent. Michael was thinking again.

"This time you can come back with us if you want to."

Maggie's heart started to pound. In one of its secret places she'd hoped he'd say that but it was a big step.

"I can't do anything until all this is sorted out. We'll see what happens then."

The next week went by in a blur of day trips, shared meals and conversations. Maggie told him stories about her life and he told her about his.

Finally Michael had to call a halt to the feeding Maggie was giving him. She was in the process of killing him with kindness.

"My cholesterol will be off the charts."

"It's only a few cooked breakfasts."

"Every day since I got here – my heart can't take it."

"We'll go for a walk after breakfast and we can burn it off."

They got their coats and left the building. It was only eight thirty so the roads were choked with early-morning commuter traffic.

"We'll go up through the town and up the long lane by the hospital."

"Whatever you say."

"It's nice up there. It's a small road so we might escape some of the traffic. There's a good hill so you can burn off your breakfast."

Michael was amazed at Maggie's stamina. The roads were taking more out of him than her. When they were well outside the town and the last house was behind them Maggie felt like she was back in the country again. She needed this. Just a little taste of her other world. They stood leaning on a gate looking across the fields.

"I'd be happy to go back with you when all this is sorted out. If you still want me."

"You know we do."

"I don't have a lot of time to drag my heels."

"Maggie Breslin, you've got to stop saying that."

She looked at the ground.

"You're only seventeen years older than I am. You're sixty. How can you think you're old?"

She examined his face closely. They could hear traffic in the distance; it was almost drowned out by a rookery of crows high above their heads.

"I believed I was old."

"I don't understand what you mean."

"It was like rot. I felt like I was trapped inside a rotting body and it was going to give out before the girl inside got a chance to live. But I feel younger every day now. I'm just afraid. Things keep changing and they could start changing back. Now I'm open, open to everything good and bad. I don't want to let in pain and disappointment."

"There are lots of good things in the world as well. Just let yourself go. Hiding won't keep out pain and disappointment – it will keep out everything."

"What would life be like for me in Boston?"

"You'll have endless coffee shops – you can prowl around them all day. There are loads of parks – you can get a cup to go and sit and watch the world go by. You can get another dog you can walk and she won't run off to the neighbours. You can get a job."

"I haven't had a job since I was in the laundry."

"You need to erase that memory for a start. You could even do volunteer work."

"Volunteer work? Around here only millionaires or people looking for work experience would do that."

"What are you good at, Maggie?"

"I don't know. I haven't tried much."

"You're a good cook."

"Simple foods!"

"Maggie, I've wanted to say this for the last few days but I don't want to insult you." Maggie's face dropped and she felt a sudden pain in her gut. She tried to brace herself for what he was going to say. It had to be bad.

"Maggie, my parents are dead, my adopted parents." He faltered again.

"I know what you mean." She laid her hand on his arm. "They were your parents."

"They are both dead and my wife is dead. My wife's mother died when she was young and her dad lives in New York. I'm floundering as much as you are, Maggie. I have two almost grown children and they're my total responsibility. I have to work very hard to make sure they have everything they need financially but I neglect the home badly. The house is cold and uncared-for. We never have a home-cooked meal. All the house responsibilities fall on Trudy. She's starting school soon. What I'm trying to say is we need you to live with us and bring the life back into our home."

Maggie was stunned. The beginning of this conversation suggested something completely different than this.

"I've insulted you, haven't I?" he said. "I should never have asked you that."

"I don't understand what you mean. Are you asking me to help you look after your family?"

"I am. They need a mother but a grandmother is just as good. I don't mean you to be a servant for us. We can all pitch in and we have a housekeeper that comes in three mornings a week. But she only does the basic cleaning. She doesn't add any personality. I'm very bad at this. I don't want you to think I'm doing a Pascal and expecting you to give up your life."

Maggie interrupted him. "Don't be silly. My home with Pascal was a grim place."

"We have a totally different life than that in mind for you, Maggie. You don't have to lift a finger if you don't feel like it. Just cook some of these delicious meals you've been fattening me up with!"

Maggie's eyes shone now. She was going to be a grandmother. She was going to look after her family. Maggie wasn't going to be alone.

"I'd be honoured." She was too choked up to say anything else.

"You might change your mind when you get there. We can be demanding."

"I'll get the dog in that case and I'll spend my time with him."

Michael hugged her. "We'll get you a dog anyway, maybe a Boston terrier – you'll love them. Come on, I'm freezing, let's go get a pot of tea."

The temperature had certainly dropped. The

bushes were high on either side of the road and swayed long shadows over them. The sky had darkened and any moment now the clouds were going to burst open. They hurried, making better time as the roads were all downhill. They were both quiet, examining their own thoughts. When they got to the roundabout at the hospital a car went around the complete circle and then again. As they headed down the Port Road the car pulled up beside them. Maggie turned as the driver rolled down his window. She thought it was someone asking for directions.

The smiling face of Jason looked out at her.

The smile consumed the bottom of his face but for the first time Maggie was aware of his penetrating eyes. She wondered why she'd never noticed that before.

"Maggie. I was worried about you. How are you?" His voice was even.

"Jason! I'm fine. I'm living in the town now. Home is a lonely place without friends."

"I was looking after you."

"By running out on me with Alan dead in my utility room!"

"Maggie, I saved your life that night. I panicked when I realised what I did. He could have hurt you."

"You hit him with a shovel. He was only talking to me."

"Why did you call me then?"

"It was an accident."

"An accident. How do you accidentally call someone?"

"Like you accidentally called the police and sent them up to me." Maggie was standing square, glaring into the car.

For a moment he stared back. "That wasn't me. They got an anonymous tip. Why assume it was me?"

"You went to move his car and you didn't return. His car was still outside when the police came."

"Maggie," Michael said, "he just admitted killing him, in front of me."

"Prove that." Now the coldness of his eyes intensified and his voice hardened in direct contrast to his talk with Maggie. "You're just trying to save your *mom*. Who do you think would believe you?" He turned his head like a dog as he spoke, his lips curling over his even white teeth. He never took his eyes off Michael's. Maggie was shocked at the evident hatred.

"What evidence is there that I was even there that night?"

"None," Michael said.

"*Exactly!*" He pronounced the word with gusto as though he just proved a point and the vague smile returned. "I was at Duffy's."

"So was Alan," Maggie said.

Jason darted his quick blue eyes in her direction now.

"Alan came to warn me of danger. He heard two people talking under his window. He never got to finish. You hit him to shut him up."

"Two people, Maggie? First I'm out to get you and now there are two people."

"No wonder you got there on time," Maggie continued. "For some reason you knew he heard you. That's why he was speaking so urgently. He knew you were right behind him."

"If all that's true, Maggie, why didn't he go to the police?"

"I don't know. He'd still be alive if he did and you'd be in jail."

"Speculation, Maggie!"

"He came to warn me first in case you came to harm me."

"You misjudged him then, didn't you, Maggie?" He looked back to Michael and spoke in a conspiratorial voice. "Maggie hated Alan. She used to hide on him when he came to the door. She thought he was her prowler. Maybe he was, Maggie. If he wasn't, do you think you're still in danger? Maybe there were three of us." He burst out laughing. "We're multiplying." A car beeped behind him; he was causing a roadblock. "Got to go, I'm in the way. I'll see you around, Maggie."

They watched him drive away.

"He's insane, isn't he?" she said.

Michael was still looking after the car. "He's unstable, for sure."

"He gave himself away, didn't he, but we're not credible witnesses. He's so clever."

"We need to call James and speak to the police."

"What's the point? There's no evidence and it's my word against his."

"Over-confidence will bring him down."

Maggie looked at a spot behind his ear. "Maybe the mistake that gives him away is the one he'll make when he kills me."

Chapter 30

Maggie was cold. She always turned cold when she was upset. Jason her friend was now her enemy. Did he set her up to make her dependant on him? Why would he bother, she wondered.

Dolores Blaney was a good woman and she'd been a good friend. Jason's father was a reformed alcoholic. Maybe there was childhood trauma that contributed to this. She knew she was clutching at straws. Her father was an alcoholic who never reformed. He just chose not to drink and then went on massive benders. None of her family turned to violence because of it. Maggie believed that bad people made bad choices. She didn't believe in evil because she thought it left them off the hook. It made them the victim, the victim of a disease of the soul. Evil was something demonic that took them over. Something that needed to be cast out, like devils in to swine and then they were saved. No, Maggie saw a person who had two paths and chose the path of evil. No matter what Jason's circumstances were, he chose the path he walked on. The victims were Pascal, Seán and Alan.

It had been many days now since she'd spoken to any of her family. Brian stayed for two days. That was an awkward time. Once he knew she saw him as a spy and not her benefactor he seemed disturbed by her company. Maggie had always been the little one they had to look out for. Suddenly he was looking at a sixty-year-old woman with no use for him. They could have become friends but Brian didn't seem capable of that role with her. She felt bad about it. He was a good person, a kind person even, but the tools of his kindness were pity, charity and condescension. If he'd been more empathetic and understanding they could have got along.

Brian wasn't Olivia or Pascal and Maggie held no ill will towards him but he couldn't be allowed to steal her power and undermine her. She was never going to let that happen again. So she let him twist in his confusion and allowed him to go home, his thoughts jumbled. He'd come over with such purpose, determined to save the day and reach out to his new nephew. He was going to be charitable and Maggie stole the opportunity from him.

That afternoon Maggie and Michael tried to put Jason out of their minds. Father Landers phoned Maggie after lunch. He was visiting a parishioner in St Patrick's. Brian had given him her number. Typical, Maggie thought. I won't let him undermine me himself so he gets someone else to do it.

The priest arrived at two-thirty.

"Maggie, how are you?"

"I'm fine, Father. Sit down. I'm just making tea."

"No." Michael stood up. "Both of you sit down. I'll get it."

"Thanks, Michael." Maggie knew the priest made him uncomfortable. He needed something to keep himself occupied.

"How's everything back home, Father?" she asked.

"Fine. Kate isn't doing too well. People are worried about her."

"In what way?"

"Just rumours. I don't want to spread gossip."

"Is she ill?"

"No. She's just out a lot."

"Oh."

"How's Eddie?"

"He's retreated into a shell. He doesn't talk to anyone and he never attends Mass now. He misses your family, I think. Brian spent a bit of time with him. I had tea with them. Brian got back all right?"

"He did, Father. It was only a flying visit."

"Two trips since Christmas under bad circumstances." He shook his head sadly. Maggie nodded. What could she say?

There was silence as they waited for the tea.

"The flat is lovely."

"I like it here. It's still quiet but I can get around

without help. It makes a big difference to be close to shops and that."

"Have you been meeting many people?"

"No."

The silence returned.

After a few minutes he turned to her. "Don't turn your back on everyone, Maggie."

"Father, I'm turning my back on no one. Nobody has contacted me since . . ." Her voice trailed away.

"They don't know what to say. They ask me about you all the time."

"Nosiness, Father!"

"Maybe they care."

"Who asked?"

"Dolores was very worried about you."

Alarm bells started ringing in Maggie's head. "Dolores?"

"Yes."

"Your neighbours care. Jason has been keeping an eye on the place with Eddie."

"Jason is the cause of all this. I saw him kill Alan. I suspect he killed Seán and maybe Pascal. Do you think I'm lying?"

"Maggie, nobody thinks you're lying."

"So I'm just losing the plot and lashing out at people who come to my door at night?" The priest looked very uncomfortable and lowered his eyes to the ground. "If there is anything you'd like to discuss with me, Maggie, I'm here."

Maggie had to count to ten before she said something

she'd regret. She decided to ignore his hint for her to make her confession.

"Who called the police that night, Father?"

"Kate did."

"What?"

"She saw Alan drive like a maniac up your road in his car. She didn't see him come back. She walked onto the road to see if she could hear anything and she heard shouting coming from your house. She was understandably cautious after what happened to her family so she called the police."

"Was the shouting between yourself and Alan that loud?" Michael asked.

"I don't know. It seems loud in my head but I don't know if it was in reality. It must have been though. But why didn't she see Jason follow him?"

Again the priest lowered his eyes and stared at his shoes.

Maggie pinched the loose skin on the back of her hand. "Jason swung the shovel and I'm being looked at for murder."

Father Landers looked even more uncomfortable and struggled to answer.

"Father. how could I have hit him so hard? He was over six feet. Even the police don't believe I did it. I think they feel I'm involved or hiding something. Three suspicious deaths in or around my yard since Christmas. I know I'm innocent and even I find it hard to believe I wasn't involved. Do you know if Jason has even been questioned?"

"Oh, he was questioned all right. Of course he'd have to be. But they must have been satisfied with his answers. Dolores would have called me if he were arrested. Maggie, I'm not saying you're guilty but I've spoken to Jason and he seems so sincere."

Michael was pouring the tea now but he was still deep in thought. "Kate called the police because a car goes up your lane and she hears some shouting. Isn't that a bit like overkill? I mean, people argue every day."

"She's just on edge. Her son was killed recently leaving Maggie's house. She was concerned."

"I suppose so." Michael still seemed distracted.

After Father Landers left, Michael turned to Maggie.

"What's this Kate like?"

"She's very nice. She's a friendly outgoing person."

"Is she young?"

"She is. Well, let me think. She's in her thirties some place. She's a nurse so she's very fit. She has a lovely figure, always wears nice clothes."

"Is she pretty?"

"She's very attractive."

"Why is she married to Eddie? You pointed him out to me. He's no oil painting. How old is he?"

"Eddie is a couple of years younger than I am."

"And he's married to a girl in her thirties . . ." Michael sceptically raised his eyebrows.

"Well, she's closer to forty and he's not yet sixty so I suppose there's maybe twenty years in the difference."

"Even so. Don't you think that's a bit unusual?"

"When they got married Kate was only twenty and Eddie was nearly forty. She's one of those strange women that appears to get younger with the years instead of older. She was settled and quite frumpish back then. She seemed older and Eddie seemed younger."

"The age gap is very noticeable now, is it?"

"Yes, it is. Now. What are you trying to say?"

"I don't know. It just doesn't seem right that Kate called the cops."

"Why would it be strange? She heard shouting."

"I don't know. Plus she saw Alan's car but she saw no sign of Jason."

"Maybe he walked up from the village."

"But you said he came from the pub after Alan. He could only have kept up with Alan in a car. Does she know Jason well, do you think?"

"The same as we all do, I suppose."

"Do you think there was something going on between Kate and Jason? I mean Eddie is twenty years older than her but Jason is almost twenty years younger. Maybe she's evening the score."

"That's a bit far-fetched, isn't it?"

"I don't know."

"Don't say 'I don't know' again!"

Michael jumped at her sharp tone.

Maggie got up, walked into her bedroom and slammed the door.

"Shit!" Michael said to the silent room. "Think, Michael, think!"

Maggie lay on her bed. Kate and Jason, it was a ridiculous thought. There was no evidence of it whatsoever. But it was a bit strange that she called the guards. Maggie thought back over the last few months. Was there anything different about Kate? The only thing she could think of was the day she found her creeping around the house. From the mountain she did look like she was creeping. It was only when she gave her explanation that it seemed normal. What was it she said? Alan called in and told her he was worried about Maggie so she went up and checked on her. That was the morning Alan peered through the window and frightened the life out of her. No. She couldn't think of anything besides that which made Kate a figure of suspicion. The only thing that was a little strange was the amount of time Seán spent with Maggie. It wasn't odd at the time but was Kate out all those nights? That would explain her anger towards Maggie, if she were away with someone . . . like Jason . . . She must be feeling very guilty, now that her only son was dead. Or! Maggie's mouth froze and her stomach squeezed into a little knot. Of course Michael could be right. Perhaps she is having an affair with Jason and now she suspected him of murdering Seán. Maybe she sent the police up when she saw Jason rushing past after Alan and the two cars turning up her lane.

The night that Seán disappeared he was thinking about that silly tiff with his father but he was also voicing his suspicions about Jason. Was there a connection? Did he know about an affair between Kate and Jason? Had Eddie found out and was that why he was disappointed with Kate and her children? Maybe he was looking at old photographs because life with Abigail wouldn't have led to that.

She'd told Seán he was wrong. That night she thought he was keeping something back from her. His little mind was troubled. Would he confront Jason or Kate? Questions were whirling around in her head. They didn't seem so strange now. A relationship with a younger man could account for her youthful bloom. It was really in the last few years she'd changed. It was around the time her daughter went to England. When she was around Jason would have spent a lot of time in the Molloy's. Himself and Rita were close friends in school. Maybe Jason and Kate comforted each other after she left.

Maggie came marching out of her bedroom. Michael opened his mouth to speak but she got there first.

"I want to go and visit the farm if that's all right."

"Sure."

"Now."

"Can I get my coat?"

"Sorry, Michael. I'm very upset."

"It will be dark soon, Maggie."

"Not for a couple of hours. We'll have a bit of time."

As they passed the Molloys' Maggie glanced at the house. There was smoke from the chimney but there were no cars outside and the house looked deserted. There was a line of washing in the orchard so Kate had been around recently. Eddie certainly didn't do laundry. Then she thought, of course Rita would be home. They turned up the lane and drove up to Maggie's house. As they entered the yard the house stood in front of them neglected and lonely. The house seemed to have darkened and absorbed all the negative atmosphere of the last few months. The windows looked blindly onto the yard. Maggie slowly stepped from the car and leaned against the bonnet.

She looked at the door and wondered if she could go inside. Her thoughts were disturbed by a sound at the mountain gate to her right. Eddie had opened it and stepped into the yard. For a moment nobody spoke. Maggie was the first to lower her eyes.

"Maggie."

"Yes, Eddie," she said softly.

"I know you didn't do it, Maggie. I've always known it."

The tears Maggie had held in check all evening spilled out and down her cheeks.

"How could I think you did it? I know you longer and better than I know my own wife."

"I haven't seen you since Seán, Eddie."

"No. Maggie, you know the one who did it. He's one of us. One of us, Maggie." Suddenly Maggie knew he was referring to Jason but he was finding it hard to put it in words.

"Eddie, this is Michael, my son."

"I've seen you around – I'm pleased to meet you." Eddie sniffed and stiffly held out his hand, the jacket flapping behind him. He looked more like a wounded crow than usual. He cleared his throat.

"Kate is away working. Would you like to come to the house for a cup of tea?"

"We'd love to," Maggie answered before Michael got a chance.

Chapter 31

The lane was dark now. The three of them got into Michael's car and drove to Eddie's house. Maggie was glad of that. She didn't think she'd ever be capable of walking this lane again without fear. As they passed the small junction to the Foy's farm she couldn't help glancing up the lane. She felt like she did as a child looking in the ditch for rats on her way to school even though she was terrified of them. But the lane was so overgrown and dark even a battalion hanging out there would be concealed in the shadows.

They parked the car and followed Eddie into the kitchen. Rita was inside with her back turned to them washing the dishes. Maggie remarked in her head on how mature she looked. She was barely twenty and from the back she looked like a middle-aged matron. She still wore her hair as usual in a tight little bun on the back of her head, sitting just above the line of her neck.

"The kettle's boiled." She spoke without pausing in her rinsing.

"Thanks," Eddie said, hanging his jacket on a hook by the door. He went into the utility room and rinsed his hands.

Maggie stood, willing herself to speak. Rita still wasn't aware of their presence.

Moments passed and Rita dried her hands on the dishtowel.

"I'll get your tea, Dad. You sit down." She turned to the table and her eyes opened in shock. "Maggie!"

"Rita, love. How are you?"

Rita blushed deeply. "I'm fine."

Eddie stood in the doorway. "Maggie was up at the farm. I invited her in for a cup of tea."

Rita stared pointedly at him but he seemed not to notice.

"Dad!" She was desperately trying to get something across to him.

"Maggie and Michael, sit down," he said, ignoring his daughter.

With panic in her eyes Rita grabbed his arm. "Mum is due back any minute."

"I know." He spoke in an even voice. "There's plenty."

"That's not what I meant."

"Rita, this is Michael, my son," Maggie said, hurrying to change the subject. It worked momentarily.

"Your son!"

"Yes. It's a long story. He was adopted when I was seventeen."

"I never knew."

"Nobody did."

"Maggie, I don't mean to be rude but this really isn't appropriate."

"You are being rude." Eddie's voice had risen an octave. "Maggie is staying for tea and that's that."

"Fine!"

Tea was poured in silence.

Maggie was sorry to drag Michael into this and he was looking very uncomfortable but the more she thought of Kate knowing something, the more it made sense. If she were honest she'd noticed that day she came off the mountain that something was different about Kate. She couldn't process it then. Kate was her friend. Could a mother really have something to do with her child's death?

"Is there any more of that rhubarb tart?"

"Mum made that."

"I know."

"I'd like a piece – and offer some to our guests."

In silent hostility Rita rose and got the dish. She cut a large piece for Eddie and two small ones for Michael and Maggie.

"No, I'm all set," Michael said.

She slapped it onto his plate nevertheless. She stood for a moment with her eyes fixed on the tablecloth and the usual rosiness of her cheeks had receded to mere dots. Her eyes were narrowed to slits.

"Sit down, Rita."

"No, Dad. Until I know what happened to Seán, I won't eat with her."

"She had nothing to do with it."

"Maybe it was him." She turned her eyes to Michael.

"He wasn't even in the country."

The opening of the porch door caused them all to turn at once.

Kate stood frozen, looking at the assembled group in her kitchen. Her uniform was crumpled. There was a yellow stain on the front. Her cardigan hung open from her drooping shoulders. Dark circles made her eyes look like black orbs. Her face was gaunt and pale. Maggie was shocked. Kate usually looked so immaculate. Her uniform was always a pristine white. If she spilled something on it during the day she changed – she had a couple of spares in her locker. Maggie was expecting anger when they came face to face but instead she saw fear, distinct fear. Her eyes darted around and she looked like she was about to bolt from the room.

Eddie sat rigidly in his chair and went back to his food, ignoring the discomfort of his wife. Michael watched him closely. Whatever was going on Eddie had a gut feeling, at the very least, as to what it was or maybe they'd always had an acrimonious marriage. Rita went to her mother's side.

"Mum, sit down. I'll make you a cuppa."

"I think we'd better leave," Maggie said, standing up.

Michael stood up, relieved. "Yes, I think we should."

Kate didn't speak. She just walked to the chair by the range and sat down.

Maggie laid her hand on Eddie's shoulder. "Thank you."

He smiled. "We'll see you soon."

Rita sniffed as she poured the tea, then she turned her back on the visitors.

When they were in the yard and the door was closed behind them Michael turned to Maggie.

"Please don't ever do that to me again. That family is falling apart. I was never so uncomfortable in my life."

"I know." A smile lit Maggie's face. "You were right. Eddie was always gentle and considerate of Kate as long as I've known them. He's not a cruel person. Kate is a mess."

"Her child did just die, you know."

"I know but there's more to it than that."

"What?"

"I don't know. My eyes were closed for the last two months. Not any more."

"But do you believe the worst of everyone now so nothing takes you by surprise?"

Maggie felt uncharacteristic anger rising again. "You put the idea in my head."

"I know. I was throwing out ideas."

"Well, it was a good one."

They were still standing in the yard. Suddenly behind them, a volley of shouts erupted from the house. They couldn't hear the words but a full-scale war seemed to have broken out.

Maggie smiled again.

"What's so funny now?" asked Michael.

"Let's go," she said.

They got into the car and drove off.

A short distance down the road Maggie abruptly said, "Stop. Pull into that gateway there and turn all the lights off."

"What?"

"Please."

Michael did as he was bid.

Maggie opened the car door and got out.

Bewildered, Michael got out and joined her at the gate.

"Look!" she said quietly.

From where they stood they could see Eddie's house and yard.

"What do you expect will happen?" he asked.

"Just wait."

They were standing there for about five minutes and Michael was starting to worry about his mother's sanity when the door of the house opened and Kate ran across the yard. Michael chided himself for his lack of faith.

Rita stood in the doorway and shouted something after her mother but Kate stopped and gestured to her to go back inside. Rita hesitated and Kate shouted at her again. Rita turned and closed the door and a minute later her bedroom light came on. By that time Kate was heading up the road, oblivious to the two silent watchers.

"You sure shook up that house tonight," Michael whispered.

"I know." Maggie's face was alight again. "Now let's follow her."

"Are you mad?"

"No."

Before he could stop her she had set off up the road after Kate.

When they left the house behind, he whispered to Maggie. "What if we lose her?"

"It's all right. I know where she's going."

"Where?"

Maggie made no answer, just walked along the road. When they got to the end of her lane, she hesitated and listened. They could just hear a voice further on. They moved stealthily up the lane, Maggie leading the way. The wall of darkness was slowing Michael down – he was terrified of stumbling. Soon the voice became clearer and they could make out the words.

"Look, I'm sick of this. Hurry up."

Maggie could see a little glow up ahead and the outline of Kate's white uniform. She'd stopped and was talking on her mobile phone. The light faded and she started to walk again. They waited a while, then followed silently behind towards Maggie's yard.

They stopped at the edge of the yard, concealed in shadows, and watched. Kate crossed towards the house door. She took a key out of her pocket and opened it. She closed it behind her and a faint light could be seen through the window.

"A candle," Maggie whispered.

"Come on. Let's go see what she's doing."

"No. Jason will be along any minute. He's too dangerous to mess with."

"How do you know?"

Maggie didn't answer. She tugged at his sleeve, indicating the bottom of the yard. They went behind the pier of the gate and circled the yard from the outside. It took a couple of minutes because the ground was rough.

Directly below the house at the bottom of the garden Michael stopped suddenly and clamped his hand over Maggie's mouth. Her heart beating wildly, she grabbed the back of his hand. Her terrified mind couldn't even come up with a reason why he would do this. Then she realised that he was pointing to the bottom of the garden inside the wall. At first she was too scared to see anything. Her eyes were swimming in tears of fright but then she stopped struggling. A dark shape standing inside the wall appeared out of the haze and a tiny red glow of a cigarette proved its existence. He was here already. Oh my God, Maggie thought. He was checking to see if Kate was followed. She thanked God for her own quick thinking in circling the yard from the outside and Michael's sharp eyes. They stood like granite statues watching the tiny red light appear and disappear.

He didn't seem in any hurry. Finally when they thought they were all going to be there for the night he moved slightly. He pulled a mobile phone out of his pocket and the green glow lit his face like a Middle Earth creature.

His voice shattered the silence. "I'll be with you soon." Then he hung up.

He put the phone back in his pocket and finished his cigarette.

Maggie was starting to tremble and her heart was pounding. Michael wrapped his arms around her and willed her to keep still.

Finally Jason must have felt satisfied Kate wasn't followed as he moved towards the house. Only when he was safely inside did Maggie have the courage to let her breath out. Her legs gave way from under her and she sat on the ground.

"Are you all right," Michael asked, sitting beside her.

"I am. He's a clever little thing, isn't he?"

"He is," Michael agreed.

"We're not so slow either."

He silently thanked God for that. Michael still couldn't control his pounding heart.

After a couple of minutes Maggie's heart had slowed sufficiently to stand up.

"Well! Now we know. They're as thick as thieves."

Michael turned to her. "But how can we prove that?"

"I don't know. I want to go and see what they're doing."

"No way!"

"I have to."

"No!"

"But we've come this far!"

"Look, Mom, you stay there. I'll go. I'll be back in a moment."

"All right." Maggie had to admit if she had to run she wouldn't get very far. "Be careful."

"I will." He muttered the words, very unhappy with his plight.

Maggie pointed to the left. "There's a little gate down there. Don't use it. It creaks but the wall is low beside it and there are no bushes so you'll be able to climb over quietly. There's a line of shadow by the edge of the wall – follow that. Be very careful. If you're caught run as fast as you can. I know my way back through the fields. We'd be safer apart."

Michael hugged her and crept away. He felt like he did as a kid reading the Hardy Boys mysteries.

He kept to the shadows and gingerly climbed over the wall where Maggie told him. The wall was loose and he dislodged one of the stones. It fell to his side with a soft thud. His heart hammered as he waited in the darkness but no other sound came to him.

With the darkness embracing him he approached the porch. Again he halted and listened. He was just outside the front window of the porch. The porch was in darkness. Jason must have closed the door into the kitchen. He moved around the side of the porch and edged towards the kitchen window. He heard a bird call somewhere close to where he had left Maggie. He had to take a chance, so moving silently and swiftly he got to the lit window.

Kate was sitting in a chair facing the window. She was crying but softly. He couldn't see Jason. Where was he? he fretted. Five minutes or more passed. He was going to run as the fingers of fear massaged his spine but a sudden sinking feeling caused him to turn around. Could he have come out the back door and circled him? He stood back against the wall and listened, training his eyes on the shadows. Nothing suspicious could be seen but still that silent fear remained.

Michael turned and looked back into the room and there Jason was, standing by Kate's chair. A small puff of breath escaped through Michael's lips. He hadn't realised he'd been holding it. At first they were just talking. Jason sat against the table with his back to Michael. Kate's face was ghostly white in the light of the candle as she looked up at him. She looked young and vulnerable and totally in awe.

Jason extended his hand and smoothed the hair off her forehead. Her face broke into a hopeful smile. His caressing hand wound its way into her hair and he massaged her temple. She tilted her head towards his palm and closed her eyes, but immediately they opened in pain. He had grabbed a clump of her hair and now he dragged her out of the chair, pushing her roughly against the wall. In shame Michael continued to watch.

Jason pulled up her uniform and roughly prised her legs apart. One of his hands was pressed against her throat and with the other he unbuckled his jeans. Michael felt a ringing in his ears and an intense pressure on his bladder. He thought he was going to throw up.

When he was finished Jason retied his buckle and

sat back on the table. Kate was still against the wall like she'd been hung on a peg. After a moment or two she smoothed down her uniform and ran her right hand through her hair. She sat beside Jason. Michael had tears running down his face. He couldn't control them. A silent sob escaped when she smiled and laid her head against Jason's shoulder and he talked to her, smoothing her hair from her face and gently kissing her nose before patting her head and pushing her into a standing position again. They seemed to be gathering themselves to leave. Michael retreated back down the yard into the shadows.

Almost immediately he heard the door open. Jason and Kate walked into the yard and crossed towards the mouth of the lane. The last thing he saw was the white blur of Kate's uniform. He waited until they were well away and then he returned to where he left Maggie. He was careful this time not to knock down any more of the wall. He whispered to her as he got closer. There was no sound. He walked to the end of the garden wall, still no sound. He retraced his steps calling her name in a low voice, but she was gone. Maybe she got nervous and went back. She was slower than he was so maybe she thought it safer if she went ahead alone.

He turned towards the lane. He remembered the time when Jason wasn't in the room. Had he gone back and harmed Maggie? No. She'd be back at the car. It was cold. He walked towards the lane. Was he waiting for him down there now? The lane loomed dense and black. He was afraid to risk it. He climbed over the ditch into a field and then tried to figure out what direction he was facing. The moon had come out now and he could see the boundaries of the field he was in. Hoping he was going the right way he walked across the field towards where he thought Kate's house was. When he got to the opposite fence he heaved a sigh of relief. He'd been going completely wrong but now he could see the lights. Praying silently that Maggie was in the car he climbed over the fence and walked towards the house.

Chapter 32

Michael realised that he was in bad shape. His chest burned and he knew if it weren't dark, he'd be seeing black spots. He was in the field behind Eddie's house. If anyone caught him out here there would be no way to explain it. He circled the house and walked along the fence beyond it. The fence was high and overgrown and he couldn't find a way out. The blackthorn trees and furze bushes not only covered the fence but were encroaching on the field as well. The field was reclaimed from mountain and the mountain was trying hard to claim it back. Suddenly a stinging pain burnt its way across his shin and he was brought to an abrupt halt on his hands and knees in the damp grass. "What the hell?" He put his hand down and immediately withdrew it. The ground was crisscrossed with briers, which had grown from the fence and into the grass. They were as taut as a ship's ropes and he had fallen right over them.

Gingerly he picked himself up and continued on. When he got to the end of the field there was a gap in the other fence with a closed gate across it. He tested it for safety. It held fast. He climbed that and checked the next field. There he found a hole in the overgrowth where he could climb through. Branches tugged at his hair and scratched his face as he lowered himself onto the road. He hoped Maggie hadn't had to do that. He approached the car from the rear but even before he got there he knew she wasn't in the car. His stomach was heaving with fear.

Maggie had heard the thump of the stone when Michael dislodged it from the wall. She was too scared to breathe. At this point she thought Jason had some type of demonic power. He seemed able to anticipate her every move. It was dark where she stood and the trees were too dense to see where Michael walked. The night was silent again. Seconds ticked by, though it seemed longer and as she strained her eyes to catch a glimpse of Michael in the yard, a noise behind caused her to turn.

"You weren't long," she whispered.

A hood was lowered roughly over her head and a strong hand covered her mouth before she had the chance to call out. Everything was pitch black now and a sharp pain caused her ears to ring. Silence followed and Maggie's body lay limp against her attacker's torso.

Kate had been due to come up to the house to see him tonight, but neither of them had expected her visitors.

He knew Maggie. When he'd heard she was in the house with Eddie he knew she'd figured out about him and Kate and she wouldn't stop until she stumbled on proof. He guessed either her or *the son* would follow Kate. He heard them as they whispered on the edge of the yard. He thought they would just walk to the window, look into the house at Kate, wait for a while and when they realised she was alone leave. Not Maggie! She knew he would be there, so she'd circled the yard. He had to admit it was a clever move but of course he'd got there first. They didn't make a sound and he couldn't see them, but he could sense exactly where they stood. A Mexican standoff! At first he hoped they'd sneak away. Maggie was an old woman, for God's sake. But they obviously thought he'd no idea they were there. They thought he would obediently enter the house, then they could call the police.

He smirked to himself. Someone had to move. He walked quietly up to the house and entered and found Kate sitting at the table.

"What kept you?" She hissed the words at him.

He placed a finger against his lips and dug the fingers of his other hand into her shoulder.

"Ouch!" she yelped.

"Shut up. You were followed."

"Are you sure?"

"Yes. Sit there and act like I'm not here."

"What."

"You heard me." He increased the pressure on her shoulder.

"Okay. I understand." She turned back and once again concentrated on the crack on the table as he quickly and quietly let himself out the back door.

Nobody knew Maggie's yard better than he did. He knew every rock and weed. It took him less than a minute to silently skirt the yard and come up behind Maggie. He wanted to watch her but he didn't have the time. He'd taken a pillowcase from the utility room when he let himself out. It didn't take much to get the pillowcase over her head. Then he turned the side of his hand and used it to crack the back of her neck. That was how his father taught him to kill rabbits. It took a bit more skill to get a rabbit. They practically had eyes in the back of their heads. Maggie was more like a duck sitting patiently in the bushes. As soon as her legs crumpled he picked her up and moved swiftly along a narrow track which led away from Maggie's house and down the hill towards the fields behind Eddie's. She was a tiny little thing. He barely felt any extra weight. But he knew he couldn't take her too far. She wouldn't be unconscious for long. He stopped and put her on the ground. He had some builders' line in his pocket. He used that to tie her up and some tape to gag her. Putting the pillowcase back over her head, he deposited her behind some bushes. He'd come back for her later.

He quickly but silently made his way back to the house and stood watching Michael look in the window at Kate. There was so much to watch tonight and no time to enjoy it. As he moved *the son* must have sensed his presence because he turned, twitching in the shadows, trying to smell the air for intruders.

Jason moved quickly, going around the house from the other side to avoid detection and to make some time. The moon had come out in the last few minutes so he had to be more careful now. He entered the room in character and sat by Kate, turning his back on the window.

"Coast is clear."

Always the hunter, now he was being watched. He threw himself into the role. Kate's fear and surprise turned him on even more. He knew as he entered her that *the son* was still out there watching them. It was the most intense experience of his life. He really was becoming a master of manipulation. They were like putty in his hands. He didn't want Michael to feel too secure so he quickly gathered himself and Kate to leave. In his mind's eye, he could see Michael clambering along the wall back to Maggie, thinking they were calling the shots. His pleasure made him uncharacteristically affectionate. He wrapped his arms around Kate and kissed her. "I really enjoyed tonight."

"Me too," she said, though she didn't look too sure. Cracks were spreading like spider webs in her reality and she knew that pretty soon her world was going to implode. She was trying to hold on as tenaciously as she could to what was left. Jason had assured her he had nothing to do with Seán's death but somewhere in her soul a mist of doubt was penetrating. Despite his reassurances that's why she called the police that night to Maggie's; she convinced herself it was because of Alan but in her heart a deeper fear lurked.

Michael was sick with fear now. He went to the door of Eddie's house and knocked urgently on it. He felt terrible waking them up but he knew something was wrong. A light went on in a room upstairs and at the same time footsteps sounded on the gravel behind him. He whirled around and met the frightened eyes of Kate. The door opened and a spear of light cut through Michael and Kate, trapping them in its glare. It illuminated her eyes. They glittered and danced in her face as she took in the scratches and dirt on Michael's face. The tension in her was palpable from ten feet.

"Will someone tell me what's happened?" Eddie asked.

Kate brushed past them. "I'm going to bed."

Michael grabbed her wrist. "Maggie is missing. Jason knows what happened to her."

She halted immediately. "How would he know?" She tried to sound confident but her voice cracked.

"We followed you. He was waiting in the yard for us. He came in the front door, didn't he? Then he left straight away by the back. He was gone long enough to snatch Maggie."

She laughed. "Don't be ridiculous!" But then she seemed to doubt her own faith. "Where would he take her?"

"You saw him tonight?" Eddie asked.

She gave Eddie a cold look and once again went to pass. But he stood in her path.

"If he has Maggie you'd better tell us," his voice held an uncharacteristically harsh edge. He turned to Michael. "Tell me what happened."

Michael went red and looked at Kate.

"Tell me!" Eddie shouted. "You don't need her permission."

Kate swayed and leaned against the door. Her face was snow white and Michael felt real pity for her. He really didn't think she'd committed any greater sin than infidelity and blind faith. He could see the evidence of a deep struggle going on in her mind as she listened to what he had to say and tried to rationalise her own fears.

At last he gently touched her hand. "Does any of that sound like the actions of an innocent man?"

She shook her head with her eyes glued to the ground.

"Where did you leave him?"

"He walked me to the end of Maggie's lane and then he turned back. It's quicker back to his house cross-country."

"How did you ever get together with him?" said Michael.

She looked back at Eddie. "I didn't like my life."

Eddie stood there static in the doorway. Michael's eyes flicked from one to the other and in his mind's eye he could see a demure old-fashioned young woman meeting a steady older man who would take her out of her life and give her a home. But the home she needed was a step on the road, like school or college. Eddie had reached maturity; Kate was only beginning her journey. The home became a prison and Kate a bird trying to escape. He felt sadness and pity for both of them. But that would have to wait.

"Kate, we have to find Maggie. Haven't there been enough deaths up there?"

She flinched at the words. "Seán. Did he kill Seán?" Her eyes were round and glassy.

Michael ignored the question. "Where would he hide Maggie?"

Her lips were barely moving and the name of her son was just audible.

"We have to call the police," Eddie said. "We have to search for her now or she won't stand a chance. Kate!"

The sudden tenderness in his voice took her by surprise and she looked at her husband.

"Come inside and sit down," said Eddie. "You too, Michael."

Michael followed him and stood just inside the door. Kate sat by the dying fire. Eddie left the room and went to search for Rita to take care of her mother, leaving Michael and Kate alone.

"What did you see tonight?"

Michael blushed again.

"I thought so. He knew you were there."

"I guess so."

"Oh God!" She groaned and buried her head in her hands. "What have I done to everyone?"

Michael sensed a moment of self-pity and he didn't want to indulge that. He liked Kate better right now stripped of her defences.

"It can't be helped now, Kate. We need to focus on Maggie."

"Of course!" She hung her head again.

Rita and Eddie entered the room.

"Oh Mam!" She ran to her mother's side and knelt by her chair.

"I've called the guards," Eddie said. "Come on, I think we should go up to the house and look around ourselves. I have a couple of lamps here."

He held one out to Michael and they left the house side by side. They retraced Michael's steps from earlier that night, all the way to the yard. Then they took the same path around the perimeter to the spot where Maggie stayed when he left her. There was nothing there. The night was silent.

"Well, we know one thing."

"What's that," Michael asked.

"He took her from here and he went that way." A small narrow path no more than a sheep track stretched away from them disappearing out of the beam of the flash lamp, leading away from Maggie's house.

"How do you know?"

"If he went the other way you would have seen or heard him."

The simple logic of Eddie's words was hard to contradict.

"Where does it go?"

"Just goes on for a bit down the hill towards my land at a forty-five degree angle to Maggie's lane, then it doubles back and connects with Maggie's lane just at the end of Foy's Lane. There's a gateway there right opposite Foy's Lane blocking the entrance to the end of this path."

"I know where Foy's is. I don't think he had enough time to get that far."

"He's fit and fast. He used to run with Finn Valley."

"Is that an athletics club?"

"It is, produced a few good runners in its time. He was one of them, a nice child, friendly little fellow. Makes you wonder."

"Eddie, we haven't time to wonder. Come on."

"Right."

They followed the path Jason must have taken. There were some semi-dried puddles on the path, which were studded with deep footsteps that looked fresh. They would be deep if he was carrying someone. Towards the end of the path the ground became firm and stony and they lost the footprints. The two men opened the gate and crossed the main lane and stood at the base of Foy's Lane. It was pitch dark up there and overgrown.

"Do you really think we should go up there yet?" Eddie asked. "The police should be along any minute."

"That could be too late. There are two of us."

Secretly they both thought one and a bit, but they ploughed ahead anyway.

They turned the torches off as they got to the gate. The house looked like a skull in the moonlight. They stood and listened but could hear nothing except a fox barking in the distance.

"I don't think he's here," Eddie whispered.

They opened the gate and crossed to the house. There was no way to effectively search the houses without their lamps. They walked to the gaping mouth of the ruin and listened.

"Did Maggie tell you about the paint and rope she found up here?"

"No," Eddie said.

"It was in a shed. She thought it was paint used to paint graffiti on her walls."

"Graffiti?"

"Yes. Jason helped her get rid of it."

Eddie sniffed. "He really had his feet under her table, didn't he?"

"Well, even you thought he was a nice kid at one stage."

"I know, always very charming, with a very free personality. Even when he was a wee one he'd greet a stranger with his hand out."

"He doesn't lack confidence now either, does he?"

Eddie sniffed again, shaking his head.

Michael looked at him. "Why do you wear your jacket like that? My kids used to wear their coats like that when they were in elementary school."

Eddie turned his back, ignoring the question. "That shed would be around the back."

The sound of his Wellingtons could be heard flapping against his calves as he walked off. Michael smiled after him, despite the gravity of the situation. He was a likeable old guy despite the gruff exterior. He was like a goblin in the gloom as he rounded the building. It was a pity his life was in such a mess.

Slowly they searched all the buildings, listening outside for any sounds. Then flashed their lights quickly inside in a wide arc. The farm was deserted. They really didn't think he'd be there. Maggie knew about this place and it was close to Eddie's house. Like Seán he'd taken her far away. They were standing at the gate again looking back at the house. Michael suddenly had a thought.

"Seán was found near Glenveigh, right?" He could sense Eddie stiffen beside him.

"Yes."

"Does Jason have connections up there?"

"Let me think. Jason was born here. So was his father. But his grandmother came from up there some place. His grandmother used to work around here when she was young. She worked on a farm as a maid. She was a good friend of my mother."

"Really!"

"Um, I thought she courted Pascal Breslin for a while but when I teased him about it one day he denied it and got angry with me. He was a funny old buck, Pascal. I really miss him."

"So was their relationship a secret or what?"

"Well, like Maggie I'm a lot younger than Pascal was so I wouldn't be aware of things like that. But I grew up here and spent most of my childhood with the

Breslins and I overheard Pascal and herself talking one day over by the boundary fence. I heard Pascal saying what's past is past. She slapped his face and walked off. I was only about nine or so and not very wise. I said to Pascal 'Oh, what did you do to Mrs Blaney?' and he shouted at me to get out of his sight. He was very upset. Years later I told him his girlfriend was in the yard and he lost his temper with me again. So I thought it was wise not to mention Mrs Blaney to him. I assumed it was an old romance gone sour."

Michael's nose was twitching again. "What was her name before she became Mrs Blaney."

"I don't know. That's all we ever called her."

A sound broke into his thoughts. They could see lights approaching and hear the squad cars coming up the lane so they went down to meet them.

Chapter 33

For the rest of the night the police swarmed the area, moving methodically over the land and the lanes, trying to find any indication as to where Jason and Maggie might have gone, but they found nothing. The detectives who'd been in charge of Maggie's interrogation were now in charge of finding her. They sat in Eddie's house going over again and again the events of the evening leading up to her disappearance.

"Mrs Molloy, how long has your relationship with Jason Blaney been going on?" Detective Grant asked.

"About eight months, I think."

"You think? Did you have any reason to suspect he had violent tendencies?"

"No. I mean he had everyone fooled, didn't he? Even Maggie believed he was her friend, looking out for her. She phoned him all the time to check on the house or yard for her."

"Did you suspect that he might have harmed your son?"

"No!" Kate shouted at her.

"Mrs Molloy, did your son know about your relationship with Jason?"

"No."

The detective raised one eyebrow.

"No. He had no idea."

Eddie was sitting quietly by her side. "I think he did know."

"What?" Kate turned to him.

"Why do you think that, Mr Molloy?"

"Shortly before he disappeared he saw me one night looking at photographs of my first wife. I'd come back from the pub a bit steamed and I was upset. A buck at the pub started teasing me about Kate and Jason. It got to me. Seán came in and sat on the chair there."

He pointed to a chair sitting between the two doors leading out of the kitchen. He hesitated in his mind's eye, seeing the boy looking at him.

"I didn't see him at first. He asked was I sorry my first wife died. I didn't answer him. Then he asked 'Would things have been different for you if she had lived?' I shouted at him. I shouted at him." For a moment he sat there reliving it in his mind before continuing. "He said, 'Yourself and Mum aren't happy, are you?' I just stared at him. You miss your first wife and Mum . . . Mum is . . .' He never finished the sentence, just got up and left the room. He knew something about Kate.

What else could he have known about her? Maybe he had a go at Jason about it and asked him to stay away from us."

"Or he saw Maggie's prowler outside the house and tried to be a hero," Michael said.

"Maybe you are both right," said Detective Ryan. "He saw Jason prowling outside her house, recognised him and confronted him then."

"Maggie said Jason didn't like Seán."

"How could he not like a young fellow like Seán?" Kate started to sob again. "Perhaps Seán threatened Jason's relationship with you," said Grant. "Mr Blaney seems quite territorial. Perhaps he doesn't like to share his toys. He didn't want you having to choose between him and your son, in case he lost."

Kate flinched at his words.

Maggie had lain in the damp ferns listening. Gradually she'd wiggled out of the hood and tried to determine where she was. Try as she might she couldn't get rid of the gag. Not long afterwards she heard someone approaching her hiding place. A dark shape loomed over her in the moonlight. A torch shone in her eyes for a brief second, then everything went dark again.

"Well, look who's awake! Come on, Maggie, we have to get out of here. You're a popular lady. There'll be a posse up here soon looking for you. Come on."

He leant down and tenderly picked her up from where he had left her in a little hole in the dense undergrowth behind some bushes. At first she was disorientated, and unsure where she lay. But then he turned back up the lane towards her house. She'd no idea where he'd take her now. Anywhere local would be searched before morning so it would have to be somewhere far away from here. His strength and agility amazed her as he moved swiftly along with her in his arms. Granted she was light, but still he wasn't very big either.

He went through her yard and out onto the mountain and took the turn towards his own house. He kept slightly uphill. After about ten minutes his breathing was labouring slightly. The path they took crossed a back road. It was silent and deserted. That didn't surprise her – this road went up into the forestry where another old house used to stand. It was just another mountain ruin now. The mountainside was peppered with decaying farms. From top to bottom this road saw no more life than the occasional rabbit. He walked down the road as if he was heading home. Surely he couldn't be going to hide her there. That would be the second place everyone looked.

The road came to an end at a crossroads. The left turn led to his house. It was only a few hundred yards.

"Now, Maggie, I have to go get my car so you stay here quietly and wait for me."

Once again he dropped her behind some bushes. Maggie couldn't figure out whether he was insane or brave. Her arms ached from the awkward position he'd tied them in. Her head ached from the blow he'd struck her.

He was only gone a short time until he returned with his car and parked it beside Maggie. He jumped out quickly and opened the back door, then lay her across the seat.

They drove along the dark roads, in silence at first. He seemed to be taking the back roads, in the Letterkenny direction. These roads crossed miles of mountain and at this time of night they would probably be deserted. Finally, after the car had eaten up a chunk of the road, Jason turned and looked at Maggie.

"You must be confused as to what this is all about."

Maggie's hazel eyes penetrated his but she didn't make a sound.

"You have a right to know what's happening. Maggie, I'm going to tell you the story of my life. My family is like yours, full of secrets. You'll be surprised to know that some of our secrets overlap. You knew my grandmother Mrs Blaney. She was such a stern woman." He flicked the light on for a moment and looked back into Maggie's face. "Her maiden name was Breda Ward. She married Peader Blaney in nineteen forty-four. A horse killed him three years later. My father was her only child. The father of her child abandoned her and then her husband died. It's like a Greek tragedy. Is it any wonder she was a tough lady? She had to be. She brought my father up by herself, two miles from his natural father. Pascal never once acknowledged him and she was too proud to ever go back to him because it would mean explaining to the world that she pawned her child off as another man's son. Over the years she broke my father. She ruled him with a rod of iron. Keeping him from being like his real father, I suppose. To this day the man is a shadow. Don't you think so?" Once again he flicked the light and looked back at her. "You're not saying much." He laughed. "My father is an emotionally bankrupt man. I heard that phrase once on *Oprah*. Do you know he goes days without speaking? He's an alcoholic. He stopped drinking thirteen years ago and since then he's barely left the house. He'd go to the mart or the co-op for grain when I was young, but when I was old enough to do it for him he stopped doing that as well. All my life he's sat around with his red-rimmed eyes darting around the house, nodding when you speak to him. From my early childhood it's been my job to fill the spaces and communicate for my father because Pascal Breslin had morals. We were both victims of his morals, Maggie. Oh, by the way, your prowler and the man who whispered in the door to you that night – wait for this – that was my father. You and Pascal have always been the only people he'd leave the house for – how ironic is that now?"

Maggie struggled in the back. She wanted to speak.

"Calm down, Maggie. You have to wait your turn. I've listened to you often enough. He heard about your American son. I bet you're wondering how he knew. Do you remember the waiter who served you dinner in The Beachwood the first day you met with Michael? Well, he plays hurling with my brother. We had some interesting dinner conversation that night. Afterwards Dad went ballistic. He went to the pub and got blind drunk. He told me the whole story while I tried to stop him chiselling his fingers off in his workshop. He was making some stupid little statue. Therapy, I suppose. Sorry, I digress. He walked home with Pascal that night you were locked in and had it out with Pascal. They fought and then Pascal took it out on you and locked you up. Dad was outside. He heard the whole thing. Pascal was so upset he forgot to lock the door going to bed and Dad was too angry to go home yet, so he went in to speak to him again. Pascal was already in the middle of an attack. Dad watched him reach for his inhaler and stood on his hand and watched him die. You would have thought that would be the end of the tragedy, wouldn't you? But no! Dad barely speaks to anyone for most of his life and that night he chooses to taunt you through the door. You had to break your way out, the police got involved and you're too bloody stubborn to explain the door and having been locked in. You made it look suspicious. I went to my dad that night when I heard him come in. He was drunk again and agitated and I knew something unusual had happened. He refused to tell me what but you helped me piece it together. I caught him in the act the night he threw the stone through your window. I told you I heard him going towards Molloy's but I was actually at home that night, not the pub, I met him going home across the mountain. I suspected it was him but I had to catch him in the act.

He stopped when I interrogated him. Your family have been the ruination of mine. Your mother walking across the hill to my grandmother, telling her about her clever children and her hard-working son Pascal and how well he cared for you all, while my grandmother struggled and laboured to bring up a boy alone and take care of her farm and then to have to lower herself for harvests and lambing to ask the almighty Pascal for help. My dad was out breaking his back at ten years of age to do the work of a grown man. He left school at twelve to work on the farm. He told me that was why he drank so much. He's practically illiterate, you know. He'd fool you with that one. My mother was married to him before she knew. The one time she offered to teach him how to read he went crazy and beat her so badly he cracked two of her ribs and knocked out her two front teeth. She told all of you she was knocked off the old horse into a wall."

Maggie's eyes were welling with tears. Poor Dolores, she remembered that incident well. They had a long chat about it and Maggie never suspected a word of it to be a lie.

"Then the Yank came back."

Again Maggie struggled trying to break free.

"You'll only dislocate that shoulder, Maggie. I've tied you up like a young hog."

Maggie knew he was right – the pain was starting to numb her shoulder.

"His rages were legendary. None of us escaped without at least one beating. Age seemed to be slowing him down until he heard about your son. Recently, he's like a man possessed. He'd started drinking poitín out in the mountains. Any time I tried to talk to him he'd explode in anger. I'd been seeing Kate for nearly a year the night Seán disappeared."

Again Maggie couldn't control her emotions and tried to shout.

"I know, Maggie. I may as well say it. I killed the little shit. Now are you happy?"

Maggie pounded her feet off the side of the car in rage and grief.

"Leave the car alone, Maggie."

The coldness of his voice made her stop.

"As I was saying. At some stage Seán copped on that I was shagging his mother. Seán left your house that night and went over to ours to speak to me about Kate, being the little man's arse that he always was. He saw me go into the barn and went to ask me to stop seeing her. I was talking to Dad. Dad was shouting at me and telling me all we were going to do to you, to try and get even with the Breslins. Seán heard everything, Maggie. The little twerp couldn't keep his nose out of anything."

In the back, tears streamed down Maggie's cheeks.

"He waited till Dad stormed out of the shed and came in to have it out with me. I would never have hurt the stupid little prick if he had minded his own business."

Again Maggie kicked out at the side of the car.

"Will you stop that? This is a new car. Let me

finish. I know, he thought it was his business to stop his mother from being a slut. But I had to do something to shut him up or my father would go to prison. He didn't take much. He wasn't very big. I burned his clothes and stuff and placed him in the lake in Glenveigh. I knew the area well. I just didn't have the time to bury him so I put him in the water to wash away any trace of me. You know it felt nice sometimes sneaking around in the dark in my black clothes. Do you remember the night I was in your kitchen? I knew my father wasn't out but I went over anyway to keep an eye on you. You forgot to lock the door that night just like Pascal did. The door banged in the wind shortly after I entered the kitchen. I could almost smell your fear. If you'd turned on the light (the switch was just behind you), I'd have had to kill you. But I thought the most likely thing was you'd get a heart attack. Wouldn't that be perfect? Get rid of both of you and neither look like a murder. Alan overheard myself and Dad arguing behind Duffy's, the night he died. Dad suspected I knew what happened to Seán. He had no ill feeling towards anyone else just you Breslins. He'd happily pull the plug on all of you. He told me once the best present I could give him was to get you all together in one room and burn it."

Maggie listened to him and knew he wouldn't tell her any of this if he intended to let her live. Jason was going to kill her next.

"Kate's a very messed-up woman, you know, Maggie."

He really was crazy. What did that have to do with anything? Once again the car lapsed into silence as it sped along the back road.

"When were you last up at Malin Head, Maggie? I've been doing a bit of rock climbing the last few years and I know the place pretty well. There's a place there called Hell's Hole. It's a deep subterranean cave, about two hundred and fifty feet long and eight feet wide. The tide rushes right in there, boiling up into powerful foam. I thought you might like a swim."

Maggie's head was spinning. She knew everything and the dawn was breaking. She could see a softening of the darkness. So that was it. She was going to be thrown into the sea. He'd lost everything. There was no way out for him. Everyone would be looking for her now and they must know it was him that took her. He was going to prison if he was caught. Of course the solution would have to be permanent.

The car rumbled on. Somewhere in the middle of Jason's story she lost all track of time. She was sick with fear and sadness. Pascal Breslin had a lot to answer for. His one stupid decision to abandon his child caused all of this. How could he let Maggie keep hers when he'd chosen to abandon his? Breda wouldn't have stood for that and who would have blamed her?

An urgent interjection from Jason interrupted her thoughts.

"Hold on, Maggie, we need to change direction. There's a checkpoint up ahead, probably for drunk drivers."

Jason calmly turned off the main road and down a narrow back road. But suddenly sirens split the night.

Jason put a hand back and stroked Maggie's forehead.

"It won't hurt for long, Maggie. Seán didn't suffer either."

He turned his attention back to the road.

Maggie rolled around the back of the car as Jason careered around bends and jumped over bumps and potholes. Maggie knew horrific crashes happened on these roads. Outside she was helpless but inside she prayed.

Chapter 34

Immediately after interviewing Kate and Michael, the police called to Jason's house. Dolores told them he'd been there less than half an hour before to pick up the car. As they questioned her, Detective Ryan noticed the unease of David Blaney. She turned to him.

"Mr Blaney, do you have any idea where your son might have gone with the car?"

He shook his head.

"Did you see him?"

Again he shook his head.

Dolores anxiously watched her husband. Only she was aware of his hyperventilating and palpitations. All the times she'd held him in the night when, under a veil of darkness, he cried in her arms. She had begun to despair in the preceding weeks. He'd started drinking again and his moods took on the blackness of when he was a younger man.

She could see why the detective had honed in on

him now – even she was suspicious of the expression on his face. But she went to her usual spot by his side with her hand on his arm. Her touch might soften the black stone that seemed to have replaced his eyes.

"Jason isn't here and we don't know where he went," she said to the detectives. "He drinks in Duffy's."

"Ma'am! Duffy's is closed," said Detective Grant, his tone deepening her embarrassment

She blushed. The sharp voice started the whispering again in the centre of her brain. It was pushing unease and suspicion, emotions she never experienced before, to the surface. Something was happening to her family. Jason never went out this late. Her husband knew what was going on; she was certain of that and she was just as certain he would never tell her what.

The detective saw her discomfort and decided not to pursue questioning David at this time. The waiting game might be more productive. He turned away. "We will be leaving an officer outside, just in case he comes back. We need to find Miss Breslin. We believe she's in a lot of danger. We hoped Jason could help us. We'll keep in touch."

As soon as he left the house he put out an alert all over the county for Jason with a description of his car and the number plate. In less than thirty minutes a call came through. They were in pursuit of Jason's car in the Moville area of the county. He was heading further north. The pursuing car could see no sign of Margaret Breslin. Cars from all the substations were on their way out to try and intercept him.

The detectives got into their car and drove in a northerly direction. They wanted to be on the spot when Jason was caught, to question him about Maggie's disappearance. At that point, like the hands of the clock approaching the top of the hour, they were all heading towards Malin head in the extreme north of the county.

Terror had invaded the car and both Maggie and Jason were consumed by it. Suicide had never been part of his plan. Jason was afraid to die. The ghosts of Pascal Breslin and young Seán were waiting for him. Maggie's mouth was still taped but her whimpers were audible above the screech of the tyres as she fought to control her panic. The car careered around bends, throwing her about. First her head, then her back would thump painfully off the seats. Her stomach was turning over and she was trying to breathe evenly, to avoid vomiting. If she did, she knew she would choke and nobody would be able to help her. Through her fear she could hear the sobs of Jason as his fear and panic escalated.

"Decades of misery caused by the evil old bastard, decades of misery – my whole family has been ruined because of Pascal Breslin and now the prodigal son is back, back to find his mom! Well, now it looks like Mom is gone! I think we're both for it now, Maggie!" His voice was cracking and his breath had turned to short sharp pants as his words tumbled over each other.

Without warning he put back his hand and ripped off the tape from her mouth. She drew in large breaths.

"Jason, watch the road!" she screamed through bleeding lips.

The car swerved but he corrected it.

"Jason, you're going to kill us!"

"What else can I do now, Maggie?" he sobbed.

"Jason, a life sentence isn't life in Ireland. You'll get twenty-five years, half that for good behaviour!"

For a moment they were silent except for Jason's laboured breath.

"No," he sobbed. "You've got to go. Pascal is gone, now you've got to go."

After that, time seemed to slow down to a painful crawl. She could see Jason turn back to the road and the look of horror spread across his features. The car turned and she slipped down against the side of it, crunching her neck bones painfully against the door handles. The car seemed to be travelling on two wheels. The only sounds she could hear were the sirens and Jason's screams. She could see his elbows in the air and knew his hands were no longer on the wheel. He was covering his eyes from what he could see in front of him and then the other sound started. The terrible haunting screech of metal on metal and finally the bang as the car hit something solid. She knew it was turning over and then everything went black.

Whirring! Maggie's head hurt and all around her she heard whirring like a jet engine. She tried opening her eyes to see how close it actually was but that made the pain worse. Maybe it was bees, she thought. Again she tried to open her eyes but the bees got angry. She relaxed and gradually the bees seemed to retreat and the pain subsided. Time had no meaning, wherever she was. It couldn't be measured in lengths of time but more like quantities of moments scattered through the buzzing darkness. The moments of clarity were when she tried desperately to see someone she knew, someone to ask what was going on and to tell her where all the bees came from.

Finally Maggie opened her eyes. The pain was bearable now and the room was quiet.

"Hey!" Michael's smile lit up the room. "Wait a moment. Don't try to speak."

Fear grabbed Maggie again as she realised she couldn't speak. Her mouth was obstructed.

"Hold on." He grabbed the emergency button and rang for a nurse.

In a few moments one came in and quickly cleared Maggie's airways. A doctor spent a few minutes checking her vitals.

When they were gone Maggie looked around her and saw she was in a private hospital room. The room was full of flowers and the smell permeated every corner. Maybe that's what attracted the bees. He held her hand and it felt warm and solid. For a moment, blissfully unaware, she savoured its touch, but suddenly realisation came back and she remembered Jason.

In a hoarse whisper she asked, "What happened to Jason?"

Another nurse arrived by her bed and interrupted his answer. When she'd finished updating Maggie's chart she left them alone.

"He's dead, isn't he?"

Michael nodded. "You're lucky you're not."

"Where did it happen?"

"You were approaching Malin Head. Jason lost control on a bend and ploughed into an oil lorry coming in the opposite direction."

For a moment Maggie tried to remember but she couldn't remember the actual crash.

"Was anyone else hurt?"

"The driver was treated for shock. It was you we were worried about. You were unconscious for days. You seemed to come to a few times and then you would slip away again. My kids are here."

"They are?"

"Yes."

"Are they in the hospital?"

"They went down to the town to get some air but they'll be on their way back soon. All your family are here as well."

"Where are they?"

"It's only ten o'clock – they're not in yet."

Maggie started laughing.

"What's so funny?"

"I'm costing them more in the last few months than I have in my life. Poor Brian! Three return tickets to New York!"

"He can afford it."

"Can he?"

"Believe me, Maggie. He talked through a bottle of wine the other night about his portfolio. He's doing okay."

"What happened to Kate?"

"Rita has given up her job in London and herself and Kate are renting a place in Letterkenny. She and Eddie have split up."

"I guessed they would. Is she still working?"

"She is. There will be a court case but she was as much a victim as anyone else. She lost her son, her marriage split up, and her lover turned out to be a murderer. If stupidity and bad luck are capital crimes they'll throw the book at her."

"Will she be charged as an accessory?"

"I doubt she knew much if anything."

"Can you get me a drink? My throat is very sore."

"Of course! Hold on a minute. I'll go ask the nurse for a jug of water. I drank that one."

"You've a great bedside manner, son."

He laughed. "Thanks, Mother. Now take it easy. I'll be back in a moment." He left the room.

Maggie's eye wandered around. She couldn't reach any of the bouquets to see who wrote on the cards. She closed her eyes and relaxed. Her head was starting to throb again.

The creak of the door woke her up.

"David!" Suddenly Jason's words and David's actions came flooding back

David Blaney stood at the foot of her bed. He

looked awful. He'd lost a lot of weight. His face was pale and thin and his eyes were their usual red-rimmed selves. He was pulling a thread that had loosened itself from the bedspread.

"Why did you come in here?" she whispered.

"I just wanted to make sure you were all right."

"You wanted to see what Jason told me."

"Did he talk to you?"

"He told me everything."

"Everything!"

"Yes, David. I know you're my nephew."

Tears were sliding down his face as he finally managed to draw the thread from its home. He nodded as though confirming something to himself before he spoke.

"Pascal destroyed me and my mother and you killed my son."

"David. I didn't kill Jason and I'm not going to say anything about the night Pascal died."

"I know you're not, Maggie. I won't let you."

"David! Let it go." Wildly Maggie looked about the room but there was nothing close enough for her to use as a weapon and she had no way of getting out of bed and past him.

"Let it go? I lost most of my life because of him. Look what he did to my mother!"

"Look what he did to me, David. I was his victim too."

"Well, you got your son back, didn't you? I just saw him talking on the phone."

Oh God, Maggie thought. That's why he wasn't coming back. Someone called him. He could be ages yet.

Maggie tried to shout but her throat was so sore because of the tubes that she was unable to raise her voice above a loud croak that barely crossed the room.

"No, Maggie. Don't do that."

He moved closer and she could smell the overpowering odour of stale sweat as he leaned towards her. He pressed one hand heavily on her chest, just below the base of her throat and with the other hand he closed off her nose and mouth. At first she tried to consciously hold her breath and not panic but as the air in her lungs tried to complete its cycle and return to the world outside the pressure in her chest felt as though it would explode. The weight of his huge hand on her chest was stopping her chest from rising, escalating her panic and making the urge to breathe more extreme.

Maggie's eyes were turning glassy as she stared wildly up into his face.

Cold penetrating eyes looked back down into hers just like they must have done into Pascal's all those months before. Gradually Maggie could feel herself slipping into unconsciousness. As she was about to succumb the pressure released suddenly from her chest and his hand moved from her face. His shape moved away from her bedside and landed heavily against the bed trolley, pushing it against the wall and landing him on the ground. Dishes and vases of flowers smashed to the floor and Maggie could hear heavy footsteps crunching through the broken pieces. As clarity returned she could see Michael banging David's blood-soaked unconscious head off the skirting board.

"*Michael! Michael!*" she cried desperately.

Maggie's voice finally penetrated Michael's thoughts and he turned to face her. He saw the snow-white face trying to reach out to him, then he looked down and saw the blood on his hands and the ruined face of David Blaney. As though stung, he jumped back from what he'd done. He'd never fought any human being with such ferocity, hadn't even known that such violence existed within him. He felt sick. As he stood up a blur of white and navy rushed past him and tried to revive David. People were shouting for security to come and help them restrain Michael but he just walked the short distance to Maggie and held her hand as the police were called.

Days passed while Maggie and Michael's family surrounded them in a protective huddle as they told their stories over and over.

David suffered a fractured skull, broken nose and a cracked jawbone but miraculously he survived and would eventually be able to stand trial. Dolores joined the ranks of the grey divorcees along with Eddie.

"Maggie, you've got to come back with us once the trial is over." Michael looked into her face, examining the changing array of emotions.

So much had happened for Maggie over the last

year she didn't think she could ever rebuild her life here. But could she start a life so far away from everything and everybody she knew? All the images from her life were flashing slowly like an old movie reel through her mind. Pain and some pleasure, people she was scared of and who controlled her life, friends like Eddie who she loved as a brother but still overall there wasn't much to keep her here. Anything worth revisiting would be here when she came back for holidays. Maybe she'd even get Eddie to take off that jacket and get on a plane.

"Okay." She turned and faced Michael.

"I'll come to live with you but you must promise if it doesn't work out there will be no regrets and I'll come back."

"Yes, Mom." With his face lit by a broad smile he kissed the back of her hand.

In two days Maggie Breslin's life would change forever. In her new life she had a family of her own, which was more than she'd ever dreamt of. Maggie saw a future filled with hope and she'd finally left silence and recriminations behind. Yes, Maggie was looking forward to her new life. At last, she was going home.

the end